D1277382

Foamers

A Novel of Suspense

Jon Berson

scribner

SCRIBNER
1230 Avenue of the Americas
New York, NY 10020

Copyright © 1997 by John Feffer

Designed by Brooke Zimmer
Set in Columbus Monotype
Manufactured in the United States of America

10   9   8   7   6   5   4   3   2   1

Library of Congress Cataloging-in-Publication Data
Berson, Jon.
Foamers : a novel of suspense / Jon Berson.
p. cm.
I. Title.
PS3552.E767F6 1997
813'.54—dc21   97-2491
CIP

ISBN 0-684-83586-X

For Karin, my ideal reader

One looks from the train
Almost as one looked as a child. In the sunlight
What I see still seems to me plain,
I am safe; but at evening
As the lands darken, a questioning
Precariousness comes over everything.

—RANDALL JARRELL

contents

before

The bayou blazed. An inch of diesel oil covering the water burned orange in the dark.

Half the train sat properly aligned on the bridge. The other half veered off at an angle—like a compound fracture—dropping off the low bridge and into the water. One car balanced precariously in mid-air.

The fire turned the bayou into a raging fuse. It provided the only light by which the rescuers could pull the survivors to safety. Flashlights were virtually useless in the thick warm water.

The passengers from the intact half of the train stood together on one side of the bayou. They talked quietly, traded their experiences back and forth—the jolts, the sounds, the fear. The light of the oil fire licked at their faces.

The other passengers—wet, burned, and numb—sat on the opposite bank. Several quietly nursed their wounds. Some cried or moaned. A man clutched at any passing arm for help in finding his child.

On this same bank, but several hundred feet downstream, a woman lay whimpering in the mud. She had been reading in her sleeper when the train derailed. After struggling to open the compartment window, she had held her breath and pushed past the inrush of black water. Dimly she heard the explosion of the engine. She kicked through the plants and silt and up toward the light. She surfaced in the middle of an inferno.

Her face was now covered with burns and her lungs were scorched. She lay in the mud on the bank, breathing in tortured bursts, her torso still in the water.

A figure appeared above her. She looked up into the narrow beam of a flashlight. I've been rescued, she thought somewhere in the middle of her pain. She tried to speak.

"Very messy," the voice behind the light said. "Here, let me help you."

Tucking the flashlight beneath his armpit, the man bent down to push the injured woman through the mud back into the bayou. Pressing her head into the shallow water with one foot, he removed a microphone from the pocket of his fishing vest and extended it into the darkness. He waited for the thrashing to subside. Then he carefully replaced the microphone, covered up the tracks, and continued about his business.

part one

ONE

Larry McBryde watched the trees darken along the highway and reflected on how little he enjoyed train accidents.

Sure, they looked fine in photos. A well-taken black-and-white could turn even the worst tragedy into something elegant. And like most train enthusiasts, McBryde owned a few of these fine-looking tragedies. There was, for instance, his stunning photo of the runaway that had smashed into Washington's Union Station in the winter of 1953. The print offered a surreal tableau of the mammoth GG1 engine collapsing through the terminal floor and into a basement baggage room. Two tiny workmen peered cautiously at the engine from the safety of a balcony. Hanging serenely from the ceiling above the destruction was a sign that read WAITING ROOM.

McBryde could certainly appreciate the artistry of such photos—their composition, the play of light and shadow. He just took no pleasure in the accidents themselves.

"An emergency meeting," the voice on the answering machine had said. "About train accidents."

Their last "emergency" meeting had focused on the new commemorative railroad stamp. The "emergency" before that concerned the menu for the annual awards dinner. The term "emergency" no longer had any meaning. It was used as recklessly as exclamation points in tabloids or "brand new" in advertising. They would probably discuss some new book on train accidents. Or perhaps someone had managed to get hold of some rare pictures from the Internet. In any case, a wasted Sunday evening.

McBryde darted around cars on the expressway. He had a horror of tardiness, related probably to his disgust for trains that couldn't keep to schedule. The boathouses along the Schuylkill River came into view, their facades outlined in bright lights like dots of vanilla frosting on gingerbread. To his left, the Museum of Art looked down upon the river. In front of him, Thirtieth Street Station rose above the train yards, long festive banners hung vertically between the station's massive columns. The expressway took him beneath the tracks and the city streets. Clearing the station, McBryde began to pull away from the Schuylkill to enter West Philadelphia.

He craved a cigarette, but had none. Six months ago he'd given up smoking. Except in his imagination. McBryde could almost feel the fresh plastic zip of a new pack, the twenty white fingers inside, the ten that he would smoke in a day, the one that would pop into his hand and then be lifted to his mouth. Only a cigarette could dampen the faint nausea that was spreading upward from his acid stomach to his tightening throat. Clearly he was allergic to train accidents.

Some train fans, however, just couldn't get their fill. Prim, asthmatic Georgia Huxley, for instance. McBryde had politely leafed through her morocco-bound albums, skimmed the clippings from local newspapers around the country that described the sudden impacts and tragic deaths—all neatly mounted and lovingly labeled. Another enthusiast he knew worked as an assessor for a large insurance company and kept souvenirs from wrecks: broken Amtrak dishes, rails snapped like kindling, bloodstained upholstery. Normal people—they held down jobs, brought up children. But the stuff they kept in boxes at home, well, it just made you wonder.

Then there was Ron Jordan. It was fitting to hold an emergency meeting about train accidents at Jordan's house. Measured strictly in pounds, he was easily the biggest train buff in the area. He was also one of the few blacks to travel in rail-fan circles. What made him famous in the community, however, was his collection of accident photographs, probably the best of its kind in the country. Not that he had many competitors. There might be twenty bona fide collectors altogether in the United States and only a handful, like Jordan, who actually took their own shots.

The Jordans lived on a quiet West Philadelphia street lined with two-family Victorian row houses. McBryde checked his watch before pulling into a parking space. Despite all the time he'd spent in Rosemont drinking coffee and saying good night to his ex-family, he'd arrived ten minutes early.

As usual, the front door of the house was unlocked. A wind chime, hung from the ceiling just inside the entrance, rippled with melody each time the door touched it. McBryde balanced his coat on a crowded peg in the foyer and walked into the familiar living room, the site of so many past board meetings. He waved to Jordan, who was in the kitchen throwing chips and salsa into bowls. The children would be asleep upstairs, Jordan's wife reading in the bedroom.

Georgia Huxley, tight-lipped and well-coiffed, was sitting with a cup of tea cradled in her finely manicured fingers. She always took a cab back and forth to these meetings and was invariably the first one to arrive. McBryde joined her on the couch.

"People aren't happy," she reported. "Even if it's only twelve dollars."

McBryde sighed. "We're running a deficit, and unless folks want more taxes—"

"I'm just telling you what I hear on the street."

The fare increase for public transportation had just gone into effect. Whenever city government insisted on such unpopular measures, McBryde discovered all over again why no one in their right mind would want his job. Head of the customer service department for SEPTA, the Southeastern Pennsylvania Transportation Authority? When fares went up, you might as well roast babies for a living, that was the amount of respect you received from the general public.

The other board members gradually trickled in, wind chimes

announcing their entrance. Clarence Brown, tall and shy, tried to slip into the room unnoticed. Brown was into $7\frac{1}{4}$ gauge, the model trains that fell halfway between Lionel and the real thing. He was building an enormous course for his steam trains in his backyard. As usual for board meetings, he wore a pin-striped engineer's cap and overalls.

Leticia Gompers, the lesbian classicist and fan of exotic foreign trains, greeted everyone with a loud "How y'all doing" as she slipped her leather knapsack off one shoulder and onto the floor. She kicked off her sandals and folded herself cross-legged in a straight-backed chair, sweeping her jumble of black curls behind her neck with the back of one hand and a twist of her head. Finally, with many apologies for being three minutes late, Marty Stein the jazz disc jockey galloped in on his stubby legs and landed with a thump in his favorite armchair, an overstuffed Victorian monstrosity with faded needlepoint upholstery.

The executive board of the Philly Foamers was now gathered for their fourth emergency meeting of the year.

They called themselves the Philly Foamers despite the insult embedded in the name. Amtrak personnel labeled them "foamers" because they pestered conductors with questions, tried to ride in the engine cab, took photographs of everything from axles to seat cushions, and literally foamed at the mouth over every last aspect of trains. "Sure we foam," McBryde had argued in his winning defense of the name, "but we're damn proud of it!"

Every month, the Philly Foamers met to discuss the latest line of rolling stock, the hottest news on supertrains, the resting place of favorite steam engines. The fifty regular members came from all backgrounds, were employed in all professions. Under ordinary circumstances, they'd have had nothing to say to one another outside of the weather, hit movies, and the Eagles. But as the Philly Foamers, they united as close friends to celebrate the glorious past, the miserable present, and the hopeful future of the great iron beast, the railroad.

McBryde and his five friends had been serving together on the executive board for the past four years. At the time of each new election, the group-at-large unanimously voice-voted them into successive terms. This was more a practical consideration than a lapse in democracy. The larger monthly meetings, held in the Mario Lanza Room of Rizzo's Family Style Restaurant in South Philly, resembled Super Bowl Sunday get-togethers: loud and boisterous with over-eating, overdrinking, and overlapping conversations. Very little business was ever accomplished. Because of the confusion of these free-for-alls, the Philly Foamers actually planned their many activi-ties and coordinated the work of the committees only at the board meetings. The rest of the group happily allowed the Group of Six to steer from above—as long as the subscriptions to *Railpace* and *Pas-senger Train Monthly* arrived on time, the yearly excursion to the Horseshoe Curve went off as planned, and enough dishes of Rizzo's famous fried calamari were ordered for meeting night.

Jordan walked in from the kitchen balancing a tray of snack bowls and clinking glasses. He distributed the drinks and then set-tled into the special extra-wide rocking chair that had been custom-arily left empty for him.

"So what's this all about?" McBryde grumbled, after taking his first swallow of beer. He was eager to discharge his irritability. "This better not be another emergency meeting about a new passenger line or first-day cover or—"

"No," Georgia Huxley cut him off. The others, who had been on the verge of laughing good-naturedly at McBryde's complaint, qui-eted at the somber note in Huxley's voice. "No," she repeated. "This is an emergency meeting in the truest sense of the word."

McBryde could see that Huxley was a very good business-woman. The words she chose quickly commanded attention.

"I was the one who called this meeting," Huxley continued, "and I apologize for bringing you out here tonight." She sniffed. It was a trademark sandpapery sound she often made (the result, she told any boor who asked, of asthma and a persistent sinus infec-tion). Then she removed something from the pocket of her dark blue wool blazer and placed it carefully on the coffee table next to a bowl of salsa. The five other foamers leaned forward.

"Is that the musical selection for this evening?" Marty Stein said with a half-smile, waving his glass of orange juice toward the table.

The comment went unnoticed as everyone looked from the object to Huxley and back again. Her dramatic presentation both irritated and impressed McBryde.

"It doesn't have any music on it," Huxley replied after a moment's pause. "That tape cost me five thousand dollars."

No one dared laugh in disbelief. Georgia Huxley, renowned for her lack of humor, remained sober and slightly disapproving at all times. In its rest position, her mouth turned down slightly at the corners. When she smiled, she managed only to straighten her lips. She never laughed. It was rumored that her parents had died when she was very young, that this tragedy had cast a long shadow over her life. She never talked about her past.

"Isn't that a little steep, Georgia?" Jordan asked, still perched on the edge of his rocking chair. "What could be on that little thing that's worth so much?"

"We all have one or two tapes from that audio outfit All Ears, correct?" she said. "And we've all met one or two tape junkies."

"This guy had a booth at the Trenton show," Jordan recollected. "He claimed to have two thousand tapes. Every major train in the world."

"Wouldn't you call yourself a tape junkie, Marty?" Clarence Brown turned to the deejay.

Marty Stein squirmed in his seat with pride and embarrassment. Everyone knew about his collection—it was legendary among foamers all over the world. Stein collected the sounds of toilets flushing on trains. It was said to be the best and indeed the only such collection in the world. Complete strangers would send him recordings of the gurgle of a Singapore commuter or the rumble-splash of a Kenyan express.

"I never heard of any tape costing five thousand dollars," Marty Stein said, trying to sound definitive.

Huxley sipped her soda. "Well, this is a tape of some very unusual train sounds."

"The last ride of the Patagonian Express?" ventured Leticia Gompers. "The Khyber Pass Local pulling out of Peshawar?"

"These are certifiably domestic train sounds," Huxley continued. "In fact, the trains themselves are not unusual. But the circumstances are." She held up the cassette and sniffed. "This is a tape of train accidents."

It took a few moments for the information to sink in. Jordan was the first to speak. "You mean, it contains recordings off the CB frequencies."

"That's not all," Huxley told him. "This particular tape has the actual sounds of three derailments, two head-ons, and one rear-ender."

"But how's that possible, Georgia?" McBryde wanted to know, his end-of-weekend depression suddenly forgotten.

"That I can't tell you," said Huxley carefully. "You can hear for yourselves. It's all there. The crash, the explosions, the screams, the ambulance sirens."

"Five thousand dollars," murmured Clarence Brown the machinist.

"For a tape," Marty Stein said.

"Who made it?" McBryde asked.

"I don't know," Huxley answered. "Really, I don't. I have a friend, James, who is rather a follower of train accidents. No one you know. He lives in Colorado. He has a full set and sold me this one."

"There are *more* of these?" Jordan exclaimed.

Huxley nodded. "Five or so; maybe more."

"And your friend knows who made them?" McBryde asked.

"No. He sends the money to a post-office box in the Caymans and a tape arrives in the mail with a different postmark each time. Naturally there isn't a return address."

"You sure they're not some recording-studio mock-ups?" McBryde pressed.

"I checked them against my clippings. My friend has gone further. He submitted them to a sound analysis. That's his job, you see. He does them for airlines, sometimes for the police. He gives these tapes an eighty-five-percent credibility rating. From what I understand, that's pretty good."

"How come he sold this to you? Why not just make a copy?" Jordan asked.

She tapped the case. "The person who mixed the sounds embedded a high-frequency code. Try to make a copy and all you get is static. Copies can only be made on a special machine from the original, if it still exists. Can you back me up on this, Marty?"

"Yeah," Stein said, looking confused. "Yeah, I guess that's possible. But listen, I—"

"Is this the only copy out there?" McBryde interrupted. "Or have others paid five thousand dollars a shot for these?"

Georgia Huxley's mouth straightened into its parody of a smile. "There's a limited audience for tapes of this nature. Perhaps only ten people in this country. Another ten overseas."

Clarence Brown whistled softly. "A hundred thousand dollars for each run of tapes. Half a million for a batch of five."

"That's not a lot, considering the risk," McBryde said.

"Listen," Stein said, "I still don't get it. You called us here just to confess that you paid far too much money for this little old tape?"

The group turned its attention to the deejay. A fast talker, he was notoriously slow on the uptake. It was Leticia Gompers who finally decided to fill in the gaps.

"For Christ's sake, Marty," she said. "How do you think this person, whoever it is, made these tapes?"

"I guess he goes on a lot of trains and, well, he—"

"Don't be a fool!" Gompers exploded. "You've been on hundreds, thousands of trains in your life, and how many accidents have you ever been in?"

"Well," Stein began. "There was that derailment outside of Topeka back in seventy-eight and I once saw this freight train get shunted onto the wrong—"

Gompers groaned. "Look, Marty, let me put it into plain English for you. Whoever made these tapes must have been prepared for these accidents. And the only way they could have known something was going to happen was for them to *make* that something happen. Q.E.D."

"Oh," Marty Stein exhaled, deflated.

McBryde looked around at his fellow foamers to gauge their reactions. Jordan was still leaning forward in his rocking chair, following every word of the account, his immense head cocked to one side. Clarence Brown was meditatively considering the issue, his long slender fingers paired off to form a spire, the thumbs pressed gently into his lower lip. Leticia Gompers, still flushed from her mini-tirade, waited impatiently for more information, her legs crossed and one hand buried in her black curly hair. Marty Stein had sunk deeper into the stuffing of his chair.

McBryde was worried. This was not a group prepared for real emergencies. "So," he said cautiously, "what's your thinking on this one, Georgia? Have you contacted the police?"

Huxley nodded. "They didn't believe me. They said, 'Sure, lady, we'll look into this.' "

"Try again." Marty Stein emerged from the padding of his

chair. "Someone's setting train accidents, we let the police handle it. Doesn't take a Latin scholar to figure that out."

Leticia Gompers fumed. "You *do* realize, don't you, Marty, that it's one of us out there doing this."

Stein looked around at the group with widened eyes.

Gompers unscrambled her legs and nearly flew out of her seat. "Not one of us in this room, you avocado head! It's a foamer doing this. Someone who knows trains inside and out. Someone who knows that these tapes could fetch a high price."

McBryde mulled over the information. "But I'd like to know whether this fellow's goal is to make money or simply cause the accidents."

"I don't honestly know," Huxley answered. "But you do all see why the police didn't listen. They already consider us bad sorts. Trespassers. Troublemakers. Thieves. We get our share of reprimands for removing objects from old stations or even from train wrecks themselves. They neither believe us nor take us seriously."

"They'd do a lousy job," Jordan added. "They'd screw up the investigation because they don't know the first thing about trains." As a city employee, Jordan had plenty of friends on the force, so his word carried a good deal of authority.

"But we could help them out," Stein offered. "As consultants or something."

Gompers said, still irritated, "They wouldn't take our help."

"Then we go to Amtrak," Stein persisted.

"That's even worse. To them, we're persona non grata."

"But we buy tickets! We're Amtrak's best customers! That's hardly non grata in my book," Stein protested.

"They wouldn't give a damn about your book or how many excursion tickets you bought last year, not at a time like this," McBryde replied curtly.

Stein scratched at his thinning hair. "I'll bet the police have already put someone on the case."

"I doubt the police recognize these as any more than routine accidents," Huxley said. "We all follow the rail news religiously. Has there been any mention of a police inquiry, on either a national or local level?"

They shook their heads.

"Ronald, you should give a listen," she continued, turning to Jordan. "The head-ons and the rear-ender were easy to identify. There's also a long segment from that Mobile disaster—the Sunset Limited that crashed off the bridge and into the bayou two years ago." She sniffed and a hardness came into her voice. "You can even hear someone drowning. Right there on the tape."

"I don't understand," Stein said, retreating again into the cushioned recesses of his chair. "I don't understand what you want to do."

They turned expectantly to Georgia Huxley. She offered them her horizontal smile.

"It has to be one of us," she said. "One of us has to track down this foamer. And stop him. We're the only group that can do this quickly, before anyone else gets hurt."

"Please." Stein sighed. "We're not vigilantes."

"This isn't vigilantism," Huxley said. "Once apprehended, he'll be given over to the proper authorities."

"So, Georgia, who'd you have in mind?" Jordan asked.

"There's really only one person who can do this," she replied.

This time all eyes turned to McBryde.

"Oh no," he began to protest, "I don't think—"

Huxley began to enumerate on the tips of her painted fingernails. "You're the only one with a gun. You're the only one with any kind of security experience. You know the system backward and forward. Look, I'd love to go after this . . . this piece of shit." Five jaws nearly snapped in amazement at this addition to her vocabulary. "But I simply don't have the proper skills."

McBryde began to sweat. "But hold on, I've got a vacation coming up, my first real one in three years and I—"

"Perfect," Jordan interrupted, caught up in the emotions of the moment. "Buddy, that's perfect! It'll give you the time to nail this guy."

McBryde snatched at any excuse. "I don't have the experience you're talking about, and besides which—"

"What about that story we pulled out of you," said Leticia Gompers between compulsive mouthfuls of corn chips. Her hand let a few chips slip onto her lap. "From when you worked for that security company out in Oregon and interrupted that robbery in progress . . ."

Jordan picked up the thread of the story. "And how you held them at gunpoint in the yards for six hours until the police came . . ."

"And how you shot one of them dead when he tried to draw on you," finished Clarence Brown softly.

McBryde shuddered as he tried to dam the images. If he hadn't been drunk that time at Cavanaugh's, he'd never have let the story out. "That was almost ten years ago."

"Should we vote?" Huxley said.

"How you shot him dead." Clarence Brown raised his voice. "And then waited for the police for six hours because they'd torn out the phone lines and smashed your scanner and there wasn't nobody there but you."

"A vote?" Huxley asked again.

"Six hours with that dead body and those three other thieves? No, sir, not me, I couldn't have done it," Brown said.

The group members paused to consider the scene. None of them had witnessed McBryde's terrifying stand-off, but it was etched all the same into their imaginations with the clarity of lived experience.

"Six hours," Brown said into the silence. "How'd you do it, man?"

"We should vote," Huxley said.

"It'd be unanimous," Jordan said.

Stein objected. "I don't like holding a gun to Larry's head like this."

They waited expectantly for a signal. McBryde stared at his hands. He hadn't fired a gun in almost a decade. He was not, at heart, a courageous man. Several times in his life he had been called upon to do brave things. But shooting that poor boy in the face had certainly not been one of them.

"Larry?" Jordan prompted.

Even if these accidents were real and had been planned, one cassette tape was not much in the way of a clue. If lucky, he might track down this criminal foamer in a month. But if the trail was well-concealed, the investigation might drag on well past his month-long vacation. Investigation?

"Hell," McBryde began, "I don't know the first thing about an investigation like this. You better find yourself a professional . . ."

"A professional?" Leticia Gompers laughed. "You know everything there is to know about trains. And you've got the rest of us to help. I can't think of a better candidate. Ecce homo!"

"Give me the tape," McBryde said with an effort. "And give me some time to think it over. No promises." He looked at the tape that had been thrust into his hands. He fingered the black plastic shell and tried not to see in his mind's eye those long-repressed images of pulsing, puddling blood.

TWO

Pierre, South Dakota? Everyone agreed: Pierre was Siberia. In FBI lingo, "Siberia" formed a constellation of unpopular offices where the willful, untrustworthy, or just plain stupid were exiled. And Pierre, they said, was the worst that Siberia had to offer, particularly for a woman. It was the FBI's last all-male field office, a mixture of flighty blond secretaries and well-muscled agents.

Or so Jennifer Szczymanski had heard. Before she was sent to Pierre, South Dakota. Alone.

"Kick butt out there, you hear?" Laura Barnegut said to her as they waited for their flights at Washington's National Airport.

"I think I'd rather stay at Quantico for four more months of training," Szczymanski said.

"This is not the Jennifer I know. Dickson nearly wet his pants every time he went up against you in martial arts. And he was a fucking state wrestling champ!"

"I'm going to South Dakota."

"Eh." Barnegut dismissed these fears with a wave of her hand. "If anybody can break those Pierre studs, you can."

Pierre had not been Szczymanski's choice. Two representatives of the Bureau's personnel office had approached her at the Academy one afternoon as she left a forensics class. Would she participate in a new program to diversify the field offices? They needed an answer immediately. That was so typical of the FBI. They threw you curveballs and never allowed you enough time to adjust your swing. Without giving the proposition much thought, Szczymanski had agreed to participate. A month later, just before graduation, they told her about Pierre. After hearing the rumors and gossip, she had petitioned for at least one more woman to go with her, either a new recruit or a transfer. Sorry, the Bureau responded: not enough of you to go around. Typical.

With her last week at Quantico so hectic, Szczymanski only began to formulate a strategy on the plane. This was not, she immediately recognized, the proper time for the Pert Young Recruit approach, which had worked quite well in many of her classes at the Academy. And the Bored Cynic routine, so useful around machismo, would probably err in the opposite direction and put the Pierre agents immediately on the defensive. She riffled through her conceptual deck of strategies—Trusty Confidante? Cold Worker Drone?

The Pierre operation, she decided finally, called for the Nuclear Posture—flexible response followed if necessary by massive retaliation. She would adapt to the new environment, giving firm indications that certain behavior was unacceptable but otherwise offering to become "one of the guys." If this flexibility failed, however, a showdown would follow. The Bureau would back her up. They were sending her to Vladivostok to comply with new affirmative-action guidelines established by a presidential task force. Any signs of further discrimination would only look bad for the Bureau. Still, in order to survive her two-year stint in Siberia, she'd have to demonstrate a certain degree of accommodation. It would be a tricky balance.

She was met at the Pierre airport not by a chest-thumping cowboy but by Doggett.

"S-so sorry," stammered the bespectacled young man holding a sign. He looked uncomfortably underfed, with the sallow complexion of someone forced to live for years on crackers and canned food. His sign read SZCZYMANSKI. The first letters were large and clear—after the M, however, the remaining letters crowded together until the final I nearly disappeared over the edge of the placard. Putting the sign into a briefcase, the young man guided her to the baggage-claim area. "I'm terribly sorry. Oh yes, and I'm Doggett. Agent D-Doggett. The room at the hotel won't be ready until after five P.M. But we w-were sort of hoping that you'd come by the office. Folks are real eager to m-meet you."

To her great surprise, the Pierre agents turned out to be warm and open and self-effacing in a midwestern way that she instantly appreciated. And the secretaries were far from bubbleheads. All female, to be sure, and a little heavy on the makeup for her tastes—but they also talked with her quite knowledgeably about FBI work and the often underappreciated pleasures of South Dakota living.

The entire staff welcomed her with a coffee-and-doughnut party in the first-floor conference room. She was presented with a fashionable black cowboy hat. The desk in her office on the second floor came equipped with a bouquet of white roses. They'd even converted a closet near her office into a women's bathroom (MEN read the handwritten sign on one bathroom; the airport placard, with its lopsided SZCZYMANSKI, was affixed to the other). There was no patronizing and no hostility. She was their first female agent and everyone treated her with respect and good humor.

"Everyone" included Rudy Blaine, the Special Agent in Charge. He was tall and fleshy enough to have played football in his college days. A regular Genghis Khan, according to the gossip at Quantico. But Szczymanski saw that he was too laid-back and bland to commandeer a band of pillaging Mongols. "Anything I can do for you, just ask," he told her that first day. During her welcoming party he stood against the wall with arms crossed. If they hadn't been introduced, she might have mistaken him for a security guard. She noted the wedding band on his finger: Genghis caged.

Flexible response it will be, she decided. She could return the weapons of massive retaliation to their silos and comfortably focus on learning the ropes. She'd always been happiest in a new situation, picking up the rules, listening for the right rhythms, memorizing the routines. It was the most exciting part of any job, before the learning curve flat-lined, before everything became rote.

She was assigned to the "Pushers," the anti-drug team. "Welcome to Siberia," they told her over beers at her hotel that evening. Not a bad office, really. Blaine's a good guy. Straight hours. Nice bennies. Pecking order can be trying after a while but, hey, that's the FBI for you. "S-suck it up and drive on," philosophized Doggett, a fellow Pusher.

Doggett and company were not the only ones to make a special effort. In her first month in Pierre, Blaine too went out of his way to help her acclimate. When mice overran her first apartment, he called around to his friends and found her another that turned out to be larger and cheaper. He let her take home a company car before all the paperwork had been cleared. He made sure she received a new Smith & Wesson 1076 semiautomatic, even though several other agents were still stuck with the old .38-caliber revolver. He even lent her his own camera to photograph evidence.

Then he asked her over to dinner.

Szczymanski accepted without hesitation, without even consulting the Pushers. She'd heard wonderful things about his wife and child. Doggett had once told her that Betty Blaine was the most interesting woman in the whole city.

But when she arrived at the Blaines' modest brick house, Betty and their baby girl were nowhere to be seen. The dining room table, quickly glimpsed as she was ushered in through the front door and escorted into the living room, was set for two.

"My wife had to go to her mother's," Blaine explained, taking Szczymanski's coat and grinning sheepishly. "She took Amanda with her. One of those last-minute things. I hope you don't mind London broil."

The dinner was thoroughly uncomfortable. Blaine studiously avoided talking about his wife and child, and Szczymanski deflected all questions about her own personal life. She tried to keep the discussion centered on the history of Pierre—the old fur-trading routes, the Lewis and Clark pass-by in 1806, the building of the original Fort Pierre. And all the time she was thinking: What does he want?

But he made no passes. When she got back to her apartment that night, she immediately called Barnegut in Atlanta.

"Is he handsome?" her friend asked over the phone.

"Come on, Laura, that's not the point."

"Aw, I'm just teasing you. But listen, all he did was invite you over for some meat. That ain't no crime."

"He's my boss. He shouldn't be doing things like that."

"How big's Pierre?"

"Oh, I don't know, fifteen thousand tops."

"Fifteen thousand? Hell, Jennifer, you're living in a small town. You and me, we're Chicago girls. Sometimes we just forget what friendly is, that's all."

She decided to tell no one else. In the several days that followed, Blaine merely smiled at her and spoke only of business matters. By the end of that week, however, he approached her with an offer to see a movie. Szczymanski pleaded a headache. She put off a proposed lunch with the excuse of too much work. Another dinner invitation could not be accepted because a "friend" was coming to visit. The SAC absorbed these polite refusals with a smile and a shrug. Szczymanski wondered if she should feel sorry for him. His marriage might be unhappy; his wife might have decided to leave him. But she operated by certain strict rules: Never date married men, never get involved with co-workers, never rush into things.

She tried as much as possible to ignore Rudy Blaine and concentrate on her work. She might only be in little Pierre, but this job was what she'd always wanted.

She'd interviewed with the Bureau immediately after college, when she was still too young and inexperienced. The recruiter laid out the options: police work, National Guard, engineering, accounting. And law. Szczymanski had taken this last route. Those years at the University of Michigan Law School had been all lost time, three years indentured to a profession she had no intention of pursuing, three dry years of torts and writs and going through the motions. Nevertheless, she topped her class and was pursued by the best New York law firms. She held to her original goal. The FBI, eager for agents with legal backgrounds, snatched her up and sent her to Quantico.

No one understood how much joining the FBI meant—not her

friends, not her law-school classmates, not her parents. But at Quantico, her loneliness quickly disappeared. She roomed with Laura Barnegut, a mordantly funny redhead, and they immediately hit it off. The training program was rigorous, demanding, and thoroughly enjoyable. Though she didn't remember the content of the law, she had absorbed its style, and this prepared her for the classes in interrogations and forensics. Three years of daily workouts at the University of Michigan gym—sit-ups, barbells, swimming, aerobics—gave her the stamina to meet the tough demands of the Bureau. Clenching and unclenching progressively larger balls of clay strengthened her hands, so she could squeeze off rounds from dozens of different weapons. She knew the FBI adjusted its physical requirements for women. But she wanted to do as well as the best agent, female or male.

As she had throughout her life, Szczymanski excelled at Quantico, earning high marks and the praise of her instructors. Quietly and patiently, she transformed herself into one of the FBI's prized recruits. They sent her to Pierre, alone, because they knew she could handle it.

And handle it she did, breaking cases that had been moldering on other agents' desks. As weeks stretched into months, the work absorbed her and Rudy Blaine became just another co-worker. She often worked late into the night, long after her colleagues had gone home. It was not uncommon for her to spend sixteen hours at the office.

One night, on the verge of identifying a pattern in a drug-smuggling case, she completely lost track of time. When she looked at her watch, it read nearly 2 A.M. The office was very quiet, with only the white noise of the heating system and the coffeemaker.

Then she heard the cough.

Szczymanski swiveled around in her chair. Rudy Blaine was standing in the doorway, holding a bunch of white roses.

"Busy?" he asked, his smile wide. "These are for you."

She indicated the empty vase on her desk.

"Hungry?" he asked.

She shook her head. The room seemed to collapse around them, and her breathing became irregular.

"A beer then?"

Again she shook her head.

"I—I—" she tried to dig out the words from the back of her throat. "I was working."

"Commendable." Blaine was still smiling.

"I think we've got the evidence on Case fifty-three." She held up a bank statement.

He stepped closer to look at the photocopy. Her hand trembled. He touched her hand. "You're so pretty."

It was then that she should have acted, should have pushed his hand away, should have reminded him of professional ethics, of his wife, of his child. But her mind went blank and her muscles grew mysteriously heavy.

Blaine took the paper from her hand and laid it on the desk beside her. He leaned over and placed his fingers delicately on the armrests of her chair. Now his face was close to hers. She could see the droplets of sweat glistening on his temples and several black hairs poking out of his nostrils. His face had turned an unpleasant shade of pink.

He tried to kiss her. Stunned, Szczymanski didn't jerk her head away. She simply pushed at his large shoulders. But his lips were already pressing against hers. She pushed more violently but couldn't get any leverage. The heat was pouring from his mouth. She slipped a hand between their faces. "No," she said forcefully. He pushed her hand out of the way and again pressed forward with his lips.

Suddenly, as if activated by some hidden switch, she burst into action. Grabbing Blaine's elbows, she jackknifed her legs around his knees, sweeping them to one side as though scything two stalks of wheat. By pushing at his elbows she managed to topple him onto his back. Without pausing for breath or reflection, she sprang from the chair to straddle his stomach, careful to keep one of his arms trapped behind his back and the other secured with her knee. The movements came naturally, a standard exercise from the Academy martial arts training course.

"I would appreciate," she said carefully, "if you'd never do that again." His broad chest heaved beneath her. Szczymanski was only a couple inches shy of six feet tall and she weighed a taut 145. She knew how to handle people twice her size, even former football players. Yet her heart was racing and needles of doubt jabbed at her. New recruits were not supposed to upend their SACs.

"Let me go," Blaine said. Anger was staining his face progressively darker shades of red. Small bubbles of spittle collected at the corners of his mouth.

"Do you promise never to do that again?" She found this further physical contact with him nauseating. It is a drill, she told herself.

"Let go of my arm," he said. "I didn't do anything."

She put more weight on the knee that pinioned his arm. "You kissed me."

"I didn't do . . . anything," he repeated, his voice edging higher from the pain.

This is going nowhere, she decided. The drill is over.

She stood up and backed away from him. She paused on the threshold, her pulse still racing. "If you expect me to say that I'll pretend this never happened, you're wrong."

"No one will believe you." He withdrew his arm from behind his back and massaged it but otherwise did not move. "I can make a lot of trouble for you." His voice quavered slightly.

Szczymanski stood for a moment looking down at the supervisor's supine body, rapidly assessing her likely future. He was right. Without the necessary proof, she probably could not make the accusation stick. She had never mentioned any of his approaches to the Pushers. She couldn't even be sure that they would support her in the end, since the SAC was popular in the office. And Blaine could indeed make a lot of trouble for her, even suspending her from the force for some imaginary infraction of the rules. Perhaps it would be best to forget about the incident and hope that it wouldn't be repeated.

Then she caught sight of something on the shelf near the door and noiselessly appropriated it. More than anything, she hated being jerked around. To hell with flexible response. It was time for massive retaliation.

"You're wrong," she said, aiming. "I'll be the one making trouble. For you."

The flash from her FBI evidence camera lit up the room.

THREE

With increasing irritation, McBryde skipped through the entries in the index: Bulimia, Drumming, Growth, Mantras, Self-Healing. None of these topics could help him. They didn't have anything to do with train accidents, inexperienced gumshoes, or murderous foamers. He wanted to call his foolishly optimistic sister and complain to her about this "self-help" book. Not that *Accentuate the Positive* had ever helped her. She still couldn't manage her three children from two failed marriages or hold down the simplest job for more than a year. "This will inspire," she had inscribed on the inside front cover. "May it bring joy and light into your life." Hah!

It was still early enough on the West Coast—the three-hour time difference made it only 10 P.M. in San Diego. But he hadn't talked with his sister now in six months, not even to thank her for *Accentuate the Positive* when the Christmas present arrived by mail over a month ago.

No, he didn't want to talk to his sister.

He wanted to talk to Rosalind.

He wanted to wake her up and hear the worried, sleep-hazy "Hello?" of someone expecting tragedy. He wanted to break the group's vow of secrecy and tell her everything about the emergency meeting, about the tape that lay on his bedside table, about the dreadful decision he had to make. She wouldn't provide him with any guidance, he knew that. Rosalind was never very good with answers. She was much better with questions. "And how do *you* feel about this?" she would ask. "Is this what you *really* want to do?" She should have been a psychologist, not an editor. But it was not her psychologist's patter that he wanted—he had more than enough between the covers of the book in his hands. He just wanted to hear her voice, wanted to hear the familiar ways her mind moved, wanted to hold the phone close to his ear and let her lullaby words pacify him.

Rosalind was his ex-wife. She'd left him nearly a year ago. When he returned from Lancaster's Seventeenth annual Spring Meeting and Railroadiana Show, she'd already cleared out her belongings from their Germantown house and carted off their daughter to a friend's apartment in Bala Cynwyd. Soon after, she was introduced to a computer-science professor who worked at a nearby elite college. Three weeks later she moved in with this home wrecker, in what for his ex-wife was an unusually hasty decision. It is a sign of her desperation, McBryde had thought at the time, and she will move out just as rapidly. But there she remained, Rosalind of Rosemont.

Accentuate the Positive claimed that mourning lasted for half the period of the relationship. For the scientifically minded, the book even provided an algebraic equation that considered several additional variables (age of the former lover, income at time of breakup). Four years? Would Rosalind lounge in his imagination, alluring and magnetic, for four long years?

If not for Melissa, he would keep as much distance between himself and Rosalind as possible, for only distance could make his heart grow colder. Ah, Melissa. A six-year-old whirling dervish, she alternately delighted and exhausted him—for two weekends a month. This weekend, she'd been particularly feisty. That morning, for instance, she'd woken him up at 6 A.M. to watch *The Little Mermaid* for the fourth time in twenty-four hours. Later, over breakfast, she made suggestions for the day's schedule.

"Paris," she said, her mouth full of cinnamon-honey-nut oatmeal. Her mother had just returned from a business trip to Paris with a T-shirt that Melissa had so far refused to take off during her stay. It was pink and depicted the Eiffel Tower in silver spangles, with little clouds of oatmeal that she'd added that morning.

"Submarine," she tried, after being told that Paris could not be done in a day. McBryde gently vetoed this suggestion as well. He was making pancakes on a hot griddle, concentrating on his batter-dripping technique.

"Daddy!" Melissa complained. "You never wanta do what I wanta do!"

"Suggest something sensible."

"Zoo," his daughter decided finally, slapping her spoon into her bowl. Oatmeal splattered onto the tablecloth and created another cloud on her shirt.

"But it's very cold outside," McBryde pointed out.

"Zoo."

The batter sizzled on the cast-iron surface. "You could read a book while Daddy did some work."

"Zoo!"

In the end McBryde had relented. He'd do anything to prevent his daughter's tears. She could be persistent to the point of mulishness. But that was not the only way in which Melissa resembled her mother. They both pushed their hair behind their right ears with their thumbs. They hugged their knees right up beneath their chins when sitting in bed. They squinted when confused. Finally, neither showed any interest whatsoever in trains. Perhaps Melissa copied him in some ways, but McBryde couldn't identify these passed-on traits. He was too busy finding the mother in the daughter. Once fun, now gut-wrenching, it was a game he couldn't stop playing.

McBryde looked down at the hardcover book in his hands. The first half of *Accentuate the Positive* was well-thumbed, dog-eared, and lunch-splattered. In the second, unread half, the pages remained squared off and compact. He turned to a page three-quarters of the way into the book, to a chapter about learning to express true feelings entitled "Saying Yes to No." He tore the page in half, horizontally. There. That felt better. He tossed the book into a pile of dirty clothes somewhere at the foot of the bed.

If only he could dismiss the tape so unceremoniously. No matter where he turned his thoughts, from his sister Eileen to Rosalind to Melissa, they inevitably returned to this compact, sixty-minute symphony of death and destruction.

McBryde looked at the tape on his night table. With the light of the lamp on it, the cassette case seemed to glow. He was suddenly seized by an irrational fear that it threw off deadly emanations like a chunk of radium. He turned his back on the table, burrowed deeper beneath the bedcovers. But the sounds continued to reverberate inside his head.

Considering the circumstances, the tape quality was exceptional. Whoever mixed the sound had gone to considerable lengths to achieve professional standards. Not only were the accidents themselves reproduced with astonishing clarity, but different sources had been spliced together seamlessly: the desperate voice of the engineer crackling over the CB, the click of the wheels as they disengaged from the track, the deliberately calm reassurances of the conductor speaking over the intercom, the distant wail of the ambulances as they approached the accident site, the horrible splashing of a drowning person. There must have been bugs everywhere, from the intercom system to the train's undercarriage. But how had they captured the voices of the ambulance orderlies? Who could have done all of this? A disgruntled conductor? A group of crazed foamers?

It would be difficult to forget the sounds he'd heard that evening. The worst was from the Fort Lauderdale head-on, the voice of the engineer just as he realized that a signal error put him in the direct path of an approaching freight train. Desperately he braked and barked orders over the CB to the oncoming train. But in mid-order, the engineer stopped. His scream was cut short by the tearing and telescoping of metal. Next came the shaky voice of a paramedic radioing for additional trauma units and her clinical description of the more gruesome injuries. The engineer had been decapitated. A conductor in the mail car had been impaled on a foot-long bolt.

Three times he'd listened to that engineer's last scream, three times he'd gone cold inside when the paramedic's voice cracked as she described the conductor's injuries. The tape contained nothing as terrible as that modulation in her voice. ". . . a bolt pierced above the sternum causing instant . . . causing eventual death . . ." Her voice had shifted up a notch on "eventual." What had she seen to change her diagnosis? She didn't say.

It reminded him of that Sunday morning almost a decade ago when he'd still lived in Oregon and his boss at Mortimer Security pulled him out of bed after a Southern Pacific hotshot veered off a bridge outside Eugene. When he arrived at the site, they posted him on the shore, near the bend in the river. Although his back was to the reclamation project, McBryde still managed with occasional sidelong glances to follow the action. A crane pulled the engine from the river bottom. Water cascaded from the Espee's open wounds—large gashes in the crumpled cab, in the turbine casing. The arm of the crane swung slowly over to a muddy area bristling with cattails. Its winch grinding, the crane gently set its burden down. Then the special-operations men went to work removing the engineer. Or, rather, the pieces of the engineer. Six hours in the water on a hot summer day and the poor fellow's body had become so bloated that it had to be cut out of the maze of metal with acetylene torches. The work was interrupted only once, to rush a new recruit into the open air where he vomited into the mud and underbrush.

From then on, McBryde had associated train accidents with nausea and dismemberment. He tolerated Jordan's photographs because Jordan was a friend. He refused to look at Georgia Huxley's album of neatly labeled mishaps after that first, uncomfortable time.

But this tape was the worst of the lot. On the first listen, he'd felt as though he were surreptitiously leafing through a porno magazine. By the second and third run-throughs, however, he realized that this was no ordinary pornography. This was the stuff he'd only heard about—with animals, with knives. The tape he was listening to was the foamer equivalent of a snuff film. Georgia Huxley should be spending five thousand dollars on psychotherapy, damn it, not on illicit audio cassettes!

McBryde threw back the bedcovers and snatched the tape from its resting place. He'd listened to the tape more than once because on that first listening something had caught his attention. But he couldn't quite pinpoint the familiar sound. He kicked aside some dirty clothes, stubbed his toe on the book, cursed, and padded over to the boom box. He pushed the tape inside. He slid back under the covers to the sounds of wheels clicking irregularly over the imperfections in the continuously welded tracks. He turned off the light.

In the darkness, the derailment became the only reality. His room became a sleeper. His body tensed at every click for the corresponding tremor from the chassis of the sleeper. His eyes expected the periodic swath of light from passing stations. Then the sounds of wheel on wood, on gravel, on grass, on rock. Something in all of those sounds on the tape was poised to trigger a memory. He tried to concentrate on that something but gradually felt himself grow disoriented. Drifting off to sleep, McBryde gave up his pursuit of this buried connection. The trains passed farther and farther away into the night.

By the time he awoke in the morning, even the memory of the memory had evaporated. Indeed, the whole incident with the tape lay forgotten. Then, on his way to the shower, he caught sight of the cassette case and his dilemma blindsided him. His stomach dropped. Groggy and irritable and unhappy that his problems hadn't disappeared during the night, McBryde leaned toward rejecting the group's plan.

"Say yes to no," he growled to himself beneath the lukewarm drizzle of the shower. "Accentuate the negative."

As he toweled himself dry, McBryde tensed at the thought of a day filled with angry commuter complaints. The public was digesting the fare increase as easily as syrup of ipecac. Carefully maneuvering the electric shaver through his stubble, he looked at the way age had conspired with gravity to pull his face downward. In a flash he saw the future, and it consisted largely of jowls.

"You're a handsome man," Rosalind had told him some months after the separation. "You'll have no problem finding someone else."

But since she left me, I've found no one, he thought, the razor now forgotten as it whirred an inch from his face. Thirty-two years old, I'm stuck in a job that once seemed promising. I'm separated from the only woman in the world who has ever understood me. And my book?

He hadn't even thought about his book in over a month, hadn't written a page in over a year, hadn't had proper enthusiasm for the project for nearly three. It was to have been his life's great work: a grand scheme, elegantly presented and relentlessly argued, for a new American ultra-high-speed rail system. Funded by a comparatively small surcharge on gasoline, the new system would have as its centerpiece an enormous magnetic-levitation network—Maglev—with intricate intermodal connections. Maglev would make trains accident-proof. Every derailment and collision infuriated him because they signified an America past its prime, in its dotage, without the sense to invest wisely in the future because it could not conceive of a future in the first place. Train accidents rarely happened in Japan. The French TGV was exceptionally safe. By eliminating grade crossings, upgrading the rails, and installing state-of-the-art safety mechanisms—or better yet, by creating an entirely new Maglev system—the United States could make accidents as ridiculous in this post-modern era as sailors dying of scurvy or farmers gored by oxen.

All of his research, including three notebooks filled with densely packed information, lay in a file cabinet in the second bedroom where Melissa spent her periodic weekends. The file cabinet and its identical partner holding SEPTA-related papers supported a slab of wood that functioned as a table for his computer. The hard drive and backup floppy disks contained several copies of the thirty-page introduction to this impassioned book-length essay. Roughly one page for each year of his life. At that rate he'd have to achieve a biblical life span to finish the project.

McBryde still received information on a weekly basis about the various legislative attempts to boost funding for Maglev. These letters, xeroxed congressional bills, clippings, and newsletters lay unread in a filer tray next to his now dusty computer. He'd been saying to himself for the last month that after the furor over the fare increase died down, he'd look at this material carefully. I will print out another copy of the draft. I will take a fresh look at the summary and outline of the book as a whole. I will not think about the promise made to an interested publisher nearly a year ago that a rough draft would be finished and sent off in six months.

Suddenly aware of the whirring razor, McBryde finished shaving. His life was succumbing to the unavoidable drag of friction. It was slowing to a standstill. Soon he'd begin moving backward, until the day of pain and bewilderment when he'd leave his life as he once entered it.

Rosalind's heart-shaped face appeared next to his in the mirror, her chin resting on his shoulder, as she used to do for so many years when he shaved. Shaking his head to dispel the vision, he nearly took off the tip of his nose with the razor.

He needed a vacation. He needed a cigarette.

A glance at his watch told McBryde that he had only ten minutes to get to the subway station four blocks from his home. He dressed hurriedly.

The decision.

On one side of the scale he placed the weights of civic duty and responsibility to his fellow foamers. The police were certainly capable of blowing the case. Then the press would get hold of it and start spreading their usual lies. A nationwide scandal could ruin the train industry and keep passenger travel in the dark age of the airplane and automobile—and just at the moment America was making up the lost ground, was about to rebuild its system in the image of the Europeans and the Japanese.

But the weights were much heavier on the other side of the scale. First, there was fear. Second, there was fifty-five-pound Melissa—he'd been wanting to spend more time with her. Finally came the weight of Maglev. If he took those four weeks as a true vacation, he could actually return to his project. He could get through the latest material, update his introduction, perhaps even make some headway on a first chapter. To hell with this crazy foamer. The group had agreed that if he turned down the assignment they would hire a private detective, someone both discreet and reliable. A poor second, they'd told him.

A poor second it would have to be. His days as a security guard—to the limited extent that they had ever existed—had long since been laid to rest. If he wanted to be a writer, there was only one choice: to write.

Then the phone rang. It was Jordan. An early-morning freight train out of Detroit heading southeast had crashed into an idling Amtrak train outside of Pittsburgh. Among the casualties were two little girls, both six years old. McBryde readjusted the scales. The voice of the paramedic echoed again in his ear. Still on the phone with Jordan, he made his decision.

FOUR

At 10:30 A.M., on the first day of her new assignment, Jennifer Szczymanski was half-squatting in the cafeteria of the FBI's national headquarters, her back pressed against a wall, sweat beginning to form at her hairline, and pain as she had never before known gripping her leg muscles.

"That's the lactic acid you're feeling, babe," agent Peña explained. "It builds up in your quads. Nothing you can do about it. Three minutes tops."

The position had looked absurdly easy. They'd instructed her to sit as if upon a box with her back against the wall, thighs at right angles to calves. There was, however, no box. Still, with the wall to push against, it should have been a snap.

It wasn't.

The pain had begun as a faint tingle and had rapidly transformed her legs into cottage cheese. Szczymanski clenched her fists resting on her thighs. Pain did not concentrate her mind. On the contrary, her thoughts leaped from one topic to another in a vain attempt to elude the heatless fire.

The pastel-orange cafeteria walls reminded her of children's aspirin. She shouldn't have eaten the entire cinnamon-almond muffin for breakfast at the hotel. Agent Peña was short and slim-waisted, with hair the color of blackberries, a pert nose, and dazzling blue eyes. An apartment. Immediately after work she'd have to resume her search for an apartment somewhere in the District.

Szczymanski blinked a drop of sweat from her eyelid. Granite.

She had an appointment in an hour to see her new supervisor, a Special Agent in Charge named Granite. The pain continued to intensify. Granite? "No kidding, babe," agent Peña had said, going over the day's schedule. Steadman Granite. Szczymanski pressed her back more firmly against the wall and felt the secondary pain of bruised vertebrae. Had she brought a toothbrush to work for after lunch? Yes, the toothbrush, it was blue, bought at a . . . a blue toothbrush . . . blue . . .

A grunt slipped from her lips.

Peña consulted her watch. "That's already two minutes. Not bad." She looked at the other women who formed a semicircle around Szczymanski. "Think she'll make it?" Peña's question was met with shrugs and guesses.

Time solidified. Her backbone no longer protesting, Szczymanski dug her fingernails into her palms, hoping that the new discomfort would detract from the great waves of pain spreading up from her legs. It had all begun as a discussion at breakfast. The four women who stood with Peña seemed to elongate, their necks lengthening and their heads coming together like the tops of neighboring trees seen from the ground. Someone had read about this position, a wall press that few people could hold for more than a minute or two. Crystal City. Thank God she'd be out of that suburban outcropping. That space station on earth. An apartment. Any apartment. With a bed. A soft couch. A Jacuzzi.

"Thirty more seconds, babe. Then you can relax."

The others had all tried it. Last week. Peña. Only Peña had made it to three minutes. "I'll do it for three minutes," Szczymanski had said. Stupidly. Not thinking. No strategy. The pain was freezing her lower body, cutting it off from the rest of her. Her legs were trembling. She looked down at her knees through lowered eyelids. She was afraid her legs would shoot out from under her. She deserved it. For not developing a strategy. Deserved it. The toothbrush. Granite. An apartment.

"Apartment," Szczymanski said through clenched teeth.

Peña tapped her wristwatch. "That's it. Three minutes. I'm impressed."

The others murmured their approval.

"What . . . did . . . you . . . do?" Szczymanski forced out the words, maintaining her rigid posture.

Peña looked down at her, uncomprehending.

"Your . . . time."

Peña's blue eyes sparkled. "Oh, I think it was three minutes and thirty seconds. Ain't that right, Metaxas?"

Szczymanski didn't hear the confirmation. She pressed her head against the wall and sucked her upper lip into her mouth to bite down upon it. Releasing the lip, she breathed, "Four. Four minutes."

Peña looked at the watch again. "That's another forty-five seconds, babe. Not a good idea. Don't know what that lactic acid's liable to do."

"She's gonna faint," one of the observers said.

"No," Szczymanski grunted, forcing her eyes to look up at the treetops so far above her. Go away, she instructed the lactic acid. Go away for forty more seconds. Take a lactic holiday. Now her midsection was growing numb as well. It was blue. Blue.

"Toothbrush." She spat the two syllables.

"What's she saying?" someone asked.

"Let's pick her up by the arms."

"No," came Peña's faraway voice. "It's only twenty more seconds now. This is what she wants."

"Toothbrush," Szczymanski spat again, trying to focus on the individual bristles. How many were there? Fifty? White ones around the edges and red ones in the center. The toothbrush was blue, with white and red bristles. She brushed her teeth with the American flag.

Szczymanski couldn't tell if her body was swaying or if it was just her mind swimming from side to side within her brain.

Suddenly she felt hands beneath her armpits lifting up. Her

knees unbuckled. Then, pain flashing to the roots of her hair, her calves dropped and her feet touched the ground.

"Four minutes," Peña said, now looking up at her.

The two women on either side of Szczymanski eased her weight down. She tentatively shook one calf, then the other. The pain was gone, replaced by prickling pins and needles. She shivered and let herself be supported by women on each side until the numbness too receded. She'd never been around so many FBI women before.

"We're all tough here. Ain't that right?" Peña appealed to her colleagues, who only shrugged. "Playing this little game has nothing to do with rappelling out of a helicopter. Doesn't mean you'll be able to shoot the dick off a bank robber with the last bullet in your gun."

Now standing on her own, Szczymanski said nothing. Someone pushed a Kleenex into her hand so she could wipe the sweat from around her eyes. They were in an alcove of the cafeteria, near a water fountain and some trash receptacles.

After motioning for the others to disperse, Peña escorted her back to the main section of the cafeteria, back to the same table vacated only four minutes before. Szczymanski's coffee cup, still half-full, waited with the better part of her strawberry-filled doughnut, its jam leaking onto wax paper. It seemed to her a meal she'd abandoned hours ago.

Her legs, now pleasurably warm and rubbery, felt as if they'd kicked through two miles of lap swimming. Into the space of her mind once occupied by pain rushed a mixture of emotions. She felt exhilarated and ridiculous and angry that she'd used such a party trick to establish credibility. Could four minutes of lactic acid endurance prove that she belonged at national headquarters? Did it eliminate the memories of her humiliating interrogation at the hands of OPR, the Office of Professional Responsibility? Of course not. It had been a needless way of calling attention to herself. She toyed with her doughnut.

One week ago she'd been in a windowless room somewhere in D.C., participating in the OPR investigation and convinced that her FBI career was finished. She'd filed the complaint out of anger and defiance, not with any hope of victory. OPR, she figured, would throw the cold water of reality in her face.

The internal investigation had been an insult. Her interrogators had been thoroughly unpleasant. OPR was renowned for its pitiless staff. The old joke was that OPR—the Office of Professional Rectums—had been created to keep all the assholes together in one place. They probed her sexual history, her psychological profile, her capacity to become enraged. It wasn't good cop, bad cop. It was bad cop, worse cop. The investigation differed little from the four-mile run in hundred-degree heat that had initiated her sixteen-week course at Quantico.

But she was fully prepared to pass these tests of character and courage with dignity. Not collapse halfway through. Not complain in breathless bursts for the entire distance. Not lose her composure and the contents of her stomach in the weeds at the end of the course.

She performed evenly during the interrogation. Her strategy—the Mannequin—was calculated to challenge the usual stereotypes of women as hysterical, unreliable, or hypersensitive. But she still hadn't held out much hope. Blaine had pull in the organization; she was a green recruit. The photos of him lying on the floor near her desk provided some corroboration, but she was enough of a lawyer to realize that they were by no means incontrovertible proof.

When the verdict came down, then, she'd been thunderstruck. Not only had she been vindicated, she'd been reassigned, promoted even, to the national office. And now she felt she had to prove the merit of her reassignment. But with a wall press? She was betraying her age, not her resolve.

"Four minutes," Peña said reflectively, opening the orientation packet. "Amazing how much pain can be packed into such a short time. And why the hell would anyone want to practice those things, huh? Leaves me cold."

Szczymanski didn't answer. Only now was her heart settling down, crawling back into its cave.

"Okay, look, let's get back to work and cut to the chase. Granite's a pigdick," Peña said, fingering the multicolored papers that lay between them. Her soft voice belied her harsh opinions. "But he's our pigdick. He's straight up, don't worry about that. He just wants perfection. Save the President of the United States from assassination and he'll want to know why you didn't file a travel-expense report on time. Now, the packet . . ."

Szczymanski tried to concentrate on the materials—the mauve pamphlet on health coverage, the teal flyer on paid leave, the gold handout on tuition waivers. But her attention kept wandering back to the wall press. Acting foolishly was bad. Worse, however, was acting without a strategy. Her public behavior was always supposed to follow a plan, a circumspect exploration of the hypotheticals. But she had acted out of control and now the wall press controlled her. A stupid, meaningless four-minute dare imposed its logic upon her future.

The lactic acid stunt signified TB^2, no way around it. She hadn't employed TB^2 since her days of Quantico role-playing. Perhaps it wasn't the appropriate style, considering the circumstances surrounding her promotion to the national office. But actions set expectations into motion. And strategies, as she was all too aware, confound those expectations only at great risk. Cart before the horse, tail wagging the dog—whatever her reservations about the applicability of this particular strategy, a Tough Ball Breaker she'd have to be—TB^2 for short.

"After that," Peña was saying, "we'll take you for a retinal photo. Pierre's the last regional office without one. Don't those cowboys worry about security breaches?"

Szczymanski shook her head. "It's generally pretty quiet out there."

"What about those crazy Indians who shot the agents back in the seventies?"

"That was on Pine Ridge Reservation. Not in Pierre."

Peña fixed her with a penetrating stare. "They'd still better install a new security system. Things are getting bad all over."

Peña turned back to her summary of security considerations— all of it detailed on four pieces of hot-pink paper and all of it familiar territory for Szczymanski. With half her attention she monitored the flow of information to ensure that no surprise nugget turned up. With the other half, she reflected on her colleague's personality.

Minutes after meeting her that morning she'd had Peña typed. Most agents were Pluggers, who did just the minimum to get by. At the bottom were the Doggers; you hoped one never became your partner. At the top, however, were the Risers. All Risers were tough, smart, and driven. But some, like Peña, were entirely selfish. They treated law enforcement as a peripheral interest, a means to an end. They didn't have any ideals, didn't care about truth or justice. Agents like Peña aimed for top Bureau positions or, if the opportunity arose, choice jobs in the private sector. Such agents were alternately chatty and brusque, as though unsure whether to consider you a friend or a competitor.

"Szczymanski." Peña had struggled with her name during the initial introductions that morning. They stood by the security desk near the visitors' entrance to the J. Edgar Hoover Building. "What the hell are all these letters about?"

Szczymanski pronounced her name. "The beginning was originally pronounced 'shch.' Like in 'fresh cheese.' "

"Fresh cheese?"

"It's Polish."

"Figured it was one of those Russian-type names."

"Polish, actually."

"Okay, Fresh Cheese. I'm Puerto Rican. If you hadn't figured that out already." Peña had looked at her questioningly, as though trying to detect signs of bias. "You originally from South Dakota?"

"Chicago."

"Good." Peña visibly relaxed, smiling for the first time. "You got some street smarts then, I guess. Last thing we need around here is another dumb farm girl."

Szczymanski cringed, said nothing, and followed Peña through the building. She'd visited the FBI's national headquarters several times during her Quantico days. An eleven-story monument to function over form, it was composed of two large concrete boxes at an angle to one another. It occupied a full city block on Pennsylvania Avenue, surrounded by the more classical facades of other federal buildings. Inside, the hallways were grimly uniform—beige walls and black doors. In Pierre, the agents had decorated their walls with colorful calendars, and the squad room kept its Christmas lights strung from the ceiling all year round. But the national office was all business. J. Edgar Hoover had been colorless; so was his building.

After Szczymanski's first routine briefing with the harelipped division-office manager, agent Peña had picked her up at the door and led her like a first grader to the cafeteria on the eighth floor.

There she was introduced to a group of FBI women who met for coffee at the same time each week. They provided Szczymanski with the real orientation: this agent admired Mussolini and gag ties but otherwise had a good heart; that agent had a pathological fear of spiders and split infinitives; this SAC's hairpiece was perpetually skewed; that SAC was a racist SOB; the secretaries in External Affairs made the best coffee; it was wise to bring a bagged lunch except on Fridays, when the kitchen produced credible pizzas. Szczymanski didn't ask how they felt as women in the Bureau, and no one offered any insights. She hoped that these confessions would come later, in more intimate conversations.

Gazing around at the other agents in the cafeteria, she must have wandered in her thoughts, for suddenly the women were talking about lactic acid and wall presses and she had no idea how the topic had come up. Still adjusting to the new environment, she fell into a comfortable listen-only posture. But something about Peña's boast—that she could take more pain than the others—irritated her. Perhaps if her feisty guide hadn't earlier disparaged farm girls, Szczymanski wouldn't have risen to the implicit challenge. Most of her relatives in Poland still farmed and remarks about dumb farmers offended her only slightly less than dumb-Polack jokes. Later she discovered that Peña used the expression "farm girl" to refer to anyone who hadn't grown up in the heart of a big city.

Szczymanski licked the jam out of her doughnut. The rest of it was stale. Peña was describing the changes in orientation that had taken place since the dark days of J. Edgar.

"Read the latest bio?" she asked Szczymanski suddenly.

"Of Hoover? No."

"Dressed up in skirts. That's what it says."

"Do you believe it?"

"Summers are a bitch here," Peña said, wiping imaginary sweat from her forehead. "Wouldn't blame the man for wearing a dress. Much more comfortable."

Szczymanski smiled.

"Don't get me wrong," she continued, "there's no room for fruits in this organization. Bad for morale."

"Of course," Szczymanski replied indifferently.

"Men hitting on men? Women sniffing after women? That just creates the wrong atmosphere."

"And men sniffing after women?"

"Well"—Peña smiled—"that just makes things more interesting."

Szczymanski dropped the subject. "What about this two-to-five slot in my schedule?"

Peña shrugged. "Maybe that's for sightseeing. I've been here going on three years and I still haven't done the White House tour." She brushed powdered sugar and doughnut crumbs from the orientation materials and assembled the trash of their coffee break. "You'll just have to ask Granite."

Which she did, within seconds of meeting the SAC.

"The afternoon?" Steadman Granite repeated. Szczymanski passed the schedule to him. He withdrew a pair of horn-rimmed glasses from his shirt pocket. "Ah yes, you'll be very busy this afternoon. We've assigned you an urgent case." He looked at her over the top of his glasses. "You're eager to start, I expect."

Szczymanski nodded, swallowing her curiosity.

Granite was a straightforward, straight-talking man. In a cowboy hat, he could have advertised cigarettes. The only flaw in his otherwise photogenic appearance was a small scar, a pale rivulet that ran from his left ear several inches down his neck. Granite didn't smile and he didn't waste time trying to make her feel comfortable. What did Peña call him? A pigdick. Pigdicks were fine in her book, as long as you knew their worst qualities at the outset.

"You're here under unusual circumstances," he said, putting the glasses back into his pocket.

Szczymanski braced herself for a discussion of the Pierre debacle. Granite fished around for a file and passed a paper to her across the desk.

"I'm not sure I understand," he continued, "how you demonstrated your abilities so quickly. Or why they saw fit to send you to me."

The sheet of paper was a recommendation for transfer. It briefly described her successful assignments in Pierre. It mentioned her firsts in academics and defensive tactics at Quantico. It discussed the importance of utilizing her skills at a more "dynamic" office.

It was signed, at the bottom, by her previous supervisor, SAC Rudolph Blaine.

"Well, sir," she said, looking up into Granite's eyes.

"No matter," he cut her off. "I'm only interested in what you do here and now. The past doesn't concern me."

But the past still concerned her a great deal. Now she understood the real reason for her transfer. The damage controllers worked up a dummy recommendation because they wanted to pretend that the "affair" in Pierre had never happened. Hush her up with a promotion. They were afraid she'd go to the press. Just like that African-American who had charged the CIA with racism and won his battle after several years of painful disclosures. Sign this, Rudy, and you're off the hook, they told him. One more fuckup and we'll tuck you in bed without your dinner. She angrily clenched her toes.

Granite reached over to pluck the paper from her hand. "It's not standard procedure to show you these documents. Don't want you to get a swelled head."

Swelled head, indeed! She forced her toes to unclench, her body to relax. At least she hadn't been branded a troublemaker. The FBI was not an organization that treasured dissent. Success is the best revenge, she reminded herself: Give me a case and this Tough Ball Breaker will crack it. As for Rudy Blaine, well, perhaps remaining in Pierre was punishment enough.

"A critical issue," Granite was saying, searching for something on his desk. He located a folder and passed it across the desk to her. "These are the latest stats from DOT. The Department of Transportation. You're familiar with our train system, right? Sixteen Class One roads handle the freight, Amtrak carries all the passenger business."

Szczymanski gave an indistinct nod.

"Amtrak's subsidized by the government. But it's still a private company, operating for profit and answerable to the feds only to the extent that it must account for the use of public funds. Those"—he indicated the folder—"are the accident bulletins and grade-crossing figures. I've also included a collection of clippings drawn from both national and regional press. Study them carefully."

Szczymanski riffled quickly through the enclosed documents.

"You're probably wondering if this is a test." Granite leaned back in his chair, folding his hands across his stomach. "A Leavis test, for example."

Leavis was a notorious professor of evidence at Quantico. He administered not tests but "challenges." They were more like trials by ordeal. Eight times in his month-long course, Leavis distributed increasingly irrelevant texts—a section of Gray's *Anatomy*, the third act of a play by an obscure seventeenth-century playwright, an instruction manual for a chain saw. These texts functioned as keys to unlock mysteries at test time. Sometimes the pertinent details were buried in a footnote, sometimes in a chapter heading. In order to solve the test problems, you had to memorize virtually the entire material—from the fonts on the title page to the back-cover quotes, and everything in between. On one occasion, the entire "challenge" had been coded and the number of keys on a harpsichord had to be plugged into an algebraic equation that yielded the formula to decipher the code. Those who forgot this crucial detail couldn't make heads or tails of the exam. They sat at their desks sighing with frustration, inserting random numbers into the algebraic equation. Szczymanski had never once failed these challenges. Her memory was excellent, her eye for detail superb.

"But this is no test," Granite continued. "We suspect that a recent upsurge in train accidents is statistically significant and potentially a result of deliberate design. I want you to determine the cause of these accidents and identify the person or persons responsible."

The tips of her fingers vibrated as though she'd just gulped down a double espresso. This wasn't paperwork or routine surveillance or a bonehead job for a novice. This was a project of national significance. It might be a group of domestic discontents or stateless terrorists. She would be involved in protecting the national interest, in saving lives. She could now safely put the professional doubts behind her. She could forget about lactic acid, about the OPR investigation, about the whole Pierre experience. She could refocus on matters of life and death.

"If it were up to me, I wouldn't give you this job," Granite said, returning to an erect sitting position. "But the decision was made by others. I will support you with whatever resources you need. But if you don't appear adequate to the challenge, I will take the case away from you. That, Agent Szczymanski, is my prerogative."

Peña was right. A true pigdick. His threats, though, were irrelevant. She'd take whatever was thrown at her—sexual harassment, malevolent interrogators, lactic acid—and come through in the end stronger than ever.

FIVE

Unbelievable," Ron Jordan said after the tape faded into silence. "Simply unbelievable." He was shaking his great head back and forth. He had listened to the noises of the accidents like a reluctant voyeur, his disgust leavened by fascination. For the entire sixty minutes he hadn't said a word.

"Do you know which ones these are?" McBryde asked.

"Sure, no problem."

They sat close to the speakers of the stereo system in Jordan's living room. The remains of dinner—Jordan's specialty of fried lake trout, mashed potatoes and gravy, and stewed okra—lay on the dining room table, waiting to be cleared away. A grandfather clock chimed ten o'clock. Pulling himself up from a slouch, McBryde fought valiantly against the drowsiness that the heavy meal was producing.

While Jordan fished around in the kitchen for a pen and a pad of paper, McBryde glanced around the familiar living room. Most rail fans used every available space to display their valued possessions—number plates and old calendars, signals and cowcatchers, spikes and couplers. Hazel Jordan, however, had laid down the law: no railroadiana in the living room. The photographs and accumulated "junk" had been relegated to the basement, to a large space adjoining the darkroom. Instead, Jordan's wife had decorated her living room with hand-embroidered samplers on the wall, a patchwork quilt covering the sofa, thick art books on an end table, and their children's swimming trophies on the fireplace mantel. You'd never know that a foamer lived here.

Jordan returned with a yellow legal pad and a ballpoint. He flipped the cassette over for a second hearing, turned the volume control on the receiver down a notch. "Okay?"

"Of course, of course," McBryde said, shaking his head to clear away the fuzziness.

"Another cup of coffee?"

"No, thanks." He'd been drinking coffee all day long—another cup would provide as much stimulation as warm milk. And tomorrow, Tuesday, would be just as hard—another round of memos, complaints, and threatened public protests. The flow of anger wouldn't abate before Thursday. His "vacation" began on Friday evening.

"Ready?" Jordan squatted down to bring his ear closer to the speaker.

McBryde nodded, pen poised above paper.

Jordan hit the "play" button and began to concentrate on the sounds. "That one there, with the double click of the wheels, that was the derailing and then rerailing of several cars. And there? That's the derailing and decoupling of, yes, three cars, the last three cars. That would be, unless I'm mistaken, the derailment of the westbound Pioneer on March fourteenth last year between Nampa and Ontario. Yes, there certainly are a lot of screams, but actually no major injuries were sustained. There, that little snip of CB contains it"—he rewound the tape and played the crackly voice once more— "that's the station code of Ontario, Oregon. The accident occurred just inside Oregon territory and the engineer radioed ahead first for help. Cause of accident was determined to be a track defect . . ."

McBryde copied down the information, marveling not only at Jordan's powers of recall, but at the way his whole manner changed when he talked about train accidents. Ordinarily his friend was the jovial, back-slapping sort who hated formality and wanted only to put his friends at ease. But when he discussed his favorite topic, train accidents, Jordan developed a fanatical glint in his eye and recited minute details in a dry, clinical tone.

"That one's unusual, a collision in the train yard. The code, 304T, indicates a fatality that occurred when someone was struck by moving on-track equipment. Only one casualty for the past year. I can find out who it was if it's important. That rear-ender took place near Benson, as the Texas Eagle was heading west to Tucson. Cause of accident was an improperly lined switch. Several injuries but no fatalities. I probably have an article about it in *Pacific Railroader* . . ."

McBryde continued to transcribe the information. Jordan was impressive, all right. His mind contained a map of the entire United States, veined with railroad lines and littered with symbols denoting different types of accidents that had occurred over at least a fifty-year span. Most people, including Jordan's own wife, considered his talent to be just plain weird. But what of the sports fan who could give Pete Rose's complete stats for the 1975 season? Or the student of politics who could rattle off all the top officials in the Harding administration? The first one gets applause and free drinks at the bar, the second gets a Ph.D. And what do foamers get? Rolled eyes and smirks.

Which made it all the more important for foamers to stick together.

McBryde fondly remembered the humble origins of the Philly Foamers. Six years ago he had been scheduled to give a presentation on light rail at a city-sponsored conference on public transportation. He stood at the podium in a large, drafty room of City Hall and surveyed his audience. Seven people, three of whom McBryde had dragged over from his office across the street, sat on the gray metal chairs set up in neat rows—ten rows of ten chairs apiece. Seven people. He had expected, had been promised, a turnout of at least thirty.

He evaluated the four strangers: an older woman eating a hamburger, a man in a suit who checked his watch every few minutes, a young woman of college age unsure whether to stay or leave, and a man as large as a sumo wrestler occupying one and a half chairs in the front row. Balancing a fresh yellow pad on his lap, the enormous man looked up at the podium expectantly, his pen held at ready. McBryde figured him for a conscientious journalist from a local paper. If not for this chance of media exposure, McBryde would have crumpled up his notes and dispersed his small audience.

The college student left her seat and tiptoed out of the room, closing the creaking door behind her.

Despairing of a larger audience, McBryde cleared his throat, introduced himself, and began his presentation. The journalist furiously covered his pad with notes. His excitement proved infectious and McBryde soon worked up a sweat in the cold room.

When the presentation ended thirty minutes later on a cautiously optimistic note, both the woman with the hamburger and the businessman with the watch had departed. McBryde's three colleagues flashed thumbs-up from the back of the room before scurrying back to the office. The man in the front row raised his hand to ask a question, oblivious to the fact that he was the only audience member left.

Later, when Ronald Jordan introduced himself, McBryde discovered that he wasn't a journalist after all but a fellow city employee and that the notes had been entirely for personal purposes.

"Great presentation," Jordan said, and McBryde could see from the man's eyes that the sentiment was genuine.

Within minutes, after a conversational route that took them from light rail in Portland to the steam trains of China, they were talking about Japanese bullet trains.

Not only had Jordan heard of these technological wonders, he'd even ridden the Shinkansen's famous Osaka-Tokyo line, which covered the 320-mile route in two hours and fifty-two minutes. McBryde had always dreamed of visiting Japan, had studied its train system thoroughly but only from a distance. The two men left the room trading statistics about the bullet train.

"Ninety-nine percent on-time record," Jordan cited.

"Nearly three billion passengers carried without a single passenger fatality," McBryde marveled.

By the time they had descended from the gee-whiz facts to the finer engineering details, he and Jordan were sharing a pitcher of beer at the Napoli, an Italian holdover in Chinatown that served six-dollar pitchers.

As that evening wore on, the discussion expanded beyond specific trains and both men were compelled to call their wives from the pay phone outside to report that they'd be late returning home. They had discovered a startling similarity in their backgrounds. Both had been loners throughout high school and college, having found no one else to appreciate the beauty and grandeur of trains. They had married women who could not tell an engine from a caboose. Voracious readers with tremendous memories for detail, they could, and eventually would, spend hours together debating why railroads temporarily lost out to canals in 1812, or sifting through the reasons for the Pennsylvania Railroad's bankruptcy. They both kept notebooks of their favorite rail quotes, particularly from novels that touched on trains—*Murder on the Orient Express, The Great Train Robbery, The Octopus.*

Most importantly, he and Jordan shared a mutual fascination for new technologies. While they could certainly find merit in a historic steam train, like the 2-8-2 Baldwin built for Pennsy's East Broad Top, it was the cutting-edge transportation that inflamed their blood, that really raised the floodgates of their salivary glands. For Jordan, supertrains like Japan's Shinkansen registered just a notch below accident photography. McBryde, on the other hand, devoted himself exclusively to the silent, gleaming trains that floated like hovercrafts and sped across his imagination like rockets.

"I will be the Theodore Judah of Maglev," he said beerily to Jordan that evening, "and I will see my trains up and running during my lifetime."

Theodore Judah had raved like a madman about his idea of a transcontinental railroad. Without his single-minded obsession, tracks would never have united the country. But Jordan reminded him that Judah never saw the final golden spike driven in.

"He died, man, long before the big day. Yellow fever. Going overland across Panama."

"Yeah, yeah," McBryde replied, knowing all too well the sad story of Theodore Judah. He ordered a second pitcher of Ortlieb's and changed the subject. Mention of Judah's death had depressed him. "When it comes to trains," he announced, "the United States is a Third World country."

"Let me count the ways, O Lord," Jordan replied, thumping the table for emphasis.

"They're always late," McBryde began.

"Lousy food," Jordan continued.

"Heating never works."

"Tickets cost too much."

"They're so goddamn slow. Takes forever to get from here to Chicago."

"Won't take you to all the places you want to go. Won't set up sensible schedules. Won't listen to consumer complaints."

"Nothing like Europe."

"Nothing like Japan."

They stopped for a moment to regain their breath.

"But we love them anyway," McBryde said into his beer.

"Amen."

Together they imagined a very different America, one that used airplanes only for international travel, that produced and sold half as many private cars, that built new magnetic-levitation lines and supertrain tracks to crisscross the country and connect every munic-ipality in a high-tech, high-speed matrix. These new trains would be safe, efficient, and comfortable. They would move people—in both senses of the word.

As a third pitcher erased the melancholy and restored the earlier excitement, they shook hands on their vision. Without realizing it, they had created the Philly Foamers.

The group grew slowly at first. For the first six months, in fact, the still unnamed club consisted of only Jordan and McBryde him-self, eating free chicken wings every Friday evening at Cavanaugh's, a bar with a muted Irish theme located across from Thirtieth Street Station. As they tore at the greasy wings, he and Jordan complained about American trains and sketched out their plans for a rail renais-sance. Numbers, Jordan insisted. Without an organized group of angry train advocates, America would plunge deeper into its trans-portation sinkhole.

Gradually, with ads in the local paper, they recruited other train fanatics to join them for drinks on Fridays. First came Georgia Hux-ley, the owner of a Center City plastics firm, who immediately found a soulmate in fellow accident nut Ron Jordan. Then Clarence

Brown, a machinist on disability, and Marty Stein, a jazz disc jockey, joined them. Leticia Gompers, who taught classics at Bryn Mawr and wrote lesbian erotica, was not far behind. Soon the table at Cavanaugh's became too cramped. With an influx of ten new members at the end of the first year, the Friday beer sessions spiraled into official monthly meetings with bylaws and budgets. Only he and Jordan kept up the weekly tradition at Cavanaugh's. McBryde could not deny that as a larger group they more successfully persuaded local politicians of the need for better trains. Still, he often grew wistful for the days when the entire chapter of the Philly Foamers, on the spur of the moment, would pile into the Jordanmobile for a trip to the train museum in Scranton or cluster around the television in McBryde's living room for yet another showing of *The Lady Vanishes*. That was why he cherished the Friday get-togethers with Jordan. They reminded him of simpler times. Of married times. Of Rosalind of Rosemont.

"Larry?" Jordan had switched back to his everyday voice.

McBryde looked at his notebook and discovered he'd missed the last entry. "Um, could you just repeat that last one again?"

"You thinking about The Unmentionable again?" There was a standing agreement among his friends not to refer to his ex-wife by her name. She was called The Unmentionable if they could not avoid mentioning her.

"My nightmare," McBryde lied. He didn't want people to think that he was pining away, that this woman who had left him nearly a year ago could still exert such control over his concentration. "Damned thing happened again last night."

"May I suggest therapy?"

"You have. I'd prefer Alka-Seltzer."

"I shouldn't have made all that fried food for you, man."

"Don't be ridiculous. I loved it. I just shouldn't have eaten three portions." His hands moved to his hips to feel his love handles. Less love and more handles.

Jordan returned from the kitchen with a glass of furiously bubbling water and waited for McBryde to drink half of it. Then he repeated the description of a derailment on the Southern Pacific line, the only pure freight train accident on the tape. This accident stood out from the rest for another reason as well. Losing its brakes as it approached a suburban community outside Los Angeles, the freight rounded a curve at over fifty miles per hour—the maximum allowable speed—and left the tracks like a rock from a slingshot. The cars smashed into an embankment, miraculously missing the buildings overlooking the tracks. However, one of the cars had been carrying LPG—liquid petroleum gas. A spark from the wheels kicking up gravel ignited the gas, setting off a tremendous explosion and destroying a good number of town houses in the nearby community. Five people had been instantly incinerated.

"This tape alone has, let's see, about sixty dead," Jordan tabulated as he settled back into his rocking chair. "Georgia said there are about a half dozen more of these. We're dealing with a mass murderer here, Larry."

McBryde nodded uneasily.

"She was real happy you agreed to do this, you know."

McBryde shrugged. "Georgia's just happy we don't spend money on a private detective."

"I'm glad too. And I'm not talking expenses here. You're the best man for the job." Jordan shifted his weight on the rocking chair. "But you and I both know that this could get dangerous. Someone who knocks off a dozen people in an accident and tape-records instead of saving a drowning person is not going to think twice about putting a slug between your ears, buddy."

"Thanks for putting it so delicately." McBryde veered away from the topic. "What do you think about the idea," he began slowly, "that maybe it wasn't just one fellow? Maybe it was a group of them."

"I was just about to try that one out myself."

"A group of foamers gone bad," McBryde continued. "A group of ordinary people just like us. They get together every month or so and talk about normal, ordinary things. Then something happens and this idea gets hold of them. They start setting these accidents, taping them, distributing them."

"But what's this idea that gets hold of them?"

"I don't know. Maybe it just started as a dare. 'If you know so much about trains, then why don't you . . .' "

"Could be, could be." Jordan went over to clear dishes from the dining room table. McBryde offered to help, but Jordan motioned him back. "Relax awhile. I'm just going to put these in the dishwasher. Ain't but room for one in the kitchen. Those are some of the latest mags."

McBryde pawed through the pile of magazines on the end table next to his chair. A familiar collection. *Trains* was the premier glossy with the best listings and classified section. He and Jordan regularly wrote letters to correct the magazine's articles ("Dear Editor: The caption beneath the photo depicting Engine F7 No. 82A was mislabeled No. 87A . . ."). Also on the table lay the magazine devoted to the trains of the Northeast, *Railpace,* the glossy British monthly *Railway,* and McBryde's personal favorite, *Passenger Train Journal.*

He picked up this last one, leafed through it, put it down. I am falling away, he thought; my pulse no longer quickens, my concentration no longer sharpens. It was not just the fault of too much trout and mashed potatoes. At one time, he could sit for hours reading from cover to cover all the latest rail magazines.

McBryde smiled sadly at these memories. He'd since lost that sense of belonging to something larger, that feeling of serving the greater good by preserving the history and the future of American trains.

The other foamers would never understand. They never seemed to be afflicted with these crises of faith. Being a foamer meant never having to think twice about an excursion. His friends could ride trains back and forth across the country, day and night, for the rest of their lives. A year ago, McBryde would have been first in line to buy such a lifetime ticket. A year ago he too would have eagerly spent his entire vacation curled in the cocoon of a sleeper or stretched out in the observation car with a magazine across his lap, awed as if for the first time by the Montana flats or the breathtaking ravines of the Rockies unwrapping themselves before his eyes. Not long ago his great love had been intact. Now his past seemed the lifetime of a different person.

Jordan returned from the kitchen drying his hands on a dish towel. "Nothing interesting this month?"

McBryde glanced down at the pile of magazines and rubbed his eyes. "I just didn't feel like reading. Spent the day poring over documents. You know how it is."

"Complaints?"

"They're burning us in effigy down in South Philly. And it's just a tiny little increase," McBryde said, trying not to sound vexed. "Lucky I only have four more days of this. Vacation starts at five o'clock on Friday."

"More or less."

McBryde nodded. "Commitments."

"Can we talk some more about this tomorrow evening? I've got a couple of ideas to pursue."

"I'm going to Rosemont after work tomorrow."

"Ah."

"To make arrangements."

"Of course. After you get back then," Jordan said.

"I guess I might have to do some traveling for this."

"There might be something in Pittsburgh. But I don't think a trip to the Caymans would get us much."

"This friend of Georgia's in Colorado? He might have some thoughts."

Jordan shrugged. They were now both exhausted.

"Damn it," McBryde said, suddenly full of despair. "I wish this whole thing hadn't come up."

Jordan said, "Think of it as an adventure."

"It's an adventure when it happens to someone else." McBryde finished off the Alka-Seltzer. "When it happens to you, it's just another bad dream."

SIX

Szczymanski eagerly looked over the materials in the packet that Granite had given her. An urgent case about trains? She'd always thought them a faintly humorous topic, perhaps because of a college acquaintance who'd been obsessed with model trains. He had stretched track throughout his dorm room, had shown her his carefully constructed tunnels, the painstakingly designed stations, the trees, the smoke pellets that went into a compartment just above the wheels of the engine. She'd never understood his absorption in that miniature world of matchstick trees and plaster-of-Paris mountains. On beautiful summer days, when the sun bathed the campus in warm light, he would sit in the permanent dusk of his room playing with his toys. It was, she decided, a boy thing.

As for the larger varieties of trains, she was aware of them only as vehicles, not even as parts of a larger "rail" system. She preferred either the flexibility of a car or the speed of an airplane. The train seemed to her a leftover from the nineteenth century, waiting to be phased out, like the steel-nibbed fountain pen or the manual typewriter.

The accident bulletins were thick and covered in green cardboard, with two fat staples for spines. Szczymanski quickly became absorbed by them, by their graphs and charts, their definitions and classifications. Despite Granite's remark, her task indeed seemed to resemble a Leavis challenge. Somewhere in the tangle of data was the key.

The bulletins reported fatalities connected to "switch improperly lined"; casualties resulting from "excessive slack action"; injuries from "moving on-track equipment"; accidents caused by snow, ice, mud, or "other acts of God." Trains smashed into cars at grade crossings, struck and killed trespassers in switching yards, collided with one another releasing hazardous materials referred to as "hazmat." Here was a world where everything went wrong, where hump retarders routinely failed, oversized loads were frequently misrouted, and railway employees could not prevent themselves from slipping, tripping, and falling in every state of the union. She had no idea that calamities could come in so many distinct and unusual packages.

The newspaper clippings in the folder, culled mostly from small-town dailies and regional weeklies, were downright gruesome. Szczymanski imagined that compared to a journalist's usual articles about school-board meetings or petty thefts, a noisy, bloody train accident was the big time, the closest to being a war correspondent that most of them would ever get. One clipping described the decapitations of several passengers. Another detailed the instantaneous combustion of a conductor. Virtually every one, even referring to the simplest derailment, devoted a block of copy to the harrowing stories of the survivors.

After several hours of immersion, she surfaced from the materials. She walked over to her only window, a small square that looked out onto the Bureau's courtyard, with Pennsylvania Avenue in the distance. It was a clear but very windy winter day. Employees were leaving the building, threading through the concrete pillars and descending the concrete steps. Even in the courtyard, the wind whipped the leaves of the ivy on the walls and the branches of the lonely trees struggling to survive amid all the heavy concrete. She looked back over to the clock on the wall above her door. Incredible: it was nearly five o'clock. She'd been reading about train accidents for over three hours. Suddenly she was aware of a pinched feeling in her stomach. She'd forgotten lunch altogether. She would wait until later for dinner. After her victory over lactic acid, she could easily master a few stomach grumbles. She sat back at her desk and picked up the materials again. In another hour, she'd make some apartment calls from the office before heading back to Crystal City.

The assignment would not be easy. There were no leads, no evidence. She had only a statistical increase. In the past two years, derailments had gone up 5 percent, collisions 10 percent, and highway rail impacts 6 percent. These increases would have seemed insignificant if not for the gradual and steady decline in such figures over the previous decade. Caught up in the first flush of excitement over the new assignment, she hadn't really grasped the nature of her task. She was being asked to turn a statistic into a culprit. It was the hardest FBI assignment—nailing an "unsub," an unknown subject. In the absence of any other proof, it was almost an abstract exercise. The latest accident, according to a wire report paper-clipped to the front of the folder, had taken place just that morning, outside of Pittsburgh. She would want to start there.

There was a knock on her door.

Agent Peña poked her head into the office. "You don't have to stay here all night, you know."

Szczymanski gestured at the papers on the desk. "First day, you know how it is."

"Couple of us going out for a beer. Interested?"

"Well . . ." Szczymanski stared helplessly at her work.

"Put it on ice."

"I've got to make calls tonight about apartments and—"

"Call from the bar."

"And I haven't eaten anything since—"

"This place has the best chopped barbecue sandwiches for miles around."

She'd promised herself after the incident with Blaine that she'd no longer form any connections with her co-workers. But as she looked at Peña, at her smooth, wide face and large blue eyes, Szczymanski realized that this was something different. This was a potential friendship between equals, between women—something she hadn't had since Barnegut. She shouldn't hold a resentment simply because of one dumb crack about farm girls. Maybe Peña wasn't a selfish Riser after all, just a scrappy fighter.

"Just one beer?" Szczymanski said, gathering together the materials.

"You a one-beer queer?" Peña asked, throwing up a shoulder in an attitude of mock belligerence. "Shit, any woman who can take four minutes of lactic acid can down at least one pitcher of horse piss. Am I right?"

Szczymanski checked herself. She'd almost forgotten her new strategy. TB^2. Get out there and break some balls.

She jabbed a finger in Peña's direction. "Damn straight, babe!"

It didn't look anything like a bar. The parking lot behind the nondescript building was large, full of cars, discarded beer cans, and plastic bags that danced in the swirling wind. Three concrete steps led down to a gray-painted metal door with a hand-lettered sign on it: "No peddlers. No Chinese menus. No exceptions." The windows facing out onto the parking lot were boarded up. There were no neon beer signs, no warning for underage drinkers. It looked like the employees-only entrance to a warehouse.

"It's called Lucky's," Peña explained from the driver's seat of the bucar—a Bureau car complete with inside gun rack and cellular phone. Peña was so small that her head just managed to clear the steering wheel. "He's been in everything—OSS, CIA, FBI. They say he was the only survivor of the 1961 Albanian operation. He spent two weeks on the Adriatic coast eating nothing but raw clams."

"Lucky man," Szczymanski murmured. She stared through the windshield at the sign on the door. Why did people in cities get so bent out of shape about Chinese menus?

Agent Metaxas sat rigidly in the backseat, as though steeling herself for a parachute jump.

"Out front's the grocery store," Peña continued. "Lucky's wife runs that. Back here, they don't let you in unless Xavier recognizes you."

"Sounds like Prohibition," Szczymanski said.

"Security," Peña said.

"What about a retinal scanner?" Szczymanski joked.

"Hey." Peña brightened. "Why didn't I think of that?"

Metaxas looked on impassively. She didn't seem like much of a drinking partner. During the drive over, while Peña nattered on and Szczymanski made an occasional attentive noise, Metaxas had said nothing. She was a big-boned, middle-aged woman of Greek descent. Her dirty-blond hair was pulled tight into a bun at the back. Her face had a peasant stolidness—deep-set eyes with dark puddles underneath, a mouth that was perpetually pursed—as though she had just come to America after surviving many harsh and profitless seasons.

"Here are the rules," Peña said, tapping the steering wheel with her palm after each point. "No getting shitfaced, no dancing, no sitting on the pool tables, and above all, no shop talk."

"What's the point of all the security if we can't talk shop?" Szczymanski wanted to know.

"Moles." It was Metaxas's first contribution of the evening, not counting her initial, barely audible "Hello."

"Remember," Peña added, "this is FBI, CIA, DIA, NSA, the works. We don't always want the right hand to know what the left hand is doing. Especially if the hands belong to different arms."

"Cross-fertilization?" Szczymanski suggested.

"Doesn't work that way. Otherwise we'd all work in one big happy organization."

They piled out of the car and crunched across the gravel of the parking lot toward the imposing door. Peña gave a syncopated knock.

Xavier the bouncer, a brown-skinned behemoth wider than he was tall and with arms the size of Szczymanski's thighs, passed them in with a nod of recognition at Peña. They walked down a dark, dusty hallway and emerged into the bar's swirl of color, noise, and smoke. Despite its unassuming exterior, Lucky's looked on the inside like any other drinking establishment in the Washington area: an assortment of rickety wooden tables, several pinball machines that emitted frequent cartoon noises, two pool tables with worn felts, a dartboard, and a brightly glowing jukebox. The bar stocked hundreds of different beers, judging by the crowded display of bottles on a long shelf above the bartender.

"Lucky!" Peña shouted.

The bartender looked up from pouring drinks. In his late sixties, Szczymanski estimated, and well-preserved; he looked like a chubby Popeye, with shaved head, black marble eyes, and a tattoo of an emerald dragon on his neck. His weathered face creased into a wide smile on seeing Peña. "Penny! How's it hanging, luv? Getting any trim?" He gestured lewdly.

Peña laughed. "No more than usual."

"I'm always here for you, luv." Lucky made a fist and tightened his biceps. He was wearing a tank top. Through the gray folds of skin, a set of surprisingly large biceps stood out in relief.

"Then make it a pitcher of the usual. For starters. And bring over three chopped barbecue. With the hot sauce."

The place was crowded, with customers two deep at the bar and drinkers clustered around tables jammed with pitchers of beer and baskets of glistening french fries. They found a space near the juke-box. As soon as they sat down, the music kicked in, serenading them with Benny Goodman and his orchestra. Szczymanski glanced at the titles: all big-band music.

As they waited for their pitcher, Peña launched into the story of her latest boyfriend, a computer programmer with the International Monetary Fund. She updated Szczymanski on the particulars. Metaxas sat with the stony countenance of a chaperone who didn't speak the language.

Listening with half her attention to the soap opera of Peña's life, Szczymanski thought about her own case. After only one day on the job, her desk was already piled high with materials. She wanted to solve this case with dispatch, to prove to her superiors that they had not mistakenly given her such an important task. Particularly Granite. She wanted to see his face glow with the pleasure of her success. Or at least pucker up with envy. Here finally was the opportunity to prove herself worthy of the FBI. She very much wanted to interrupt Peña with stories of train accidents around the country.

But no shop talk. They were depriving her of the only good reason for going out for a beer with colleagues. She hated just hanging out. It seemed like a waste of time, like watching television or smoking dope. For the most part she'd avoided chitchat in high school and college, concentrated instead on work, on athletics. She began by staying away from boys who had nothing to say. And ended up staying away from most men. Life was too short to waste breath on empty talk.

The pitcher arrived with three glasses. As she tilted the glasses and poured the beer, Peña continued her blow-by-blow account of the affair with the computer programmer. How he would never show up on time. How he would forget her birthday. How they would have a great week together and then spend a month shouting at each other. Szczymanski smiled and tsk-tsked at the appropriate moments. Metaxas said nothing, roamed the room with her eyes. Peña seemed genuinely appreciative of Szczymanski's more engaged style and didn't seem to notice its superficiality. As she drank more beer, Peña seemed to develop a slurring affection for her new friend. She glanced more in Szczymanski's direction, directed more of her comments that way.

"They're beasts, just beasts," Peña said, clinking her empty beer glass against Szczymanski's half-full one. "But we can tame them, can't we? Now, how about you, Szczymanski, got any special friends here in D.C.?"

"I just arrived here."

"Well, we'll just see what we can do for you, then, right, Max?" Peña turned to Metaxas. "Between the two of us I'm sure we can drum up a dream beast for you."

Metaxas gave a barely perceptible nod and took another controlled sip of her beer.

"Now, babe," Peña said, "what do you like best? Bulls? Stallions? Or cuddly little terriers that—"

"Don't worry about me," Szczymanski said. "I have enough work to last me for—"

Peña shook her finger violently in front of her face. "No, no, no! Remember: no shop talk. This is fun time. Only fun topics allowed. Right, Max?"

Szczymanski combed through her mind for a "fun" topic but drew a blank. The beer, meanwhile, was having a strong effect on her empty stomach. Fortunately, Peña was moving on to another discussion of her own devising: the disproportionately large number of women in the D.C. area. Szczymanski gave herself over to the role of student to Peña's instructor.

"They got us over a barrel, see," Peña lectured. "They got their pick. I can't begin to list the number of beautiful, intelligent women out there who just can't get a date. Like Max here."

Szczymanski flashed a sympathetic smile at Metaxas. She couldn't imagine any man going out of his way to ask this close-mouthed woman on a date. Except an Alaskan prospector who ordered his brides by mail.

"It's not fair, I tell you," Peña continued. "I just hate seeing all these big shots strutting around like buyers at a hog show." Her voice deepened into the affected drawl of a Southern plantation owner. " 'No, suh, Ah believe Ah want one with whitah teeth, please. Yes, an' a thinnah waist, biggah boobs, and pret' little ankles.' "

Szczymanski laughed, felt a smidgen more comfortable. Peña refilled her glass and drained the last of the beer. "Drink up," she commanded of Szczymanski, "we're getting another." Before she could say no, Metaxas had seized the empty plastic pitcher and marched off to the bar.

Peña leaned over close. "She doesn't talk much, but I trust her with my life."

"She seems, um, nice."

"Fuck nice," Peña responded. "I've seen her rip the guts out of a drug pusher and not blink an eye. But like I said, she's dependable and a good friend. Una roca. A rock. I've just been trying to get her to loosen up a bit."

Before Szczymanski could ask how Peña hoped to achieve this result, Metaxas returned with another pitcher of beer. As she filled mugs all around, Peña continued with her castigation of Washington men.

Szczymanski glanced at her watch. One landlord had mentioned 6 P.M. as a good time to call and she didn't want to miss him. The sooner she got an apartment the better. She was tired of living in Crystal City. Waiting for Peña to pause to take a breath, she asked, "The phone is . . ."

Peña jerked her thumb upward. "They got one in the store upstairs." She gestured for Szczymanski to follow her to the bar.

"Hey, Lucky! My friend here needs to make a call. Can you show her to the phone?"

"International?" the bartender grunted unpleasantly.

"Relax, Lucky," Peña replied. "Into D.C. She's looking for an apartment."

"Oh yeah?" The old man's face lit up. The dragon on his neck undulated as he drank from a can of soda. "I got an extra room for her if she wants."

"Yeah, extra room in your bed. Just show her the phone, Lucky. And buy yourself a shot of the good stuff on me."

Lucky reached for the gin bottle.

"After you show her the phone," Peña bargained.

Grumbling, the bartender pushed aside some empty beer bottles and flipped up a section of the bar to let himself out. "Cover for me, Alice," he said to a gray-haired woman with bright-orange lipstick sitting on a stool and knitting a scarf.

Szczymanski followed the old man's crooked gait into a hallway that ran along one side of the building. Framed and occasionally autographed photos of famous criminals—Pretty Boy Floyd, Sirhan Sirhan, Charles Manson—lined both walls.

"To Lucky," read the dedication from Gary Gilmore. "Thanks for everything."

Lucky unlatched a chain that restricted access to steps leading up and flicked a switch that flooded the stairwell with light. At the head of the stairs, he unlocked the door and pushed it open. The light from the stairway dimly illuminated the room. Szczymanski saw a scantily stocked convenience store, the kind that exists in poor neighborhoods or off rural highways, with rows of canned goods on wooden shelves and stacks of cheap white bread in colorful plastic bags. Lucky leaned over a counter to their right and pulled up from the depths on the other side an old black telephone with a cracked plastic rotary dial.

"Just close up when you leave. Door locks automatically." Lucky began to return down the steps. "And don't let no one else up here, okay? The store's closed for the night." He descended two more steps and turned again. "And drop two bits on the bar when you're through. This ain't no tourist information center, luv."

Szczymanski stood in what appeared to be the main aisle of the store. Refrigerator units to her left murmured with electricity. She couldn't decide whether the grocery store was a legitimate enterprise, a front for the bar downstairs, or just a tax write-off.

The phone balanced on her shoulder, Szczymanski fumbled in her purse for the slip of paper with the prospective landlord's name and number written on it. Just as her fingers closed upon the paper, however, the receiver slipped from its perch, bounced once on the counter, and clattered on the floor on the other side.

She could have simply pulled the receiver up from behind the counter by its tangled black cord. But the plastic was frayed, exposing the colored wire viscera inside. Reeling in the phone might snap the cord altogether.

So she moved farther into the dark store until she found a break in the counter and stepped around it into the proprietor's space. The back side of the counter too was lined with shelves stocked with institutional sizes of mayonnaise, tomato paste, and canned corn. As she bent down to retrieve the phone, Szczymanski knocked a can of corn from its perch with her elbow. Reacting quickly, she reached a hand beneath the can only to lose her balance and fall heavily against the shelf, displacing several more items.

"So goddamn clumsy," she breathed, irritated as only a tall person can be when forced to maneuver in areas designed for the smaller and nimbler. Gathering up the fallen cans, she realized that this middle shelf of the counter was unexpectedly shallow, containing only one rank of food. The upper and lower shelves accommodated cans three deep. The middle shelf evidently had a false back. She quickly restored the phone to its cradle and, suddenly curious, bent down again to remove all the cans from the middle shelf, carefully laying them one after another on the floor. After a few minutes' probing, she discovered a catch that let her pull the wooden board out. The dim light revealed a metal box, three feet long, with a padlock at one end.

A safe, she imagined. This was where Lucky kept all the quarters he collected from phone callers. Or the meager daily take from the grocery store.

She didn't know why, but she was suddenly motivated to pick the lock. She was not given to foolhardy gestures. She took risks only if they helped her achieve particular goals, not for the sheer excitement of meeting a challenge.

Perhaps it was the secrecy surrounding the bar. Being an FBI agent had so far involved little more than filling out paperwork, sitting in meetings, and reading reports. The railroad case had whetted her appetite. Now she found herself in an establishment chockfull of spooks. How else to explain her impulse to act like James Bond and pull a hairpin from her purse, insert it into the padlock, and, with a few expert twists—a specialty she had cultivated at Quantico—throw the catch?

It didn't contain quarters. Nor any money. In fact, it wasn't even a safe.

Szczymanski stared at what seemed to be a piece of stereo equipment. Across its face was a staggered row of several dozen holes, which on closer inspection turned out to be for headphone plugs. On top of the console rested a pair of headphones.

She stood up, walked around the counter, and closed the door leading down to the bar, throwing the little grocery store into complete darkness. From her purse, she removed a pocket flashlight. With the narrow beam of light guiding her, she returned to her position kneeling among the cans of corn and plum tomatoes. The once-bright labels of these heavy cans had faded to pastels, making her think of rations in a bomb shelter. How long had they concealed this device? Since Lucky had returned from his clam-eating expedition to the Adriatic coast?

A flick of a switch at the top left corner of the console made the machine hum softly. Szczymanski plugged the headset into one of the jacks. A knob on the right side controlled the volume of the voices she heard.

". . . understand why he charges more for this domestic shit," a male voice was saying. "I mean, taste it. This is ale? Ale?! Pilsner, maybe. But not ale."

She pulled the plug out, inserted it into another hole.

". . . ten for twelve from the floor. And that was in the first half," a different male voice was saying. "Then they trade him! So he can't sink his foul shots. What do they want, Jesus of Nazareth?"

She tried several more jacks, finding similar conversations. The idea amused her tremendously. Spooks spying on spooks. What was Lucky's game? Who would be interested in CIA agents talking about sports, FBI agents complaining about beer? Perhaps Lucky's was an off-site, a place to run undercover operations. In any case, it wasn't her business. The FBI often kept off-sites like this—fake bars, fake stores, fake offices. She was about to replace the headphones and lock up the console when, on the last jack, she picked up female voices. She didn't have to listen for very long before recognizing the whispers.

"What does she know?" came the voice of Metaxas.

"Only that she has this case, something to do with train accidents," Peña responded.

"Train accidents?"

"Yeah, Department of Transportation's been pressuring us to look into train accidents. But you know what it is. They just want to shift the blame. They've been asking us to look into it for six months. Granite's put them off."

"Until now."

"He needed something to give her. Told her it was, get this, urgent!"

Szczymanski breathed quietly even though she knew that they couldn't hear her. The blood pounding in her head seemed to make a deafening sound. So much for the rule against shop talk.

"I wanted to tell you back in the office. Didn't have a chance."

"You can see, right, if she comes back?"

"Got my eye on the corner, babe. There's no other way back."

"As long as I know now," Metaxas said, matter-of-factly. "Why'd you invite her along then?"

"We have to get tight with her. Gain her trust. That's why Granite assigned us to her. She's probably a man-hater. So, the sooner we start, the better. I was worried she'd be beyond our control before we even knew it."

Fidelity, bravery, integrity—Szczymanski was violating the entire Bureau credo. She was behaving treacherously, cowardly, shamefully. Everything in her training insisted that she pull the plug and turn off the infernal machine. But the very first words had captured her. They were speaking behind her back. Wasn't it fair to turn the tables?

"I think we can expect," Peña was saying, "that she'll be wasting a lot of time here in D.C. going through papers and interviews. In fact, there are a few already set up for her. That was Granite's idea."

"Where was she before?" Metaxas asked.

"Pierre. As far as she knows, it's a promotion."

"Problem out there?"

"Whistle-blower. Sexual harassment. Nobody believes her."

"And she doesn't suspect the reassignment?"

"They say it's what she's been angling for. She's a Riser, all right."

"And?" Metaxas asked.

"And we watch her."

"How long?"

"As long as it takes."

"Until?"

"She quits."

So that was their plan. Was it OPR's doing? Szczymanski controlled her sudden desire to take up a family-size can of corn and smash the machine.

From the headphones came the sound of beer being poured into glasses. When Peña spoke again, her voice was at normal pitch. "It's not bad here tonight. Couple of cuties."

"This is neither the time nor the place," Metaxas said with disgust, her voice still low.

"Anytime, anyplace."

Szczymanski lifted the headphones from her ears. She turned off the console, restored the padlock, and clicked it into place. The single row of canned vegetables once again concealed the false back.

Szczymanski leaned for a moment on the counter. Peña's words began to penetrate. Granite had lied—about the train accidents being high-priority, about the national importance of the case. They didn't trust her. She felt a sudden, dizzying vertigo. She'd made the decision to devote her life to the Bureau and they simply didn't trust her. Breathe slowly, steadily. Keep your head, woman!

Downstairs, she dropped a dollar on the bar, winked at Lucky, and zigzagged back to her table. Peña and Metaxas looked up with smiles when she approached. Peña had a wide and impish grin. Metaxas looked as if she were bravely putting up with a toothache. Either way, the smiles were false. From now on, Szczymanski realized, everything would be false.

"Washington men," Peña resumed where she left off. "They spend as little money and time on you as possible. Shit, they treat their pets better!"

Watching this small, animated woman speak, Szczymanski was suddenly struck by a dismal conclusion: The Academy had released her into a world of deceit and hypocrisy. In her classes, the morality had been clear. The FBI was on the side of right, and the drug traffickers and terrorists and Mafia hit men were always in the wrong. In Pierre, with the notable exception of Rudy Blaine, the agents had leveled with her. But here they lied.

She steadied herself with two hands on the edge of the table. What were her options? She could simply work away at the statistics, prepare a desultory report on the possible reasons for the marginal increase in accidents, and otherwise keep her conduct above reproach. Such an unimaginative approach neither appeased her anger nor satisfied her strategy of TB^2. And switching strategies mid-stream might make Peña suspicious. Much better, she decided, to go gung-ho at the case and uncover some actual malfeasance. It might not be the terrorism that she had previously hoped for. But some illegality might be lurking in there somewhere, perhaps a case of criminal mismanagement or bribery or corruption of some sort. She would uncover whatever there was to uncover and then present it to the Bureau. She would prove her innocence by identifying the guilty. She'd force them to believe her.

The chopped barbecue sandwiches finally arrived. Szczymanski smiled weakly at her companions and rolled up her sleeves.

"I think it will be a real pleasure having you around, babe," Peña said, raising her pint of beer. "To Fidelity!"

Metaxas lifted her glass a few inches off the table and grunted, "To Bravery."

Szczymanski clinked glasses with the other two agents and thought to herself—To Hell with you both. Then she rallied her forces and sang out in a deceptively hearty voice, "To Integrity!"

SEVEN

Dust thickened around him. McBryde couldn't move his limbs, could barely breathe. His elbows were pressed tightly against his sides. His thighs were pulled up against his chest as though he were about to cannonball off a diving board. Cold walls enclosed him on all sides.

He wasn't frightened at first, only bewildered—didn't know where he was, didn't know how he got there. But the familiarity of the situation leaked into him like ink onto blotting paper. Then the fear began, intensified. His muscles tightened. His neck became rigid with horror and expectation. He tried to hug his limbs closer, tried to absorb them into himself.

The explosion came with a blinding white flash. He felt himself shrink before this great light, his arms shriveling to stumps, his legs twisting and disappearing like strips of burning paper, his torso becoming a small knot, his head consumed like the charcoal tip of a matchstick. He was screaming, the pain unbearable . . .

McBryde lay in the darkness of the room, sweating, waiting for his heartbeat to return to normal. A simple nightmare. It was short, intense, and frightening. But described to other people, even if sympathetic, the nightmare seemed prosaic. He was almost embarrassed at its lack of grotesque imagery and fantastic details.

Over the past year, McBryde's nightmare had turned his friends into amateur psychiatrists. Leticia Gompers explained that the enclosed space symbolized the womb of his mother while the light represented the glare of the hospital delivery room. He was obviously angry at his mother and had projected these feelings into a rage against his own birth. Jordan, meanwhile, insisted that the enclosed space was a coffin and the blinding light was the presence of the Lord. Georgia Huxley figured it for cremation anxiety. Marty Stein suggested half-seriously a fear of being flushed down a toilet. McBryde found none of these explanations satisfying. He wasn't particularly religious, didn't worry about cremation or toilets, and suspected that Leticia Gompers had projected her own maternal anger into his nightmare.

Once, over the summer, he'd been alone in the small elevator in his office building when it abruptly stopped between floors. The electricity shut off and he was forced to wait in the hot darkness of the metal box for nearly ten minutes. When service finally resumed and the elevator brought him down to the ground floor, he walked out on elastic legs, dark circles of sweat expanding under his arms. It was bad enough in dream-state. The terror multiplied a hundredfold in real life. Fortunately, however, the dream rarely stayed with him during his waking hours.

On this Tuesday morning, for instance, it had retreated into the shadows of his unconscious by the time he settled behind his desk at work. Atop his extra foam cushion, with a cup of coffee at his elbow, transit updates scattered in front of him, and the telephone perched on his shoulder, McBryde had no time for interpreting dreams.

Instead, the angry voice of Councilman Calhoun pounded into his ear.

"These are poor people," the councilman was saying. His office in South Philly's First Ward was inundated with complaints over the fare increase. "They're tired of paying through the nose for what should be a free public service."

"How can it be free?" McBryde reached without thinking into

the side drawer of his desk for the packet of cigarettes next to the paper clips. His hand moved like a spider among the office supplies. No cigarettes. That's right, his conscious mind told him; we've quit, you and I. "You, sir, know that our city can't afford free buses and subways."

The councilman was not deterred: "I've done some research and there are several cities that provide free transportation. Seattle, San Antonio, Stockholm . . ."

McBryde waited for the list to end, then patiently explained the limitations to these "free" systems and why Philadelphia couldn't implement them anyway. He recognized the councilman's argument for what it was: an attempt to win votes in an election year. The hypocrite. He was always complaining at press conferences about the city's budget deficit.

"Yeah, yeah," the councilman interrupted. "All I gotta say is this: If my constituents organize a boycott, I won't stand in their way."

At the mention of a boycott, McBryde involuntarily moved his elbow, knocking his coffee cup onto the rug. The coffee splattered his pant cuffs and soaked into the dirty carpet. "Shit!" he exclaimed.

"That's right," Calhoun responded. "I'm glad you finally see the seriousness of this situation." The councilman rang off.

Injustice permeates the world, McBryde thought as he wiped at his pants with a saliva-wettened napkin. And the people of the First Ward can think of nothing better than boycotting public transportation to save a lousy twelve dollars a year? Calhoun, the son of a bitch, was being investigated for sweetheart contracts with the construction workers' union. A boycott could certainly offset that publicity. He might even organize the damn thing himself!

McBryde casually put a budget from the previous year over the spill on the carpet. By the end of the day it would look like all the other stains. His secretary had been making fun of his recent clumsiness and he saw no reason to give her more ammunition.

He sat back in his chair and looked out the window. His office was on the top floor of the City Hall Annex, not far from the buckles on William Penn's five-foot-long shoes. For the longest time the statue of Philadelphia's founder that graced the top of City Hall had been the tallest point in the city. An informal building code had prevented developers from elevating Philadelphia's skyline. Then, in the late 1980s, the construction of several immense office buildings had nullified this informal pact. As a result, the tapered glass needles of Liberty Place One and Two now watched like immense sentinels over the development westward from Broad Street to the Schuylkill River. Poor Billy Penn was dwarfed, his horizons blocked off. City Hall, despite its recent overhaul, looked gray and shrunken. McBryde's office once afforded a magnificent view of Center City. Now it was just another space. Business had taken clear precedence over politics.

The other day, walking down Ben Franklin Parkway, he had watched the rain pour off Billy Penn's hand. From that angle the hand was just visible at waist level, and it looked as though the great man was urinating on the city. A fitting response. When he reached his office, it was difficult to resist opening his window and joining in the fun. For McBryde also felt passed over, in the shadow of others, forgotten. The book on Maglev should have made his name. But he was still behind the same desk. He was blending into the scenery as surely as the carpet stains. The Maglev czar? The next Theodore Judah? Hah, he would end up as Count Ferdinand von Zeppelin, the man who thought dirigibles were the bright future of transportation.

He gazed past Billy Penn at the building on the other side of City Hall. On the site of the old Broad Street Station squatted a rectangular eyesore, what the architects of the 1950s had imagined a bank should look like. Progress. The grand terminal, with its red brick Frank Furness addition, had fallen victim to the wrecker's ball in 1952, long before he came to Philadelphia. He had a photograph somewhere of Eugene Ormandy and the Philadelphia Orchestra playing on a special platform car for the passengers of the last train departing the station.

So many of Philadelphia's rail landmarks, for better or worse, had been torn down. The infamous Chinese Wall, a thirty-foot brick wall that ran along Market Street and hid the train tracks connecting Broad Street Station to Thirtieth Street Station, had been replaced by commercial buildings—and that probably was for the good. But what of the renowned Baldwin Works at the corner of Broad and Spring Garden, which once produced most of the world's trains? Or the stations at Ninth and Green, at Front and

Norris, at Third and Burkes? All gone. Only the Reading Terminal survived.

Growing up on the West Coast, he'd read about the great train cities of the Northeast, and particularly Philadelphia, a hub for the Reading and the Pennsy and the B & O. But when he finally moved to the City of Brotherly Love, these giant lines had been reduced to mere spots on a Monopoly board.

McBryde swiveled in his chair to look at the rest of the office through his open door. His staff was busy handling the fare complaints. Everyone had received a sheet of "talking points" for guidance—a comparison of the fare hike to cost-of-living increases, the state of the city budget, a graph depicting transportation expenditures versus revenue. He could hear them fluidly and patiently fending off the enraged consumers. His staff was excellent, fresh from college, destined for much better jobs at salaries considerably larger than his.

"Line three, boss," his secretary said over the intercom. When she called him "boss," he knew immediately the identity of the caller. The Timer.

"It leaves one minute early," the Timer said over the phone in his rapid, high-pitched voice.

"I'm sorry?"

"You don't know what I'm talking about, Mr. McBryde? Aren't you the boss? Aren't you in control?" The Timer was a schoolteacher from the Main Line. His complaints invariably focused on time.

"Can I help you in any specific way?"

"It's the R5. It leaves one minute early from the Merion Station. I've been out there. I know."

"I'm sure you do."

"Do I detect a note of sarcasm? I hope not. One week ago I missed my train because it left one minute early. All week now I've been timing it."

"Perhaps the watches of the conductors are not properly synchronized." The Timer had a son high up in the mayor's office. Otherwise McBryde long ago would have instructed his staff to ignore the schoolteacher.

"That's the excuse you used three months ago when I pointed

out that the R5 consistently left Suburban Station two minutes late. A full two minutes, mind you!"

"I'll make some calls," McBryde said wearily.

"Tomorrow morning I'll be there with my watch. It's digital, very accurate. And another thing. I see there's been a fare increase."

"A small one."

"The proverbial straw!"

"Actually I have a meeting I must attend—"

"I hear there might be a boycott."

Jesus, news traveled fast. He'd better cut the oxygen off to this particular rumor. "I really don't think—"

But the Timer was ready to sign off. "See you at the barricades!" he said with a final squeak.

EIGHT

On Tuesday morning, Szczymanski found a note on her desk. The SAC wanted to discuss protocol with her. Protocol, it turned out, consisted of two matters.

First, Granite reiterated the importance of her case, the considerable prestige riding on a successful outcome. He indicated, however, that the case—"a devilishly complicated mess"—might take up months of careful research and that she shouldn't become "frustrated." Szczymanski understood the deeper meaning. The case did not concern train accidents but the infinitely less resolvable question of her own reliability. She imagined a surreal scenario in which she spent an entire career in the FBI doing nothing but proving her loyalty to the organization.

Second, he identified both Peña and Metaxas as her new associates.

"They'll be your resource people," Granite told her. "Since you're new to the landscape here, they can help out with any of your research needs. You'll be a team."

In other words, her associates would always be available, even if she didn't need them. *Particularly* if she didn't need them.

The qualities of Steadman Granite that on the previous day had seemed acceptable, even reassuring, had become profoundly unsettling. The SAC's smile now struck her as sinister, his size menacing, his straightforward manner perversely deceptive. For the first time she noticed a tic that periodically convulsed a small muscle in his upper jaw—a mannerism that made him appear less solid, less confident. He scribbled on his desk calendar with his right hand and cast sidelong glances to his right: a good sign of lying, according to the rules she'd learned in the kinesics seminar at Quantico.

He's a pigdick, Peña had said, but he's our pigdick. Szczymanski gritted her teeth: he's certainly not my pigdick.

Back in her office after this brief meeting, she reclined in the desk chair with hands interlaced behind her head and elbows akimbo. The FBI didn't trust her. They had given her a low-priority case and placed her in a lose-lose situation. Her associates were her informers. Moreover, she had no real evidence to back up her charges. Even if she had the goods—for instance, a tape of last night's conversation between Peña and Metaxas—to whom could she turn? The FBI director? The attorney general? The American people?

No matter how sharp the pain of betrayal, she'd have to be extraordinarily careful to conceal her knowledge. A new strategy was required, something appropriately duplicitous. On the outside she'd continue with TB^2 and dish out at least as much as she absorbed. But on the inside she'd be Scheming Feline. Quick, fickle, and surefooted, she'd carefully observe her observers and locate some method of extricating herself from this terrible bind.

At Lucky's last night, she'd been forced by circumstances to split her behavior down the middle. The three of them drank beer, played pinball, shot a couple games of cutthroat pool. Once she had settled her stomach with some chopped pork barbecue, Szczymanski competed with complete self-assurance, bragged about her Quantico achievements, and sought to demonstrate that mastery over lactic acid was not her only talent. This performance, which received high scores on the pinball machine and a string of victories at the pool table, earned her enough free drinks from her partners to cover at least two more excursions to Lucky's. Through it all, she monitored her monitors, hoping that the alcohol and the competition would loosen their lips. But they, too, were careful. She was confident that ultimately they would slip—long before she would.

At a deeper level, however, she felt terribly betrayed, far more than after the sexual harassment in Pierre. Blaine, after all, had been a mere individual, his actions a result of lust, not conspiracy. Now she was confronting an institution, an imperfect institution to be sure, but *her* institution—the one to which she'd devoted her life.

Szczymanski had long taken pride in having no illusions, ever since her great awakening as a teenager. When she was fourteen, her best friend Dorothy stole the boy that she'd begun to date. Just like that—without an explanation. One day, she was necking with Garcia in the alley behind the Polish-American Friendship Society; the next day, at a movie with another friend, she saw Dorothy and the little heartbreaker glued to one another in the back row of the theater. She never talked to either one again. Just like that—without an explanation. She didn't return calls, ignored letters, spurned the mediation attempts of their mutual friends.

From then on, Szczymanski no longer expected others to live up to her expectations. People were, in general, irresponsible, thoughtless, and inconsiderate. In those rare moments of apparent altruism, they concealed ulterior motives: lust, greed, false modesty. She didn't even completely trust her friends—Barnegut in Atlanta, the few comrades from college and law school she still kept up with. Perhaps trust was not the right word. It was realism. She'd grown a second, more calloused, layer of skin. Her first layer protected her from the elements. This second skin shielded her from people.

Her "strategies" sprang directly from this philosophy. After the betrayal of Dorothy and Garcia, Szczymanski realized that multiple personalities gave her a better chance of surviving in the real world. Her private self, that set of slowly evolving hopes, fears, and desires, would remain consistent throughout. Depending on the circumstance, however, an arsenal of masks would protect her from further betrayal.

She thus considered her life illusion-free. Nobody could hurt her. Friendships went just so far. Relationships with men were destined to end. Colleagues were not to be depended upon. Only by scaling back her expectations could she forestall disappointment.

The FBI shared this dim view of human nature. In fact, not content simply to round up criminals, the FBI deliberately tempted people into wrongdoing: showering a lonely old man with offers for mail-order child pornography; approaching legislators with bribes from phony Arab sheikhs; luring suspected drug addicts into crooked deals. We live in a fallen world, Szczymanski reflected, and only institutions such as the FBI prevent society from splitting apart at the seams, from becoming entirely dog-eat-dog, from devolving into a war of all against all. Only the FBI and its constabulary cousins keep the playing field at a gentle incline favoring the dishonest and the psychotic, rather than at a more precipitous and sinister grade.

But the FBI too was imperfect, which she had always known but only now understood completely. Like all institutions in a fallen world, it was buffeted by the same forces of greed and stupidity that warped souls everywhere. Gather people into a group and they will showcase their worst tendencies, regardless of the scattering of virtues found among the members. Still, the FBI should have attracted the best, Americans of the highest caliber.

These last illusions, rooted so deeply in her psyche, died the hardest. She hadn't expected her superiors to lie in such a grand fashion. She hadn't expected the Bureau to turn against her so thoroughly. To put her under surveillance? How much lower could they go? It would have been better if they had just fired her.

Sitting at her desk, with the accident bulletins and crossing incident charts arrayed before her, Szczymanski finally felt the full weight of her predicament. Whom was she kidding? TB² and Scheming Feline? Her new two-edged strategy was tantamount to using sunglasses to protect against a nuclear blast. She looked at the notes she'd been making on a yellow pad, an attempt to find a pattern amid all the tangled data. What was the point of it all? Even if she did achieve the impossible and pull an unsub out of the hat, a cloud of suspicion would still hang over her. She'd never been in such a position before, hemmed in on all sides. On this, her second day on the job, after a roller-coaster ride from exile to vindication and back again, her confidence was faltering. She felt weak, ugly, and stupid. And ashamed of these feelings.

The phone rang.

Peña's rapid-fire voice shot from the receiver. "Partner? We got an interview with the head of the Federal Railroad Administration in ten minutes."

"We?"

"Metaxas is bringing the car around."

"I have a lot of reading to do."

Peña laughed. "Mañana. This was his only available time."

"I like to be prepared for my interviews."

"Then think of this as a prelim. We can always go back. Hell, this thing might stay with us like a bad case of the runs."

"Look, if we're going to be working together as associates . . ." Szczymanski began.

"Then we're going to have to cooperate," Peña finished. "So let's not keep Metaxas waiting."

The Federal Railroad Administration was housed in one of the U.S. Department of Transportation's immense sugar-cube buildings located just south of the Mall. They flashed their FBI badges at the door and were escorted to the tenth floor, the office of the administrator. "Anthony Marinetti" the nameplate on the door read.

Marinetti's office looked suspiciously clean for a bureaucrat. The bookcases were empty except for a few volumes of thick loose-bound documents. The Department's calendar from the previous year, with June featuring a sunny photo of an engineer waving from the cab of a locomotive, hung askew from a pushpin jabbed into the wall. On the desk lay several computer manuals, tented open with cracked spines. To one side of these manuals was a sleek notebook computer. Behind the computer sat the administrator, concentrating. He was a smooth-faced man, his hair thin but his eyebrows unusually bushy. He wore a bolo tie with a large turquoise stone at its center, an ornament that jarred with the machinelike minimalism of his surroundings.

"Please sit down," he told the three agents without taking his eyes from the screen. "I'll be with you in a moment."

"Take your time, sir," Peña said.

Szczymanski groaned inwardly. She'd never met a bureaucrat she liked. Employed at the public expense, they rarely returned the investment. They were paid, it appeared, to keep you angry and to keep you waiting.

Metaxas didn't seem to mind. She sat straight in her chair, staring at a point several inches above the administrator's ear. During the car ride over, she had spoken perhaps five words in all. No matter; the space had been amply filled by Peña. Peña on food. Peña on the weather. Peña on the best Swiss Army knife to buy for a backpacking vacation in Maine. Now Peña was sitting in sycophantic silence, drawing elaborate geometric patterns in the margins of her notebook.

"Performance," the administrator grunted, finally tearing his eyes from the computer. "That's what I demand from a computer. And this computer outperforms every single competitor in its class." He stood, cracked his back with a sharp downward tug of his shoulders, and extended his hand in turn to each woman. "Marinetti. Tony Marinetti."

He put the computer to sleep and slid it across the desk. Inserting pencils as bookmarks, he overturned the manuals and stacked them together. "Now, what can I do for you?"

"Accidents, sir," Szczymanski said, pleased to see that Peña was deferring to her. Metaxas took out a yellow pad and assumed a secretarial posture. Peña too was ready to make notes. Szczymanski reached into her pocket and pulled out a pocket tape recorder. She placed it on the desk, depressing the "on" button. "You don't mind, do you?" she asked.

"Model 457 is much better." Marinetti picked up the recorder to turn around in his hand. "Better sound quality." He set it down on the table in front of him.

"This one will do for the moment," she replied, checking once more to see if it was ready. Again she had to depress the "on" button. A slick bureaucrat, no less.

Marinetti rearranged himself in his chair. "Accidents, you say? You're going to have to be a little more specific, young woman. Are you interested in highway crossings or track defects? Derailments or collisions? Vandalism or obstructions?"

"Accident rates per million train miles, sir." Szczymanski had read enough of the materials on her desk to cut through at least some of the usual bureaucratic doublespeak. "Collisions up ten percent. Derailments five percent. According to the estimates provided by your department for the last two years."

"Accident rates can rise for any number of reasons," Marinetti replied. "Deteriorating rolling stock. Human error. Or deliberate design."

"And you think deliberate design," said Szczymanski.

"I leave that to the FBI to decide." He looked from one agent to the next. "It is not my business to speculate. I am here to ensure service and world-class performance. I leave speculation to others."

In addition to courtesy, Szczymanski thought. "Do you think the deterioration in rolling stock has caused the increase?"

"It's all in the numbers," he replied. "The average federal appropriation for the passenger train industry is thirty million dollars a year. The annual depreciation is one hundred seventy million. We have old trains, old tracks, ancient bridges and tunnels. I'd be surprised if the accident rate had not gone up over the past two years."

"What about human error?" Szczymanski pressed.

"We've laid off people all around the country. Each employee now has to do the work of several. Errors are inevitable."

"Then why would anyone think there's a deliberate design behind all of this?" Szczymanski was approaching exasperation.

"I never said that anyone did."

"But—"

"Simply this, my dear woman," Marinetti continued, reaching over to shut off the tape recorder. "It would be more convenient for us here at the Department of Transportation if the accidents were caused by someone else. Do you understand?"

Szczymanski plucked the recorder from his desk and pocketed it. "I understand perfectly, sir. We're sorry to take up so much of your time. Perhaps after the results of our preliminary investigation come in, we'll arrange another interview."

Peña and Metaxas looked up from their notepads with eyebrows raised.

Marinetti's own eyebrows rippled like fat black caterpillars. He fingered his bolo tie, then pulled his computer back into position in front of him. "World-class," he said, looking up as the agents rose to their feet. "Eventually I want this department to oversee a world-class transportation system. Are you on my side?"

Szczymanski became aware of an acidic taste in her mouth. Was this the flavor of dislike?

"Naturally," Peña said brightly. "It would be wonderful if—"

Szczymanski interrupted her. "If I need more information from your office?"

"My assistant will give you his card."

As Metaxas negotiated the Washington streets, Szczymanski tried to control her anger. The whole affair had begun to smell more and more like a Leavis exercise. She remembered one particular occasion when Leavis informed the class that a student had been randomly selected to be an undercover Russian agent; their job was to unmask the unsub. The first person to rout the mole would win a pass to the final exams. As Leavis retreated behind his *Washington Post* and refused to answer further questions, class members began to confer among themselves, establishing this and that vetting process to screen out the Russian. But after ten minutes of going over the matter in her own mind, Szczymanski stood up and announced that the Russian agent didn't exist. "Why not?" demanded the professor. Economy of means, explained Szczymanski. The idea of an agent was more destabilizing than an agent itself. The professor could not rely on any of the students to maintain cover, so it would be easier simply to plant an imaginary agent among them. Finally, she said, the exercise was infinitely more interesting without a real mole.

The professor gave one of his rare smiles. "Very good. But beware, Szczymanski. The true answer is not always the most interesting answer."

Was Leavis right? She was confronted with a very uninteresting solution indeed: the railroad accidents could be attributed to unintentional factors. She could spend a year poring over accident patterns, trying to tease the smallest chain of malfeasance from them. But, in the end, she'd have to report to Granite a total lack of evidence. The Department of Transportation simply desired a scapegoat—just as the FBI had suspected. It was a make-work assignment.

"I still had some questions," Peña pouted from the passenger's seat.

"Then think of this as a prelim," Szczymanski replied.

"Why'd you want to leave so soon?"

"Other things to do."

"Oh?"

She let Peña's exclamation hang in the air and gazed at the wide expanse of the Mall, the Indian atop the U.S. Capitol, the two wings of the National Gallery. It seemed like a very attractive city. Sequestered at Quantico forty miles south, she'd never really had the opportunity to see it properly.

"Would you like an introduction to some of the Bureau services?" Peña asked, suddenly conciliatory.

"For instance?"

"Faxes, on-line bulletin boards, tele—"

"I may need," she interrupted, "some mainframe computer time for number crunching. Would you be able to arrange that?"

"Of course," Peña said. "No problem. Tomorrow I'll explain your security clearance and what forensic services you'll have access to."

Szczymanski brooded: they'd control her access, and monitor it as well. In such a closed system, she could shield important discoveries from her putative partners only with great difficulty.

She hated to admit it, but she needed help. In this fallen world, in this organization of smoke and mirrors, she needed to find someone on the inside whom she could trust.

NINE

Upstairs, Lenin was reciting a nursery rhyme, mixing up Mother Goose and Mother Hubbard and laughing at his own confusion. Lenin was his ex-wife's lover. That wasn't his real name, just an observation of McBryde's (Rosalind preferred to call it an unfortunate joke). His replacement was a computer-science professor who sported a goatee, favored small round wire-framed glasses, and possessed a gleaming bald head. If you just saw him at a glance or from a distance, he looked much like the Russian revolutionary arriving by train at Finland Station—a picture McBryde had once seen in a book on Russian trains. The one discernible difference between the two was that Rosalind's Lenin, like an anesthetized Bolshevik, always seemed to be smiling.

The Unmentionable smiled at him from across the blond-wood-and-glass coffee table. Trying to find a way to broach the subject, McBryde looked down into his now empty coffee mug, emblazoned with the call letters of a radio station to which they had pledged thirty-five dollars two years ago. His thumb caressed the small chip in the handle. He looked at a *Casablanca* poster on the wall, Bogie and Bergman so in love. He averted his eyes in embarrassment and tried to read the headlines of a computer magazine upside down on the table in front of him. Giving up, he looked into the kitchen at the remains of dinner. If he concentrated, McBryde could just capture the lingering aroma of stuffed peppers, his favorite dish from their life together.

Rosalind followed his gaze. "Stephen cooked tonight. He makes better stuffed peppers than I do."

"Is nothing sacred?" Once again, Lenin had proved his superiority.

"Ever since we became vegetarians he's taught me an enormous number of new recipes."

"I suppose he has you spraying ketchup on fur coats."

"It wouldn't hurt you to cut down on those hamburgers and hoagies. I bet you haven't done your sit-ups in months. Am I right?"

He squeezed the ring of fat encircling his midsection. "As soon as I get through this week, I'll—"

"Yes, I've heard that before."

"I gave up smoking. It was a fattening decision."

"You need exercise."

"I suppose Lenin jogs every day and plays tennis on the weekend."

"He keeps fit."

Feeling suddenly light-headed, McBryde leaned across the coffee table and lowered his voice. "Are you happy?" he asked.

He regretted the question as soon as it left his mouth. Why couldn't he control himself? It was inevitable. After spending more than ten minutes with his ex-wife, he always blurted this very same question, the one that followed him everywhere like a shadow.

Rosalind paused and before she could speak, McBryde forged ahead, oblivious to the objections of his conscious mind. "Because if you're not . . ."

She pursed her lips. "Larry, why do you keep asking me this? You can see that I'm happy. You should work more on being happy yourself."

He grunted and straightened up. Of course she was happy—

only an idiot could misread the signs. He retreated into his office persona. "Like I said over the phone, I might be going out of town. Starting this weekend. And I might be away for a couple weeks."

"This is rather inconvenient," Rosalind said. "We planned to go skiing the weekend after next. Stephen hasn't taken a weekend off in months."

"Neither have I!" McBryde protested.

His wife's eyes registered no sympathy. "We hoped to leave Melissa with you as usual."

"Your mother?" he suggested.

Rosalind pursed her lips.

"Your friend Claire?"

She raised an eyebrow.

"Look, Rosalind, I wouldn't ask you to do this unless it was important. I'm just looking for a little flexibility."

"I don't want to stand between you and your vacation."

"I told you, it's not exactly a vacation. It's work-related."

"A West Virginia short line? The last of the great Oklahoma steam engines?" Said with a trace of mockery in her voice.

"Work-related," he repeated, refusing to be more specific.

"A convention? A rare-mileage ride?"

"Look," McBryde exploded, "have I missed one child-support payment? Or one weekend with Melissa so far? Have I been a bother to you in any way?"

Rosalind immediately softened at these reproaches. "No, Larry, you haven't. I couldn't dream of a better ex-husband."

A buzzer went off in the basement. "The laundry," Rosalind said, standing up. McBryde was left in the living room, free to consider his status of ex-husband.

It was, he decided, an unenviable position. While the separation made Rosalind more charming and independent, he'd become only sullen and impatient. He'd tried to start over, to date, to seek out "relationships." A blind date with the daughter of one of Jordan's colleagues felt like a job interview, with firm good-night handshakes exchanged at the end. He went on dinner dates with a neurotic food stylist who criticized the color of their entrees, a functionally mute secretary who went to the bathroom every five minutes, and a veterinarian who insisted on discussing intestinal worms over their pasta entrees. He even went out with one or two female foamers. But mixing trains and sex had been a turn-off.

He hated dating. It made him feel like a junior high schooler. Ex-husbands shouldn't have to go through such trials. Ex-husbands should be allowed to skip these ridiculous preliminaries. He wanted to step into a relationship mid-stream, to wake up one morning to find a familiar face next to his on the pillow. He wanted someone who looked and acted like Rosalind. Or, even better, someone identical but without those little habits that used to drive him crazy— like forbidding him to talk while they watched television together or insisting that he remove his shoes at the front door before entering the house. But, truth to tell, he'd even begun to miss these traits. McBryde looked down at his socks. They were worn thin in places. He hadn't bought clothes in over a year.

He stood up. It had been a mistake to come out to Rosemont. He should have arranged everything over the phone. But there was Melissa, he'd wanted to see her again. McBryde shifted his weight from foot to foot.

"Larry!" The computer professor appeared at the bottom of the stairs. He gestured at the sofa. "Sit, sit, we see so little of you. In and out twice a month. Rosalind has invited you for dinner, hasn't she?"

McBryde nodded. He sat down again, stared into the kitchen to avoid looking at his adversary. He felt like a child misbehaving at an adult party.

"Hungry?" Lenin asked. "There's a left-over pepper. We nuke it and you'll have dinner in a minute."

McBryde shook his head.

"There was an article in one of these," Lenin said, sweeping up a magazine from the coffee table and brandishing it. "About trains. About a new computer guidance system. Something to do with the new high-speed system."

That was too much: the Devil quoting Scripture. "I'll have to track that one down," McBryde said without thinking.

"Oh, very good!" Lenin was bubbling up with mirth. "Track that down! I must remember that one!"

McBryde detested puns.

"So," Lenin chuckled, flapping his arms like a bird, "you're going on vacation. Flying somewhere special?"

"Actually it's work-related, not a vacation," he said tentatively.

"Well, that's wonderful too," the professor answered, his eyes twinkling, the pink of his scalp glistening like stretched bubble gum.

McBryde wondered if he might be brain-damaged. Or perhaps he was one of those strange idiots who could teach medieval English but needed help tying his own shoelaces, who could play perfect Beethoven on the piano but drooled uncontrollably down the front of his shirt. McBryde looked around the room in embarrassment, hoping for Rosalind to return and rescue him soon. Again his eye fell on Bergman and Bogie cavorting on the wall. Didn't they ever get tired of one another?

"Hey, did you hear the one about the blind xylophonist?"

McBryde shook his head. Bad jokes were only one step above bad puns on his moron index.

"He left his . . . his . . ." Lenin suddenly looked troubled. "Oh drat, hold on a minute." He moved to the door to the basement. "Oh, Ros? Do you remember the punch line to that joke about the xylophonist? The blind xylophonist?" He went down the steps into the basement to confer with his wife.

McBryde heard the low rumble of conversation. Then Rosalind appeared at the top of the stairs.

"I'm sorry about Stephen," she whispered, sitting back down across from him. "He's had a hard day at school. He's still a little bit cranky. I've left him down there to fold the laundry. That'll lift his spirits." She crossed her legs, pushed a sprig of hair behind her ear with her thumb. "Okay, Larry, I've thought it over. We'll postpone the skiing. But you're going to have to do something for us in return."

"And that would be . . ."

"I haven't decided yet," Rosalind said wickedly. "But for the time being, you're in my debt. Now say good-bye to Melissa and skedaddle. It's already past her bedtime."

Melissa's room was filled with stuffed animals, paper flowers, an assortment of foam-rubber sports equipment, and enough multicolored building blocks to create a kaleidoscope city. The scattered profusion of color suddenly reminded him of the model train set of his youth, the parts distributed around the basement: the coal-black engines, raspberry-red cabooses, orange and yellow and brown sidecars, green tufts of trees, and yards upon yards of silvery tracks. He paused for a moment in the middle of his daughter's room, as if inhaling the memory, then shook the image from his mind.

Underneath the covers of the bed, he glimpsed a small body, only a few wisps of blond hair displayed on the pillow. Melissa was trying to stifle her giggles. The memory of the train set and the sight of his daughter's hair pushed aside all the accumulated resentments of the evening.

"Now where is my little princess?" he asked, as her laughter became harder to conceal. "Is she hiding behind this door? No! Is she over here, behind this bookcase? No! Maybe the fairies have taken her away? Or maybe she is where she should be. Right *here!*" And he bounded over to the bed to tickle her beneath the sheets.

Gasping for air, Melissa popped her head out from the covers. "Daddy!" Then, becoming suddenly serious, she scampered out of her bed and began to build an unsteady house out of the multicolored bricks.

The building crumpled before it could reach a third story.

"That was pretty," he encouraged her.

"It was," Melissa pouted, her hands deep among the scattered bricks to rescue the small furry trolls that had been brief tenants in the building. "But it's gone now. Why don't they stay?"

"If they stayed, you wouldn't be able to build anything else."

The Unmentionable hovered on the edge of his thoughts.

He remembered the first time the gang of thieves broke into the Portland yards. They gave the guard dogs huge steaks with coiled springs inside and made off with several pieces of expensive equipment. The dogs were discovered behind the air hoses, yelping with pain. Their stomach acid had dissolved the steaks. The springs had then slowly uncoiled, mincing their innards into hamburger.

That, McBryde decided, is how I feel when I see my ex-wife. Each time our eyes meet, the wire uncoils just a bit more.

"Would you like a nice wooden train set?" he asked his daughter. "It could take your little dolls around the cities you build."

"A train?" Melissa looked up at him, tucked her hair behind her ear. "Yuck."

He picked her up and returned her to the bed. Sitting up, she drew her knees up until they almost reached her chin. "Daddy, next time we go to Paris?"

"Do you really want to go to Paris?"

"Next week."

"But I won't see you next week." He held up two fingers. Peace, my little one, he thought, afraid of what else would come from her mouth.

"Next week," Melissa repeated. "Saturday. With Mommy. And with . . . with . . ." She squinted at him. "With Mommy and with . . ."

McBryde looked away. Then, turning back, he kissed his daughter on both cheeks and straightened the covers around her shoulders. "I love you," he said simply. As he turned off the light and made his way downstairs, he felt heavy and tired and terribly alone.

Back at his apartment, he phoned Jordan.

"So," he said, "I'm off the hook with Melissa for another two weeks. I'm ready to roll. All revved up and nowhere to go."

"How about the Lake Shore Limited leaving New York this Sunday?" Jordan said.

McBryde laughed. "And why would I want to start there?"

"Because," Jordan said, suddenly solemn, "that's where the next accident will be."

TEN

It was a late Wednesday after-noon and Szczymanski was fading as quickly as the sunlight. She'd remained in her office all day with the door shut, hadn't eaten anything since a hurried breakfast at the hotel. Hour after hour she'd pored over the data, tried to find a pattern, any pattern. If only she had access to a computer, she could process the data so much faster. Peña had promised a computer orientation by early next week. Early next week? Bureaucracy or deliberate obstruction—take your pick.

Her stomach growled ominously. Wasn't there a candy machine near the elevators on her floor? But she wanted to avoid Peña and Granite, didn't have the presence of mind to deal with their lies. It was almost four-thirty. Could she hold out for another half hour without a chocolate bar? Of course. There were several more geographic variables to test. Leavis would be pleased at her persistence, but disappointed with her results.

A chocolate bar filled with caramel? And almonds? And maybe coconut sprinkles on top? Did such a candy bar exist? Her mouth remembered something of the sort. Actually she'd settle for M&Ms, for licorice sticks, for Mary Janes. The mere thought of sugar accelerated the blood flow in her veins. Hell, she'd even take one of those dreadful peanut-butter-sandwich crackers. She pushed her chair back and stood up. A spell of dizziness forced her to lean against the desk. Then, her hand sifting through the change in her pant pocket, she strode to the door and opened it.

On the other side of the door stood a strikingly handsome man, his hand raised to knock.

Smiling sheepishly, the man lowered his hand. He was Asian-American, with a wide face, high cheekbones, and black hair cut short on the sides but left long on top. Several strands hung down into his eyes. He brushed them back with splayed fingers. "Busy?"

Szczymanski shook her head warily, backing into her office.

"Martin Chao," the man said, extending his hand. "That's Chao, like Puppy Chow, but most everyone calls me Chaos, like chaos theory."

"Chaos? I don't get it."

"I'm married, see." He held out his hand so she could see the gold band. "And we have three little ones. Now, they're the best, don't get me wrong. Suzie's ten, Nora's eight, and Jimmy's only three. Great kids. But they're kids, and kids can be a little wild. So when we go anywhere as a family—and that's most of the time—people always say, 'Here comes the Chaos.' Here comes chaos. Make sense?"

"Sort of."

He took a pen out of his breast pocket, a notecard from his back pocket, and wrote "Chao" and then "chaos." He held it up. "Ever watch 'Get Smart'? The old TV show? That was the name of the other side's spy unit. They were a group of bunglers, remember? So that's kind of a joke too. Because, well, I never bungle." He grinned at her and swept the rebellious strands of hair away from his forehead.

"Chaos," she repeated.

"Beats Puppy Chow. Or," he went on, a shade more seriously, "Chow Mein."

"You never bungle?"

"That doesn't sound very modest, does it? But it's true, I think. I know my machines inside out and they never fail me."

"Your machines?"

Chaos suddenly looked confused. "No one's told you about me yet?"

"I don't think so . . ."

"I'm in the Engineering Research Facility. Computer section. You've heard of us, right?"

Szczymanski had taken an entire four-week course on the facility. Having thoroughly read all of the class materials, she felt that she knew ERF quite well indeed. "Triple I," she said. "Big Floyd."

His face broke out in a wide smile that exposed the bright-red gums above his upper teeth. "Those are my two favorites. You know we're updating Triple I? Soon—but don't tell your friends—the states will allow us to keep all the criminal records on line. Then watch out!"

"Please, sit down. How rude of me. I guess you haven't moved into the separate facility yet." The ERF, she knew, was moving to West Virginia for pork-barrel reasons. She returned to the other side of her desk.

Chaos, after closing the door, sat down across from her. "Not the computers, the mainframes. Next year, I hope."

"And have you nailed anyone yet with Big Floyd?" At Quantico, she'd written a paper about Big Floyd, an artificial intelligence program being used for labor racketeering cases, and in it had made suggestions for improving its logic. The professor had been so impressed with the paper that he had forwarded it anonymously to the research group in charge of the program.

"Still experimental," Chaos said. "It's a darn good program, probably the best AI we have. But still hasn't learned to fly."

She couldn't help herself. "Do you remember a little paper about domain-independent algorithms?"

His face lit up with pleasure. "With the five proof-transformation operators?"

"And the five domain-independent control heuristics."

Chaos laughed, clapped his hands together. "That little paper saved us six months of work and tens of thousands of dollars!"

She grinned so hard it hurt.

"You?" Chaos pointed at her. "Well, ma'am, you could knock me over with a fractal! We had some follow-up questions but never found out who sent it to us."

"I'm just glad it helped."

"Delighted to finally meet you," Chaos said, rubbing his hands together. "I'll send over the latest on the project. Love to get your feedback. Where'd you get your ideas? Dietterich?"

"Segre. Studied AI in college. Kept up with the literature in law school."

"Impressive. Anyway, Granite told me to stop by for a chat. See if there was anything you needed."

Oh, Granite. She felt deflated. Was Chaos just another person assigned to monitor her activities? He seemed like a pleasant and honest guy, but that could merely be a front. If Granite was behind this, then she had to suspect Chaos. She gestured to the papers on her desk. "Well, I think I have enough right here to keep me going for a while."

Chaos glanced in the general direction of the materials but did not attempt to read them. He looked pained. "Couple of key searches and a computer could boil down everything you need to a couple pages."

"I . . . I like to start out the old-fashioned way." God, this was worse than chocolate. She craved computers so.

"But what you're working on lends itself so readily to computers."

"Oh?" She didn't like the idea that her case was so widely discussed.

Chaos, sensing her resentment, became apologetic. "Granite gave me the general outlines of your project. He thought, because you're new here and we'll probably be working together and all . . ."

"That's fine," she said in a monotone. "I look forward to working together."

Chaos looked uncertain. "I have to say that I'm particularly interested in toxic waste."

She did a double-take. "Excuse me?"

"Toxic waste. I'd love to nail those polluters. And with my computers we'll be able to knock them off like birds glued to a post.

Each one leaves a chemical fingerprint and it's just as if the corporate logo floated right there on top of the swill."

"I'm not working on toxic waste," Szczymanski said flatly.

Chaos gave a little start. "I'm sorry, I don't think I quite heard what—"

"Trains," she replied. "My case is train accidents."

He fumbled in his pocket and came out with a slip of paper. "Lisa Grumbach?"

"Jennifer Szczymanski." She smiled and waggled her fingers at him as if in greeting. "Pleased to meet you."

"Room 512?"

"Next one over."

"Oh." His face crumpled. Chaos suddenly looked like a little boy separated from his mother at a supermarket. He rose to leave.

Should she risk it? If she didn't do something soon, they'd have her completely tied up. He looked as if he could be trusted. Computer jocks tended to be straight shooters. And weren't her gut instincts often correct?

"Wait," she said before he reached the door. "I'm going to need some help. Some professional assistance."

Chaos turned around slowly. "If you submit a request—"

"No," she interrupted. "This can't go through the normal channels."

The computer specialist looked uncomfortable. He twisted the slip of paper in his hands into a corkscrew.

Szczymanski scrambled around in her mind for a viable reason. "You see, I think there's a conflict of interest somewhere in the office."

Chaos's nostrils widened in curiosity.

By lying to the computer expert, she was now playing a more dangerous game. If word were to get back to Granite about an undercover internal investigation, she would inevitably be fingered as the source. But what choice did she have?

"I can't yet tell you who or what. And I need your promise not to reveal your work on this matter to anyone."

"Someone in the office." Chaos meditated on the words for a moment. "This is a very serious charge."

"Will you promise?"

"Perhaps."

"Look, as soon as this is over, you and me'll sit down for a serious talk about Big Floyd. I think Segre's latest work might be applicable."

Chaos tilted his head, looked at her curiously beneath his black forelocks. "Train accidents, you say?"

"I need a pattern." She took in the contents of her desktop with a sweep of a hand. "If someone is causing these accidents, then I'll bet there's a pattern somewhere. Can you find it for me?"

Chaos moved closer to pluck a booklet off the desk. "Federal Railroad Administration Office of Safety. I'm sure we have this on CD-ROM." He glanced at several other titles. "I could run the tests after hours. Any guesses of variables for the pattern? Geography? Or time period?"

"The last two years," Szczymanski said. "That's all I know. But if you find me a pattern, I'll know what to do with it. With a computer we might even be able to predict where and when the next one will be. I want to be on that next train."

"Someone in the office," he repeated, rolling up several papers from her desk into a tube and inserting it in his back pocket.

"Oh, and Chaos? Have you heard anything interesting about me?"

"Fresh cheese," he said, now standing by the door. "That's what they're calling you."

She laughed. "It's not the worst nickname. Anything else?"

"You're the lactic-acid chick, right?"

She blushed.

"Didn't take you long to get into the thick of things."

"Life's short, crime's long. And hey, I appreciate your help."

"Help? What help? I'm afraid I don't know anything about your case." Again Chaos brushed back his recalcitrant wave of hair. "Anyway, you're the one who saved us all that time and money. Fair's fair."

"You'll have something in a couple days?"

"Let's shoot for tomorrow. I have some time this evening, but then it'll get hairier."

"Shall we say eleven A.M. by the water fountain near the public relations office? Know the one?"

"Excellent drop."

"By the way," she added mischievously. "I thought you said you never bungled."

"I was speaking metaphorically." He winked at her and slipped out of the room.

They were forcing her to do it, Granite and the others. She felt strongly about never departing from procedure. But she also hated being jerked around.

That night she moved into her new one-bedroom apartment near Dupont Circle. Standing on the well-lit sidewalk of Swann Street, in front of the painted brick town house whose entire third floor would be hers, Szczymanski watched the movers carry item after item out of their truck, through the iron gate and the lovely wooden door, and up the narrow staircase. They placed these jigsaw pieces of her life willy-nilly in the new apartment—in the kitchen, the floral-wallpapered bedroom, the old bathroom, and on the living room's wall-to-wall mint-green shag carpeting that looked as if it could use one more thorough cleaning. Szczymanski felt sad and displaced as she carried in a few plastic bags of stray items. She liked new jobs but not new apartments.

When the movers left, she sat down on the edge of her futon frame, on the mattress still wrapped in plastic. She felt like succumbing to inertia, letting the undertow of melancholy pull her in. She could take a straightforward legal job—good money, no risks. She could give up on trying to save the world.

Szczymanski lay back on the plastic, saying to herself that it would only be a minute. She would look at the cracks on the ceiling and think a little more and then unpack.

Then she said to herself: I'll just close my eyes and in a moment I'll be refreshed.

Then it was morning.

Chaos was waiting for her at 11 A.M. at the water fountain near the public relations office. Szczymanski smiled at him and bent down for a drink. Taking a quick swallow, she prepared to strike off in another direction.

"Oh, miss?" Chaos said. "I think you dropped this?" He held out a mailing envelope, unaddressed, with tape sealing it closed.

"Ah, yes."

Several people walked past them in the hallway, paying no attention to their dialogue.

"It looks very valuable." Chaos winked. "You should be more careful."

Szczymanski hurried to her office, eager to see the results of the computer search. She locked her door and carried the precious envelope to her desk. Sitting down, she slit open the top and saw several sheets of paper inside. And something else. She dumped the contents onto her desk. The papers were filled with equations and statistics and figures highlighted in lemon yellow. A little handwritten note was paper-clipped to something.

The note read: "My best guess. Took the liberty to buy these for you. Figured it would save time. Charged it to my account. The Bungler."

Attached to the note was a round-trip train ticket. To Chicago on the Lake Shore Limited. Leaving that Sunday evening from New York.

part two

ELEVEN

Awaysickness began with a slight electric charge that tickled the hair on his forearms. Then, as the departure date approached, the feeling moved to his fingertips, which throbbed as though he'd thrust them first into snow and then into hot water. On the morning of the departure, the excitement seeped from his fingertips into his muscles and his whole body twitched with anticipation.

McBryde loved travel, loved motion through space and time. Most people preferred a sense of permanence. They wanted a patch of ground they could claim as their own, a staked-out parcel of the globe's surface that could, when they were off in distant lands, elicit the peculiar emotion of homesickness that McBryde never could understand. He grew attached to people, but never places. Home for too long, he became restless, like a nose tackle waiting for the snap of the football. He felt truly at ease only when listening to the click of a train's wheels on tracks or watching the blur of countryside from a curtained window.

"There isn't a train I wouldn't take, no matter where it's going," Edna St. Vincent Millay wrote, and McBryde couldn't agree more with the poet. Airplanes, cars, and buses could not ease his awaysickness. They offered conveyance, not travel or genuine transport.

Seven months ago he'd taken Melissa to Portland for a week with his parents. To save time they flew. His daughter had been ecstatic, thought the DC-9 a giant carnival ride. McBryde recoiled at her enthusiasm. He had the deep loathing for airplanes that others reserved for modern cannibals or genocidal diseases. Airplanes were expensive, uncomfortable, and woefully inefficient. They turned people into substanceless creatures who could not appreciate the slow poetry of distance. Such blinkered human beings conceived of the world only as discrete points to be connected. They did not understand movement through a landscape. Ah, but what of Maglev and its superfast speeds? His soul divided, McBryde loved both leisurely ambles through the countryside and the idea of rapid trains that knit the country closer together. From both the slow doodlebug and the rapid Maglev, you saw what you traveled through, not like a plane and its passage above the clouds. He was secretly pleased at Melissa's in-flight nausea; he hoped it would inoculate her against the jet-setting disease.

It was almost a year since he had last traveled on an intercity train. More than once during this time, McBryde had worried that he'd lost his idiosyncratic longing, as others shed their homesickness after a period of accommodation. More than once, he'd questioned whether he was still, at heart, a foamer.

But yesterday, Saturday, when he'd fingered the coiled spine of a new spiral notebook in the drugstore, the sensation reappeared, and he'd greeted it like an old friend, like a favorite shirt unearthed from a corner of a bureau drawer. All day the awaysickness intensified, curbing his appetite and making him jittery and restless. He awoke Sunday morning out of breath, almost feverish. On the subway ride to Thirtieth Street Station he was afraid he'd hyperventilate. He felt like a boy nervously returning to his girlfriend after a long separation. Did she still love him? And would he still thrill to the sight of her?

He very nearly swooned upon entering Thirtieth Street Station itself. It was beautiful. He'd been too busy at the office to follow the renovations closely. Sometime in the last two weeks the work had been completed. Now the scaffolding was gone from the vast hall. The fluted columns, topped by gold-leaf capitals, were newly clean. The terminal ceiling was repainted in soft tones of beige, peach, and the old Tuscan red of the Pennsylvania Railroad. The Art Deco chandeliers were restored. The commercial areas were redesigned to accommodate new bakeries, cafés, and seafood markets. The tall, narrow windows on all sides, scrubbed clear, let in great rivers of light. Thirtieth Street Station glowed in the late-afternoon sun.

It was a glorious station, certainly his favorite in the country: more human than Grand Central Terminal, more exalted than Penn Station, and more accessible than Washington's Union Station. Philadelphia's major terminus was emphatically a *public* place, expressing the true meaning of America—large and welcoming and democratic. Walking into Thirtieth Street Station seemed more genuinely civic than entering a voting booth. And it made him proud to be connected to the enterprise, however obscurely.

Despite its obvious virtues, Thirtieth Street Station generated on average a complaint a day for his office.

"Why the hell isn't there an underground connection between the station and the subway?"

"It was too dangerous," his assistants would counter. "It was removed."

"Parking's too expensive."

"Try the meters by the post office."

"That ugly statue, the one near the door, well, I don't like seeing an angel carrying a corpse to heaven every time I'm going to board one of your trains."

So don't look, McBryde wanted to say, you've got free will.

A city could do nothing without generating complaints. If the city council approved a plan to give every man, woman, and child a hundred dollars in transportation rebates, his department would receive a dozen calls the next day complaining that the money wasn't enough, was too much, wasn't distributed properly, should have been used for something else. The Parks Department routinely received complaints about the number and variety of flowers planted on traffic islands. The Office of the Superintendent of Schools was flooded with calls taking exception to its free spring basketball clinic. And these were the positive aspects of city government! The flaws and fuckups and messes and failures that were the inevitable result of metropolitan life produced a constant deluge of complaints.

His job was as unrewarding as whitewashing graffiti in North Philadelphia. The next day there was always more ugliness to confront.

McBryde stood in front of the "Departures" board, surrounded by tumult. As gates were posted, travelers laden with luggage rushed to their trains, elbowing each other, one or two of them stepping on McBryde's shoes. He stood his ground, jaw set. They rushed around the terminal oblivious to the grandeur of the space, taking for granted that all train stations were automatically clean, well-lit, and comfortable. Rail passengers expected their connections waiting for them. Consumers bought their cappuccinos and grilled vegetables and calzones as though the businesses had been established for their benefit alone. As though the thousands of workers who toiled daily to maintain these spaces were part of a natural machinery. As though some beneficent hand wound up the labor force in the morning, oiled their parts in the evening, and provided replacement drones when necessary.

Was anybody ever thanked for the system when it worked? If they were, he and his colleagues in the Department of Bitch and Moan never heard about it.

Again the "Departures" board fluttered into action. McBryde's connecting train appeared at the bottom of the list, scheduled to depart in twenty minutes. It would get him to Penn Station in New York with enough time to buy a newspaper, pick up a sandwich for the train, and even get his shoes shined—before boarding the Lake Shore at 6:40 P.M. Clearing muffin crumbs from a wooden bench, he sat down with his duffel bag between his knees and waited for the boarding announcement. It was a perfect cigarette moment. Without a smoke, his hands felt idle. He tapped the flats of his fingers on his thigh.

Perhaps if he were smoking a heavy Gauloise, he'd feel better about playing the part of a private detective. A dick without ciggies was like a foamer without a scanner. Then again, perhaps he wouldn't have to playact. After all, this idea that the crazy foamer was following a pattern didn't make any sense. Ron Jordan's explanation had sounded so tenuous.

Still, Jordan was so rarely wrong, especially about trains.

"It was nothing, man," his friend had said when explaining how he'd hit upon the pattern. "I had this feeling, you know, like when the answer to a crossword puzzle clue is right there in your mind but you can't quite pull it out. I got messed up looking at all the trains. Things only started to click when I narrowed in on the *passenger* trains. First I tried the names, the names of the trains, thinking it might be alphabetical, something simple. But that didn't work. Then it hit me, Larry. The numbers. I know it'll sound crazy, but here it is: The passenger train accidents are separated by multiples of thirteen. The most recent one, the collision outside of Pittsburgh, was Amtrak train number fifty-one. The passenger trains on the tape we have are numbers 142, 129, 116, 103, 90. I'm not sure how the freight accidents fit in since they're numbered differently. And I don't know about a pattern to the accidents on the other tapes. But the Lake Shore is number thirty-eight."

"Isn't number twenty-five the Southwest Chief? And number twelve the California Zephyr?"

"That's right, buddy. But he won't get that far. Am I right?"

"Then how do you know it's going to be this Sunday?"

"We have four elements here: the train, the date, the type of accident, and the location. We look at the numbers and we get the specific train. The date is relatively easy. The accidents have been happening closer and closer together, first months separating the targeted trains, then weeks, now days. The type of accident and location are a real piece of work. This guy's got a thing for anniversaries. Cornfield meet outside Pittsburgh happened on the same day as the famous East Palestine head-on—same line. This Sunday'll be the one hundred forty-fifth anniversary of the Utica disaster. The Cincinnati Express went right off the wooden bridge. It's the same line the Lake Shore now takes. But my guess is he'll shoot for something closer, like the Colonie Bridge outside of Albany. It's a relatively new trestle and there haven't been any accidents near or on it yet. Virgin territory. It's just a hunch, though; the accident locations don't conform to any pattern that I can figure out."

"But why a pattern at all?"

"An obsessive-compulsive. They need patterns like we need three squares and a warm bed."

"And you think he'll be on the train?"

"For the extra thrill. And to make sure the bugs are set properly. He'll get off, though, before the fireworks."

McBryde hugged his duffel bag between his knees. Inside the bag—along with two changes of clothes, his toiletries, and a cellular phone—was the gun, a .45, newly oiled. It lay unloaded in a shoe box, packed all around with excelsior. A blackjack also nestled under that green plastic grass, along with ten rounds of ammunition. He hadn't used these weapons since leaving the security firm. If it came to a fight, he preferred the blackjack—it was cleaner, more efficient. The short hardwood handle and its deadly pouch fit neatly in his grasp. With the gun, he was sure his hand would shake, spoiling his aim. In Portland, during that first year with Mortimer's, he'd practiced daily—perforating the heads of silhouettes, squeezing off shot after shot as though knowing beforehand that he would have only one chance to stop the kid. He hadn't fired a gun since that night, neither at a shooting range nor in real life.

Although the connecting train was listed "on time," the gate still hadn't been called. With four minutes to go, they were cutting it close. The Timer would have thrown a fit. McBryde wasn't worried. Most of the trains along the Northeast Corridor, Amtrak's big-money line, had acceptable on-time performances. The Lake Shore, however, was a different matter. Amtrak's longer runs frequently arrived between two and six hours late. Six hours late on an eighteen-hour run! No other industrialized country would put up with such mismanagement. Small wonder his non-foamer friends were all frequent flyers.

He'd done the Lake Shore run two years back with Jordan and Marty Stein on a Memorial Day weekend. They had taken the train out on a Friday night, passed along the Hudson River up through Croton-Harmon and Albany to Schenectady before veering west and pushing on toward the Great Lakes. In Chicago, where they'd arrived miraculously on time, they spent the day wandering the former site of the Pullman Palace Car Company before boarding the eastbound that evening. The plan had been to arrive back in Philadelphia in time for a Sunday dinner with their families at Rizzo's.

But the return train had been five hours late. Monitoring their CBs, they discovered that a headlight malfunction kept them for an extra fifteen minutes at Toledo. That delay cost the Lake Shore its right-of-way over a freight train at Cleveland. That additional half-hour delay forced their train to make a longer-than-usual stop at Erie, and so on. On Sunday morning, the passengers had to suffer through a series of increasingly apologetic announcements over the intercom. Expecting an afternoon arrival, the kitchen had not stocked food for dinner. Hungry travelers demanded their money back. Amtrak distributed complimentary packets of potato chips and pretzels, but after all the beer and soda had quickly sold out, the thirsty passengers only grew more hostile. Never relying on Amtrak to provide food, McBryde and his friends had brought their own emergency provisions. They calmly accepted the revised schedule. They sat in the café car with their hard-boiled eggs and tuna-fish sandwiches and thermos of iced tea, happy for a few extra hours on the train and not in the least disappointed at missing the family dinner.

McBryde started from his reverie to observe a line forming at a nearby gate. He hurried over with his suitcase. Now he was feeling something new. This time the flutter in his chest was not awaysickness. It was fear.

TWELVE

"**T**he Bureau's a great place," Chaos told her when they met after work at The Last Drop, a 1960s relic of a coffeehouse off Dupont Circle. "But I've had it up to the hairline with the you-can't-do-this and the you-can't-do-that. I felt just like a kid again running your correlations—hanging out after work, doing everything secretly. We're seriously backlogged. But it's not every day I get a thrill like that, with all the stupid forms we have to fill out in triplicate, with countersigned authorization and . . . well, you know how it is."

Szczymanski had felt fairly confident that Bureau staff would never visit The Last Drop. Dark and cluttered, it cultivated the atmosphere of a bar after closing time—chairs pushed askew, clothes scattered about, waitresses ignoring the customers. A cork bulletin board near the entrance was stuffed with note cards advertising cheap sublets. Colorful murals on the wall proclaimed peace, equality, freedom, and the right to enjoy oral sex. Customers fell into two categories: young punks in anarchist black and middle-aged hippies in original grunge.

Chaos curled his tongue around the froth in his cappuccino. "My staff, you know, they hate to follow orders. I spend almost all my time riding herd. No time left over for the AI research."

She didn't want to talk artificial intelligence. It was already Thursday evening. Sunday was fast approaching and she needed information. "The Lake Shore?"

"Right." He smoothed back his hair. "Fed in the data. Computer spit out the answers. And this is what we got."

"We?"

Chaos laughed. "Me and the computer. Don't worry." He picked up the papers lying between them. Szczymanski followed his finger as it moved authoritatively down and across the pages. "First we looked at all the accidents for the year. No pattern—that figure there. Then we looked at various subgroups—derailments, head-ons, so forth. Again, here you see, some patterns began to emerge, but after the third or fourth variable they all collapsed."

She absorbed the information quickly, feeling her proficiency for algorithms and statistics return like a tennis stroke or a piano piece.

"Finally," he continued, "I began to impose patterns on the data to see if the computer would verify them—geography, time, weather, all sorts of cross-tabbing. Look over here. For the period September to October of last year, a grade-crossing accident occurred every day between five P.M. and six P.M. in areas of the country where the temperature reached a high in the seventies."

"Significant?"

"Not at all." He smiled mischievously. "Patterns sometimes simply appear. They mean nothing more than pure randomness. Why are there so many southpaws on my son's Little League team?"

"I don't know."

"Nobody does. Luck of the draw."

A guitar player began testing his microphone on the small stage set up at the far end of the café. He tapped it with a finger but it gave off no sound. After he wriggled the cord about, a high cicada-like swell of feedback filled the room. Switching off the microphone, the musician shrugged apologetically. The few customers in the booths and tables looked up momentarily during the feedback and then quickly resumed their conversations.

The musician looked like Rudy Blaine, same build, same strong jaw. She tore her eyes from him. "Are you saying the pattern you're giving me is also pure chance?"

"There's no guarantee. You asked for a pattern and I'm giving you the most likely one from the data. If it doesn't work, we try again."

The musician began to strum his guitar softly and mumble some rhymed lyrics. The buzz of conversation in the restaurant did not noticeably abate.

Szczymanski exhaled wearily. On a second viewing, he didn't look like Blaine at all. "So how'd you get lucky?"

"After a while I decided to focus on passenger trains and only then I noticed something new. Each passenger train has a number. Did you know that?"

She thought back. "I suppose so."

"They have names—the Big Apple and the Keystone and the Palmetto. But they also have numbers. Every Texas Eagle leaving Chicago for Houston is number twenty-one. On the return trip, it's twenty-two. I never knew that. So, on a whim, I asked the computer to check for a pattern among the numbers. And there it was."

"In the numbers?"

"Unlucky thirteen. A cluster of accidents have been happening on this series here—you see on the chart? With escalating frequency. This graph here shows the accidents coming closer and closer together. According to my calculations, Sunday's the next point on the line."

"Thirteen?" Szczymanski shook her head unhappily. "I don't know what I expected."

Chaos looked up from his graphs and squinted at her. "Does it strike you as silly? Remember: a pattern is just that. It doesn't explain anything. It's just a way of connecting events. That's all I was looking for. Naturally the rest is up to you."

"Did your computer happen to tell you where the accident would take place?"

"No. But you'll have some time to look around. None of the accidents have occurred within a hundred miles of the point of origin. Don't ask me why." Chaos patted the table and arched his eyebrows. "So?"

She looked at him quizzically.

"Aren't you going to tell me more about this assignment?"

"Absolutely not," she replied firmly.

"I have a higher security clearance than you do. I might be able to help you more than you think."

"I'll keep that in mind."

"Suit yourself. I'm not just a numbers man, you know."

"I'm still at the beginning of the process. I'll let you know when I need your help again." She tried to invest a measure of warmth into her voice.

"And in the field?"

"I like to work on my own."

Chaos looked suddenly uncomfortable. "Oh . . ."

"Something wrong?"

"Well . . . I . . . I sort of arranged something for you."

"Excuse me?"

"He'll be on the Lake Shore."

"Excuse me?!" Her voice trembled.

"Don't worry." Chaos held up a placating hand. "He's Bureau. And absolutely dependable."

"An agent?"

"Well, yes."

"Call him back. I don't want his help."

Chaos squirmed in his seat as if suffering from acute indigestion. "I can't do that. He's already on the road. I'm sorry. We were talking this morning and he mentioned that he was traveling to Buffalo this Sunday. I asked him if he'd take the train instead of flying and he agreed. It's nothing official—don't worry. Just a favor. It seemed like a good idea at the time."

"Why didn't you call me?"

"I didn't, um, have your phone number."

"Jesus Maria!" she exclaimed, trying to control her temper. "What's his name?"

"He likes to be called Jigsaw."

She groaned.

"He loves a good puzzle. And he's got a mind like a wolverine—

once it bites into a problem it won't let go. He knows what you look like. He'll introduce himself."

"Lovely. Jigsaw."

"I didn't tell him anything about the pattern or the accidents. He'll just be there if you need him." Chaos gestured at the sheets of computer-generated figures and graphs. He kept his eyes cast down. "I thought it might be dangerous and having someone around could be useful."

To disguise her anger, she asked him to explain the figures once more. Jigsaw. Just what she needed—a man with a wolverine mind. He was probably just another of her monitors, another Peña. She'd put him on the bathroom detail to record the comings and goings of passengers. This is what happened to rogue operations. They ricocheted like a pinball in and out of your control.

She clenched her fists and concentrated on Chaos's finger, which was again moving through the charts like a bee around a flowering bush. She could see how he had zeroed in on a pattern, selecting it out from the background clutter. His results looked so obvious, the answer almost leaping out from the page. But she knew this could be a dangerous illusion.

Long ago, as a child, she'd read a book about a precocious astronomer who devoted himself to the search for Planet X. Every night, after finishing his apprentice chores, he pored over photographic plates of different segments of the starry sky, trying to catch the faintest shift in position of one of the multitude of small white dots. The task didn't take genius or any particular creativity. It simply required a crazed determination. In those pre-computer days, the young astronomer quite nearly burned out his eyes from the effort. But in the end he succeeded. He discovered Pluto where other, more experienced astronomers had failed.

This scientific fairy tale was intended as an object lesson in the rewards that come to those who work hard. A perverse little girl, she asked the school librarian for biographies of the astronomers who had destroyed their vision in vain, who had devoted their lives to searches that yielded nothing. These books, she was told, did not exist. Immediately she realized, at the advanced age of eleven, that success was never inevitable and that failures weren't worth mentioning.

The pattern chosen by Chaos and the computer might set her

off on a statistical wild-goose chase. She could end up riding trains back and forth across the country searching for a culprit who didn't exist, pursuing a pattern that had a reality only in the circuits of a computer. She wouldn't burn out her eyes like those forgotten astronomers. She'd simply burn out—lose energy, drop behind, become a Plugger.

That night in her apartment she tested Chaos's pattern from every angle. It held. Everything pointed to the Lake Shore Limited, the one leaving that Sunday. But if it was truly accurate, why would someone deliberately embed such an arbitrary pattern into their handiwork? The hook was baited with a tantalizing tidbit. Was she foolish to nibble?

On Friday morning, she found a new folder on her desk with a note from Granite. The note advised her of a meeting later that morning.

The folder contained her new identity.

According to the attached backgrounder, she now worked as a correspondent for the *Arlington Star,* an imaginary weekly the FBI had created a dozen years back. Anyone who called the number provided on the press pass or reached the paper through directory assistance talked first to a "secretary" who then patched the caller through to an "executive editor." These agents sat across from one another in a cloistered subdivision of External Affairs. They spent the day impersonating a wide variety of people, from peevish French diplomats to obsequious telemarketers—whatever an operation required.

Her cover name was Darla Kubb. Copies of several articles with her byline had been included in her packet. Szczymanski thumbed through these articles, amused to discover that she'd written on horticulture, Russian foreign policy, and the changing technology of the book-glue industry. Across the top of each reprint was emblazoned the *Arlington Star* logo, a bald eagle with feather quills in its claws instead of arrows. The newspaper's motto was scrolled modestly underneath—"To Inform a Sensible Public with Sensible News."

How convenient. Just as she was about to go undercover on her own, the FBI provided her with an identity.

Turning to the press pass, Szczymanski stared at the face sheathed in the laminated plastic. It was round as a cabbage, with a high red color in the cheeks, a chin like a wedge, and straw-colored hair as matted and brittle-looking as shredded wheat. She would have preferred a more flattering portrait, but the FBI's public relations department had used her Quantico graduation photo. The point, of course, was not to impress. It was to deceive.

"These covers will allow you free range to ask questions," Granite explained when, later in the morning, Szczymanski and her two colleagues sat in an arc around his desk.

"Subjects clam up around reporters, sir," Peña said.

"That's not the point," Granite said. "We don't want anyone to know the FBI's involved. The last thing Amtrak needs is a panic."

Metaxas nodded slowly. "The Department of Transportation is very clear about this."

"But if we break the story, sir," Szczymanski disagreed, "the unsub might stop."

Granite didn't blink. "Catching the unsub is not our only priority. We must apprehend without undermining public confidence in the rail system. Or, for that matter, in the FBI. That damn Medicare story broke this morning."

Szczymanski looked to Peña for an explanation.

Peña sighed. "We sold thirty-five cards to a suspected fraud operation. Then we lost control of them."

"Can't you just cancel the cards?"

Granite shook his head. "They're real cards. It would wipe out the benefits. Damn Florida office. Must have been sunstroke."

"No chance of anything like that happening here," Peña assured him.

Granite stared intently at Szczymanski. "All the same, I want to meet every Friday morning for a briefing. It'll be a useful way of keeping up to speed. And no one will be left in the dark about their responsibilities. That's key for an underop."

Undercover operations—underops—made Szczymanski deeply uncomfortable. She would've joined the CIA if she wanted the cloak-and-dagger life. The FBI, preferring informants, or "cooperating individuals," rarely indulged in underops. Probably because it was so bad at them, such as the COINTELPRO surveillance of antiwar protesters and the inept break-ins at the Socialist Workers Party headquarters. Other underops had simply spun out of control, like the time the Operation Recoup investigating team set up a used-car business to lure racketeers but managed only to sell hot vehicles to unsuspecting consumers. That had cost the Bureau millions of dollars. Operation Frontload, Iranscam, now this Medicare fuckup: these rogue undercover operations were the Bureau's greatest fear. A criminal gets away and the FBI can blame local and state law enforcement. But if an agent runs amok, then Congress jumps on the Bureau's back and appropriations get cut. "We are investigators, not spies," the instructors at Quantico had emphasized, "and our purpose is to uphold laws, not break them." Fine with me, Szczymanski had thought, just as long as I nail the bad guys and put them where they belong.

But now she was embarking on a very questionable enterprise indeed. Not only was she going undercover in search of an unsub, but she was about to leave the orbit of Bureau supervision altogether. She'd take the Lake Shore to Chicago on Sunday and, except for Chaos and this wolverine named Jigsaw, not one of her coworkers would know a thing about it.

An operation could not be more roguish than hers.

Working on her own didn't bother her. Indeed, if presented with a choice, she preferred to work alone. The Bureau, however, valued team players who could survive in a rigidly hierarchical environment. Agents just starting out were freighted with so many rules and regulations that their every movement seemed preordained by Bureau policy. As a good Catholic, Szczymanski knew that freedom could flourish even among such restrictions. As an ambitious American, however, she wanted only to lose those administrative fetters and strike off on her own.

Granite began to crack his knuckles. "Now, tell me what you have."

Szczymanski was taken aback. There had been nothing in the note about furnishing preliminary findings. She looked at her two partners. They didn't appear surprised at all.

Metaxas spoke up first. While Granite bent and pulled on his fingers, the solidly built woman squared her shoulders, opened her small notebook, and began to summarize her findings as though reading chapter and verse from the Bible. Szczymanski could see from a distance that her handwriting consisted of very neat and very small block letters.

"Conducted phone interviews with a selection of conductors

and brakemen from trains falling into the accident category." Metaxas spoke in a monotone and never lifted her head during her recitation. "No leads provided that could help identify the unsub. Inquiries conducted by the railroads established that several accidents had been the work of teenage children, either placing objects on the rails or deliberately altering the switches. I have requested all files pertaining to state and local criminal investigations into these particular incidents."

Metaxas flipped through the pages of the little book with a firm thumb. "Have begun certain researches into the relationship between railroad accidents and terrorism." Her thumb peeled away several more pages. "In this country, there have been numerous examples of terrorists targeting airplanes, ships, and even buses. But only one comparable instance of a terrorism-inspired attack on a train—the work of that neo-Nazi group in Arizona several years ago. There've been no copycats. I've also assembled documentation on several Mexican cases of terrorism. On another matter, I've begun to compile a list of cases in which disgruntled railway employees have destroyed company property and endangered passenger lives. I hope to make these findings available early next week. Finally, I have submitted my data to ERF. They are backlogged at the moment but promise some computer results next week."

Granite located the appropriate folder, flipped it open, stared at the contents. He looked up to nod approvingly at Metaxas. "So, terrorism's a bust."

Instead of answering, Metaxas turned to Peña, who cleared her throat. "Sir, I've been looking into ARES, the Advanced Railroad Electronic System. It's not yet up and running, but when it is, private and semi-private railroad companies will be able to access government-operated satellites to track trains around the country. They tell me merchant ships use something similar to find themselves at sea."

"But trains must know where they are," Granite interrupted.

Peña nodded. "On-board computers hook up to the satellites and can instantly find out about trains on other tracks. Doesn't take an FBI agent to figure out why a terrorist would be looking at this thing. DIA is sending over their files on possible security breaches."

"Good. So terrorism's still a go." Granite moved his neck slightly to pick out Szczymanski with his eyes.

She tried to hide her astonishment at the quantity of her colleagues' research. The terrorism angle was also something new. The dead-end assignment suddenly seemed a hot case. Why the sudden change? Or was this all for show?

"I've carefully read over the materials from the Department of Transportation." She paused.

"And?" Granite raised his eyebrows.

"I haven't found anything yet, sir."

They waited for her to continue.

"The interview with Marinetti . . ." Peña prompted.

"Yielded nothing," Szczymanski finished.

The scar on Granite's neck seemed to pulse.

Szczymanski used the silence as a weapon. In addition to being surprised, she was furious. She had no revelations to share. She came out looking like a slacker, a real Dogger. Let them remain in the dark as to her thinking, her plans, her strategies. They were hardly her allies.

"Marinetti did say," Peña added tentatively, "that the DOT very much wanted a scapegoat on this one."

"I imagine so," Granite agreed. "But I think this is a live one. I'd like to see more on these Mexican terrorists. Maybe they're moving north."

Szczymanski coughed. "Sir, if that's all . . ." She rested her hands on the armrests of the chair and raised herself slightly. She knew she was violating the Bureau norm of deferring to superiors. It was Granite's responsibility to organize and dissolve such meetings. She also knew that calling attention to herself through these minor acts of insubordination was stupid. But she couldn't help herself, not with the anger raging inside her, the anger that had been building up now for quite some time.

"My in-box is full," she said by way of an excuse and marched out.

Ordinarily she maintained a comfortable distance from her emotions, releasing them in smaller or larger quantities like a scientist testing the effects of a drug on the circulatory system. To rise in a career, she knew that her inner life had to be strictly controlled.

Women were expected to be emotional, unpredictable, unmanageable—perpetual slaves to the hormonal cycles of the body. This capacity for emotional self-control, together with her portfolio of strategies, had always served her well. But sometimes she felt a little too mechanical.

Her control mechanisms had now jammed.

The anger tightening her muscles had nothing to do with hormones, with natural cycles or menstrual ebb and flow. It was the anger of helplessness. She had little choice but to keep Peña and Metaxas in the dark, to mislead Granite. Only Chaos knew that she was going outside Bureau rules. And she'd already lied to him. She wanted to lay all her cards out on the table, to come clean. But the others would still keep their hole cards hidden. So she could only remain silent and angry and helpless.

Before she could properly settle behind the desk in her office, Peña burst in, already talking. "So, what didn't you tell Granite?"

Szczymanski shook her head.

"You spent all this time reading these reports and that's all you got to say?"

Stick to strategy, Szczymanski reminded herself. She'd played Scheming Feline at the meeting. Now it was time for TB². "And what about all that information you and Metaxas uncovered? When were you planning to fill me in on ARES and your terrorism angle?" She added petulantly, "I thought we were a team."

Peña seemed to relent. "Okay, on Monday, you, me, and Metaxas'll sit down and plot a strategy. Okay?" Suddenly Peña was leaning forward, intense. "We're going to make stats on this baby. You with me on this?"

Was Peña trying to make a low-priority case seem truly important? Or had her recent research led her to believe that the accidents indeed resulted from terrorist attacks? Did she think that she could use this case to rise in the FBI hierarchy?

Szczymanski hesitated too long before answering. Peña moved closer, her fists balled on top of the desk.

"I've heard the stories—what you can do with guns, what you got upstairs," Peña went on in a low voice. "You're supposed to be some pretty hot shit."

"Hot shit? I wouldn't say that."

"Look, fuck this modesty routine, okay?" Peña's blue eyes narrowed. "All you have to know is that I can be a real bitch to work with if I want to be. I like you, Szczymanski, but don't fuck me around, understand?"

She felt the smallest surge of satisfaction. Peña had expressed a real feeling. It wouldn't be long before she slipped up in the heat of the action. And that would be Szczymanski's chance.

THIRTEEN

His heart beat furiously against his chest. At first McBryde thought that he was still reacting to the last-minute rush at Penn Station—the several minutes of anxious foot-tapping and wristwatch-glancing as the deli counterman dawdled with his corned beef on rye and wrapped his complimentary pickles with painstaking care, then the frantic maneuvering past the crowds down the stairs to his platform, and the final leap onto the Lake Shore moments before the conductor closed the door and the train lunged forward. But no, his heartbeat should have slowed by now. It wasn't his final dash that was still unsettling him. It was his seatmate.

McBryde was sitting next to the most beautiful woman he'd ever seen.

He sat in the aisle seat, she by the window. Whenever he turned to look out at the Hudson River, he saw her profile. She didn't attract him with the golden, sinuous features of a *Cosmo* cover girl.

No, she was striking in a way only he could appreciate. She reminded him of all his previous crushes and love affairs.

She had Rosalind's pointed nose, which his ex-wife bitterly complained made her look like Margaret Thatcher. She was as tall as a favorite high school sweetheart. She cut her hair in a fetching pageboy, the same style as Suzy, the stewardess he'd dated after college. And she possessed a delightfully round face, just like little Peggy Ann, the girl next door he'd mooned over through pre-adolescence.

Most important of all, however, she had chin: a flying buttress of a chin that made his heart stutter long after he should have recovered from his Penn Station scramble. McBryde never fully understood his fascination for chins, any more than he understood his love of trains. Regardless of reasons, he considered the chin the most sexually charged attribute of a woman. Rosalind led with her chin, all of his previous girlfriends had. He considered a chinless woman to be asexual, neutered, recessive in every sense of the word. He'd never told anyone about this near obsession (he disliked the term "fetish"), not even Rosalind, not even after periodically cupping his hand over her chin during lovemaking. After all other confessions had been aired—about masturbation, fears of impotence—his obsession with chins remained a secret.

Like flies drawn to an open jam pot, his eyes repeatedly settled on his seatmate's chin. He tried to control himself, but couldn't. How could the discrete features of his former loves blend so harmoniously together on one face?

He hadn't planned to sit next to anyone, hadn't wanted any company, any distracting conversation. And if that counterman had not lavished so much attention on his pickle-wrapping, McBryde would have boarded in plenty of time to find a pair of free seats. Instead he'd discovered a train crowded with tourists returning from a weekend in New York City. Only single seats remained empty. Mopping his brow with a deli napkin, he'd looked for a sleeping senior citizen or a morose college student engrossed in a fat book. Then he caught sight of the blond pageboy from behind and immediately thought: Suzy! What was Suzy Horton, a stewardess, doing on a train?

When he drew up level with the pageboy, however, it turned out not to belong to Suzy at all. He shifted his weight from one foot to the other, unsure of what to do. Her bag rested on the aisle seat beside her. Should he ask if the seat was free? Or should he just drop to one knee and propose? She looked up at him and even in annoyance she was unmistakably beautiful. He didn't know what to say. He wondered if she could hear the blood thundering in his ears. He forgot entirely why he was on the train in the first place.

Finally she transferred the bag to the floor by her feet and McBryde took his place by her side. He felt the breath leak out of his body, as though someone were applying a steady pressure to his chest. She's married, he thought. But she wore no ring. She won't speak English. But she spoke the language with no difficulty. She'll be cold, uninterested in conversation. But after the initial annoyance she seemed quite warm and animated. And God, what a chin!

She introduced herself as Darla Kubb, a journalist traveling to Chicago to cover an environmental conference. A book lay across her lap, the blue-and-white globe on its cover oozing a tear.

"I'll have to come and go a bit," she said after he'd settled into the seat. "If that's okay with you." She smiled. McBryde was immediately thrown back to fourth grade, little Peggy Ann pressing a Valentine's Day card into his hand after school, smiling just like that before turning red as a waxed cherry and running to the other end of the jungle gym to rejoin her friends.

"Just, um, say the word," he replied unsteadily. "I'll be walking around a bit myself."

For the next half hour, she neither turned back to her book nor excused herself to go to the bathroom. McBryde gradually remembered his purpose for being on the train, knew that he should be looking for familiar faces from train conventions, searching for suspicious characters, playing the private-detective role. But he couldn't drag himself away from the conversation. Just ten more minutes, he told himself, just one more meaningful exchange.

"Five stories a week?" he repeated, awed.

"Plus features," Darla Kubb replied.

"That's a lot of writing."

"You get used to it. A job like any other."

"Not like mine."

"You said you work for the Philadelphia city government? Department of Transportation?"

"Department of complaints," he clarified. "When everything goes right, no one knows who I am. When everything breaks down, suddenly I'm a celebrity."

"Like Lee Harvey Oswald."

He laughed, came dangerously close to giggling. Quick, funny, simple: her reply was straight out of the Rosalind tradition. Both women kept their humor dry. They produced funny lines as if they were ordering at a fast food restaurant.

Stop comparing, he commanded himself. He'd never see this journalist again. And he wasn't being fair, because he liked her not on her own merits, but for the qualities she shared with all the women who had parachuted in and out of his life.

"Just the other day," he began, apropos of nothing, intending to tell her about the councilman and the bus boycott.

Suddenly she sat up straight and made little motions to indicate that she wanted to get out. McBryde stood in the aisle to make room for her. He watched her retreating figure adjust to the motion of the train.

Then he quickly pulled himself back from his adolescent fantasies. Chin or no chin, he wasn't on a pleasure cruise and he didn't have time for an onboard romance. According to Jordan's intuitions, the Lake Shore might meet its accident at a vulnerable trestle bridge just beyond Albany. He had roughly three hours to prevent the derailment and identify the party or parties responsible. Unless Jordan's intuitions were will-o'-the-wisps and a train somewhere else in the country was hurtling toward an accident. But Jordan's guesses were all he had.

Three hours and no idea what he was looking for. A crazed, wild-eyed freak? A cool, calculating robot? An ordinary, three-piece suit? Or perhaps he should be looking for a foamer, someone wearing an engineer's cap and a vest overgrown with train buttons and badges. It seemed so hard to believe. Foamers might become obsessed with train wrecks but they'd never set them. Most foamers were pencil-necks, stay-at-homes, the pocket-protector and Coke-bottle-glasses types. They might have problems communicating with people. They would never kill them.

But I've killed someone, McBryde remembered suddenly. With a single bullet through the mouth.

He shouldered his bag for his first trip through the train.

Threading his way down the aisle, he avoided protruding elbows and feet. Soon he regained his train legs, that ability to walk in a straight line on a surface that shifted like a slippery rug. One lurch of the train could send a man into a young woman's lap, a grandmother's steadying fingers into a clergyman's nostrils, a toddler's pacifier into a neighbor's tumbler of soda. The passengers were not at fault. Trains didn't have to wobble. Amtrak could lay tracks that permitted travel as smooth and level as an automated walkway. But that cost money, which the freight companies that owned the tracks didn't want to spend.

Now that his eyes weren't fixed upon a chin, he realized that his car was an old Pennsylvania Railroad coach built in the 1960s. Amtrak had reupholstered it in the standard burgundy, added new curtains for the windows, refitted the undercarriage. On the outside, the car would have more pronounced ribbing, all of it repainted Amtrak's color scheme of platinum mist. Lacking equipment when it started out, Amtrak cannibalized from its predecessors. By now, however, it had flushed most of the old cars out of the system, making this Pennsy a real jewel. In homage to a past age, Amtrak had even retained the original lounge areas at each end instead of knocking down the partitions and adding seats. He parted the burgundy curtain that closed off the men's lounge. Inside were two Naugahyde chairs and a wooden coffee table, enough room for a cocktail party of four. A sink bolted to the wall was stacked high with paper towels and little bricks of soap. A narrow door opened onto a small toilet. Compared to Amtrak's usual cockpit-size bathroom, the Pennsy's spacious lounge was civilized. It wouldn't be long before they decommissioned the old car, he thought sadly.

McBryde walked from one end of the train to the other to determine its consist. The other cars were all Amtrak stock probably built in the early eighties. Behind the engines came at least one mail car before the sleepers began. Between the sleepers and the coaches were a diner and a café car. Behind the sixth and last coach—his Pennsy car—was the observation car, half of it reserved for smokers. In the café car, he bought an iced tea in order to give his stroll a purpose.

He lingered in the café, sipping his drink and looking over the passengers in their booths. Among the gray-haired ladies and little children, one passenger stuck out. The man sat by himself, his head bent close to a magazine. Long, stringy hair hung in front of his face, only a large nose visible through the strands. He looked like Hollywood's image of a child molester. McBryde casually approached the table. The man was reading a rail magazine, open to a picture of a train cutting through a mountain pass.

"Seat free?" McBryde asked, trying to remain calm.

The man looked up. The hair parted to reveal sparkling blue eyes and an unexpectedly handsome face. "You will want to move my crutches, yes?" he said with a French accent.

McBryde looked down at the empty seat, at the pair of supports lying there, the kind with metal bracelets that fit around the elbows and plastic dowels for handgrips. A disguise? He looked beneath the table. One leg right-angled to the floor, the other ended abruptly in a stump. How could such a man plant microphones the length of a train?

"You are welcome to sit, my friend." The man gestured.

McBryde smiled, backing up a step. "I'll be back in a minute or so," he said weakly.

He retreated to the service counter to survey the customers waiting on line. No one there struck him in any way as unusual. He watched them select from an impoverished array of snacks. It was always the same overpriced hot dogs, limp tuna and egg-salad sandwiches in triangular plastic cases, and packages of potato chips whose contents had not only settled but virtually disappeared during shipment. The food in the dining car, one step closer to first class, was no better: hamburger patties from the freezer, pizza from the microwave, spaghetti sauce from jars, soups from cans, salads from hell.

Once, between Chicago and Denver, McBryde's train had been running seven hours late for no good reason. Just as in his previous trip on the Lake Shore Limited, the kitchen ran out of food. But this time, a conductor radioed ahead to the stationmaster at the next stop. When their train pulled into McCook, Nebraska, a truck waited for them, its flatbed piled high with boxes. The crew loaded the boxes into the train and then marched down the aisles distributing the different components of a fried-chicken meal. First came biscuits, cold and greasy, then cups of watery mashed potatoes in congealed gravy. The coleslaw and the soft drinks had been unappealingly warm. Finally they received the entree. McBryde had never enjoyed a Kentucky Fried Chicken breast more, despite its tepid sogginess.

The U.S. train system in a nutshell, he thought at the time. We're so hungry and angry and impatient, and then we're so damned grateful for the little crumbs they throw us. It's the only game in town. Eat or starve.

Although McBryde dreamed of a brilliant, streamlined Maglev future, some retrograde part of his consciousness yearned for the glorious heyday of train travel when the restaurant car served you real food on real plates. Along the tracks now covered by the Lake Shore once ran the Twentieth Century Limited, bound for Chicago on the same water-level route through upstate New York. Back in the golden age, the Twentieth Century Limited set the standard, using classy china, embroidered linen, and the best wood trim in its cars. In those days of high varnish on the high iron, you could sit in a salmon wing chair in a mahogany-fitted drawing room, read a penny dreadful bought from the news butch who scurried between cars, wait for your turn with the train's barber, and anticipate with relish the evening meal of roast pheasant and fresh-baked apple cobbler. To keep service tip-top, spotters hired by the Pullman Company masqueraded as passengers to test the food, run a finger along the washbasins, and assess the manners of the porters.

Penn Central eventually sold the Twentieth Century Limited to the Mexican National Railroad, which renamed it El Tapatio. Boy, did the Mexicans get a great deal. America would never again see the likes of the great trains. At a rail show, McBryde once bought a coffee mug with the inscription "Amtrak: The Train of Today." Yesterday's trains guaranteed splendid service. Tomorrow's trains promised speed and safety. But today's trains were just one misfortune after another.

Walking slowly back through the train, McBryde looked at everyone as unobtrusively as possible. In one coach, a group of octogenarians was bound for an alumni gathering. Each wore a card that announced: "Hi! My name is . . ." In the adjoining coach, some high school girls on a midwinter trip had converted half the seats into a temporary party room. One foursome played Trivial Pursuit, passing the board back and forth across the aisle. Another pair kneeled on their pillows, their chins resting on the top of their seats, and gossiped with the girls behind them. Notes were sent airmail, the paper tightly wadded into balls. A sextet tried to remember the lyrics to a rap song. Their two exhausted supervisors complained in whispers. McBryde could tell at a glance that the other passengers in the car resented the girls' antics. Privacy was a rare commodity in coach.

The rest of the passengers came in singles or pairs: young European backpackers in bright travel gear, businesspeople typing on their laptops, Florida retirees recounting their best golf shots and pinochle games, a few Albany politicos bent over briefing papers, a scattering of older men reading Louis L'Amour and older women reading Sidney Sheldon. There were also a couple of deadheads, off-duty rails returning home after putting in all their hours in one direction.

McBryde recognized no one. Nor did he see anyone who might vaguely count as a suspect. No one eagerly checked a watch and compared the times to a schedule. No one looked nervous and sweaty. No one even looked cool and psychopathic. The Lake Shore was abounding in normality. The suspect might not be on the train. The bugs could have been set in the yards, to be removed later by someone else. McBryde thought about trying to locate these hidden mikes. But he wouldn't even know where to begin. Discouraged, he returned to his seat, no better informed than when he'd left.

The journalist was reading her book, with one finger poised to flip the next page. She looked up. "How's the café?"

He pulled down the tray table for his iced tea. "Sorry, I should've asked if you wanted something."

"Oh no." She smiled. "I brought my own." She indicated a brown paper bag sticking out of a pocket of her traveling case.

"Smart."

"Forewarned."

"I'm curious," he began. "Why'd you decide to take a train to this conference instead of flying?"

"Something new."

"With all your deadlines?"

"I needed a rest. This is the only piece I have to do until Tuesday. Thought I'd catch up on my reading."

He glanced at the title of the book—*Matricide.* "Background for your conference?"

"It looks like I'll be doing a series of articles on the environment," she replied. "Then, if I'm lucky, I might be able to pull together a book on the subject."

"A book?" McBryde knew that he should just let the subject pass, move on to something else. But the words were out of his mouth before he could strangle them. "Actually, I'm working on a book too."

"Oh?" She didn't look as though she believed him.

He felt himself flush. "But it's not finished. It's not . . ." His voice trailed off.

"What's it about?"

"Maglev."

"A desert in the Middle East?"

"Magnetic levitation. The next generation of trains." He cursed himself inwardly for ever bringing up the subject. He wanted to impress her, to reveal that he too worked with words and not just with angry people. But with only thirty unpublished, unpolished pages to his name, he came perilously close to being a fraud.

But the journalist looked interested. "So you're sort of a train buff?"

"You could say that."

"Tell me about this Maglev of yours." She settled back into a listening mode, arms crossed and chin just above her breastbone.

Rosalind does the same thing, McBryde thought, the same hangdog drop of the head when she's listening to something. It was the latest mannerism that Melissa had picked up from her mother. He gripped the seat's armrests and thought about his book instead.

"Maglev will transform the United States from a Third World country to a pioneer in transportation," he quoted from the first sentence of the manuscript.

"A Third World country?"

"I'm talking here about our trains. We used to be a leader in train innovation." He pointed to the passing utility poles. "You know how fast this train is going?"

She looked out the window. "Ninety miles per hour? A hundred?"

"Top speed on this line is seventy-nine miles per hour. Amtrak runs only two lines in the country that even approach a hundred. In 1893, steam locomotive number 999 pulled the Empire State Express at 112.5 miles per hour. That was over a hundred years ago. We haven't gotten very far since. The latest, cutting-edge engine? The Genesis, General Electric's AMD-103. That stands for Amtrak diesel, 103 miles per hour. Pathetic."

"Maglev is faster?"

"Three hundred miles per hour."

"Sounds dangerous."

"That's the beautiful part. The train wraps around the guideway. There's no way it can come off. So no more derailments. And the propulsion system prevents trains from colliding with each other. From either the front or the back. No more accidents."

"No more accidents," she repeated, nodding her head.

"They've got a demonstration project up and running in Orlando. You know, for Disney World. If they finally decide to do it, the Las Vegas–Anaheim route will be the first true Maglev. But Germany'll probably get there first with the Transrapid between Hamburg and Berlin."

"They just float, right?"

"Six inches, generally, both above and below the guideway. No friction. The smoothest ride imaginable." McBryde was warming to his subject. "A lot of people are pushing just for high-speed trains, like the French TGVs or Japan's bullet trains. Don't get me wrong, they would be a lot better than what we have. TGVs go up to 185 miles per hour, the bullet up to 170. But compared to Maglev, they're just yesterday's technology. Japan's investing in second-generation high speed. Europe, too. We get their hand-me-downs— the Swedish X2000, the German ICE—and our tracks still can't handle them. Want me to describe a possible future for us?" He blushed. "I mean, for America."

"Please do." A smile curved gently around the side of her face.

"The subways will be all Maglev. No noise, no jostling. Just a smooth, clean ride to work every day. Then, between cities, a Maglev system set up along the medians of highways will provide rapid transit for local commuters. It will be elevated. That will eliminate grade crossings, the major cause of train accidents. A set of special lines will provide express service between larger cities. And finally, to put a stake through the heart of the airline industry: evacuated tubes running across and between continents. Maglev trains will run through these tubes at Mach three. Montreal to New Orleans will take only fifty minutes. Tokyo to London only three hours and fifty minutes. Imagine that."

"I can't."

"That's because you still think of trains as part of the nineteenth century. Billowing steam. Cowcatchers. Leisurely pace."

"I just can't see people giving up either planes or cars."

"They'll change," McBryde replied stubbornly. "Ruskin said that all traveling becomes dull in exact proportion to its rapidity. But people no longer believe that, and sometimes I think that's a shame, even though I'm a fan of Maglev and—"

"Ruskin said that?"

"Oh, I just collect things, quotes about trains. They show up in the strangest places." Jesus, why did he have to bring Ruskin into it? First the book, now his collection of train quotes. She must think he was a total goofball. *Accentuate the Positive* suggested pausing for two seconds before saying anything important to someone you wanted to impress. Maybe that wasn't as stupid as he'd first thought. Ruskin would never have survived a two-second pause.

The train suddenly slowed to a halt. They were between stations, in a field of weeds. "What's wrong?" she asked.

McBryde pulled his scanner from its hip holster. He switched it on, volume low, zeroed in on the right frequency, and brought it close to his ear. The engineer was talking with the stationmaster at Rhinecliff-Kingston. They were being held up because of a switching delay.

"Just a little traffic jam at the next station," he told her, putting away the radio.

"That's a neat little thing," she said, pointing. "Carry that wherever you go?"

"It's pretty standard foamer gear."

"Foamer?"

"Just another name for a train enthusiast. You know, rabid, foaming at the mouth."

"Oh?" Again she wore the intensely curious expression of a journalist onto a lead.

"It's Amtrak's little term of abuse for us. They joke around behind our backs, talk about giving us bibs."

"Do you know what time it is?" Darla Kubb asked suddenly.

"Eight twenty-five."

She pulled up her sleeve and checked her own watch. "Just making sure it's accurate."

"That's what trains did, you know." Again he forgot to pause. Too late. "Back in the nineteenth century. Before the railroad, each city went by a different time: five, ten, fifteen minutes different. There wasn't any reason to make it all the same. But then the railroad came along and these small discrepancies began to cause accidents. That's when the time in Philadelphia and New York had to become exactly the same."

Her pen resting against her lips, the journalist asked, "So, you seem to know a great deal about train accidents. Is that part of the foamer repertoire?"

McBryde chose his words carefully. "Some foamers. Personally, however, accidents don't interest me."

"No?"

Why this sudden interest in train accidents? he wondered. "People get hurt in train accidents. I'm interested in saving lives, not endangering them."

"Could you tell me a little about foamers who are fascinated by accidents?"

At that moment, a man walked quickly down the aisle toward the front of the train, hands in pockets, head down. He was tall and thin, wearing a red corduroy shirt, loose jeans, and a baseball cap. Both McBryde and his seatmate turned their heads sharply to follow him with their eyes. He wasn't a conductor, simply a passenger, but he moved with the deliberate speed of someone on official business.

"Friend of yours?" she asked.

"Nope. Probably just waited too long before going to the bathroom," he replied casually. "Which reminds me . . ." He got up and excused himself.

He hadn't moved fast enough. Two of the giggling girls from the class trip had interposed themselves between him and the other man. Balancing hot dogs and sodas in cardboard trays, they walked with exaggerated care, each trying to make the other spill her burden from laughing. The aisle wasn't wide enough to pass. McBryde watched over their heads as the man slipped into another car, still moving rapidly.

"Excuse me," he tried. But the girls only seemed to slow down and giggle harder.

He tried to remember what the man looked like in case he had to search for him among the seated passengers. But he hadn't seen a face, only the red shirt and the baseball cap. He walked along for a few moments in an agony of frustration before hitting on a plan.

"Do you know," he whispered to the blonde below his chin, "that sometimes you can see deer out there, near the edge of the field." He bent over to point through the window.

"No way!" the girl screamed delightedly, turning to face the window. "Hey, Maggie, hear that? Deer! Over there!" They both turned, sloshing soda onto the laps of the passengers sitting by that window.

McBryde slipped around the two girls and hurried down the aisle. When he entered the next car, the man was already gone. Had he passed on to a farther coach? Returned to his seat? Or perhaps even taken advantage of the delay to jump off the train?

As he hurried through the car, McBryde eyed the passengers, looking for the man. No luck. He continued on to the vestibule, a dark passageway between the cars. But before he could push the square black button that opened the sliding door to the next car, the train suddenly came to life and the overhead light sputtered on.

To his right, McBryde glimpsed a red shirt, the rapid movement of the bill of a baseball cap, and the metallic flash of a sharp object.

FOURTEEN

In movies, they conjured up glamour and mystery. But in real life, Szczymanski thought trains slow and dirty, only one step above buses. Trains also discriminated. They serviced only the largest American cities, making grudging stops at the smaller towns only at the most awkward times. Amtrak even bypassed South Dakota altogether, something she had discovered when planning her Thanksgiving trip to her parents in Chicago. But the worst aspect of trains was their schedule. They were always late. Or else you were left at the station with too much time to kill before your connection.

Like the three hours she had to spend at Penn Station waiting for the Lake Shore Limited to depart.

She'd planned to eat a late lunch at the station to fill the time. But the restaurants in the Penn Station concourse repelled her. Outside, she walked for twenty minutes before finally deciding on an upscale Chinese restaurant. There, bent over a plate of General Tso's

Chicken, she leafed through Peña's file on ARES, occasionally splattering plum sauce on the xeroxed pages. The file contained nothing new. The system was nowhere near operational—all schematics and artists' renderings. It was clearly a red herring. Her case was in the here and now, while this computerized satellite guidance system wouldn't come on line until the next millennium. She ordered cold sesame noodles to go for dinner on the train and made it back to the station with plenty of time to board the Lake Shore Limited ahead of the crowds.

In vain she tried to find a coach that didn't smell stale. But the sweat and dirt of thousands of passengers seemed to have soaked into all the seats and carpets. Everything about the train depressed her—the sticky plastic fold-down trays, the Amtrak glossy that pretended to be an in-flight magazine, the dim overhead fluorescent light that ran the length of the aisle. It was all so 1950s. Worst of all, the train was not built for tall people. She could cross her legs comfortably in her seat, but not stretch out. She didn't look forward to spending the night braided in upon herself.

The Lake Shore slowly pulled out of New York, coming up to speed in the tunnels and across the bridges of Manhattan. The crush of passengers looking for empty seats dissipated.

She was not thrilled about meeting Jigsaw. Perhaps at some point he might prove useful. But right now she didn't want to deal with him. Problem was: Chaos hadn't even given her his description. Turned out that theirs was entirely a phone relationship. All very suspicious.

So when the man with the walkie-talkie fastened to his belt stopped by her seat and stared at her intently, she immediately assumed him to be the agent. He was pleasant-looking, even boyish. Roughly her height, he had curly red hair and a sprinkling of freckles on his cheeks. She challenged him with her eyes, expecting that only Jigsaw would pick up the gauntlet. When the man stayed rooted to his spot, she cleared the seat next to her of its bags.

She introduced herself as a journalist. He twisted his body around to face her. Staring into her eyes, he occasionally squinted as if in recall, as if recognizing her from somewhere. She repeated the name of her paper, the *Arlington Star*, confident that if he couldn't match Chaos's description to her face, then surely he'd react to the

FBI's phony newspaper. He gave no such indication, simply nodding at her words and smiling dreamily.

After half an hour, Szczymanski gave up trying to fit him into a slot in which he clearly did not belong. He was just another guy. Worse: Larry McBryde was a bureaucrat. He exuded tedium like body odor.

Before this McBryde character could launch into a boring anecdote, she bailed out of the conversation, maneuvered into the aisle, and embarked upon Plan Two: exposing herself to the train passengers and seeing if the real agent would bite. She wanted to settle the Jigsaw question as soon as possible.

She looked for the FBI stereotype: a clean-cut man with posture as straight as a telephone pole. Her gaze fell upon several prospects, but they either didn't take the bait or shot back looks of piqued curiosity. By the time she had negotiated the entire train, she'd received several raised-eyebrow proposals and even a verbal invitation to sit down in the café car across from a handsome Frenchman with one and a half legs.

It must have been during her visit to the bathroom that McBryde passed by. For when she returned to her seat he was gone. She settled back next to the window, picked up her book on the befouling of Mother Earth, and resumed reading the introduction. She pulled at a strand of her hair, imagining herself a journalist attending the imaginary conference. Her cover story suddenly seemed to have greater solidity than the supposed reality of train accidents and unsubs and mysterious Jigsaws. How nice to have a job with the certainty of deadlines, hard copy, and real people. How refreshing to know where to draw the line between fact and fiction.

"There's sickness all around us," a voice sounded near her ear.

Szczymanski jerked her head around to discover a man leaning over McBryde's empty seat as though about to throw up in her lap. It was, she remembered vaguely, the fellow who'd been sitting by himself across the aisle with a fluffy bright-orange parka piled next to him.

The man continued, "Those environmentalists are right. The world's a sewer." His protruding gut spilled over the armrest against which he was leaning. He had a pudgy face with a bulbous blue-veined nose and yellow, bloodshot eyes that looked like eggs sunnyside up doused with Tabasco. He wore the mismatched plaids of an amateur golfer and smelled faintly of overripe cantaloupe. "We're all gonna have to wear gas masks real soon."

He pulled himself upright, then swung his stomach out of the aisle and into the seat next to her. His elbow rested between them as he leaned closer to examine the book in her lap. The smell of rotting fruit intensified.

"Do you mind?" she said, pushing at his elbow.

His eyes narrowed, obscuring the blood-red yolks beneath. "I'm Jigsaw. Friend of Chaos."

"You?"

Jigsaw extracted a little red pill from his shirt pocket and flicked it into his mouth. Tossing his head back, he gulped it down dry. "What you see is what you get."

The man patted his stomach and then, without further comment, withdrew to his seat across the aisle. He folded a sweatshirt into a ball, wedged it between headrest and window, and curled his body into a sleeping position.

In her confusion, Szczymanski turned back to her book and stared at the same sentence for several minutes. Jigsaw was indeed much worse than she had expected. Perhaps if she ignored this Dogger, he'd go away. She considered moving to another part of the train. Then she steadied herself—don't judge so quickly. She'd been wrong about Rudy Blaine. Maybe Jigsaw would surprise her and turn out to be useful. But those clothes, that *stink!* She hoped fervently that what she saw was not what she got.

McBryde returned, tapping his fingers against a can of iced tea. They fell easily back into conversation. In comparison to Jigsaw, the bureaucrat wasn't so bad after all. It even turned out that he knew something about trains, was something of an enthusiast. Too bad she couldn't just switch the two men. The dozing Jigsaw, his face pressed against his sweatshirt and a hint of spittle visible at the edge of his mouth, fit her mind's picture of a foamer. This nice-looking fellow sitting next to her, who said he was working on a book, should have been the FBI agent. He didn't seem rabid at all, even when he sketched out his science-fiction scenario of magnetic trains levitating across the country and passengers propelled at impossible speeds through evacuated tubes. She generally warmed to men who cared deeply about something other than sex or possessions or themselves.

Then he mentioned train accidents. And that changed everything. The freckles and the boyish good looks had misled her. What better unsub than a foamer?

Heartbeat accelerating, she looked more carefully at McBryde as he responded to her questions. She tried to apply the body language rules learned at the Academy. Gestures away from the body indicated sincerity, gestures toward the body meant deceit. Rapid-blink rate, numerous pauses, long sentences all were supposed to signify lying. But McBryde smoothly talked about himself and about train accidents, gesturing away from his body, blinking at a normal rate, and using short sentences. Psychopaths, of course, could lie without giving any external indication. She looked at his eyes, expecting to see some sign of insanity around the pupils. But his eyes were a normal gold-flecked green. He mentioned Ruskin. Did psychopaths read Ruskin?

She pressed her forehead against the smooth, cool glass of the window to settle her feverish thoughts. The train rushed by a small town. The headlights of the cars waiting at the grade crossing flashed in her eyes. McBryde certainly knew a great deal about trains. But he talked too much to be the unsub. She'd play it carefully, picking his brain for information while keeping an eye out for clues.

Just as she turned back to ask McBryde a question, the train slowed to a stop. "What's wrong?" she asked.

He pulled out his walkie-talkie, flicked a few switches, and pressed the device to his ear. She could hear the muted crackle of voices.

"Just a little traffic jam at the next station," he reported.

She tried to pry out more information about foamers, particularly foamers interested in train accidents. But just as McBryde began to warm to the topic, his attention was diverted by a passenger striding briskly down the aisle toward the front of the train. A look composed equally of fear and suspicion crossed McBryde's face and he quickly excused himself, ostensibly to go to the bathroom. To play it safe, she waited for him to clear the first car before preparing to follow.

She managed only two steps before feeling a hand on her

elbow. She turned around, her nose already picking up the telltale scent of overripe cantaloupe.

"I got something to show you," Jigsaw said. "Let's go this way." He pulled her toward the back of the train.

"Wait," Szczymanski insisted, holding her ground.

Jigsaw leaned closer. His whispering breath was hot and fetid. "It's important. Real 007 stuff. I'll show you in the observation car." He moved down the aisle, gesturing with his hand for her to follow but not turning around to see if she would.

The observation car was lined on both sides with dusty picture windows. Orange plastic seats, placed at even intervals, were fixed and uncomfortable. The yellow carpet was frayed and stained, peeled back in several places to reveal the red rubber matting beneath. It looked more like a bus-station waiting room than a cozy place to read and sightsee.

With the sun gone and only the dust visible on the windows, the car was empty of gazers and shutterbugs. Only the smokers gathered in their half of the compartment. In the corner closest to the door they entered, a young man with a cigarette dangling from his mouth read a book with a lurid cover. Next to him four old men were telling lawyer jokes and chain-smoking out of a single packet. Across from them, a father was trying to interest his daughters in coin tricks. He, too, took drags from a cigarette, releasing the bluish smoke into the haze of the compartment's upper reaches.

Jigsaw stopped near a bank of empty seats at the opposite end of the car. As they sat down, the train began to glide forward again.

"My allergies are simply out of control today." He pulled a clear plastic bag of pills out of the pocket of his magenta-and-chartreuse-plaid pants. Inside the bag, the multicolored pills looked like an assortment of buttons. "And I think I'm coming down with something worse. Ever get these pains up here, near the temples? Migraines, they tell me. But I'm thinking tumor. Don't laugh." She wasn't laughing, not even smiling. "They come at you like stalking tigers. You don't notice a thing. Then they pounce. And why not? I'm at the tumor age. Cancer's all around us. In the air, the water. And all it takes is the slightest, the smallest, the most infinitesimal cell variation and then, boom, it multiplies faster than humping bunnies. But if that doesn't get me, then this pain over here—"

She interrupted him as he began to pull up his shirt. "Did you bring me back here to complain?"

"Am I complaining?" He looked genuinely surprised. "I was just, well . . . let me see, I was just telling you what was on my mind." He suddenly laughed, a frightening, uncontrolled laughter that revealed mustard-colored teeth. "On my mind! A tumor. On my mind!"

Jigsaw's laughter merged into a coughing fit. He put one hand out, as though to prevent her from coming to his aid. The coughs traveled through his body in successive waves. He looked like a dog shaking itself free of water.

Jigsaw cleared the mucus from his throat, swished it around his mouth, and swallowed it back down. His plump fingers rustled around his plastic bag, drawing out first one, then several pills. "The pink one's a simple antihistamine. For the allergies. There's aspirin, vitamin C, something with cod-liver-oil extract, and, let's see . . ." He peered closely at his palm. "Well, it doesn't matter." He piled all the pills into his mouth and gulped, his Adam's apple bobbing several times as he forced the pills down without any liquid.

"Look—" Szczymanski began impatiently.

"And this," Jigsaw continued, rummaging again in the bag before pulling out what seemed to be a small metal insect, "this is what I wanted to show you." With a forefinger, Jigsaw stroked the top of the insect that lay on his palm. "Is it one of yours?"

"Where'd you get that?" Szczymanski demanded, finally recognizing that the insect was indeed a bug, a miniature microphone designed for concealment.

"Oh, nearby."

"Nearby? As in New York, or as in the café car?"

A beatific smile lit up his face. "I found it rather fortuitously. Serendipity, if you will. It was like picking out a four-leaf clover from a field of alfalfa. Tell me, is it connected somehow to your case?"

"Don't know."

"And your case is? Chaos was such a closemouthed little boy and—"

"I'm looking for someone who's setting train accidents." She decided to be straight with him. Especially now that he was collecting evidence.

"Train accidents? Oh my!" Jigsaw put his hand to his rounded mouth like some grotesque parody of Betty Boop.

At that moment the train lurched as it swung around a curve. Hand still at his mouth, Jigsaw neglected to secure the bag in his lap. With a soft rustle, the pills rained out onto the yellow carpet. Jigsaw yelped in dismay and immediately fell to his knees to save the pills from scattering.

"My angels," he breathed, moving now one way, now the other in his attempt to corral the errant medication. He kept his left hand tightly clenched, careful not to lose his other treasure.

Szczymanski reached down to pick up the capsules that collected around her feet. "Are these prescribed or over-the-counter?" she asked casually.

"My angels," Jigsaw continued to purr as he gathered the pills back into the bag, along with the dirt, gum wrappers, pennies, pencil points, cigarette ash, and other detritus that had accumulated on the floor.

Szczymanski watched as the father took a final puff, pocketed his magic coins, and hustled his daughters out of the compartment. The young man stared at them over the top of his book. The old men continued to tell each other jokes.

With some difficulty, Jigsaw maneuvered his body back into the chair, one hand clenched, the other holding tightly to the plastic bag. Only when he was secure against the rolling of the train did he hold out the bag, with a narrow opening extending through his fist, to allow her to drop the pills one by one down the neck. "I don't know what I'd do if I lost my angels."

Szczymanski held her tongue. Bureau policy dictated that agents should never be "under the influence" while on duty. Possibly Jigsaw was taking only allergy medicine, vitamins, and placebos. She didn't have the pharmaceutical eye to distinguish amphetamines and barbiturates from among his colorful mix.

Jigsaw peered into the bag, his head close to its neck. He looked like a glue sniffer about to salvage a last high.

"You were saying about the bug . . ." Szczymanski prompted.

He reluctantly tore his attention from the bag. "The bug? My beautiful bug?" He slowly opened his left hand and marveled anew at the small device centered on his sweating palm. "It's precious, isn't it? It would be lovely evidence, wouldn't it?"

"It might have been," Szczymanski observed, "if you had handled it properly." She could recite the procedure word-for-word from the manual. *Place the object in a crush-proof container without touching it directly with your fingers. Seal and identify the container by writing on it in ink your initials, the date, the source, and an exhibit number.* Now, however, the bug could provide evidence only of Jigsaw's sweaty palm and whatever residues of drugs that clung to it.

Instead of becoming defensive, Jigsaw simply guffawed. It seemed that he was a man of widely varying emotions, all crowded together near his surface. "Too true, dearie, too true! But, you see, it was already too late by the time the little fellow was in my hand. All covered in dirt and grease he was. Couldn't even tell it was a bug. Took him to the bathroom and gave him a good scrub. Cleaned behind his ears!" Jigsaw brought his hand level to his eye. "Rather shiny now, though I don't think he'll be doing any listening anymore."

Washed the evidence? Szczymanski peered closer at Jigsaw. What office would put up with such a Dogger? Or was he one of those rumored bagmen the FBI hired on the sly to lean on the guilty and bypass court orders? She'd always thought of bagmen as mysterious, completely in control—not befuddled oafs.

"And you found it where . . ." she asked wearily.

"Bent down to tie up my laces," Jigsaw replied. "Between the cars. Not very smart. Train moves back and forth like a drunken belly dancer. Like a bucking camel. Like a—"

"So . . ."

"Wouldn't you know but the train screeched into a station and I lost my balance. Found myself lying flat out on that dirty metal floor." He pointed to some faint stains on the chartreuse squares of his polyester pants. "And I was face-to-face with this little fellow. Looked like a tick on the side of an elephant."

"Between which cars?"

"If we call this observation lounge the first car, then it was between the fourth and fifth." He pointed toward the front of the train.

"Are you sure?"

"Fifth and sixth, maybe. No, third and fourth." Jigsaw laughed again. "I was so upset about the stains on my pants, I was all confused. Just bought these suckers, and this kind of grease never comes out in the—"

"And where was the bug precisely?"

"Right underneath the edge of the platform where it couldn't be seen. Just lucky that my head fell in just the right position. Otherwise—"

"I don't understand how you came face-to-face with something that was lying beneath the metal floor."

"Aw, I was just speaking figuratively." Jigsaw's bloodshot eyes gleamed wildly. Again Szczymanski wondered if something a little stronger was mixed in with the antihistamines he had swallowed earlier. "Fact is, my fingers slipped underneath the floor and I felt the little creature. It came off in my hand. First thought was that I'd broken the train. Now ain't that a scream? This behemoth weighs a couple thousand tons and I thought I broke it by chipping off a little piece." His chuckles merged into a laugh that approached the maniacal. A malarial flush suffused his face.

Szczymanski tried to fit a listening device into her speculations about the case. Why would someone want to listen in on a train accident? To check if everything was going according to plan? Then why place it in the vestibule between cars, underneath a platform? There it would pick up only the sound of trolls like Jigsaw, tying shoes and taking tumbles. Perhaps Amtrak bugged its own trains, to monitor the sounds of the wheels. That was a question for a foamer.

"Any suspicious characters?" she asked Jigsaw when his laughter had died down.

Jigsaw wiped away the sweat beaded on his forehead with the back of his hand. "Everybody's suspicious," he reported, so charmed by his observation that he threatened once again to dissolve into peals of merriment. "Those girls going on a class trip? Bet some of them have just taken electronics lab. A little help from the teacher and there's your bug."

"I hardly think that—"

"Or that group of grandparents heading to their umpteenth college reunion? I suspect one or two of them served in military intelligence back in the Big One. They're the right age. Monte carries a couple of these babies in his dentures case wherever he goes. Wife tells him to stop installing listening devices in the hotel men's rooms but Monte just can't stop. That was his job for so many years and he likes to keep his hand in and—"

"Monte? Who's Monte?"

"Beats me. I was just improvising, and—"

"Anyone *in particular* that seemed suspicious?"

"In particular? Well, yes, I suppose. Fellow you're sitting with. Don't think this is a pleasure trip for him. No, sir, not him."

"Why do you say that?"

"Boy's got a practiced eye, I'd say. Followed him on one of his excursions up and down the train. Seemed to go a whole long distance just to get an iced tea that he didn't hardly drink."

"Concrete evidence?" she asked, pulse quickening.

"I'd have to get a lot closer for that."

"Meaning?"

"Couple pats here and there. Nothing offensive, nothing objectionable. But the train moves a lot, people jostle against one another; maybe I'm homosexual, he doesn't know, I get a little closer than maybe I ought to, but just close enough to find out what he's carrying in his pockets."

She eyed Jigsaw. Definitely bagman material. "Look, I haven't even found out who you really are and what you think you can do," she began.

"I'm Jigsaw." He reached again into the plastic bag, pulling out two more pills, seemingly at random, and depositing them in his mouth. "Go flush our little friend from the café car or wherever he is and then I'll show you what I can do."

FIFTEEN

It took **several seconds for** him to realize that he was looking into the eyes of a boy, not a man. A thread of blood trickled from McBryde's thumb where the screwdriver had nicked him. It wasn't the knife he'd initially expected, but its beveled tip could still be dangerous.

"Hey, man, you're hurting me!" the boy cried, his hand twisted to one side. The boy's height had suggested an adult, the baseball cap had concealed his punk haircut. The wisps of hair just beginning to extend down from in front of his ears placed him somewhere in his mid-teens.

"What's with the screwdriver?" McBryde demanded, his heart no longer between his teeth.

"Are you with security?" the boy asked. "Because . . ."

"Because?"

"Because I want to know."

McBryde looked more closely at the boy. Just a tall, gangly, scared kid. With acne constellations on his forehead and a nose too large for his thin face. McBryde let go of the wrist. It fell limply to the boy's side. On his baseball cap lying on the floor a Burlington Northern patch was carefully sewn just to the left of the St. Louis Cardinals emblem. Hooked to his belt was a scanner. He clenched what looked like an employee timetable in his hand. A budding foamer.

Stepping back, McBryde noticed something poking out from between two lower buttons of the boy's shirt. Pointing, he asked, "What's that?"

"It's not illegal," the boy insisted, his eyes darting around.

A silver-haired woman wearing a name tag on her blouse stopped momentarily beside them on her way through the vestibule. The boy followed her with his eyes, looked as if he might appeal in her direction. She glanced fearfully at them and then hurried away.

With the boy still distracted, McBryde stepped forward and plucked the item out of his shirt. He straight-armed the boy back and held the small object up to the light.

"Hey!" the boy protested, reaching up to retake the strip of metal. McBryde held it out of reach like a biscuit above a dog's jaws. Then, resigned, the boy repeated, "It's, like, not illegal. Aw, Christ, it's not such a big deal."

It was the identification number from one of the cars, which ordinarily was screwed in just beneath the door-release lever.

"You schmuck," McBryde muttered softly. Louder, he said, "Of course it's illegal to take an identification number. That's a Class 12-A offense, stealing government property."

"I know," the boy whispered. "But I need it for my collection."

"For crying out loud—"

"I want one from each line. I'm real close. I need, like, just three more."

"But identification numbers? No one cares about identification numbers."

"I care." The boy picked up his baseball cap. He restored it to his head and drew himself up to his proper height. "I care about identification numbers."

About to vent his disgust, McBryde suddenly stopped short. Why not collect identification numbers? Late at night, after the disappointments of grades and girls, the boy could pull out a shoe box and finger his numbered metal strips. They were tangible, could bring to life an entire train. By comparison, McBryde dealt primarily with lifeless diagrams and figures and imagined case studies. Identification numbers existed; Maglev was still mostly a dream. He gave back the treasured strip to the boy. Watching him clutch this scrap of metal, McBryde realized that nothing possessed intrinsic value. An object had value only if someone invested it with value.

"You going to turn me in?" the boy wanted to know. His pride in the identification-number collection had given way to anxiety.

"No, no. Relax. Sorry I hassled you." He'd struggled to land a marlin but ended up with only a spunky sardine.

"So, like, you're not security?"

McBryde shook his head. "Just a concerned citizen."

The kid pulled off his cap, ran a sleeve across his forehead, and glared at McBryde. "Oh yeah? You scared me shitless, Mr. Concerned Citizen."

McBryde grunted. He inspected his thumb, which had stopped bleeding. "Look, are you thirsty? I'll buy you a soda."

"A beer."

"You're not old enough for a beer."

"You just, like, added decades to my life, mister."

"Okay, a beer."

It took considerable nerve to steal identification numbers, with conductors constantly walking back and forth. At that age, McBryde too had taken risks, stupidly, self-destructively. As a teenager, he'd wandered around the Portland depot late at night, slipping in and out of boxcars, climbing on top of hoppers, breaking into the occasional Amtrak coach and searching it with a flashlight. He'd risked fines, detentions, potentially a lot worse. But he wanted to be near the huge cars and engines, wanted to run his hand along their warm metallic sides. Whenever he felt particularly lonely or misunderstood, he told his busy parents that he would be at a friend's—and then spent the night in a scrapped Pullman car that sat rusting in the corner of the yard.

I should be steering this kid in a more normal direction, McBryde thought. Look, kid, he should say, why don't you collect baseball cards? Spend your time looking at girlie mags, not *Railfan*

Monthly. Go to Great Adventure, for God's sake, not the West Virginian Steamer Museum. Later in life you'll be happier, better adjusted. People won't treat you like a freak.

At the café McBryde bought two overpriced beers, poured them into glasses, and joined the boy at a booth.

With the baseball cap on, the boy looked just old enough to be drinking alcohol in public. He took small sips, as though to make the beer last until Chicago. After wiping his mouth with his hand, he raised the glass and announced: "Crisscross."

"Excuse me?"

"You know, Bruno Anthony and Guy Haines are having lunch and Bruno says, 'Crisscross.'"

McBryde chuckled. It was from Hitchcock's *Strangers on a Train*. "You like train movies?"

"Seen them all," the kid boasted. "*Murder on the Orient Express, The Lady Vanishes, Track 29*, both *Silver Streak*s."

"The oldies? *Great Train Robbery? The General?*"

"Oh yeah!" the kid exclaimed with enthusiasm. "I just eat up that silent shit!"

"*Closely Watched Trains?*"

The boy looked suspicious. "That an American film?"

"Czech."

"I don't do subtitles."

McBryde quoted: "'I had finished a train dispatcher's course and everybody in town knew I had chosen this calling to be able to strut on the platform with a disk in my hand and shirk work all my life, leaving all drudgery to other people.'"

The boy listened intently. He asked McBryde to repeat the lines. "I like that," he said finally.

"The boy in the movie is about your age. It takes place during World War Two, when the Nazis occupied Czechoslovakia."

"What happens?" The boy leaned forward on his elbows, his beer forgotten.

"He helps out the Czech partisans by bombing a heavily guarded train loaded with German ammunition."

"Wow. Do you, like, see the train blow up?"

"You only hear the explosion and see some smoke."

"And the guy, he gets an award for his bravery?"

"He gets shot and killed by the Germans."

"Oh." The boy looked out the window and then turned back to his beer. "I like *Runaway Train* the best—that scene when the Alaskan runaway smashes into the caboose of the Granville 12 and, like, all that wood and snow and shit just goes everywhere."

"An excellent scene," McBryde agreed. "You want to be a director?"

The boy touched the bill of his cap and said softly, "I want to be a boomer."

"That's no easy job." Boomers switched trains in the yards.

"My 'rents want me to be a doctor."

"You'll make better money in medicine."

"Money!" the boy said contemptuously. "Is that all you people think about?"

"Trains aren't a secure future."

"We're riding one, right? And I don't see a lot of empty seats."

"Twenty years from now there'll be no need for boomers. The yard work will all be automatic. But hey, people are always going to get sick." McBryde paused. Given the choice as a boy, would he have taken medicine over trains? "Look, you can always keep your interest in trains as a hobby."

"A hobby? Jesus, you sound like my mom."

"Moms can be right too." Was he really mouthing these terrible clichés? Even a year ago, he would have alerted this gutsy foamer-in-training to some little-known collectors' exchanges. Now, however, he felt like telling him how trains kept people apart. But he didn't know how to put that insight into words.

It didn't matter. The kid wasn't paying attention to him any longer. His eye had been attracted to two girls eating potato chips and scouting a place to sit down. When the boy waved his baseball cap at them, they immediately fell against one another to confer behind cupped hands.

Checking his watch, McBryde said a quick good-bye and stood up. He should have been paying closer attention to the time: Albany in twenty minutes. He needed to look at the maps in his bag to determine the best time to pull the emergency brake cord, for that seemed the only way of keeping the Lake Shore Limited from its likely appointment with the Colonie Bridge.

With the adrenaline rush of the chase ebbing, he lapsed back into skepticism. Jordan had been wrong. Why should there be a pattern? The Lake Shore would continue past Albany and there'd be no accident. All these happy passengers would debark at their destinations, perhaps a little late but otherwise none the worse for their journey. And he too, lacking the nerve to pull the emergency cord, would get off in Chicago, with no further clues and no idea of where to go next.

He passed the journalist in the aisle on his way back to his seat. She nodded at him curtly. He tried to toss off a witticism as they turned sideways to pass, but his tongue lolled uncooperatively in his mouth. Her beauty intimidated him.

Back at his seat, he pulled from his bag a railroad map of the tri-city area—Albany, Troy, Schenectady. Ten miles outside Albany, the Lake Shore crossed a small railroad bridge over the Colonie River. He'd listen carefully to the scanner. Unless he heard or saw something to stay his hand, he'd stop the train five minutes after passing the Albany-Rensselaer station. He couldn't afford any doubts. Wild-goose chase or not, he didn't want to risk tipping over the Colonie Bridge and repeating the Utica disaster. Their plan was somewhat far-fetched—McBryde would pull the emergency brake surreptitiously, contact Jordan by cellular phone, and then Jordan would call in an anonymous warning to Amtrak to check the Colonie Bridge for sabotage.

His eye was distracted. Across the aisle, a man rooted around in a plastic bag of candies. One after another he selected an M&M or a Good & Plenty and held it close to his eye before putting it back in. After watching this procedure several times, McBryde realized that the bag contained not candy but different-colored pills. The man caught McBryde's gaze and leaned conspiratorially across the aisle.

"I'm just checking my supplies," he confided in an urgent whisper. He had a puffy, unevenly colored face, with thinning salt-and-pepper hair slicked back like an otter's. His prominent eyebrows seemed to be permanently arched. "By the way, you got a nice girlfriend over there."

McBryde had been in similar situations before. Sometimes you met wonderful people on the train. Other times you longed for a can of Mace. "She's not my girlfriend," he said carefully. "We just met."

"Oh yeah?" The man packed away his bag of pills into a canvas knapsack squeezed between his feet. Then he clutched the bag's strap with one hand and raised himself slightly from his seat. "Then can we switch places?"

"Excuse me?"

"Switch places," the man repeated, rising a little farther in his seat. "She's awful cute and I'd like to get her phone number."

McBryde looked incredulously at this slightly overweight middle-aged man. With his loud polyester shirt and his shiny plaid pants, he looked like a real estate agent having a night on the town. "Better make yourself comfortable where you are," McBryde said. "I'm not moving."

"No?" The man looked genuinely surprised. He left his seat, crossed the aisle, and leaned over McBryde. "That a map you got there?"

McBryde folded the map and returned it to his bag. "Just checking to see where we are."

"Didn't look like a regular map."

The man had a peculiar cloying odor that spread like bug spray. "Do you mind?" McBryde tried to push the man back with his intonation.

Instead of returning to his seat, however, the man dropped into a crouch in the aisle, bringing him eye-to-eye with McBryde's scanner. "And what's this?"

McBryde considered several options: going to the bathroom, returning to the café car, knocking the man onto his face.

The real estate agent began to tug the scanner free of its holster.

McBryde pushed his hand away. "It's not a toy," he growled. "Now would you please leave me alone?"

The man looked up, startled. "Leave you alone? Why, sure! Here I thought you was looking for some company. Silly me!" He straightened up and returned to his seat.

First a young thieving foamer and now a pill-popping Middle American wacko. He located the can of iced tea near the footrest release and drank it down in three gulps. It was terrible, too sweet and too bitter at the same time. But Albany was coming up now in fifteen minutes and the caffeine would sharpen his senses.

The journalist intrigued him. She was smart, funny, and seemed to know nothing at all about trains. And she was so beautiful. He dreamily considered her lovely, composite face. It would have been better to meet her at a Laundromat or a bookstore. Romance and detective work mixed well only in the movies.

His relationships with women always began in odd ways. Rosalind, for example, introduced herself into his life by nearly running him down as he was crossing a street with both hands full of groceries. This happened in Portland, during his first year at Mortimer Security. When she halted within inches of his thighs, he'd been so startled that he dropped his packages on the hood of the car. A carton of eggs landed on the windshield. The sight of the driver's face, panic-stricken behind the white-and-yellow trickle of the broken eggs, struck him as inexplicably funny. He put one foot up on her fender and began to laugh. Rushing to his side, she apologized over and over for her momentary blindness, for the sun's glare through the windshield, for the poor visibility of the traffic light. "You ruined my breakfast," he said, joking, pointing at the eggs. So, after they had repackaged the groceries and cleaned off the windshield with paper towels, she drove him to a diner and bought him a huge omelet.

McBryde rubbed his eyes. A profound lethargy was descending upon him. He'd never see this journalist again. Just as well; Rosalind had ruined long-term relationships for him. He couldn't imagine living with another woman, adjusting to her idiosyncrasies.

A conductor, preceded by a gust of air, charged down the aisle announcing the Albany-Rensselaer stop in five minutes and removing the seat checks of departing passengers.

McBryde's plan was to sit with his scanner in the observation car to monitor communications between the engineer and the stationmaster. He also wanted to see which members of the crew changed at Albany. He didn't want to pull the emergency unless absolutely necessary. A sudden stop could produce precisely the derailment that he was hoping to avoid. But what else could he do? The conductors would never listen to him.

The lethargy was spreading through his limbs. He didn't want to move just yet. He let his head rest against the back of his seat. Just for a minute, he told himself. My head is so very heavy and it needs to lean against something for a moment or else it will pitch forward and snap off my neck. And I must close my eyelids for just a minute as well or else they too will tumble from my face.

No—he shook his head, feeling as though he were under water—no, we are leaving Albany and I must concentrate. I must concentrate. With great effort, McBryde picked himself up out of the seat. He stood in the aisle, swaying. I must concentrate. And yet his thoughts scattered like ants around a disturbed anthill. The bathroom, he thought. A splash of cold water. That would clear his head. Then he'd be able to concentrate again.

SIXTEEN

In the end, she didn't need to flush her game. On the way to the café car, Szczymanski encountered a smiling McBryde. He seemed to have every intention of chatting with her in the aisle. But after acknowledging him with a brisk nod and a tight smile, she continued on. Let Jigsaw run his little caper. She certainly didn't want to watch. She'd rather spend a few minutes over a cup of coffee and then return after Jigsaw had collected the evidence.

Waiting on line for her coffee and agonizing over Jigsaw's reliability, she heard a voice near her elbow. "First time on the train?"

A teenage boy waited behind her in line with a wide grin and a plastic cup of beer. He removed his baseball cap in greeting. His hair was shaved close on the sides but left spiky on top like blades of grass. Two small studs in the shape of little golden spikes glistened in his earlobes. She scowled at the boy and turned back to pay for her order.

He touched his plastic cup to her Styrofoam one. "I'm not as young as I look, if that's, like, what you're thinking."

"Look, I don't have time for chitchat," she said, receiving her change. "My husband's waiting for his coffee." The attendant smirked at her in sympathy before asking the boy what he wanted.

"Um, I guess nothing," he said hurriedly and then stepped out of line to follow Szczymanski down the aisle toward the coach cars. "Hey," he said to her neck, "your husband that fellow you're sitting with?"

"Bingo, Sherlock," she said without turning around. The age of harassment had clearly dropped below the age of consent. So much for waiting in the café car. She hoped that by the time she returned to her seat, Jigsaw would be finished with his business.

"That's not your husband," the kid said into her ear as they waited for a couple to pass through the sliding door to the vestibule. "You just met him on the train today."

She groaned. A smart-ass kid with two studs and an attitude.

"I been sitting behind you all this time," the kid continued.

"Congratulations."

Szczymanski stepped across the threshold and into the vestibule between the cars. She was about to pass into the next car when he said quietly, "You're interested in accidents, right? Train accidents?"

She turned around so sharply she nearly elbowed him in the voice box.

He jumped back. "Hey, watch out, you nearly—"

"What did you say?" she demanded, crowding him into the recessed space in front of the exit door. Hot coffee sloshed onto her wrist. Holding the cup with one hand, she seized the boy's shoulder and turned him toward the window. Her fingers dug into the hollow above his collarbone.

The boy squirmed. His breath fogged the door's window. "I just heard you talking about trains, that's all. Thought you were interested in accidents. You don't have to get so jumpy about the whole thing, jeez, I mean . . ."

Behind them on the platform between the cars, a steady stream of passengers carried cardboard containers of food or held their purses and wallets ready.

She kept her voice low, pretended to enjoy the scenery with her young charge. "What do you know about train accidents?"

"Nothing, really." The boy's bluster had disappeared and he was now plainly worried. "I just said that to get your attention."

"Why'd you want my attention?"

"I don't know. Just, like, being friendly, 's all."

"Yeah? But why me?"

The boy blushed. "Because you're a babe. It's no crime to try to hit on you, huh?"

At another time Szczymanski might have laughed at this slip of a boy trying to pick her up. But now she merely relaxed her grip on his shoulder. "I suggest someone closer in age."

"You got a sister?"

She ignored his renewed enthusiasm. "Why'd you think I was interested in train accidents?"

"Look, I was just listening in on your conversation. You going to let me go, or what? You're making me nervous. Why're people so jumpy these days, huh?"

She dropped her hand from his shoulder altogether. "Are you a train buff?"

"Me? Yeah, sort of."

"Train accidents?"

He shrugged. "I like those big wrecks. They're cool. It would be way cool if this sucker went straight into another train going the other way."

"Think that might happen?" She turned him around to face her.

"No." But his eyes suddenly narrowed and his expression became conspiratorial. "But listen, I saw these two guys way back at the station in New York, and they were in the video arcade whispering about something. So I moved closer and put on my Walkman and started grooving with the music. But, like, the thing was I didn't have any music on. That way I heard what they was saying but they didn't think I was listening. Pretty sharp, right?"

"Way sharp. What did they say?"

The boy looked suddenly greedy. "What'll you give me for the information?"

"I'll buy you dinner."

"How 'bout a kiss?"

"Wrong."

"What are you anyway? A cop?"

"A journalist."

"Dinner in the café car or the dining car?"

"Dining car."

"Wine?"

"They won't serve you."

"Two entrees?"

"Two desserts."

"Deal." He thrust out his hand and they shook on the proposition. "They were talking about this train and about this bridge—"

"Name of the bridge?"

"Colony? Maybe."

"What else?"

"One guy said something about a derailment."

"Jesus Maria, Colonie's only ten minutes outside Albany!" She checked her watch. They'd be in Albany in less than five minutes. "You were the only one near them?"

"Only one close enough to hear."

"What did they look like?"

"Just two white guys. Kinda ordinary-looking."

"Size?"

"I don't know, hard to tell."

"Thin? Fat? Glasses? Beard?"

"Jeez"—the boy screwed up his face—"I can't remember. I was concentrating too much on the words."

"Could you recognize them again?"

"One of 'em. Other one was standing with his back to me."

"The one you could see—was he the man sitting next to me on the train?"

"Your husband?" The kid snickered. Then, more seriously, he said, "No, wasn't him."

"Is this man on the train?"

"Yeah, I think I saw him getting on."

"Could you pick him out for me?"

"Yeah, sure. But I'm getting kinda hungry."

They could walk through the train together. But she didn't want the kid caught up in this thing, didn't want him shot in the crossfire. No, there was a better way.

"Listen up; here's what I want you to do. I'm giving you a five-minute head start. Walk through to the rear of the train. If you see this fellow, find an empty seat behind him and wait for me. I'll finish my coffee right here and then follow you. You find this guy and I'll buy you dinner."

"Hey, hold on," the kid protested. "Dinner was for the information, you gotta—"

"Wrong," she interrupted. "Dinner is for information and identification. Package deal."

"I don't know, this is—"

"No choice," Szczymanski said, flashing her most malevolent TB² look in his direction. "If you don't help me out and quick, I'm going to rip those studs out of your face." That was putting it a little strongly, perhaps, but she didn't want this teenager jerking her around.

The boy paled at her words and nodded, started to make a joke of it, but then stopped. She sent him off on his mission with a solid clap on his shoulder.

Szczymanski leaned against the wall of the train and sipped her coffee. Several days ago she had prayed for some assistance. God must have misinterpreted her request as "some assistants." Now there were too many cooks. She was losing control of this underop. But maybe, just maybe, the kid would find one unsub and Jigsaw the other. Then she could collect them, stop the train, and wrap up the case.

The Lake Shore pulled into the Albany-Rensselaer station. She moved into the recess in front of the trackside exit to allow passengers to push and pull their luggage off the train. Cold night air poured into the vestibule. Shivering, she finished the coffee as the train swallowed more passengers and pulled out of the station. She waited another couple of minutes, then set out in pursuit.

But on her way back to her car she saw no sign of the boy. And when she arrived at her seat, McBryde too was gone.

Jigsaw was peacefully sifting through the pills in his bag.

"Hey," she said, settling down beside him. "You see a kid with a baseball cap pass this way?"

Jigsaw looked up, bleary-eyed. "Kid? With a cap? I don't rightly know. Wasn't paying much attention to the comings and goings."

She released her anger by exhaling slowly out of her mouth. "Then he's probably in the observation car. What about McBryde? Where's he gone?"

"Bathroom, I expect."

"Bathroom? Listen, we don't have a lot of time. It's ten minutes before—"

"He'll be back in a jiffy. Gave him a little sedative."

"Excuse me?" Szczymanski recoiled in her seat.

"Seconal. Two hundred milligrams."

"What the—"

"Slipped it into his iced tea. Plus some sugar to sweeten the pill. Actually it wasn't a pill, it was in liquid form. A few drops, nothing easier."

"Jesus, what if he collapses in the bathroom!"

"He won't. Doesn't knock people out like that. This is what'll happen. He'll go to the bathroom, splash some cold water on his face, stumble back to his seat, and settle down. People'll think he's had a little too much in the café car."

"That's what you think."

"Guaranteed. I know my little angels."

"But their effect on other people?"

"You'll see. When he comes back, I'll sit next to him and go through his pants while you stand next to us in the aisle. I can always check him out in the bathroom if necessary, but people go in and out of that men's lounge and I'd rather just do it right here. He's a mighty suspicious character. Had this railroad map in his bag." He removed a misfolded rectangle from beneath his thigh. "Look, he's circled this bridge here, right past Albany."

"You are not a professional," she said coldly.

Jigsaw smiled at her. "Thank you."

"I don't have time to argue. We've got only ten minutes before this bridge comes up. And I want to find this kid. On the way back we'll pick up McBryde if he's still in the bathroom." She stood up.

"What kid?" Jigsaw asked, following her down the aisle toward the observation car.

"He thinks he knows one of the unsubs."

"Is it the teenage girl? No, I bet it's Monte, that old—"

"Shut up!" Szczymanski said fiercely and in a tone loud enough to turn several heads. "Just follow me and keep quiet." They passed by the men's lounge and she resisted the urge to poke her head through the curtain. They were running out of time. Right now she had to get the kid and pull the emergency.

But the observation car was empty—except for the four old joke-tellers now playing a spirited game of pinochle, the cards passed back and forth by wrinkled and expensively ringed fingers. Where could the boy have gone? It wasn't possible for him to have slipped by them. Perhaps he'd been seized with the sudden need to use the bathroom. It had been irresponsible to rely on a sixteen-year-old, to have involved him in the escapade at all. Now she was back at the beginning and staring a derailment right in the face.

"Five minutes to the bridge. We're going to have to pull the emergency," she whispered to Jigsaw.

"Takes a full minute for a train to come to a stop."

"Oh yeah?"

"Or is it two full minutes?"

"What do you know about trains?"

"Trains?" His eyes drifted past her and out the window at the back of the car. "I've ridden a few."

"McBryde knew about trains," she replied dryly. "Too bad you knocked him out."

"Maybe I shouldn't have done that," he admitted.

"Yeah, maybe."

"Seemed like the right thing to do at the time."

"We've got four minutes. Pull the alarm."

"The alarm?" He jerked a finger at the red handle hanging from a chain in front of the back window. "Me?"

"Can I help you?"

They both turned around to face a conductor.

"Us?" they replied in unison.

"Enjoying the sights?" the conductor asked. He was a musta-chioed Latino, slight of build but with a large head accentuated by a closely cropped Afro. "For me this is the best place in the whole train. Too bad it's so dark out there. Make sure you get good seats in the morning."

"I've got this problem," Jigsaw began. "I think my seat mecha-nism's jammed." He began to lead the conductor away. "I wanted to sit back, read a book, put my feet up. But it wouldn't go back."

"It's probably stuck."

"That might be it," Jigsaw said, the two of them now parting the pinochle players and moving through the observation car. "But if you could take a look, I'd be real grateful."

They left the car. She had only a minute to decide. There really wasn't much of a choice. It would have been better to apprehend the unsub first and then appeal to the train's engineer to stop the train. Thirty seconds. They'd probably know that she pulled the handle. She'd have to come up with a convincing excuse. But that was a risk she'd just have to take. She reached for the red handle.

SEVENTEEN

His body felt disassembled, the legs walking independently of the torso, the hands and arms drifting at a distance, the head a big swirl of cotton candy floating in the air a few inches above his neck. Somewhere in the fuzz of his brain McBryde realized that he'd been drugged, probably something dumped into his iced tea—that slightly bitter taste. A splash of cold water wouldn't reassemble his body. He needed to purge his stomach as quickly as possible.

Careening down the aisle, McBryde steadied himself wherever he could—on armrests, the tops of seats, the shoulders of passengers. He could barely see, or rather, could barely connect the images on either side of the aisle with his movements between them. He jostled a tray table with an anesthetized hip, overturning a drink onto a sandwich and a twitching hand. He ran his numb fingers through the moussed hair of an elegant redheaded woman. He crunched the toes of a foot that unwisely lay in the aisle.

"Drunk," he heard.

"Watch it, buddy," someone said.

He opened his mouth to apologize and heard, as if from a distance, the sputtering of a drowning man. Faces ballooned before him but he pushed on, his momentum preserved by one word—bathroom. All else was forgotten—the journalist, the sixteen-year-old foamer, the imminent accident. Only one image, that of the welcoming doughnut hole of a toilet, remained fixed in the haze of his consciousness. The idea of depositing the drugged contents of his stomach right in the aisle never occurred to him. His mind could manage only a single linked activity—throwing up and flushing down.

McBryde floated around the corner that separated the men's lounge from the rest of the car. Parting the curtain, he found the room empty. There, in the sanctity of the lounge, he paused and leaned against the wall, centering his cheek between his outstretched hands. He breathed heavily, trying to forestall unconsciousness. He wasn't sure how long he remained in that position. As he leaned at an angle, a thought flitted briefly around his head like a bluebottle fly caught for a moment inside a box: how tenuous the connection between mind and body could become. The rest of his thoughts dangled, repeated themselves, stopped short, then continued two steps later.

Finally he pushed off from the wall. Veering to the left and then to the right, like a hand trying unsteadily to thread a needle, McBryde made for the door to the toilet. This room too, blessedly, was unoccupied. With enormous relief he swung himself inside. The space was small, but he didn't need a lot of room for the job.

Even after voiding himself of everything in his stomach—and then some—McBryde still felt the effect of the drug. It would take some time before the toxins stopped circulating through his bloodstream. He got up off his knees and backed out into the lounge. The area remained empty. At the sink, he rinsed his mouth out with water. He barely recognized the face staring back at him in the mirror. The eyes were bloodshot, the surrounding skin puffy. His nose had turned clownishly red and stood in stark contrast to the sallow skin of his surrounding face. His ginger hair, the curls usually combed neatly, now defied gravity as though he'd just slept upside down in a tree. Small dots of vomit stained the collar of the shirt poking out of his sweater. It was not a pleasant sight, but he was still too drugged to care.

The train stopped, though it seemed to McBryde that he was still swaying to its motion. It must be the Albany-Rensselaer stop. Ten minutes to the Colonie Bridge.

Returning to the bathroom, he used several paper towels to wipe shakily around the toilet rim. Flush. Did Marty have a tape of this one? McBryde flashed on the row of cassettes that the deejay kept in a corner bookcase in his den facing his wildly expensive stereo system. It would occupy a place of honor: the sound of his friend McBryde's breakfast and lunch making their way to the septic holding tank beneath the car. He replaced the lid of the toilet and again returned to the lounge area, where he sat down in one of the smooth Naugahyde chairs. He put his head in his hands and tried to think.

The train started moving again. It would happen soon. He checked his watch but the numbers streamed together on the dial face. Stop, he commanded the spinning hands, stop dancing back and forth. His thoughts piled one atop another. He had to stop the train, had to prevent whatever was going to happen from happening. He knew who the foamer was. Not the boy with the serial numbers. Not any of the smooth, potentially devious men scattered around the train.

It must be the lunatic across the aisle. Why else would he have slipped something into the iced tea?

He wrestled the Bearcat scanner out of its holster and with clumsy fingers flicked it on. A static crackle filled the small compartment. High above the interference came the voice of the stationmaster spitting out track numbers and arrival times for the engineer. McBryde tried to concentrate. They were approaching a set of switches before the bridge. If the switch was not set properly, the train would derail, slide down the embankment, and hurl into the water of the river below. Utica Two. McBryde's heart began to pound. If that happened, the electricity would go off. The cold river water would flood into the darkness of the lounge.

There was an emergency handle next to the sink. He could say that he'd slipped, that he meant to reach for the light switch, the paper towel, the soap dispenser. Then he'd have to contact Jordan so the anonymous call would go out. McBryde grasped the handle and was about to pull it when someone staggered in through the curtains.

It was the kid, the foamer. As the train sped along jerkily, the boy collided against a wall and pitched over, first against the sink, striking his shoulder, and then against McBryde's knees. McBryde let go of the emergency lever and bent over the boy.

"Sorry," McBryde began with numbed tongue. "I . . . I . . ."

It was only then that he saw the red streak the boy had left on his pant leg. He looked up and saw that the wall near the lounge's entrance had broken out in a pink flush. For a moment he thought he was hallucinating. Then he saw the boy's head pressed against the leg of the chair, his eyes closed and his face distorted by the pull of cheek against metal. A small bullet hole broke the skin of his temple. The short blond hair at the back of his head was red with blood and gray with oatmeal flecks of brain matter.

He didn't have to take the kid's pulse to know he was dead. But it took him a few moments to find the murder weapon shoved into the waistband of the boy's pants. Without thinking, he pulled it out. At first, because of the silencer attached to the end of its barrel, he didn't recognize the gun.

Then, with a start, he realized that it was his.

EIGHTEEN

Szczymanski reached for the handle of the emergency brake. Just as she was about to pull it, though, the air was filled with the screech of metal wheels on metal rails, and she was thrown off her feet and onto the floor.

She tumbled down the aisle of the observation car like an awkward gymnast, collided with the hard plastic seats, tried to keep her limbs close to her body, and finally barreled into the felled pinochle players. The noise of the braking train rose to a terrible peak and then eased. She smelled the fearful sweat of the old men. Reaching out a hand, she managed finally to steady herself against the base of a chair. When the train came to rest, the overhead lights went out. She pulled herself off the floor, helped the dazed old foursome to their feet.

"Are you okay?" she asked, concerned.

They clung to one another in the darkness, loudly refused any further help.

"Suit yourselves," she responded, brushing the dust and a playing card or two from her clothes. Her elbow throbbed from hitting something, but otherwise she was unhurt.

Jigsaw? The engineer? Who could have stopped the train at exactly the moment she'd intended?

She scrambled through the darkness of the vestibule, knocking into at least one person on her way. Her own car was a mess. The lights from a nearby highway dimly illuminated the scene. She saw everything as if through a blue filter. Baggage littered the aisles, with several people mixed in among their belongings. All around her the passengers raised their voices in confusion. A small child was crying, nearly screaming. There had been no announcement, no explanation for the abrupt stop. Those who had sustained minor injuries—banged heads from flying luggage or burned hands from spilled coffee—complained of inadequate attention. No conductors appeared. And no one went in search of them. A freight train rumbled by slowly, gained speed. After a few minutes, the Lake Shore's engine started up again and the lights came back on. The cries of distress abated somewhat. After restoring their bags to the overhead luggage racks, the passengers retreated to the safety of their seats as though afraid of aftershocks.

Jigsaw was resting comfortably with his seat back, his sweatshirt draped like a ribbon of honor across his chest, and his plastic bag of pills just peeking out of his pant pocket. He opened his eyes when she leaned over him.

"You do this?"

Jigsaw shook his head.

"Where's McBryde?"

"Seat works nicely now." He smiled.

"McBryde," she demanded, "the guy you pumped the Seconal into."

"In the bathroom. I'm still waiting for him to come back. That's what I'm doing. Waiting." He wriggled snugly in his chair, like a baby in a papoose. His eyes shone glassily and he licked his lips. Then, softly, he began to sing a popular TV jingle for hemorrhoidal cream. "In the end you'll be happy, in the end you will see . . ."

Some potent combination of drugs had rendered Jigsaw almost useless. Why had Chaos burdened her with this incompetent? She reached over for McBryde's bag and deposited it on the seat beside Jigsaw. "Make sure no one takes this."

Jigsaw broke off his singing to gurgle an indistinct response. Then he resumed, off-key, "From the bedroom to the bathroom, you will sit comfortably . . ."

Szczymanski hurried to the bathroom, hoping that no one else had gotten there first. She planned to search McBryde's pockets and then pull him back to his seat.

She was not prepared for what she found.

The scene in the lounge reminded her of a gangland rubout. It wasn't the amount of blood so much as its distribution—on the wall, on the edge of the sink, in a puddle on the floor. The blood didn't bother her. She'd visited enough morgues and hospitals. The sight of the baseball cap lying next to the boy's elbow, however, made her tremble. Her young accomplice had indeed found the two men responsible for the train accidents. And they, in turn, had killed him. A bullet through the head. From the entrance wound she guessed a .45.

She drew her own gun out of its concealed shoulder holster and flicked off the safety. Then she stepped gingerly around the body and looked into the toilet area. Empty. McBryde had disappeared, leaving behind only a few specks of vomit on the toilet rim.

Back in the lounge she saw that the emergency handle was down. The poor kid. He'd probably run into McBryde and the only way to defend himself had been to pull the emergency.

It was her fault. She'd deputized him, sent him into battle. Her shoulders began to jerk, her neck muscles tightened. But she couldn't afford the time to indulge in guilt or grief. She had to gather the evidence and get out fast. If someone discovered her—either a passenger or a conductor—she'd have to blow her cover, identify herself as FBI, assist the criminal investigation, and bring in the whole troop from national headquarters—Peña, Metaxas, Granite. That, she knew, would spoil her plan. The risks were high. But she was already in too deep. It was for precisely these contingencies that she needed to be a Tough Ball Breaker.

Swallowing back tears, she pulled plastic gloves from her purse, quickly slid them on, and removed a small leather kit containing the necessary tools. She scanned the area for a murder weapon, for a bullet or a shell casing, but found none of these. She bent over the body, feeling the back pocket of the boy's jeans and finding his wallet. Inside was fifty dollars in cash. They hadn't had enough time to set it up as a robbery. With a gloved finger, she slid out a library card. Jackson Long. Teaneck Public Library. A Jersey boy. She pushed the wallet back into his pocket.

With tweezers, she removed several hairs from beneath the boy's fingernails and placed them in a small cardboard envelope. She scanned the area for objects that might have fallen from a suspect's pockets, but found only a wadded-up paper towel. She took a blood sample from the wall of the lounge, careful to scrape the blade of her pocket knife across both stained and non-stained areas, and collecting the flaked material onto separate pieces of paper. She returned to the toilet and removed a sample of the residue from the rim.

Finally she performed the most difficult task—going over the boy's body for hidden objects. She discovered a metal strip imprinted with a number. Then, lifting his body, she found what he still clenched tightly: a screwdriver. She examined the tip and found what might have been dried blood. She put the strip and the screwdriver into separate bags and stood up to leave.

The whole operation—from discovery of the body to collection of the final sample—had lasted no more than three minutes. Whenever someone passed through the corridor, rustling the curtain with an elbow, she froze in her position. Each time, however, the person moved on without interrupting her work.

About to slip back into the corridor, she turned for one more look—to fix the scene in her memory. Procedure called for a photograph, but she had no camera. Her guilt called for a brief, silent prayer.

Returning casually to her seat, she roused Jigsaw from his slumbers. But no, he hadn't seen anything—hadn't seen the boy, hadn't seen McBryde, hadn't seen a conductor. Szczymanski swallowed her anger. Never rely on someone else, she reminded herself, if you can do the job yourself. Chaos was going to get an earful.

"In the end . . ." Jigsaw murmured, his head dropping back down to his chest.

Again she rattled him awake and whispered, "The kid's dead

and McBryde's gone. You know nothing about McBryde, okay? We're handling the unsub. If the police find his body, so be it. Otherwise it's up to us. Is that clear?"

Jigsaw laughed. "From the bathroom to the bedroom—"

Szczymanski grabbed his chin and shook his head violently to the left and right. "Did you hear what I said?"

"You're the boss," Jigsaw simpered.

"Repeat what I said."

"McBryde's dead and the kid's gone and—"

"No." She applied pressure to his chin with a thumbnail and repeated the message.

When he finally got it right, she let go of his chin. He drifted back into his reverie. The touch of his skin nauseated her. She'd make damn sure she'd never have to see him again.

Szczymanski walked through the passenger coaches. The car attendants were busy treating the injured. She searched quickly for McBryde, explaining to anyone who asked that she was trying to locate her husband. But McBryde wasn't crumpled up in any of the corners she checked. Murderer, he would have jumped the train. Murdered, his body would be dumped alongside the tracks.

Back in her seat, she transferred the contents of his bag to her own, then folded the bag itself and packed it away with the few objects. Her own traveling bag now swelled from its additions. She kept all the criminal evidence in her purse.

Including the screwdriver. If the blood on the tip was McBryde's, then she had walked off with the most important evidence. Match the DNA from the blood to the DNA from the vomit and they had a case. Except that she'd collected the evidence improperly. She remembered enough from law school to realize that. Better she should have left the screwdriver. She'd been too eager. But it was too late to go back.

The boy's body was not discovered for a full ten minutes. By that time Szczymanski was slouched in her seat, her face buried in *Matricide*. While one attendant roped off access to the lounge, another explained to the passengers that the train was experiencing certain technical problems. Two more attendants escorted the man who had discovered the body down the aisle. He was ashen and tight-lipped, with deep wells around his eyes that gave him a haunted quality. Not believing "technical problems" for one minute, the passengers began to speculate about the roped-off area. By the time the rumors reached Szczymanski's ears, the lounge had become the scene of a mass knifing, with three dead and two injured. Passengers in the window seats stared into the darkness outside, waiting for the bodies to be carried off.

Szczymanski kept her eyes fixed on her book and tried to work out for herself what had happened. The boy found McBryde in the bathroom. Probably he hadn't known what to do, since he could no longer follow her plan. Panicking, he confronted McBryde. In the ensuing struggle, the kid drew blood with the screwdriver before pulling the emergency, before getting shot in the head. In a hurry to get off the stalled train, McBryde had been careless in covering his tracks.

This story still had too many holes. Where was the accomplice, the second man the boy had seen? Had he also been in the lounge? What was the hidden microphone for? Where was McBryde now? The case was not making much sense.

Slowly at first, but then more rapidly, the train edged backward toward Albany. A line of police waited on the platform as the Lake Shore pulled into a siding. The passengers filed out into the cold darkness and were met immediately by a group of policemen who took down names, addresses, and phone numbers, and checked these against identification. She used a false identity from her Pierre work. The station was opened up to receive the grumbling passengers, Szczymanski and the still smiling Jigsaw among them. The policemen posted at the doors to the station turned away all anxious questions. She spent the time preparing her alibi. Jigsaw curled up on the floor and napped.

Finally, after they'd stood and leaned against windowsills in the crowded waiting room for an hour, an Amtrak conductor announced that buses would soon arrive to take everyone to hotels in Albany. The next evening they would continue on their way. "Technical problems" continued to be the official Amtrak line, although the presence of all the police belied this explanation. Among the passengers, the lurid story of the multiple knifing seemed far more popular.

Before letting them board the buses, a policeman announced through a bullhorn that passengers might be called later with more questions. And that was it. No interrogations, no body searches. Szczymanski wondered at the lax procedure.

Unless they knew something she didn't.

She took a taxi from the station to the Albany airport. Waiting for the first flight to D.C., she spent the rest of the night sleeping on a plastic bench that gave her a sore shoulder and a headache. At 4:40 A.M., she hitched a ride with a private prop plane. The pilot, a Pentagon flack who spent weekends at his house in Troy and weekdays at his Arlington efficiency, used the Air Force's fields as his parking lot. His car was waiting at the base and they drove together into the District. He asked for her phone number. She gave him Chaos's, told him to call only after midnight. Partial payback for Jigsaw.

She went directly to her office. If the Albany trip had spilled over into the week, she'd planned to call in sick. At least she didn't have to resort to that tired excuse. Now, however, she truly did feel sick. There, slumped behind her desk, she slept fitfully for half an hour. Images from the previous night combined and recombined in her mind. The baseball hat appeared atop a shrunken Jackson Long, his face gashed and gory. The bug grew to the size of an armored tank. The train became a worm that traveled in and out of the holes on the boy's face and was in turn pecked at by the bug, a birdlike beak stretching metallic from its side. In the last sequence, McBryde appeared to be enmeshed in the train, his naked torso merging with an engine and two small horns growing out of his head, like a centaur. He smiled seductively, then threw his head back and bellowed, "Maglev, Maglev!"

She woke up sweating, her shirt cuff soaked through where her forehead had rested. Dreaming about a case was a sign that she was getting too personally involved. No longer did these accident figures refer to the abstract dead. Worse, she was directly responsible for young Jackson Long's death. She tried to appease her conscience by arguing that the boy, driven to confront the suspect or suspects by a fatal curiosity, would have been killed anyway. But she found such reasoning unconvincing. She tried another tack, that the innocent often get killed in the line of fire. An FBI agent had to harden her heart against such casualties. But even this rationalization left her uneasy. Work, she hoped, would concentrate her mind.

Her first phone calls of the morning yielded two surprises.

The desk sergeant at the Albany precinct responsible for the Lake Shore incident told her they had a suspect in custody. The thin, raccoon-faced man who she thought had merely discovered the body turned out to be a thief with a record. He'd worked the Lake Shore before, jumping on at Albany-Rensselaer, lifting a few wallets and purses, loitering in the bathrooms to avoid ticket collectors, and then jumping off at Schenectady twenty minutes later. A conductor had walked into the lounge to find the thief picking Jackson Long's pocket. Both Amtrak and the police were extremely satisfied to have such a prime suspect. He hadn't confessed yet, the desk sergeant told her. But they were working him over good. And a detail was combing the tracks for the murder weapon, which they assumed had been thrown from the moving train. Now she understood why the police had allowed the passengers to continue on their way with so few precautions taken.

The second surprise involved the engine.

According to the Albany-Rensselaer stationmaster, a crew had been sent out early that morning to bring the Lake Shore's unit up to Schenectady to substitute for the disabled engine of a northbound Adirondack. Just before the Colonie Bridge, the tandem engines derailed because of a faulty switch. Fortunately the damage had been minimal and no one had been hurt. If they'd been going even ten miles an hour faster, however, they would've ended up at the bottom of the Colonie River.

"Good thing the Lake Shore never made it to the bridge last night," the stationmaster told her, "or else we'd have a trainload of deaths on our hands."

"Why didn't it reach the bridge?" she asked.

"Someone pulled the emergency."

"Who?"

The stationmaster didn't know. "God," he guessed. "Or maybe that poor kid."

Neither Amtrak nor the Albany police discovered a second body—not on the train nor along the tracks. McBryde had gotten away and she probably had the only evidence that could convict him. A few more calls confirmed that the bureaucrat was indeed a bureaucrat. What, then, had been his motive? It was odd that a man who dealt with public transportation complaints should of his own accord disrupt the system. He was also unusually inept. He left his luggage and a potentially incriminating screwdriver behind. His bug had been poorly concealed.

And he talked too much. From her psychological profiling class at Quantico, Szczymanski knew that not all criminals were taciturn. There were talkers in the criminal world. But when these talkers got going, they babbled incessantly about themselves and their grandiose plans. McBryde talked about trains, about Maglev. Unless he had a split personality, such naive exuberance didn't fit the profile of someone who engineered train accidents so cannily as to make them seem like acts of God or nature. Finally, she just couldn't imagine McBryde aiming a bullet up into Jackson Long's brain. She recalled a diffident man whose enthusiasm for trains made him seem like a little boy. Trying to reconcile these impressions with reality gave her a headache. She did know, however, that the thief was innocent of murder. And she would eventually have to speak out in his defense.

The accident didn't come over the wire until later that morning. The murder didn't appear in the reports until the late afternoon. No one phoned in for her reaction. Peña and Metaxas appeared to be out of the office conducting interviews. Granite was paying attention to other matters. Szczymanski was relieved. She needed time to collect herself.

That evening she met up with Chaos at The Last Drop, the coffeehouse near Dupont Circle. He was already waiting for her at the table, with a steaming glass of hot cider at one elbow and an array of pictures fanned out in front of him.

"I just picked these up at the photo lab," he said with an impish grin. The snapshots were of his family, from their youngest child's fourth birthday party. "Not bad, eh? Little Jimmy blowing out the candles. And over here, well, he dropped his piece of cake onto the rug, that's why he's crying—" Chaos stopped. "Are you okay? I didn't see you on television this morning, so I figured everything went smoothly."

"It didn't go smoothly."

"Oh." He folded his hands together and listened to her story carefully, without interrupting. When she had finished, he said, "So, you lifted the evidence."

She passed a plastic bag across the table above the now forgotten photographs. "Extraordinary cases require extraordinary measures."

Chaos shook his head, swept back his forelocks. "I hope you know what you're doing. Running the computer checks for you was one thing. But this? If they find out about this, OPR will hang us from the rafters."

"I just need a little more help. Plausible deniability. You can say you didn't know the circumstances. That you were just doing a favor for someone who didn't know the ropes."

Chaos squirmed. He collected his photos and tried to fit them back into their yellow envelope. Several fell onto the floor.

"And another thing. This Jigsaw fellow was a total bust. Worse, he was a hindrance."

"Jigsaw? Really?" Chaos looked surprised. "He's terribly competent over the phone. His algorithms are impeccable."

"I can't say anything about his algorithms," she said, her anger rising. "But I can say that he's a pillhead. And that he knows next to nothing about evidence collection. And that he's about as on-the-ball as a narcoleptic."

"Huh." Chaos exhaled. He gathered up the stray photos, adjusted his glasses. "Sorry about that. I thought he'd be a help. He's the New York office's sweeper. Very highly recommended, not just by me. But maybe he's lost his touch."

"Lost his mind. Lost his marbles. Lost his bearings. I told him that if I ever saw his face again I'd make him snort his pills two at a time." She hoped that putting Chaos on the defensive would make him more amenable to her demands. She rested her hand on the plastic bag. "Look, it's just a few checks. I need a DNA test on samples A and B. There's also a few hairs from beneath the kid's fingernails. A metal strip with numbers on it. A paper towel with some residues, maybe prints. I've written down the name and address of my primary suspect. See if any of the prints match."

"Anything else?"

"A bug."

"Dead or alive?"

"A mike."

"Why a mike?"

"I don't know. Any ideas?"

"Where was it?"

"Underneath the metal walkway between the cars."

"They wanted to listen in on the accident. Make sure it went according to plan."

"Could you send it to one of your soundmen?"

Chaos looked unhappy.

"I tell you what," Szczymanski offered. "Set it up in the computer so that the reference number reverts to mine after, say, two weeks. It will be entirely my responsibility after that."

Chaos didn't look any happier. "I can do that. But it isn't just my butt I'm worried about. You're new here. They could really jack you up over all this."

"That's the problem. They already have." But she didn't explain. She didn't want Chaos to know all the particulars. Nor at this point did he seem eager to find out. Clearly she couldn't rely on much more from him. She tried to cheer him up, wipe the vinegary expression from his face. "At least we know the pattern's good. You and your computerized partner guessed right. Where am I going next?"

"Data suggests that the next accident will be this Saturday on the Southwest Chief. You can pick the train up in Chicago on Friday evening."

She decided to be direct. "I need one more thing."

"Don't you have anything better to do than jeopardize my career?"

"This one's easy. Please, Chaos. I just need a pattern, any pattern, for freight-train accidents. The last one, I think, was in Texas, outside Dallas. Predict me something far away from there, preferably on the other coast. And give me some plausible graphs."

"I thought we were doing passenger trains."

"We are. I'll explain later. Thanks, Chaos. You're saving a lot of lives, you know that, right? There were a couple hundred people on the Lake Shore. A good number of them would've died if the train went off the bridge."

"I may be saving lives but I don't know how or why."

"In time," she soothed. "Remember, plausible deniability."

Chaos grunted. "Dallas, then somewhere out west? I'll have it tomorrow afternoon."

As she walked home from the coffeehouse, Szczymanski felt

cold and lonely. The coffee hadn't buoyed her. An icy rain drizzled down. She pulled her scarf tighter and kept her head down until her building appeared through the mist.

Her apartment was damp. It echoed. Even switching on all the lights couldn't dispel the gloom. She turned up the thermostat and lit a burner for a pot of tea. She'd spent only four nights there. The smell of the new paint still lingered in the air's upper register. Her kitchen cupboards contained a package of chamomile tea, a can of pea soup, a box of linguini, and a few lonely spices—granulated garlic, oregano, thyme. A single jar of tomato sauce occupied the refrigerator's brightly lit interior. The empty kitchen made her want to cry. She considered a trip to the supermarket for provisions. But it was too cold outside and she was too tired.

She walked through the apartment waiting for the water to boil. Her television sat unplugged on the floor in her bedroom. She still hadn't unpacked most of her boxes. A forlorn pile of books was stacked against the wall in the living room, waiting for a bookcase that she intended to buy. She pledged to herself that tomorrow she'd go out shopping after work.

The kettle whistled and she poured the boiling water into a cup. She added the tea bag. This is me, she thought wearily. I am a tea bag that the FBI is dangling in hot water. When all the flavor is gone, they'll throw me away. The image was so powerful, so depressing that she couldn't drink the tea. She left the cup in the kitchen, went into the bedroom and kicked off her shoes. Burrowing under the covers, she was asleep within seconds.

In the morning she flirted briefly with the idea of calling in sick. But she forced herself into the bathroom and under the showerhead. Damn it, where had all her resolve gone? Hiding from Granite and Peña was ridiculous. TB^2 required an offensive defense—run with the wolves, swim with the sharks, cultivate the badass within. And hell, she'd already laid the groundwork with Chaos.

At FBI headquarters she immediately arranged for another briefing session. Marching down the corridor, she felt a new energy pulsing through her. She carried the wire reports of the Lake Shore's accident.

Granite was at his desk, leafing through his correspondence. He looked up impassively at her entrance and motioned for her to sit across from him.

"Have you seen this, sir?" she asked, brandishing the wire copy.

"I can't read from this distance."

"The Albany train accident. There was a murder as well."

Granite reached over to receive the report. He read with an index finger tracing a crooked vertical line. While he was absorbing the information, Peña and Metaxas arrived and sat down on either side of Szczymanski.

"The Lake Shore?" Peña leaned over to ask Szczymanski.

She nodded.

"So," Granite said, after his finger lifted off the final page.

"So I have a suggestion, sir," Szczymanski said, before Peña could offer an opinion. "Agents Peña and Metaxas should investigate the scene of the crime. Discreetly, of course. And only in the interests of journalism."

"The *Arlington Star* would obviously be interested in the story," Peña said, deliberating. "But shouldn't the *Star*'s star reporter come along too?"

"No," Szczymanski said smoothly. Then she leaned over to tell them forcefully what she planned to do.

"Dallas?" Peña said. "Why are you going to Dallas?"

"The freight train accident out there a week ago."

"And?" Peña was all sweet-faced suspicion.

"I've been running some applications on my computer at home." If only her computer had that kind of power. "And I think I've found a pattern in the train accidents. But only in the freight trains. I think the passenger train accidents have been red herrings. But someone out there has it in for freight trains. And I'm getting close to finding out why."

"Care to tell us?" Granite asked.

"At the moment it's just a hunch, sir," Szczymanski replied, thinking to herself that it was quite a bit less than a hunch. "But I'd lay bets that one of the Class One lines is deliberately sabotaging the others."

"Wouldn't that be easy to figure out? Sixteen Class One lines and the accidents happen on all but one of them," Metaxas pointed out.

"They're more clever than that. All the roads have suffered accidents. But some accidents are less equal than others. In any case, I'll have the charts drawn up by tomorrow. In their attempt to be clever, I think they've nonetheless left behind their business card."

Granite looked dubious. "Freight trains, industrial sabotage—this sounds rather old-fashioned."

"Why don't we all go to Dallas?" Peña interjected. "Let's forget about the Lake Shore."

"No," Szczymanski said firmly. "I might be wrong. And there was, after all, a murder on the Lake Shore. Someone should definitely go up there. And you and Metaxas seem to work so well together . . ."

She caught Granite and Peña exchanging a furtive glance. A proposal to split up directly challenged their little conspiracy. Letting her venture forth independently was precisely what they didn't want. But she relied on her nominal control over the team, a privilege she hadn't asserted before. In the end, they'd let her handle Dallas by herself. But she knew that Peña and Metaxas planned to catch up with her later.

She simply wouldn't be there when they arrived.

NINETEEN

Dazed and dehydrated, McBryde fell heavily into the past. The train was still hurtling toward the Colonie Bridge, but the boy's dead body momentarily pushed all thoughts of train accidents from his head. Seeing the gun, the blood, he couldn't prevent the night in the Portland yards from closing over him. He lost all sense of time.

The thieves were back. Killing those poor dogs with the doctored steaks hadn't been enough. They were greedy, so greedy that they disregarded the danger of hitting the yards a second time. But now McBryde was there instead of the dogs. He surprised the youngest at the roundhouse window, discovered the other three trying to break into an engine. The telephone wires had already been cut. His scanner broke when he wrestled the youngest to the ground and knocked him unconscious. It would be just he against them, no chance of assistance until morning. His mind jumped over the actual killing—the pulling of the trigger, the snap of the boy's head, the second mouth that opened up at the base of his skull. But he remembered what he'd screamed at the cowering survivors: "You want to end up like him?! I'll kill you all, damn it. All of you! Get down on your stomachs. Hands behind your back!" Wild with fright and anger, he waited with them until the next shift came on, six hours later. He remembered the pain and the fear and the boredom. He remembered parts of his crazed monologue to the three teenagers lying prostrate on the pebble-strewn ground—about violence, revenge, death. And he remembered the dead body of the fourth folded haphazardly upon itself, like a piece of clothing blown off a laundry line.

The ground in front of the roundhouse turned into the carpeted floor of the Pennsy lounge. The baseball cap with the Burlington Northern patch lay upside down like a beggar's cup. The bullet wound in the boy's forehead was puckered at the edges. He was no longer bleeding. Hadn't he read somewhere that corpses never bleed? Only the living give blood.

He knew he had to move quickly. Any minute the pill man would come through the curtain, a conductor in tow, and they'd have him . . . dead to rights. He couldn't do any more for the boy. Shot in the line of duty, like that poor Czech signalman killed by the Nazis. Even in his weakened state, McBryde realized that he was being set up. Was the journalist in on it too? She had seemed all too interested in train accidents. He was stung by the possibility.

The train was still moving and he knew that it shouldn't. He grabbed at the emergency handle, a slim wooden gourd hanging by a chain. He aimed left, aimed right, finally seized it and pulled. After a moment, the train began to brake, pitching McBryde up and over the boy and slamming his back into the legs of the coffee table. The corpse rolled over to sandwich him in, the boy's slender limbs not yet stiffened by rigor mortis. The loose objects in the lounge, soap and paper towels and baseball cap and gun, flew toward them as though magnetically charged. The boy's head pressed against his chest. He tried to push the body away but couldn't overcome the inertia. The boy's hand, clenched tightly around the screwdriver, pressed against his knees. McBryde gagged.

With a gasp and a shudder, the train finally stopped—and then pitched backward in recoil. McBryde and the corpse tumbled over one another as if in play. He disengaged himself from the body and scrambled to his feet, breathless with disgust. A small spot of gray matter clung to his sweater. He swallowed hard to keep from retching, grabbed a paper towel off the floor, and rubbed at the spot, rubbed at it until only a dark smudge remained, and then flung the towel into a corner. The lights dimmed and then faded altogether.

If he acted quickly while the train was stopped, he might have a chance. He felt about on the floor, found the gun, and bolted from the lounge. The sounds of people shouting and crying came from the coach cars. The vestibule between the observation car and the coach was quiet. He moved instinctively, bumped against a person groping in the opposite direction, and continued on. In the darkness, his practiced fingers found the release mechanism that opened the door of the train. He didn't have time to bother with lowering the steps. So he simply jumped into the night air and landed on the gravel bed, almost but not quite turning an ankle.

McBryde stood shivering on the gravel separating the northbound from the southbound tracks. He wore only a thin wool sweater over his button-down shirt. He jammed the gun, safety on, into his pocket. Fortunately his scanner had somehow remained fixed to his belt. Unfortunately his phone was still in his bag—he couldn't call Jordan. And his winter coat still lay on the overhead luggage rack on the train. Too late to go back. At least the cold air was helping to clear his head. He considered running over to the highway that paralleled the tracks. But who would pick up a blood-splattered hitchhiker?

Then he saw the white flash of an oncoming train on the horizon several hundred yards to the north. It grew larger, then stopped. He guessed by its distance that the engine had pulled up alongside the Lake Shore. He imagined the engineer of the southbound train asking the Amtrak engineer if he needed any assistance. The conversation didn't last long. The Lake Shore hadn't derailed, the tracks were clear. The southbound blew its whistle and the fiery orb of its headlight began to expand. McBryde knelt down beneath the accordion diaphragm that separated the cars. As he waited for the other train to pass, he gathered his strength.

The noise of the approaching train crescendoed. With a rush of air, it passed him. He was relieved that it was a freight train. An

Amtrak train would have offered fewer opportunities for concealment. After the Conrail engines came a set of boxcars, which he
knew would be locked. Two flatbeds then rolled by, carrying railroad ties bound together like sticks. A gondola car with rock ballast.
It was still moving slowly, maybe ten miles an hour. Nailing her on
the fly wouldn't be easy. It was something he hadn't attempted since
he was fourteen.

Finally, as the hoppers began to pass, he decided to take his
chances. He pushed off, started to pump his arms and legs, felt
exhilarated. Cold air poured into his lungs. His feet kicked up
the gravel of the bed. He knew he should be running faster, that the
drug was slowing him down. But he pressed on. He reached for
the ladder on the side of an open hopper, grasped it, but a jolt of the
train made him lose his grip. He fell back a few steps, slowed down
to a jog to let another boxcar go by. Then, determined, he pulled up
level with the next hopper. He wanted to scream, it felt so good to
be running, to be running away. Breathing hard, he grabbed a metal
supporting rod at the end of the car and hoisted himself up onto a
narrow ledge running the length of the hopper.

It was a precarious position, the toes of his shoes balanced on
only several inches of support. He was at one end, the ladder a full
car length away. The freight train began to pick up speed and the
wind was blowing hard in his face. He pressed his body between the
raised vertical seams of the car, his hands now holding on to these
corrugations. His cheek felt cold against the rough metal, and his
belt buckle pinched into his stomach. He felt the gun in his pocket.
His chest heaved. One slip and he'd fall under the wheels.

Mustering his remaining energy, he inched along the side of the
hopper, clinging like a rock climber to a cliff face, his hands reaching for the metal seams one by one, his feet shuffling along. The
wind tried to peel him off. As the train gained speed, the cars began
to sway back and forth, "walking the dog," as the old-time rails
called it. He hugged the hopper fiercely, tried to flatten himself into
its side. At last he reached the ladder and began to climb. At the top
of the huge steel container, his foot slipped and he tottered crazily
on the lip. But some survival instinct pitched him over the top rather
than down to his death on the ties.

On his hands and knees inside the hopper, McBryde drew in

several rasps of air, his ribs pressing against his chest. What had earlier felt exhilarating was now simply painful. He was too old to be jumping a freight train.

When his breathing became less strained, he took stock of his surroundings. It was a twin offset side steel hopper, roughly thirty-five feet long, with sloped plates inside that served to funnel its load through the chutes at the bottom. He'd expected junk metal or odd pieces of wood, the sort that open hoppers usually carried. Instead he found himself kneeling on a sheet of thick black plastic held down by a few sizable rocks. Finding a seam in the plastic, he slipped his hand inside and discovered a soft, granular substance underneath. He withdrew a pinch between his thumb and forefinger. In the murkiness of the hopper, the only light provided by an occasional highway arc lamp that lit up the space like a flashbulb, the substance between his fingers resembled gray silt. By its silicate sparkle, he guessed it to be sand. Anything more valuable would have gone in a sealed hopper.

Although the hopper lacked a top, its sides kept the wind out. Still, the night's temperature had fallen to near freezing. McBryde's hands were already stiff. If he slept exposed, with only his thin sweater and pants for protection, he'd die of hypothermia.

If the cold didn't get him, the police undoubtedly would.

With numb fingertips, McBryde turned on his scanner and adjusted the frequency knob until he picked up the freight's engineer. For a few minutes, he let the voices from the CB keep him company. In all the chatter about the stalled Amtrak train, neither the engineer nor the fireman nor the stationmaster mentioned a runaway suspect. He turned it off, reluctant to lose the voices but conscious of the need to save the batteries. It would take some time for the police to arrive at the Lake Shore. The pillhead (and his journalist accomplice?) would tell them everything, finger him for the murder. First the police would search the train, then everywhere around the train. It wouldn't take them long to figure out that he'd escaped not into the surrounding countryside but onto the train that had met the Lake Shore ten miles north of Albany. They would know about his scanner. Deliberately staying off the radio waves, they'd be waiting at an upcoming station, flashlights held ready for a systematic search. What then: Prison? Visits from Melissa, packages from Rosalind? Endless hearings to prove his innocence? His life ruined. He pulled the gun from his pocket. It had brought him only bad luck. He threw it into a corner of the hopper.

There was no point worrying about the future when the present offered enough challenges. He certainly didn't want to jump off the moving train. His mind had no difficulty culling rationales. It was cold, dark, and late. The police would be understaffed. They'd give up trying to find him at night. When someone remembered the freight train the next morning, he'd already be safely delivered southward. Most critically, despite his aerobic escape, enough of the drug remained in his blood supply to make his limbs uncooperative, his brain still sluggish. Even if he jumped from the hopper he wouldn't have enough energy to find a warm place to sleep. He'd die of exposure along the tracks. Better to die on a train. The hopper made for a roomy coffin.

He was no lover of the outdoors, had gone camping only under duress. Nevertheless, before sleep completely seduced him, a few survival tips bobbed to the surface of his mind. He moved several stones aside and gathered up a portion of the black plastic to fold it over. Then, using his hand as a trowel, he began to dig, scooping out the sand and piling it to one side. The finely granulated material refused to accumulate neatly and streamed back into any hole he tried to create. But a shallow depression was all he needed.

He tore out two large plastic sections, shaped one into a pillow, and laid the other at the bottom of the trench. Lying down on his side with a corner of the plastic in one hand, he rolled over in the trench and wrapped himself up like a pig in a blanket. He kept his other arm free by extending it above his head. Secure in his plastic blanket, he used his free arm to sweep the sand over his body, starting in a sitting position with his feet and legs and then, as he lowered himself backward, over his torso and finally across his chest. He made sure to get several inches of the material over his body as insulation. Then, his arm still free, he put the plastic pillow into place beneath his head. His neck and head were uncovered—no chance of suffocation. He finished by burrowing his free arm into the sand.

He was now encased. Like an Egyptian king. Like a bug in amber. It would take time for his body heat to warm up the area enclosed by the plastic. Considering the circumstances, he was making out quite well. Indeed, he had spent far worse nights on trains, vainly trying to get comfortable in the reclining seats of the coach cars.

Now that he was settled, he could think back on what had happened on the Lake Shore. That poor boy. It reminded him of the terrible scene from *The Octopus*. Near the beginning of the book, a train barreled through a lost flock of sheep, snapping their backs, throwing them against a barbed-wire fence. Their blood glistened black in the moonlight. But it wasn't the Lake Shore that killed the young foamer. That bullet had probably been meant for McBryde. The boy was a warning, a sad, terrible sign, an innocent slaughtered so that the guilty could continue with their crimes.

He tried to reconstruct the scene from the bathroom but couldn't. The exhausting tension of the day and the lingering effects of the drug combined to send him quickly into a dreamless stupor.

McBryde awoke to the rushing sound of his wildly pumping heart. His ears reverberated with the noise. It was dark, the air thick. His limbs were immobile and he had difficulty breathing. He braced himself for the explosion. Then, just as he was about to scream, he felt the plastic rubbing against his lips. And he remembered: he had dug his bed in the sand and now he was lying in it.

Somehow in the course of the night he had managed to insert his head into his plastic pillow. He unearthed an arm and cleared the plastic off his face. The sky was a dazzling blue rectangle above him. The train was passing rapidly beneath a dense crosshatching of high-tension wires. He swept aside the sand and kicked himself free of his black plastic wrap. His body was sore but intact. The sand had found its way into his clothes, rubbed unpleasantly against his skin, collected in his shoes, gathered in his mouth. No matter—it had saved his life. He got to his feet and flapped his arms to circulate the blood more evenly through his body. Sand trickled from every crease of clothing.

As he peered over the lip of the hopper, a gust of cold air eliminated the last vestiges of his drowsiness. The sun sat low on the horizon on a bed of pink clouds. It was still early morning, barely past dawn. He instantly recognized the skyline in the distance. The train was just now passing through the low, marshy land that fringed the South Bronx. Ahead the apartment buildings of the Upper East Side were framed against the midtown skyscrapers. To his right, the Harlem River sparkled in the sunlight. On his left, cars kept pace with the train along a freeway lined with low-rise apartment buildings. McBryde considered jumping down into the mud and weeds separating the tracks from the river. But it was too risky. The train was still moving rapidly, and in his weakened state he might easily break a few bones. He squatted down on the sand to escape the cold morning wind and plot a strategy. The train was probably bound for Queens, perhaps farther out to Long Island. Had the police figured out where he was yet? Would the Queens yards be safe? He spent some minutes trying to remember the geography of Queens.

When he returned to the lip of the hopper, however, he learned that the train was not heading for Queens. Having cleared the South Bronx and bridged the Harlem River, the freight was now making its way down the East Side of Manhattan. A hot, sick feeling crept into his stomach. It didn't make sense. Freights were never routed to Grand Central Terminal.

McBryde found the scanner where it had slipped beneath the plastic. After listening for several minutes, he pieced together the story: the freight was carrying construction materials needed for a "renovation project." That sounded unlikely. Why would they need sand from upstate New York for their "project"? Even if the police were not rerouting the train to make capture easier, Grand Central was not the ideal place to elude detection. Extra details would be posted at the train and bus stations in the city, the police expecting him to move southward on the way back to Philadelphia. He remembered Gregory Peck outsmarting his pursuers at Grand Central in *Spellbound,* Cary Grant dressing up as a porter to fool the cops at Chicago's Union Station in *North by Northwest.* Looked great in the movies, never happened in real life. Better if the train were going to the anonymous yards in Queens.

McBryde got back to his feet. By the time he picked out a street sign amid the dazzle of city sights, it was already 105th Street. The train entered the tunnel at Ninety-seventh Street and everything turned black. The smell of diesel exhaust hung in the air, stifling in the confined space. His eyes grew accustomed to the shades of darkness. Sodium vapor lamps, spaced at intervals along the side of the tunnel, cast an eerie orange glow on the sand in the hopper.

Even in the dim light of the vapor lamps he could see that he was a mess, his sweater and pants smeared with blood, sand clinging to him in patches. He looked like an imperfectly breaded cutlet. He was sure that his face, dirty and perhaps blood-streaked, was a fugitive's. He was determined not to make such a nicely wrapped present of himself. He wouldn't wait for the train to deposit him in the hands of the police; he'd abandon the unit at the first opportunity. But how would he navigate his way out of the tunnels?

Then, from the archives of railroadiana stored in his head, McBryde remembered a way out. He wasn't exactly sure of its location, and it might be locked. But it was worth a shot. He began counting the seconds and gauging the train's speed.

After eight minutes in the tunnel beneath Manhattan, the freight train stopped. From the scanner McBryde learned that the engineer was waiting for the congestion at the terminal to subside. He stood up to take his bearings. Eight minutes at roughly fifteen miles an hour would put the train a little more than two miles into Manhattan. If they entered the tunnel at Ninety-seventh Street and twenty blocks equaled a mile, then they were roughly beneath Park Avenue and Fiftieth Street. Perfect.

McBryde didn't wait for the highball signal that would have set the train in motion again. He retrieved his gun and shook the sand from it, then carefully climbed down to the tracks. Seconds after he left the hopper, the freight train shuddered and came to life. He waited for the dozen cars to pass him by. Lumbering slowly through the tunnel like elephants attached trunk to tail, the train finally passed out of sight. McBryde was alone in the murky orange-tinted darkness.

There were four sets of tracks, two northbound and two southbound. Rusted steel I-beams separated the traffic. Illegible graffiti and occasional electrical warning signs decorated the pitted rock walls. It was cold in the tunnel, almost as cold as the outside. McBryde leaned against a column and trembled in his light clothes.

As part of his job, McBryde frequently accompanied repair crews into the trolley tunnels of West Philadelphia or the knot of subway lines beneath City Hall. He loathed the image of a bureaucrat sitting in an office, receiving and passing on papers, like some organ in a constipated digestive system. He craved action, wanted to be part of the solution, wanted to help the crews with their job both on the ground and beneath it. Then, at public meetings, he could stand up and say that he personally had helped distribute rat poison along the Broad Street Line or that the repair work on the Malvern route was proceeding as rapidly and as safely as humanly possible. On these trips through the tunnels, McBryde always joined a knowledgeable, fully equipped team. Now he was alone, without a flashlight, ear guards, or even a warm coat.

He faced southward, toward the Terminal. Somewhere in the next five blocks, among all the branch tunnels and steam tunnels and old luggage tunnels, was a private siding that was no longer used. Finding it would require patience. And luck.

He kept to the middle of the northbound track, placing his feet carefully on the wooden ties. He eyed the third rail, kept his distance from that poisonous snake. The vapor lamps provided a darkroom glow. They were interspersed with an occasional blue light, which indicated a link to the security system. Signs with white and black horizontal stripes marked indentations in the tunnel wall where repair workers could take shelter from passing trains. The air smelled of chalk, wet wood, and sewage. His breathing resonated in the narrow space, set off against the distant rumble of rolling stock, the trickle of water, and the rustling of what he feared were hungry rodents.

After he'd gone a mere twenty feet, McBryde detected a change in the register of the distant rumble. A train was approaching. At first he couldn't determine its direction because the growing roar was all-encompassing. The steel girders in the center would provide enough protection, but still he made for the nearest black-and-white sign. A cool whisper of air touched his face and he knew the train was heading away from the station. He crouched in the recess amid the mud and broken pieces of wood, covering his ears to the sound.

The train arrived with a noise and a violence that even McBryde, who had spent a lifetime around trains, found unsettling. The tunnel amplified the sounds to a deafening crescendo and this time his ears were unprotected. The swirling light from the headlamp cast monstrously elongated shadows on the tunnel walls. He stared up in horror as the lighted windows of the Metro North commuter flashed by him. In the train's wake, a tornado wind generated a cloud of dust and ephemera that took several minutes to subside.

After the dust settled, McBryde stood up slowly and shakily. He could finally sympathize with nineteenth-century cranks like Ruskin and Thoreau who likened trains to hellhounds that snorted fire and brimstone and disrupted poets on peaceful country picnics. Another fast train and he would lose all composure, forget which direction he was heading. He had maybe thirty minutes before the traffic of morning rush hour became relentless.

Near the recess, in the ghostly light, he found an unsecured drainage grate. He pushed it aside with his foot, dropped in the gun, listened for the splash. With the weapon missing, the case against him would be more difficult to prove.

After another fifty feet, he came across a switch and a branching tunnel. The siding he wanted would, like this one, veer off to the east. But was he close enough to the Terminal? Poking his foot at the switch to test its age, he realized the naïveté of his search. To find an old private siding amid the maze of tunnels beneath Grand Central was a Herculean task. He peered down the dark branch tunnel, hoping for a posted sign or some indication of its use.

"Hey!"

The sound reverberated throughout the tunnel, surrounding McBryde. He took a step backward, scared and confused, and slipped on a rail. He fell with a gasp onto a tie.

"Hey!"

This time the voice was accompanied by a light. They both came out of the darkness of the branch tunnel.

"What the hell are you doing here?"

His tailbone felt cracked open like an egg. Painfully getting to his feet, McBryde shielded his eyes from the glare of the light. He couldn't see a thing. He massaged the base of his spine, found nothing broken. "Sorry, I—I must be lost." He immediately regretted the excuse. It sounded absurd in a train tunnel beneath Manhattan.

"Speak up, I can't hear you."

"I mean no harm," McBryde said loudly but plaintively.

"You're in my tunnel," the voice said, keeping the beam of light fixed on McBryde's face. "I don't recognize you. You're not Metro North."

"I—I don't work for any of the lines here."

"Then how in hell you get down here?" The voice was gruff. "You one of them kids? Them graffiti kids?"

McBryde shook his head. He had a sudden inspiration. "I'm a journalist."

"Speak up! I can't hear so good."

"I'm a journalist looking for an old siding. Used to be around here somewhere." He gestured vaguely with the hand that wasn't shielding his eyes.

"I'm not crazy about journalists." The voice became canny. "I'm not gonna give you my name, understand?"

McBryde nodded. "Of course not."

"You don't look like no policeman." The light wandered from McBryde's face down his body. "Looks like you been in some kinda mix-up."

McBryde remembered the blood. "I guess I fell a couple times back there. Got kind of dirty."

"Course you fell. 'Less you know where you're going, you're gonna get hurt." The voice shifted from suspicion to resignation. "Sheesh. Just follow me, okay?"

The light swung around in an arc, exposing the graffiti on the wall before boring into the darkness of the branch tunnel. McBryde now saw a man illuminated in outline, his back a silhouette. Small to begin with, the man was also slightly hunched over. He strode with confidence into the tunnel, swaying from side to side. McBryde followed warily.

The tunnel stretched for about twenty yards before banking sharply to the right. After clearing the curve, the tracks stopped. The flashlight beam picked out the end of the tunnel—a wall hung with bright pictures. The light blinked off and darkness again swept over them. When the man reappeared, he stood beside a lamp. Its light revealed an extraordinary scene.

McBryde found himself in a space the size of a modest studio apartment set up between the end of the tracks and the branch tunnel's terminal wall. The little apartment contained a mattress propped up on concrete blocks, a chest of drawers, a hard-back chair with a cane-rush seat, a bookshelf of bricks and plywood packed tightly with paperbacks and magazines, and even a threadbare area rug with an indistinct pattern. The pictures that he had glimpsed on the back wall were advertisements torn from glossy magazines and chosen, it seemed, for their bright colors—green salads, violet convertibles, flaming-pink bungalows, models in pastel bathing suits posing against lush forest backdrops.

The small man fingered his flashlight, his eyes darting from side to side as if making an inventory of his living space. His face and hands were dark from soot. A full beard filled his face like a wild hedge. His hair was a tangle of matted curls. His multiple layers of clothes ended in a dirty red down vest and oversized army surplus pants with their cuffs stuffed into combat boots.

McBryde stood in wonderment at this unexpected alcove of civilization. The man pointed to the single chair. "Sit down, okay? I was just fixing to have some breakfast when I heard you out there. Hungry?"

McBryde slowly nodded his head. Suddenly he was starving. Along with his coat and bag, he had left several undigested meals on the train. "The electricity . . ." he wondered out loud, sitting down.

"Tapped into an auxiliary line," the man said. He squatted over a hot plate with three burners, juggling a kettle, a frying pan, and a saucepan. He added some ingredients to the cookware and within seconds the aroma of sizzling butter filled the space.

"How long have you—" McBryde began.

"Eggs and beans," the man interrupted. He cracked four eggs into the frying pan and, without looking up, flipped the shells against the wall beneath the advertisements and into a box at its base.

McBryde listened to the reassuring sizzle of eggs being fried. The room wasn't nearly as cold as the tunnel. Then he saw the orange-red coils of a space heater, angled toward the bed. It reminded him of descriptions of the 1930s, the hobos sharing a meal at an encampment by the rails. Except that they were underground, beneath the midtown bustle of Manhattan, and instead of a campfire they had a space heater and a hot plate. A chipped plate with two fried eggs next to a hillock of pork and beans was pushed into his hands.

"Coffee'll be ready for after we finish." The man, still hunched over as though expecting a blow, took his plate over to his bed, where he unlaced his combat boots, set them carefully on the carpet, and dangled his feet in the path of the heater. He set to work on his breakfast, lingering over every forkful. When he had finished, he swirled his dirty index finger in the yellow-and-brown sauce and poked it in his mouth.

McBryde, too, found the meal profoundly satisfying, though it tasted of rancid butter and diesel oil, and he couldn't help but wondering how (or if) the man cleaned his dishes. "How long have you been—"

Again the man interrupted. "Look, journalist, you ain't writing about this." It was a statement, not a question.

"Of course not," McBryde said. "I'm just looking for a private siding that used to be down here. Maybe you know where it is."

"Private siding," the man repeated. "There's a lotta tunnels down here. Right now we're five blocks from Central. Closer up, there's a bunch more."

McBryde became aware of another train approaching, its initial roar like that of an insect near his ear but the noise growing rapidly to become an angry swarm. The light from its headlamp played briefly on the wall at the beginning of the branch tunnel. And then it was gone, its pitch receding.

"How do you . . ."

"Gotten so I don't even notice 'em anymore. What you lookin' for exactly?"

"A siding," McBryde said. "The Waldorf-Astoria once had a private siding off these tracks. That way they could bring FDR straight up to his hotel suite."

The little man showed his black-and-yellow teeth. "Oh, that's rich, I like that! FDR—that was the one in the wheelchair, right? Took him right up to the, what you call it, penthouse? Now they just fly 'em in by helicopter."

"Limousine, probably."

"Helicopter," he repeated. "The penthouses are way up there on top. Limousines just wouldn't do it." He went on a coughing jag that rattled his slight frame. When he finally stopped he said, "Wouldn't want to live in no penthouse. Sway back and forth up there, like living in a tree."

"The Waldorf-Astoria," McBryde prompted, worried that the man might have tuberculosis or something equally communicable.

"Yeah, I think I know what you're looking for." He picked up the flashlight and beckoned for McBryde to follow him back to the main tracks. As they rounded the curve, the light from the apartment gradually faded and then disappeared. The little man turned on the flashlight and gestured with it down the southbound tracks.

"There's a tunnel up ahead, the third one down. It's boarded up but the boards at the bottom are loose. Push 'em up and crawl on through. Go to the end of the tracks, maybe twenty yards. There'll be a door, an old sign next to it. Maybe it says something about a hotel."

"But maybe not?"

"When I first got there, there was some red carpet. Waited too long. Gone now." He began down the tracks. "I'll go with you a ways."

They walked in silence for several minutes.

The man cleared his throat. "How come you know about this siding, huh?"

"I know a little bit about trains."

"Oh yeah? When they build this Grand Central?"

"1913."

"Good. When they tear down the old Penn Station?"

"1963."

"Guess you do know a little," the man conceded. "Journalists usually don't know nothing."

Again they walked in silence. The man pointed out a tunnel branching off to the right. "That's where the Burnhams live. Nice folks. Sometimes play their music too loud, though."

"You're down here all day?"

"Oh, I work, if that's what you mean. Up there I deliver newspapers. Early in the morning in a van with some others. I was just getting home when I heard you rustling 'round like some big rat. It's good money. Long as you don't have to pay rent. Don't know what I'd do if I had to pay rent."

"It seems comfortable," McBryde said politely, amazed at this new world.

"Comfortable?" the little man snorted. "Fuck comfortable. We didn't choose to live here, okay? There wasn't no ad in the papers. Find me something better, I'm there, understand?"

"Of course." McBryde was at a loss for words. "I just meant . . ."

"I know you just meant. Next thing I know, the city's going to send all of us down here. Pack us in. Keep us out of the way, off the streets, away from respectable folks. And when they run out of room in the tunnels, they'll just dig down deeper. I don't want to see none of this in the papers, okay? I don't want to be up there on the job and see any headlines about us. Burnhams are the closest neighbors. Once or twice had to tell 'em to turn the damn music down. It's already too crowded down here."

"Don't worry. Just looking for that siding." McBryde thought about when the railroads pushed westward and opened land to the settlers. See the smoke from your neighbor's chimney, the old saying went, and it was time to move on. He should have said he was a historian. No one liked journalists.

"This is it." The man pointed with the flashlight. "If'n I see any of this in the headlines, I'll know who to go after. Remember, I'm in the newspaper business too. I got connections."

The light swung around and the hunched man left McBryde alone in the murkiness of the main tunnel with only the sodium vapor lamps for illumination. His departure was so sudden that McBryde didn't think to ask for the loan of the flashlight, to ask if the door at the end of the siding was locked. He would have made a lousy journalist. But then, his impersonation of a private detective wasn't Oscar material either.

He stood before the branching tracks. Several large pieces of plywood indeed prevented access to the tunnel. But, as the little man had promised, the boards at the bottom could be pushed aside. McBryde crawled through on his hands and knees, carefully, since the ground was littered with sharp little stones and minute shards of glass and metal. Now he was in utter darkness, without even the minimal glow of the orange lamps. He got to his feet, disoriented without visual clues. First to one side and then to the other, McBryde reached out a hand to determine the location of the walls. With only one set of tracks, the narrow tunnel spanned just fifteen feet or so. The rock faces were moist to the touch. He took a step forward and heard the sound of scurrying. Ordinarily not afraid of rats, he suddenly flashed on an image of a sea of swarming, furry bodies. His stomach churned. They only go where the food is, he tried to reassure himself, and there's no food here. Except me.

Slowly, and with his jaw clenched tight, McBryde followed the tracks. Whenever his foot touched the rail, he adjusted his trajectory, always trying to stay in the center of the ties. His ears seemed unnaturally sensitive, picking up the slightest sounds of motion. He kept his arms moving in front of him, desperately hoping that they would not encounter anything animate. He kept his eyes firmly shut. He pretended to play blindman's buff. At intervals, the idea that something lurked in the tunnel seized hold of him and he had to stop, wait for his heartbeat to subside and his body to untense. He opened his eyes to stare into the darkness but saw nothing. When he wiped away the cold sweat from his forehead, he found the touch of his own unseen hand unnerving.

I am the master of my own fate, he said to himself.

So argued *Accentuate the Positive.* Nothing lies beyond the reader's capabilities. The book's examples included: demanding a promotion from a boss; winning a tennis match after dropping the first set; and asking an attractive person out on a date. McBryde was his own boss, hated tennis, and the most attractive woman he had recently met may very well have collaborated in setting him up. Why couldn't the book advise on more relevant challenges—such as navigating through a pitch-black, rat-infested tunnel toward a door that in all probability would be locked? He had to stop again, this time to shake the fear out of his arms. "Center down," the book recommended for crisis situations. What did that mean exactly? Avoid vomiting, he decided.

Of all the items he'd left behind on the train, he missed *Accentuate the Positive* the least.

He stubbed his foot against a wall. The tracks had ended. The wall, rising chest-high, led onto a concrete floor. His fingers fluttered across the surface of the platform in front of him—pebbles, scraps of paper, a piece of some kind of fabric. The red carpet that the little man had promised? McBryde carefully lifted himself up onto the platform. The footing was safe. He slowly windmilled his arms to find another wall, but encountered nothing. Arms flying out in front of him, McBryde kept moving in what he thought was the direction of the mysterious door, hoping that he hadn't turned himself around in confusion.

"Find me a door," he said softly to himself. His voice was surprisingly reassuring. It was much better than fumbling around in the silence.

"Is it here?" he asked, remembering the game he played with his daughter. "Is my little princess over here?"

He reached the jagged ridges of the rocks on the far wall. No door interrupted the surface. He began to trace the wall back to his right.

"Or is my little princess over here?"

After dancing along a stretch of rock, his fingers finally found something different: wires. They protruded from a silver-dollar-shaped hole several inches above his head. A light fixture? He proceeded carefully, his left arm ranging lightly across the wall, his right arm waving in front of him to detect any barriers.

"Keep going," he urged himself, no longer certain whether his words were spoken or only thought.

His feet stopped short, and he nearly fell over the steps. He maneuvered around to where the steps began and slowly climbed them. Three broad steps. That led to his door, a double door, like the entrance to a stateroom. It felt like a heavy wood, oak perhaps, with cold metal fittings. He tried both knobs and nearly cried. They were locked. He rattled them. Firmly locked. His fingers found the chain and the padlock. With a sudden rage he yanked at the doorknobs.

And plucked both doors from their hinges.

As the doors clattered to either side of the stairs, McBryde toppled backward and somersaulted once before landing upright on his knees. It took a few seconds for him to realize what had happened. The back of his head throbbed from where it had hit the platform and his neck felt wrenched out of place. His tailbone had taken a second beating. He dusted himself off, felt for other injuries, and waited for the pulsing pain at the back of his head to subside.

The darkness had not diminished when he opened the double doors. The passageway on the other side was evidently as dark as the tunnel. He made his way back up the stairs and felt around inside the foyer. A large metal grille seemed to indicate an elevator. To its side was a narrow staircase. There were handrails on both sides.

He climbed for what seemed a good ten minutes, pausing to catch his breath and to feel for a door whenever the step lengthened into a landing. It felt odd to walk up flights of stairs in the dark. At certain points, he forgot whether he was ascending or descending, the actions of his feet seemed so removed from his sense of motion through space. Flashlight? Hell, why hadn't he just asked the little fellow for his favorite escape route? McBryde would have hit out in frustration if he could just have seen what he was hitting.

Finally he reached a plateau from which he could climb no farther. Another double door materialized in front of him, outlined in yellow light. He tried the knobs but they wouldn't turn. Bracing himself, he tried to pull the doors from the frame. But they remained set.

For the first time he contemplated the horror of retracing his steps—of descending the steps, lowering himself down onto the tracks, making his way back to the barricade, and crawling through to the main tunnel. The prospect of all that backtracking suddenly made him furious and desperate. He grabbed hold of the doorknobs and shook them, pulled at them, tried to tear them from the door. The yellow rectangle taunted him. It seemed as though he grappled with the two knobs for at least an hour before finally hearing the voices. And the movement of what seemed to be a heavy object. At first he worried that the noises all issued from his own throat. Only gradually did they resolve into external sounds.

"I know, Arnold, just stay back," a female voice said. "I'm sure it's nothing. Don't be silly, it's not ghosts. Go lie down. Can you hear me?"

This last line seemed to be directed to McBryde. He unclenched the doorknobs and composed himself.

The female voice sounded flat, Missouri-ish. "Can you hear me out there?"

"Plumber," he said, feeling foolish.

"What's that?"

"I'm the plumber. I've been looking at the pipes."

"The plumber? Well, how 'bout that, Arnold? A plumber! Didn't think places like this had plumbers. Bet you didn't know this entrance was blocked. We had to push this big old thing out of the way. Poor Arnold! He nearly threw his back out. He's lying on the bed now. It's his sciatica. Now, how come you just didn't come on through the front?"

"Pipes were over here," he replied. "No other access."

The woman clucked her tongue against the roof of her mouth. "Well, you might've just knocked, you know. Let's see if our key works."

"We've had a complaint," he extemporized. "If we don't flush the pipes, the toilets will back up."

"Oh!" the woman gasped. Her key rattled more vigorously in the lock. "You hear that, Arnold?"

The man's response was indistinct. The key continued to rattle in the keyhole. McBryde held his breath. What elaborate excuse would he use if it didn't work and she phoned the management? Before he had to fabricate another identity, however, the key turned in the lock and the doors opened into the room. The light and color dazzled. Everything appeared as if overexposed. McBryde stepped back, throwing an arm in front of his eyes.

"Hello, Mr. Plumber!" the woman greeted him.

He managed, by squinting, to remove his arm and consider the scene. The woman stood in front of him, arms akimbo. She was a big woman in a simple woolen dress with a rope of pearls around her neck. Her hair was done up in pink rollers. Beyond her stretched a plush suite dominated by a canopied bed, which in turn was overwhelmed by a hefty man propped up by an improbable number of pillows. She caught McBryde looking at the pearls.

"They're not real, if you gotta know," she confided. "Folks around here dress up for breakfast?"

"Some folks," he mumbled.

"Where are your tools?" the woman asked, looking him up and down.

"I've left them down there, ma'am." McBryde gestured behind him. "With the pipes."

"You're awful . . . dusty," she observed.

"Pipe burst," he replied quickly. "Lots of rust." He hoped that would account for the bloodstains.

"Let the man in already, dear," the man on the bed urged. "The sooner he does what he has to do, the faster he can leave."

"It's our fortieth," the woman explained in a stage whisper. "Our children and grandchildren gave us a whole week at the Astoria. Ain't that grand?"

"Congratulations."

"Martha," the husband said. "We wanta catch the early Circle Line."

Martha looked at McBryde closely, as though suddenly doubting his profession. "What is it exactly you gotta do?"

"Adjustments," he said. "In your bathroom. Take just a minute." Suddenly inspired, he held up his scanner. "Then I'll call down to my assistant and he'll fix everything on his end."

"Dear?" The man was attempting to roll over onto his side but, like a flipped cockroach, couldn't manage the feat. "Just show him the bathroom."

She flew to her husband's assistance, tugging here and there at the pillows in an attempt to distract him from his pain. McBryde took a tentative step into the room. His feet sank luxuriously into the plush carpet. He soaked in the room's warmth and the woman's powder-fresh scent. He gazed down at himself. He was filthy, streaked with soot and dirt and blood and caked-in sand.

"Okay, Mr. Plumber, why don'tcha just get to work," Martha cried, wrestling with the pillows. She pointed. "The bathroom's over there."

He tramped into the bathroom, closed the door behind him, and locked it. It was enormous, as large as his own living room, the bathtub alone designed for a family of four. He avoided looking at himself in the full-length gilt-edged mirror. Picking up a heavy hairbrush, he knelt down beneath the sink and rapped on the curved pipes beneath. He repeated this motion for thirty seconds, varying the rhythm and trying to give the impression of a plumber at work.

"Gotta check your water pressure," he called out.

Then he turned on the shower, stripped off his clothes, and quickly but thoroughly washed himself. Afterward, staring at himself in the mirror, he saw that despite all of the terrors of the previous night his face seemed rejuvenated. Gone were the puffiness, the lines of anxiety. With all the grime of the tunnels removed, he looked lean, purposive.

The woman knocked on the door. "Everything . . . okay?"

"Your toilet's in bad shape," he replied, looking around for different clothes to put on. He found only a pair of slightly damp socks. "Give me another ten minutes."

Using the running water in the sink to disguise his actions, he brushed his teeth with a borrowed brush, deodorized his armpits with a borrowed stick of musk, and even sprinkled his feet from a borrowed container of baby powder. He felt a sting of guilt for abusing the hospitality of these unsuspecting tourists. But necessity bred contempt (was that the expression?) and he just didn't have time for remorse. He put on his still reasonably clean shirt and, leaving aside his briefs, very carefully eased into his pants. Since they were both filthy and bloody, the pants remained a problem. New Yorkers would perhaps see them as a fashion statement. But his trip back to Philly was another matter. He picked up the hairbrush, gave the plumbing another few whacks, considered the problem. He looked into his wallet—thirty-three dollars. He had intended to visit a cash machine at Penn Station but never had the time. Now he was in a bind—that money had to get him back to Philly. Using a credit card to buy a coat was too risky. The police might have already frozen his account. No, he had to be more resourceful.

He would find the nearest coffee shop, sit down facing the entrance, watch the customers coming in, and record who was wearing what as they hung their coats on the rack near the door. When someone went to the bathroom, he'd drop a dollar on the counter next to his coffee cup, walk casually over to the rack, and take the man's coat (calf-length and fur-lined would be best). Properly outfitted and disguised, he'd grab a PATH to Newark and only then take the local trains back to Philly.

He slipped out of the bathroom, carrying his sweater in his hands but leaving his undergarments behind in a ball in the closet. Martha waited for him with her hands resting on her hips. She looked surprised at his clean appearance but didn't say anything.

He closed the bathroom door and shook his head sadly. "Don't go in there, it's not pretty. I'm going to talk with the super and then come back to do the final adjustments."

She looked queasy. "Does this always happen at the Astoria?" she asked. "Our son told us this was the best place in town."

"Back in a jiff."

Clean and confident, he glided over to the Waldorf-Astoria elevator. The doors opened and he was suddenly facing a manager in a blue serge suit and silver name tag. McBryde swallowed with difficulty.

"Can I help you?" the manager asked, an edge to his voice. Tight-lipped, he looked McBryde up and down.

"No," McBryde said, reviving. "Can I help *you?*"

They stared at each other for a moment, McBryde resisting the urge to bolt for the stairway. Finally he willed himself to step into the elevator. "Lobby," he announced confidently. "Please."

The manager looked unconvinced, but depressed the lobby button.

While the manager conferred with the desk clerk, McBryde walked authoritatively across the lobby's mosaic floor and pushed his way out the heavy revolving doors. On Forty-second Street, he found an appropriate coffee shop and in less than twenty minutes had successfully enacted his plan.

On the train back to Philadelphia, a lovely London Fog coat concealing his dirty pants and keeping him exquisitely warm, he read through all the newspapers he could find. But they didn't report on the Lake Shore murder. He'd have to wait for the later editions.

Putting the newspapers aside, McBryde reflected on how well he had handled the adversities of the previous twenty-four hours. He'd been worrying about growing soft, about sinking into the mediocrity of middle age. The enthusiasms and excitements of his youth were palling and all the color seemed to be leaching out of his body. His increasing indifference toward trains was only one aspect of the transformation. He feared that one morning he would look at himself in the mirror and a white grub would stare back.

But, he chuckled to himself, white grubs don't prevent train accidents, survive a frigid night in a hopper car, crawl through the tunnels of Manhattan, pull off a masquerade of both a journalist and a plumber, and pluck an expensive London Fog from a coffee-shop coatrack right under the eyes of the proprietor. His little adventure had provided the confidence-building of a week-long Outward Bound course. He didn't need self-help books. He just needed to rise to a challenge.

He felt so good about himself that it was only when he stood on the street outside his apartment building that he again remembered the police. They hadn't hassled him in New York, hadn't been on the trains back to Philly. McBryde looked up and down the street. No cop cars patrolled the block. He could see through the curtains into his living room, and it appeared empty. He threw a pebble against the glass and waited. No one came to look out. He tried this several more times before deciding to take the risk.

His apartment was indeed empty. It was almost disappointing. A red light flashed on his answering machine. He automatically hit the "playback" button.

"Uh, yeah, Larry? This is Harold, you know, from the group. There's, uh, an excursion next weekend. The Stoney Creek Ramble. My records show that you haven't bought a ticket yet. Should I save you one? They're going fast."

Beep.

"Larry, time to cash in the favor. We'll cover you next weekend. But you have to take Melissa beginning Thursday night the following week. Okay?"

Beep.

"Larry, man, the report just came in on the scanner. I hope you're okay, buddy. I'm a little worried. There was some code in there about a casualty, but maybe I misheard. No accident was reported. Very strange. Give me a call as soon as you get in?"

Beep.

"Larry, this is your mother. I was just calling to see how you are. It's not an emergency. The weather report says there's a cold front on the East Coast. Are you warm enough in your apartment? We love you!"

Beep.

"Larry, it's Monday, it's nine-thirty and it's Luke. Hey, it's chaos down here at the office. The phones are ringing off the hook and I . . . I'm not sure how to handle all this. The boycott began this morning down in Ward One. And it's spreading. They're forming human chains around the buses and they're not letting them move, it's a fucking nightmare. We need help. I know it's your vacation, but . . . yeah, yeah, I'll talk to you in a sec, I'm on the phone with Larry's machine . . . but hey, we need some help. So call—"

The machine cut off this last sentence, beeped three times, and fell silent.

He groaned. Luke was overreacting as usual. He shouldn't have left the office in his charge. Human chains around buses? That stupid Councilman Calhoun. McBryde didn't have the patience for such nonsense. He didn't care if the whole city became a huge parking lot because of the boycott. This wasn't the civil rights era. This was one goddamn extra dollar a month! The car owners and the taxi drivers wouldn't support the boycott. Hell, the rail commuters wouldn't even join in. Tomorrow he'd give Luke a call, calm him down.

In the meantime he had more pressing concerns. He got in touch with Jordan and they planned an emergency board meeting for Wednesday night. This time McBryde had no qualms about the word "emergency." He was way over his head, and the more collective railroad knowledge he received, the better.

TWENTY

That was pretty swift back there," Peña observed as they walked together down the corridor after the meeting. Metaxas followed a pace behind like a bodyguard. "Showed real leadership qualities, babe."

"I hope you get some dirt in Albany." Szczymanski tried to sound sincere.

"Maybe you have some ideas?" Peña prompted.

"Well, there might be a couple of—"

"Let's talk about it later," Peña interrupted her. "On the car ride over to Lucky's. And we've got some info for you as well."

"Which is?"

"A little morsel our friend Marinetti coughed up."

"Which is?"

"Patience."

"We can't talk at Lucky's. House rules."

"Like I said, on the ride over."

"Why don't we just talk about it here?"

"No time. Anyway, Lucky's is a Monday-night tradition."

"Today's Tuesday," Szczymanski pointed out.

"Metaxas had a date yesterday, so we had to postpone. Don't tell me you got something better to do?"

Szczymanski shook her head. She wasn't eager to see the bartender again, didn't want to listen to her colleagues bullshit her. But she also didn't want to arouse suspicions. And she itched to discover the tip from Marinetti, the frosty bureaucrat. Even a false tip might reveal something interesting.

On the car ride over to the bar, Peña warmed to the subject of trains slowly and only by way of her usual route.

"Another man's been taken out of circulation, ain't that right, Metaxas?"

From the backseat, Metaxas shifted position but remained silent.

"I even talked to him myself," Peña continued. "He told me it was hot and heavy."

"We had Italian food for dinner," Metaxas reported with little emotion. "Then we went to a movie. Then he drove me home."

"Gave you a good-night kiss is what I heard."

"Yes. That's true."

"Tongue?" Peña asked.

Metaxas didn't reply.

"Some tongue, Max?" Peña pressed.

"No, there was no tongue." Metaxas didn't falter in tone. She could have been describing the unclogging of her kitchen sink and not the intimate details of a budding romance.

Peña continued to complain about the disservice Metaxas did the women's community in Washington by dating such an eligible bachelor.

Finally Szczymanski could take no more of it. They were already in Arlington, ten minutes or less from the bar. "We really don't have much time left."

Peña looked at her sternly as they waited at a stoplight. "This ain't irrelevant, if that's what you're thinking."

"I can't see how agent Metaxas's date has anything—"

"That's where she got the tip."

"You mean—"

"I saw them making eyes at each other during that very first meeting."

Szczymanski recalled that the head of the Federal Railroad Administration darted his glances all around the room while Metaxas's eyes had been cast demurely down upon her notebook. Subsequent meetings had evidently taken place, and Szczymanski hadn't been invited to watch the romance develop.

"So?" she prompted.

"A match made in heaven," Peña continued. "The hot, spicy Italian and the cool, reserved Greek."

"The tip," Szczymanski said, thinking that Marinetti was about as hot and spicy as iceberg lettuce.

"Right. Max?"

Metaxas again rearranged herself in the backseat. "They have a suspect in the train accidents."

Szczymanski twisted her head around to view Metaxas. "Amtrak?"

"No, the Federal Railroad Administration. Someone in one of their regional offices."

Another suspect? They were popping up everywhere. "What's the motive?"

"Sabotage. He has a grudge against the main office."

"Why didn't Marinetti tell us this earlier?"

"They didn't have enough evidence," Metaxas continued. "And they still don't."

"What are they planning to do?"

"The suspect's been sent to Japan for four weeks. To study the transportation system there. Tony expects the major accidents will stop."

"I thought that . . . Tony . . . didn't think there was anyone behind these accidents."

"Maybe he doesn't," Peña said. "But when they get the goods on this guy, they hand him over to us and we wrap up the case."

"And if the accidents continue?" asked Szczymanski.

"That'll be somebody else's unsub. We'll have ours," Peña said.

"And what are they doing now that he's in Japan?"

"Internal investigation," Metaxas said.

"And if he jumps?"

"Then we have our proof."

"But we lose our suspect."

"Not for long."

"When can we see the evidence?"

"Tony says next week."

"Some tongue and maybe we'll see it on Friday," Peña wagered.

Szczymanski couldn't figure it out. They assign her a high-priority case that turns out to be low-priority. They tell her to find a culprit, but it's actually a covert loyalty test. Granite warns her that the case might stretch on indefinitely, but then they appear willing to scapegoat some poor slob to make some easy stats. It didn't make sense. Of course, this temporarily exiled functionary could be McBryde's accomplice—the second man on the train. But it didn't sound right. The timing nettled her. Perhaps someone worried that she was getting close to something. As far as anyone knew, however, she had merely stared at accident bulletins. And told some fabricated story about a pattern of freight train accidents.

As if reading her thoughts, Peña asked, "This hunch of yours—about freight trains—you think it might be connected?"

Szczymanski murmured noncommittally.

"I mean," Peña continued, "that could be it, right? That would tie everything together. How long you staying in Dallas? We could join you there when we finish up in Albany."

Szczymanski feigned enthusiasm. She'd leave the next station in the fake pattern on their desks just before she flew to Chicago. No point in giving them too much of a head start. Fortunately they were already entering the bar's parking lot and shop talk ceased.

Lucky's was again noisy and crowded, a press of customers at the bar and almost all the tables taken. Only their previous spot was free—in front of the jukebox, this time playing Glenn Miller's "Jungleland." The bass drum boomed beneath the babble of conversation. As Peña divided up a pitcher of beer among them, Szczymanski prayed for an early night. Chaos had promised some results. She'd call him at the office later that night. As Peña interrogated her partner for more details about the blossoming relationship, Szczymanski kept on the margins of the conversation. She whiled away the time leaning back in her chair and tapping her foot to the rhythm section.

Until Lucky came by.

The bartender appeared at her shoulder, his belly bulging out of his ribbed tank top. He jabbed a finger on the tabletop in front of her. "I got a bill to settle with you," he said truculently to Szczymanski. On their last visit, Lucky had played the curmudgeon. Now, however, an undercurrent of violence animated his gestures.

"Aw, Lucky, what you going on about?" Peña asked.

"Between me and her, Penny." He rubbed his leathery scalp and waited for Szczymanski to rise. Worried, she followed him to the back stairs, past Murderers' Row, and up into the dark grocery store. He turned on a light and closed the door, leaving the two of them in the main aisle.

"You used the equipment," he said flatly.

"Exactly." There was no point denying it. She might as well tough it out. TB^2 had so far been successful that day.

"You're Bureau. But that ain't just Bureau equipment."

"I had work to do."

"Oh yeah?" Lucky rolled his shoulders and cracked the remaining knuckles on his fingers. "And what kind of work might that be?"

"Bureau work," she said simply.

"I could get you into a heap of trouble, luv." Lucky had little eyes set back in their sockets, like nails pounded deep into soft wood. These now radiated a certain sadistic pleasure. He moved a step closer.

"But you won't."

The eyes blinked once. "And why's that?"

"I have high-level authorization," she bluffed. "How'd you think I knew where the equipment was?"

He gazed at her uncertainly.

For all his big talk, Lucky was no longer an Agency hotshot. Just a small-time barkeep. She pressed her advantage. "We're on to something big, okay? So keep your mouth shut. I may need your help later on." She remembered a phrase of Marinetti's. "Are you on my side, old man?"

The machinery of Lucky's mind chugged away behind his wrinkled forehead. "Agency know about your work?"

"Of course." The CIA?

"Ain't nothing more important than what we're doing right now."

"It's all related."

The little eyes burned intensely. "We any closer? To nailing the SOB?"

What SOB? "Now that I'm on the case we are," she hazarded.

Lucky pounded his fist into his palm. The gray flesh on his arms rippled. "I fucking hate moles. If I get my hands on the SOB, I'll feed him his own shit."

A mole! She concealed her surprise. "Better turn 'em than burn 'em," she quoted a Quantico instructor.

"Fuck that!" Lucky retorted.

"This is a delicate operation, okay? The more mole-hunters, the easier for the mole to hide."

Lucky nodded. He didn't look entirely convinced.

TB^2 was by definition a risky strategy. But with her adrenaline flowing and her confidence inflated, Szczymanski knew she could handle even twisted CIA alums like Lucky.

"I mean it." She lowered her voice to carry greater authority. "If I hear back that you've been talking, it'll mean trouble." She didn't specify. She barely knew what she was talking about. "In this case, the right hand better not know what the left hand is doing."

On the way back to the bar, she focused on the hairs sprouting from Lucky's bare shoulders. She disliked hairy shoulders. Hair should be confined to specific areas, like a trimmed lawn. She focused on Lucky's shoulders because she didn't want to think about the mole. She didn't want Peña and Metaxas to note any change in her behavior. This mole was serious. She needed time to herself to ponder the new layer of complexity.

By the time she neared the table by the jukebox, the mole had tunneled to the back of her mind, had become virtually inaccessible. She prepared herself for another tedious session on Metaxas and Marinetti, a topic she found as sexually provocative as tap water. But the conversation had shifted since she had left.

And so had the composition of the table.

Two men had joined her partners. With a start she recognized her OPR interrogators. They looked the same as before, the younger one still tanned and fit, the older one disheveled and morose. Jim and Paul, she vaguely recalled. But she couldn't remember who was who. The foursome watched calmly as she approached. The two men were not surprised to see her—Peña must have briefed them. FBI regulations, however, prevented the OPR boys from discussing her case, from even acknowledging that there had been a case. Perhaps she could turn this imbalance in information to her advantage. They'd been coldhearted SOBs. It was time for payback.

"Hiya, boys!" Szczymanski greeted them heartily. She clapped the morose one on the back. The younger one began to stand up, offering her his seat. "No, no, rest your feet a bit. I didn't know they let OPR boys in here." She stood between the two women and winked at the two men.

"So you've met Jim and Paul?" Peña said, twisting her body around to address Szczymanski. She looked genuinely surprised.

"We spent a little time together here in D.C.," Szczymanski said quickly. "Had some fun." Again TB^2 was taking her into a potential minefield. But riding high from the confrontation with Lucky, she felt like playing her hunch. If they contradicted her, she could always pretend to have mistaken them for two others. She smiled at them fetchingly, hoping to lure them into her little trap.

"I'm all ears," Peña said, leaning forward.

"Oh, it was just fun, right, boys?" Szczymanski said.

"Why, um, yes," Jim/Paul said, sweeping a tanned hand through his short blond hair. He looked over at Paul/Jim, who nodded almost imperceptibly. "Just fun."

"Oh, but that night you got drunk at the Holiday Inn cocktail lounge," Szczymanski said, placing her hands on the table and smiling broadly.

"Well," Jim/Paul said, looking disoriented.

"And when you"—she turned to Paul/Jim—"threw up all over the waitress!"

Paul/Jim shrugged helplessly.

Peña's eyes glistened with interest.

"But the best part," Szczymanski continued, "was the car chase. I didn't realize that pot can improve driving performance. But Jim really showed those D.C. cops a thing or two about city driving."

Having acceded to the mild misstatements, Jim and Paul couldn't backtrack. They eventually extricated themselves from the increasingly sticky situation, but not before Peña had grilled them on these departures from FBI procedure. It had been a delicious entrapment, like threatening an opponent's queen and king simultaneously with a lowly pawn. Peña would probably feed the new stories into the

Bureau's rumor mill. And the mole-watchers would no doubt record the incident for future investigation.

On the way back from Lucky's, Peña declared Szczymanski auténtico, a crack agent, a great partner. Szczymanski merely smiled, accepted the praise, said she looked forward to meeting up in Dallas.

In a fever of impatience, she called Chaos at work as soon as she stepped into her apartment.

"Give me another hour," he reported. "And I'll have your results."

"Is the blood on the—"

"Another hour," he interrupted her and signed off.

Her mind seethed. There was a mole. And there were train accidents. How did Larry McBryde fit into all this? She thought about Lucky and the CIA investigation while stretching in the living room. She was too revved up to sit still. She took a shower. She tried to watch television. Finally she picked up the hardcover book that had been in McBryde's bag. *Accentuate the Positive.*

It didn't seem a book that a murderer would read. Still, those who live at a perverse angle to the world could find inspiration in the oddest places. She looked for underlined words and bracketed paragraphs. A page halfway through had been ripped horizontally—a violent man? Several corners were dog-eared—significant? There was a generic inscription from someone named Eileen—an accomplice? Otherwise the book was clean.

"Your spouse just left you," she read from one of the dog-eared pages, "and you feel unhappy, depressed, sad, and lonely. Don't stay down in the dumps! Make a list of the ten things you hated most about him or her." Hated? That didn't seem like accentuating the positive. "Now make a list of the ten activities you couldn't do because of that relationship. Maybe she didn't let you play poker with the boys. Maybe he didn't want you to read poetry out loud. It's now a fresh new day. Get up, get out of your doldrums. Go play that poker! Go recite that Emily Dickinson! Think of yourself as very fortunate, as having the freedom to develop and to concentrate on YOU and YOUR NEEDS!"

Why would anyone read such trash?

She wanted McBryde to be innocent. But she didn't hold out

much hope. An innocent man wouldn't carry around a blackjack, a concealable microphone, and a map of the area with the accident site circled. An innocent man wouldn't suddenly leave the scene of the crime. Wouldn't disappear altogether. All that remained to seal McBryde's fate was the DNA test on the blood and the vomit. She checked her watch. Ten more minutes.

"Cultivate a HOBBY," she read. "Hobbies are fun and relaxing. They let YOU be YOU! A hobby will take your mind OFF your job. And that will make you more effective ON the job." Ridiculous. Hobbies were worse than superfluous. A hobby at law school? A hobby at the FBI? Sleep was her hobby. She devoted herself to it every night, religiously. Hobbies were for the clueless. Her mind, dizzy with anticipation, jumped over to the other side of the argument. What about McBryde? For a devoted hobbyist he seemed mature enough. True, he did go on about magnetic levitation as though it cured cancer. But she'd been intrigued by his enthusiasm. And his obsession—his foaming—was better than alcohol, perhaps even better than couch-potatoing in front of the television. So maybe hobbyists were harmless after all.

As long as they didn't arrange train accidents.

Finally, as she skimmed through a section on bipolar syndrome, the phone rang.

"Okay, Fresh Cheese," Chaos began, "I ran the DNA check. No go. Not enough material in the two samples. Inconclusive."

"Damn!" She closed the book with a snap.

"Wait up. That paper towel with the kid's tissue on it? We lifted prints off it."

"And?" She held her breath.

"They're from the fellow you suggested."

Fate sealed. "The rest of McBryde?"

"He's clean. But there is one interesting thing."

"What's that?"

"He's killed a man."

Szczymanski swallowed saliva down her windpipe. She covered the phone receiver with one hand and coughed into the other. Fortunately the interview was over the phone and Chaos couldn't see the surprised expression on her face.

"How'd you figure that out?" she managed finally.

"Nexus search. It was in the papers. Happened about ten years ago."

"Oh."

"He used to work for a security firm. A railroad company out in Oregon hired him out of college. One night he killed some young punk, part of a gang that broke into the yard. It never went to trial. Self-defense."

Perhaps that case deserved reopening. "Does he own any guns?"

"At least one. Oregon registration."

"Let me guess. A forty-five."

"Dead-on. You know this guy?"

"Peripherally. What about the bug?"

"Mike and bug in one tiny package. Japanese design. State-of-the-art. They're digital."

"Meaning?"

"They don't send out radio waves. Just digital information. Very sophisticated."

"Range?"

"Two to three miles."

"Someone could be in a house three miles away sitting next to a receiver and listening to everything on the train?"

"And recording it."

"What makes you say that?"

"These are top-of-the-line bugs. Very expensive. Soundman said they're usually used only if a high-quality recording is needed."

"But why?"

"Why do murderers take pictures of their victims? It gives them the illusion of notoriety, even when the crime hasn't been detected."

"Any thoughts on who would do this?"

"You haven't given me enough information to have any thoughts." Chaos sounded petulant. "Maybe you should ask your peripheral friend."

"When I catch up to him. Metal strip?"

"Identification number. Taken from one of the cars of the Lake Shore."

"Significance?"

"None that I know of."

"I see. Dallas?"

"It's not the best pattern, but it works for the last four freight accidents. They all involve a particular type of engine and a particular type of cargo. Next scheduled accident according to this pattern will be next Wednesday outside of Seattle."

"Perfect. Next topic—when do you think the Southwest Chief will meet its fate?"

"Location is still stumping us—the computer and me, that is. Highest probability is given to New Mexico, probably near Las Vegas."

"Thanks, Chaos. I'll give you a call when I get back." She had almost all the evidence she needed. And if the accident wouldn't occur until New Mexico, she'd have all the time on the train that she needed. On the Southwest Chief, she'd flush out McBryde or his accomplice or both, and Chaos would no longer be necessary. Relying so much on him was, in any case, dangerous. At any point, he could cut off the assistance or, worse, rat on her.

Chilled by the thought, she glanced at the book now lying face-down by the phone. "Don't stay down in the dumps!" the dust jacket screamed at her. "It's time to stop thinking negatively and accentuate the POSITIVE!" But the case was becoming so confusing. There were too many parallel lines, too many stories that refused to intersect. "It's time for a new game plan!" Perhaps. On the horizon was the Southwest Chief. And she knew that even parallel lines converge at the horizon's vanishing point.

TWENTY-ONE

For a good ten minutes after reading the morning newspaper, McBryde danced around the kitchen, to the Jordan children's delight. He read and reread the small article and, in between, waltzed with Hazel Jordan, hip-hopped with the two children, and even performed a little solo shuffle that Ron Jordan likened to an epileptic fit.

"Go slow, man," Jordan said, laughing in his deep baritone. "You're going to hurt yourself."

McBryde had spent the previous two nights on the Jordans' sofa, anxious about the safety of his own apartment. The absence of his name from the newspaper accounts provided little relief. He knew that the police often withheld the identities of suspects in the hopes of luring them into the open. The exultation of eluding his pursuers and scrambling successfully through the subway tunnels of New York was effaced by a grim realism.

Today, however, the fog of paranoia lifted. A small article

appeared in the *Philadelphia Inquirer*'s early edition mentioning an unnamed suspect in custody in the Lake Shore Limited case. McBryde hoped it was the pillhead. At noon, Ron Jordan came back to the house to celebrate over a six-pack. Giddy, they drank beer and told their favorite police stories. McBryde didn't know why he'd escaped the murder rap, but with three beers rolling around in his stomach he felt better than he had for days.

His good mood restored, he packed up his bag and returned to his apartment, looking forward to taking a long, hot shower and getting his mail. There was a card from Melissa—hand-lettered "I miss you, Daddy!" with a big red crayoned heart—probably a school project. More mail for some schmo, Charles Thayer, which he threw into a pile by the door to discuss with the mail deliverer. The gas company threatened to turn off his service for nonpayment. But even the gas company couldn't destroy his new optimism. On Friday he'd board the Southwest Chief, prepared with Jordan's specific instructions, and clear up the mystery. He was in such a good mood, in fact, that he decided to call the office.

"Larry, man, where you been?" Luke sounded irritated but immeasurably calmer, his voice no longer peaking hysterically at the end of sentences. "I thought you were sticking around Philly this vacation."

"Family business," McBryde replied. "Situation still hairy?"

"Arbitration," Luke said. "I'm telling you, man, Monday morning was a trip. They were seriously going to take over the city! Tuesday wasn't any better. But this morning we got them to agree to arbitration."

"You have to learn to relax, Luke. Things are never as bad as they first look." The newspaper article acted like a drug to lift his spirits and transform him into a fount of goodwill and optimistic clichés. "Arbitration always takes the steam out of them. Accentuate the positive, my friend."

Buoyed by this additional good news, McBryde then decided to call Rosalind. She didn't like to be disturbed at work. But he had good news for her.

"Rosalind Peterson." She sounded so gentle over the phone. Her maiden name, though, burned in his ear.

"Um, hi."

"Larry, you know better. I'm very busy."

"I know, I'm sorry. I just wanted to say that there's no problem with next week. I'll be in town and I can pick up Melissa Thursday evening."

"What happened to your vacation, I mean, your 'work-related' trip?"

"I'll be back early next week."

"Good. Then all debts are cleared. We're even."

He spent the afternoon in heroic reveries that involved saving the passenger train industry, putting the pillhead behind bars, making the case for Maglev on national television, and winning the heart of that strange journalist, Darla Kubb. Jordan even did him the favor of checking into her. She was legit, all right. It was absurd that he'd considered her involved in such a monstrous crime. Not a woman with such an adorable chin. Maybe she'd even call him up after his victorious press conference and profile him for her newspaper.

That evening, at the fifth emergency meeting of the year, the Philly Foamers greeted McBryde's account of his adventures with an unusual silence. Leticia Gompers, who had complained incessantly at the very outset about the inconvenience of the meeting, quietly twisted a finger through her ebony ringlets. Fast-talking and slow-thinking Marty Stein, uncharacteristically at a loss for words, opened and closed his mouth several times like a dying trout. Clarence Brown stared moodily at a patch of carpet. Georgia Huxley sipped at her tea and sniffed only once while McBryde talked.

Jordan rocked slowly back and forth in his chair. He was the first to speak up. "Like Larry said, there are a couple of strange things going on here. I've checked with the police reports and he's not a suspect. For some reason, the two people he met, the journalist and the drug addict, didn't say anything to the police. Now they've got somebody else, a drifter."

Marty Stein finally relocated his language skills. "I don't get it. If they're the ones to blitz the kid, why wouldn't they finger Larry?"

"Would have wrapped things up in a nice package," Leticia Gompers observed.

Clarence Brown looked up from the patch of carpet. His eyes traveled around the circle until they lit upon McBryde. "They didn't want you in the hands of the police."

All faces turned to Brown.

"And?" Gompers prompted.

"They got the evidence," he continued. "For blackmail."

"What evidence?" Jordan asked.

"The towel," Brown replied. "Larry, didn't you say you wiped off the kid's blood with a paper towel? Got that with you still?"

McBryde shook his head. He remembered flinging the crumpled-up paper away in disgust.

"I'll bet either the journalist or the addict has it. With your prints. They can lift them off paper these days. It's a special technique. I saw it on TV."

"Wait; I still don't get it," Stein complained. "Why'd they leave the gun behind? That was the setup, right? So the police would nab Larry with blood on his hands?"

"They changed their minds," Gompers said, more patiently than was her usual style. "First they figured the conductor would find Larry and the gun together. But Larry slipped out with the gun and it was time for Plan B. So they returned for the paper towel. For blackmail, as Clarence said."

"But what could I give them?" McBryde asked, suddenly feeling as cold as he'd been when he sat atop the plastic tarpaulin in the open hopper.

"Whatever it is, you'll probably find out on the Southwest Chief," Jordan said, quickly recapping his discovery of the pattern's four variables.

McBryde's mind was buzzing. Blackmail hadn't occurred to him. Until that morning, he'd been chiefly preoccupied with the police, worried that they were simply toying with him.

"The police," Marty Stein said. "I think it's time to stop this fooling around. No offense, Larry, but we're just amateurs."

"We're in too deep," Leticia Gompers disagreed. "It's too late to go to the police. They'd just stick Larry in jail and let the real culprits get away."

"They've got their suspect," Stein said. "I think we should be more worried about blackmail. Larry should have the choice of pulling out now if he wants."

"Leticia's right. It's too late," McBryde said, thrilling to the sound of finality in his voice. "I can't stay away from the Southwest Chief now."

"Look, Larry, they're killing people right and left. Who's to say you're not the next in line?"

"And the people dying in the accidents, Marty?"

"What are you, Superman?" Stein's voice was rising to its normal pitch. "Fat lot of good you can do for them if you're also dead. That gun of yours didn't do dick to defend you. They FedEx that paper towel to the police and you're shit on a shower curtain."

"I just wish I knew what was going through their twisted little minds," Jordan wondered out loud.

"What about bugs?" Gompers asked. "Find any concealed mikes, recording equipment?"

"None."

"So we don't even know if the Lake Shore was being recorded, right?" she asked.

Georgia Huxley sniffed again and clicked her long, finely manicured fingernails together. "Actually," she said, "we do know." She reached into her leather purse and extracted another cassette. "After I received Larry's message, I called my friend in Colorado. He sent this tape overnight delivery."

"In one day?" Stein blurted. "They did another mix that fast?"

"Demand was high," Huxley reported.

"What's on it?" Jordan asked.

"The cornfield meet in Pittsburgh and the Lake Shore."

"Let's hear them," Gompers urged.

They turned to McBryde. He couldn't hide his unhappiness.

"It's not easy for you," Gompers said. "But better now than later."

Heavy with foreboding, McBryde nodded to Jordan. His friend inserted the cassette into the tape deck, pushed the "play" button, and swung his bulky frame gracefully back into his rocking chair.

They listened first to the Pittsburgh crash. Both the freight train and the commuter had been wired for sound. The producer had fed each source into a different channel, creating a vertiginous stereo reenactment of the collision. The impact reverberated from speaker to speaker. Intact passengers helped the injured out of emergency exits, each grunt and oath and curse and hallelujah recorded faithfully. In documentary-radio style, the mixer had added sound bites from the news coverage: "In Holmsburg, Pennsylvania, today, an eastbound Conrail freight train collided with a westbound Amtrak passenger train, leaving six people dead and dozens injured, according to a spokesman for the Pittsburgh police department . . ."

The three foamers who had not yet heard the accident tapes paid rapt attention to the Pittsburgh segment. Brown stared at the speakers accusingly, as though they were the culprits. Gompers coiled her ringlets more tightly around her finger. Stein exclaimed "Jesus" at regular intervals. The Pittsburgh segment ended with a gruesome tidbit lifted from a scanner conversation. Two Conrail employees discussed the difficulties of hosing down the gore on the railbed. Stein motioned Jordan to hit the "stop" button.

"That's a professional job," he said admiringly. "They obviously cleaned up the tape in the studio. The ambient sound was reduced. That way we can hear the voices more clearly."

"Any clues there?" Jordan asked.

Stein shook his head. "I doubt it. If I spent a lot of time, I might be able to figure out what equipment they used. If I had all the acoustic gadgetry of the CIA or the FBI, maybe I could uncover something in the background—a sound print, a cough, a muffled voice, something. How much you say these cost, Georgia?"

"The price is increasing," Huxley replied. "This tape was ten thousand dollars. And it has only two accidents."

"So that's their strategy!" Gompers burst out. "Hook the collectors with the early tapes, then ratchet up the price. Even at fifty thousand a tape, the true collector won't be able to resist."

"You bought the tape?" Jordan asked.

"We need it to catch them," Huxley explained. "It's a small price to pay to apprehend these . . . these . . ."

"It's terrible," Clarence Brown murmured. "Too many more of these accidents and only suicides will ever ride the trains again."

"It's there again," McBryde said, more to himself than to the group.

They waited for him to continue.

"I don't know what it is. Something familiar. I just get this feeling. It was the same with the first tape."

"Try to be more specific," Huxley prompted.

But McBryde couldn't say. He simply sat in his chair, brooding on his faint intuition.

"Perhaps we should listen to the Lake Shore," Georgia Huxley said into the silence.

Jordan, kneeling by the stereo equipment and waiting for a signal, depressed the "play" button. McBryde braced himself.

The click of the train's wheels surrounded them like the hum of cicadas on a summer evening. A boy's voice faded into the scene, asking nervously if his pursuer worked with railroad security. McBryde swallowed hard when he heard his own voice responding negatively. Then the boy cried out, "Hey, man, you're hurting me!"—followed by the sound of a muffled gunshot. A soft gasp issued from the boy, like air being let out of a tire. A body fell to the floor. In a horribly vivid replay, McBryde retched in the bathroom. As the last dry heaves petered out, the scream of the train braking began to build. Jordan turned down the volume and they endured the awful banshee wail until it finally ceased. The last segment of the tape recorded the reaction of the person who discovered the body, the whispered conversation of two conductors as they stood in the lounge area, and excerpts from what must have been a lengthy gathering of evidence by the police.

"That's not how it went," McBryde said quickly when the voices of the police officers faded out. He glanced around at his fellow foamers. They looked back at him confused, not accusatory. "They spliced together segments all out of order. That first part was when I confronted the kid over the stolen identification number."

"You throwing up after the gunshot makes it sound like you were reacting to the murder, not the drugs," Jordan said.

"Larry, they got you by the short hairs," Marty Stein said. "You better lie low for a while."

"No," McBryde said, growing angrier. "I'm going to the next site. I'll just be more careful this time."

"The Southwest Chief," Clarence Brown pondered.

"You expect the next accident just outside Las Vegas, New Mexico?" Leticia Gompers asked Jordan.

"Yes, roughly," he answered. He seemed suddenly embarrassed. "There's a pattern."

"Which is?" Leticia pressed.

"A 'w.'"

"The letter 'w'?" Stein repeated. "Are you joking?"

Jordan held up a small map of the United States. A large "w" was indeed inscribed on the country, connecting a series of red dots. The line stretched south from Ontario, Oregon, to Benson, Arizona; northeast through Las Vegas, New Mexico, to Kansas City; southeast to Mobile, Alabama; then again northeast through Pittsburgh to

Albany-Rensselaer. "I left out this map one night with the accident sites circled. My daughter must have played connect-the-dots."

"What does it mean?" Georgia Huxley asked.

"It could be a coincidence." Jordan shrugged. "Or maybe someone has a very sick sense of humor."

"Listen, the train gets to Las Vegas around one-thirty P.M. on Saturday," McBryde said. "There's no point in getting on in Chicago and giving them a whole evening to set me up again. So I'm going to fly to Kansas City and board late at night."

"What about your kid?" Gompers asked.

"I'm not on Melissa duty until Thursday night."

"Las Vegas," Clarence Brown repeated.

"Nothing much out there," Gompers said. "That's old Katy country." Katy was the defunct Kansas and Texas railroad. "What kind of accident will it be, Ron?"

"I'm thinking a simple derailment, like the one that happened outside Raton thirty-five years ago on the same date."

"Get on in Kansas City and dynamite her," Stein said. "Clear the clock, give her the works, plug the engine."

"No," McBryde said. "Pulling the emergency will only stop her for a moment. They'll check her out and continue on. I want to catch these crooks red-handed."

"And how will you do that?" Georgia Huxley asked.

McBryde shrugged. "I'm hoping to be inspired. But I'm willing to take all suggestions."

"Stay in the public areas," suggested Gompers. "They won't try anything if you're in the observation car during the day and your seat at night. And for God's sake, stay away from the bathroom. Piss in your pants if you must. Bring a busman's companion."

"Stay awake," advised Brown. "Sleep on the flight out, take pep pills, and stay awake. You might find out the most at night."

"Stay close to your scanner," said Jordan. "That's where the clues will come from."

"Stay home," said Stein.

TWENTY-TWO

From the heart of Chicago's downtown, Milwaukee Avenue angled northwest into a succession of ethnic neighborhoods. Just beyond the Loop, on the other side of the Kennedy Expressway, the avenue bisected Greektown. Then came Logan Square and the Hispanic community with its bright red-and-yellow awnings announcing taquerías, librerías, and bodegas.

Only gradually did the Latino neighborhoods merge into Jackowo—"Yatskovo" in Polish pronunciation. Here lay a unique Polish-American world that so haphazardly blended the two cultures that only someone who grew up on its crowded streets could appreciate the hybrid. Americans were confused, Poles contemptuous. But Polish-Americans fiercely loved their stretch of Milwaukee Avenue, its grit, compactness, self-sufficiency. The world came to Jackowo, not the other way around. Five blocks away were the best taquerías in the city. But Jackowo residents went only to Mexico Hut, next to the Krakowiec Tavern, where the servers understood Polish and the tacos were so limp and pasty and bland that only Poles could appreciate them.

Szczymanski stood on Milwaukee Avenue watching her cab pull away from the curb. She lifted her eyes to take in the collage of street colors and drew deep into her the Jackowo smells of smoked ham and cheap cigarettes and loud floral perfumes. She was traveling light, carrying only an overnight bag slung over her shoulder. It was early evening and the stores were brightly lit against the gloom. She had given the cabbie an address ten blocks from her parents' house. She needed the walk down Milwaukee Avenue to acclimate. To remember.

She listened to the Polish being spoken around her. It was like a familiar melody. Who could tell that this was Chicago? The butcher shops, with their hanging skeins of sausages and their shelves bulging with thick glass jars of sauerkraut, listed daily specials only in Polish. The newspaper shops displayed the Polish-language magazines—New York's *Nowy Dziennik* and Warsaw's *Gazeta Wyborcza*—more prominently than the *Tribune* or the *Sun-Times*. The restaurants advertised their all-you-can-eat buffets with large Polish signs and, as a concession to the inhabitants of the hinterlands, smaller, misspelled ones in English.

Szczymanski spoke enough Polish to conduct day-to-day business—dzień dobry (good day), chciałbym kupić sześć funtow kapusty proszę (I'd like six pounds of cabbage, please). Maria Szczymanski told relatives that her daughter spoke lovely Polish as a child, but that after a few years in Catholic school she began to forget everything. That is for the best, her mother said, for where outside Chicago and Warsaw will anyone understand our beautiful language? Szczymanski deeply regretted losing her mother tongue. Occasionally she dreamed in broken Polish; the frustration of not finding the right word made her wake up trembling and disconcerted.

An icy winter wind swept down the broad expanse of Milwaukee Avenue, whipping the frills on awnings and rattling the street signs. The shoppers in Jackowo did not seem to mind the cold. Old women bundled themselves in coats three times their girth and wrapped woolen scarves around their heads. They clenched large plastic shopping bags in both hands and glanced at shop windows on both sides of the street for bargains. Grandchildren, in down cocoons, toddled alongside, heads bowed against the wind. Clusters of men, out of work or just off work, slapped each other on the back, laughing, looking forward to a beer at the Krakowiec or the Wilanów. Several pairs of men carried duffel bags between them, each holding a strap to share the burden.

At one time Szczymanski could have easily identified the latest arrivals from Poland. The women wore clothes that had been stylish a decade before and dyed their hair an implausible shade of red or orange. The men invariably dressed neck to ankle in denim and grew walrus mustaches in honor of Lech Wałęsa. But with Poland no longer Communist, she found it increasingly difficult to distinguish between the new immigrants and the already Americanized.

Her parents had lived in the same modest two-story house since coming to the country in 1957, first as renters, then eventually as homeowners. Inside they displayed few reminders of Poland—a hand-embroidered tablecloth with a colorful folk design, a photograph of Piłsudski, a crucifix here and there, the Black Madonna. True, the attic and the basement contained a greater number of mementos. And somewhere her mother had squirreled away fat photo albums of pre-1957 Poland. But the Szczymanskis wanted few visible indications that they'd been born and raised abroad. So their daughter grew up with American furniture, American magazines, and all the symbols of middle-class American stability: a color television, a microwave, piles of *Good Housekeeping*. Of these, her parents only became attached to the color televisions, which grew ever larger over the years.

Little Jennifer, born in 1969, represented the Szczymanskis' final break with their Polish past. Her very name, so typically American and with no true Polish counterpart, signified citizenship by birthright, not rite of conversion. As a baby she learned Polish, inevitable among so many Polish-speaking relatives. Her parents tried to speak only English to her, but the language seeped in nonetheless. When they enrolled her in a Catholic elementary school, they gave her name as Jennifer Shemanski (but out of habit kept their own names intact). Entering college, Jennifer Shemanski decided that the old way was the right way and so once again became Szczymanski, though she rarely insisted on the original pronunciation. In funky Hyde Park, she too wanted an ethnicity.

Assimilation was not cool in the multicultural 1980s. Later, the additional letters proved an asset. People remembered Szczymanski. Not precisely, of course. She was "the one with the crazy name."

Returning to Jackowo was never easy. Szczymanski strolled down Milwaukee Avenue to recall her parents' origins, their mindset, their limitations. She knew that her father's repetition of his dearly held political truths—though she agreed with them in principle—would irritate her with their simplicity. She knew that after the first two hours they would have nothing left to say to one another. So instead they would sit around the television and let it talk for them.

For all the difficulties of the visits, however, she missed the family gossip, the taste of her mother's cooking. These pleasant memories, enhanced by wishful thinking, lulled her each time into believing that this visit would be different. The first few moments were the finest. The first hugs were the most sincere, the first smiles most genuine. The first whiff of her mother's cooking made her feel so hopeful, like reading that first fresh paragraph of a new novel.

This time was no different. A hot blast of childhood smells hit her at the entrance, a mélange of smoked meat and pickled beets and sweet pipe tobacco and marjoram-flecked sauces. For all their attempts to assimilate, her parents could never completely adjust to American food. Her mother had dutifully prepared hamburgers and spaghetti and chicken à la king for her growing daughter. But gradually, Maria Szczymanski reverted to the recipes she had learned as a child and her husband could finally stop complaining of indigestion.

That evening's meal included all of Szczymanski's favorites. It began with żurek, a sour white soup of julienned ham and perfect cross-sections of hard-boiled egg. Then came the gołąbki—little pigeons—stuffed cabbage rolls bursting with ground beef and rice and tomato sauce. On the side were salads: shredded carrot, thinly sliced cucumber with fresh dill, and diced beet. For dessert, her mother had prepared her neighborhood-acclaimed poppy-seed cake. It was cooling on the sideboard underneath a dish towel. A bottle of krupnik, a rich honey liqueur, stood by waiting for the end of the meal.

Over soup, they caught up on family gossip, the babies and christenings and graduations and deaths. But the gossip soon ran out.

"Too hard you work," her mother said, adding more hot tea to everyone's glass. "Always you fly here, there. Always you travel."

Her father, a still handsome man with unfashionably long gray sideburns, noisily spooned the żurek into his mouth. "Washington is nice, yes? I would like to see very much the Monument. And the White House."

"When it gets warmer you should come visit," Szczymanski said, instantly regretting the offer. Her parents had never visited her in Ann Arbor or out in Pierre. They rarely traveled outside of Jackowo. Her mother treated a trip to the Loop like an overseas assignment. They would be a burden to her in Washington, afraid to leave her apartment, constantly in her hair.

Her mother was looking at her. Her hands clenched and unclenched beside her plate, a sign that she was debating whether to broach a subject. She sipped her tea and made her decision. "Gosia called." Gosia was Małgorzata Szczymanski, a cousin who worked as a lawyer in a large New York City firm. "Job is there. Just now."

"I have a job, Mama." The żurek was pleasantly sour. She wished her parents would concentrate on their soup.

"I know. You have job. But what kind job? There, in New York, you not have gun, you not shoot people."

"I don't shoot people now. I haven't shot anybody, if that's what you're worried about."

Her father was dunking a piece of dark bread into the soup. "Money you would make in New York. A lot of money."

"Money's not everything, Tata."

After working his way up through the management of a construction company, her father had abruptly left the company to open his own department store. Five years later, the store went bankrupt. With borrowed capital, he had built up another business, a hardware store that also sold lumber. This enterprise proved more durable and now, in their early sixties, her parents were financially stable.

"Tell me . . . what is . . . more important than money?" her father demanded between spoonfuls of żurek. "God, yes, but you cannot be nun. Your family, yes, but I don't want you sell hammers and nails."

"Right and wrong," she replied wearily. It was an old argument.

"Right and wrong," her father repeated contemptuously. "You sound like—"

"Bogdan," her mother tried to head him off.

He wouldn't be stopped. "Like the Communists, you sound. With their right and wrong."

"You don't believe in right and wrong, Tata?"

"Yes, I do!" he thundered, rapping his spoon against the lip of the bowl for emphasis. "But right and wrong is no job. It is here!" He thumped his chest. "Right and wrong is in here."

"Two pieces you want or one?" Her mother now stood by her side with a serving dish of stuffed cabbage stacked in a pyramid like gold ingots.

"Two, please."

Her mother beamed. "You eat wrong there, in District of Columbia. I know. Fast food. Not healthy."

The second course succeeded somewhat in pacifying her father. He forked his cabbage roll in half and the steam swirled up from the filling to frame his face. "You go to church for right and wrong. Not to government. They cheat and steal in government."

"I don't work in the government, Tata. The FBI often uncovers corruption in government. That's what I mean when I say right and wrong."

"You should work for yourself. By yourself."

"But Tata, that's impossible. Even successful lawyers work for someone else."

"Law," her father said contemptuously, before pushing a morsel of the little pigeon into his mouth. He had wanted her to be a successful businesswoman, running her own company. He didn't trust lawyers. But at least they made money.

"I give to you her telephone," her mother offered, her head down as if addressing her diced beets. "Gosia remembers you. From Wujek Jan's day of name."

"Name day," Szczymanski said. She corrected her parents' mistakes only when irritated by their attempts to control her. "I have

Gosia's phone number. But I won't call her. I told you, I was recently promoted. That's why I'm living in D.C. Why would I want another job now?"

"Terrible," her mother said, picking at the diced beets. "This is no good. Beets are old, not sweet."

They always pretended that their daughter's fling with the FBI would not last long. Her father expected an eventual turn to business while her mother pushed for a return to law. Perhaps together they compromised on a future as a corporate lawyer. It did no good to explain the importance of the FBI—for herself or for the world at large. Her parents maintained a selective and thorough deafness.

They would, of course, open their ears to any stories of FBI wrongdoing. Her story of harassment and betrayal would be received with pleasure. Her father's prejudices would be confirmed— the malignancy of government, the sinister workings of bureaucracy, the terrible burdens placed upon enterprising individuals. Her mother would delight in her daughter's disenchantment, eagerly looking forward to pressuring poor Gosia into setting up an interview at the New York firm. Better to present them with the shining ideal of the Bureau, to stress the fidelity, bravery, and integrity of the agents, the importance of her own mission. Better to repeat the tired lines of dialogue.

"Don't you think it's important to put criminals behind bars?" she asked.

"Eh," her father said, spooning more of the salads onto his plate. "Let the stupid ones do that." He helped himself to two more cabbage rolls.

"Bogdan . . ." her mother warned.

"Jestem głodny jak wilk." He lapsed into Polish to whine petulantly about his hunger. He pointed to the gołąbki. "Too salty," he criticized.

"Your heart," his wife said, but let the matter stand.

Szczymanski hoped her father would veer off onto the subject of his high blood pressure. Wishful thinking. Rarely could he be diverted from a topic of his own choosing.

"The stupid ones, the stupid ones," he repeated. "Stupid people should be in the police. Cops and robbers, let them shoot one to the other and leave us with peace."

He loved this theme of the mutual ignorance of the lawmen and the lawless. The latter had only recently become "stupid people." Until five years ago, he still called them "blacks," which included a variety of ethnicities. Before that, he had used more regrettable names, only stopping at his daughter's insistence.

"It doesn't work that way, Tata." She tried to be patient. "If you believe in the ideals of this country—"

"People are with sin," her mother said. She, much more than her father, held tightly to Catholicism. While he attended Mass grumbling, she trembled visibly at the words of the priest.

Szczymanski agreed. "And without the FBI, this country would fall apart, sink under the weight of its own sins." FBI the ideal, she repeated to herself; the reason I joined, the reason I push myself.

"Eh," said her father. "Your FBI sounds like ZOMO." He proceeded to draw the parallel, describing in loving detail the elaborate intelligence service—ZOMO—created by the Polish Communists. Entranced by his own words, he ignored the generous piece of poppy-seed cake that his wife put in front of him. Szczymanski bent her head over her own slice.

Before the collapse of communism, her father's moral world had been flawless and complete. In those simple times, he would have applauded his daughter for working with the U.S. government in any capacity—in the good fight against communism both at home and abroad. This resolute anti-communism had filtered down to his daughter undiluted, and it still colored her views. Since the end of the Cold War, however, her father had lost his moral bearings. He still worked conscientiously. But he no longer cared about society at large. Once he had read the newspaper from cover to cover, and everything within he could explain as some aspect of the heroic battle between communism and the free world. Now he rarely even looked at the headlines. Cut off from the present, he tried to explain the world entirely in terms of the past.

"You are smart," her father concluded. "That's the tragedia."

"Tragedy," Szczymanski murmured.

"You should be rich and happy and . . . and . . . no, I must say this, Marysia . . . married!"

It was another of his pet subjects.

"They marry when more old," her mother reported.

"Eh." He pushed himself away from the table and brushed the crumbs of poppy-seed cake off his pants. He reached for the krupnik, but for only one of the three glasses.

While her father leaned back in his chair, lit his pipe, and sipped at the honey liqueur, Szczymanski helped her mother clean up. The sweet tobacco smell spread through the house. Her mother filled the sink with soapy water, ignoring the dishwasher that had been used only once in all the years they'd lived in the house. Szczymanski shook out the napkins and the place mats, refolded them, and stored them in a cupboard drawer. Hands plunged in the soapsuds, her mother turned her head.

"Maybe you have fun in District of Columbia?" she asked.

Szczymanski knew what the question really meant. She chose simply to nod her head. "D.C., Mama. Please call it D.C."

"You have nice friends?"

"Of course."

"We meet one someday?"

"Maybe."

"His name?"

"Please."

"I wish for you happiness."

"I'm happy."

"Too hard you work."

"I like my work."

Szczymanski checked her watch. In two hours, they had managed to touch on all the key topics—work, relationships, stupid people. If she spent an entire weekend with her parents, the conversation would double back on itself and the same observations would come up again and again, in different combinations, with different emphases. Fortunately she wouldn't have time in the morning to pick up the pattern again. Although her train left in the evening, she had told her parents that she needed to be at the station by 9 A.M. That way she could spend the day in the Loop, remembering Chicago. Perhaps she'd even take a bus down to Hyde Park and stroll around the university.

She finished drying the dishes and, with her mother, joined Bogdan Szczymanski in the living room. His pipe had been put away. He fussed in front of the television like a flower arranger—

adjusting the antenna, stepping back to evaluate, striving for the best picture.

"We like very much this show," her mother said, propelling Szczymanski to the second most comfortable chair in the house. In the last several years her parents had begun watching more and more television. "Every week we watch."

Her father finished tapping the antenna and retreated into his favorite armchair. Szczymanski sat between her parents. The show began and immediately her father leaned over to identify the characters.

"Bogdan!"

"But she doesn't know."

"Bogdan, you must to tell her after."

Her father lapsed back into silence. Imprisoned between her parents, Szczymanski stared dumbly at the images of violence and semi-nudity, the wisecracking police and the street-smart criminals, the car chases and the drug busts and the shoot-outs and the lovers' quarrels.

It's not like that, she wanted to tell them. But she knew that the television was more persuasive than she could ever be.

TWENTY-THREE

Temperature-wise, inside and outside were indistinguishable. A raw wind blew across the platform at the Kansas City train station, and a refrigerator chill hung in the air of the Superliner. McBryde half-expected enormous red-and-white marbled haunches of beef to hang by hooks in the luggage compartment. So much for quality control. Superliners were double-decker coach cars introduced into the fleet in 1979 to replace the aging Heritage Fleet and attract more customers on the western routes. Superliners were supposed to set the luxury standard for Amtrak. They weren't supposed to give tourists their first taste of cryogenics.

As he followed the conductor up and around the spiral staircase to the upper level of the coach, McBryde mentioned the temperature in a low voice. His breath clouded into speech balloons.

"Sorry, sir, we seem to be experiencing problems with the heater system," the conductor whispered back.

"Have you tried turning it on?"

But sarcasm couldn't get a rise out of him. "We should have it fixed shortly."

"I guess I'll just go to another car then."

"The seats are all taken, sir. I'm sorry."

The conductor spoke in the tired and neutral tones of someone who has endured endless complaints and numerous jokes directed at himself and his employers. McBryde could readily sympathize.

The conductor's flashlight cut a path through the darkness of the aisle on the second level. At first McBryde couldn't tell whether the cargo in this car was human or merely woolen. The scene looked like a Salvation Army sorting room. Then his eyes oriented themselves to the dark and he saw a limb move here and there, an eyelash twitch, a puff of breath rise into the air. He looked for the pillhead's telltale bulbous nose. But in the jumble of overcoats and heavy sweaters he recognized none of the visible body parts. The passengers who had embarked in Chicago were dressed for the weather. Little had they known that the Windy City would follow them onto the train. Ach, Amtrak.

The conductor stopped by an open seat, flicked on the overhead light, and motioned for McBryde to sit down. In the window seat was a bundle of clothes with an ear attached on top like some strange flower.

As McBryde lowered himself into his seat, the bundle stirred and the ear swung around. A scarf slipped down to expose a stretch of skin. A hole opened up in the skin, and gray teeth glinted in the half-light.

"Ain't been right since Nebraska. They keep saying they'll fix it but I think they just want to sell more blankets."

McBryde nodded, stowed his bag beneath the seat. The Southwest Chief jerked awake and slowly pulled out of the station. The arc lights along the tracks guided them out of Kansas City. It was one-thirty in the morning. The Chief had arrived in Kansas City, miracle of miracles, five minutes early. So McBryde had had a chance to pace the platform and itemize the train. It was a typical western arrangement, with two AMD-103 diesel engines, front to back, an Ambox mail car, three material-handling cars, a baggage car, a diner with the kitchen below, a lounge car with an observation deck above it, and six "luxury" Superliners (including two sleepers).

"Eight dollars a shot." McBryde's seatmate uncoiled the scarf from his face. He was an older man, with a fully bald head and a wrinkled relief map for a face. "And they're no bigger than my great-grandchild's diaper."

McBryde knew the scam. Amtrak sold a thin souvenir blanket with its logo emblazoned on it. It was meant more to remind passengers of their glorious trip than to keep them warm. McBryde pulled his parka tighter about him. "What about the other cars?"

"Another one's just like this. Then there's one like the effin' Sahara. Only one of 'em's just right. The Goldilocks car."

"Could be worse, I suppose."

"Pizza I had for dinner last night gave me the runs," the old man confided. "And there ain't no soap in the bathrooms downstairs."

"Going all the way to California?"

"My corpse is." The old man grinned.

"It'll be warmer in here by Arizona."

The man ignored McBryde's optimism. "It wasn't always like this with trains, you know."

"I know."

"I took the Super Chief back in fifty-three. Atchison, Topeka, and Santa Fe it was then."

"I know."

The old man peered more closely. "You ain't more'n forty-two, young man."

McBryde flinched. Did he really look so old? It must be anxiety that added the years to his age. "I've read a lot about it."

"Rode in a Vistadome back then, in fifty-three. The car was made all of glass."

"That would have been the Zephyr, Chicago to San Francisco. I believe the Chief had Domeliners."

The old man snorted. The wrinkles flowed and re-formed themselves into an approximation of satisfaction. "Guess you've ridden a few in your time. So you know how the whole effin' thing's collapsed."

"A shame."

"In fifty years, they cut the railroad miles in half. In half! What do you say about that?"

"Criminal."

"Put 'em behind bars, I say. And turn off the heat in the prison." The old man cackled.

"You've got my vote."

"Glad I don't have to sit next to some dummy. Let's have breakfast together later." He wrapped his scarf back around his face, leaving a space for his mouth. Turning his body slightly toward the window, he tried to get comfortable. He had supplemented his pillow with a rolled-up ball of underwear.

McBryde checked the pocket of his parka for his Walkman. He had brought along some of the loudest, brassiest music in his collection—in case of drowsiness. He'd even brought *West Side Story* to remind him of Melissa, of trying to put her to sleep at night to the finger-snapping Jets. He'd see her soon, in less than a week.

He flicked off the overhead light and kept his eyes fixed on the door several seats in front of him. No one would catch him unawares. Soon he would roam the train, looking for the suspects. He knew he shouldn't, but he wanted to see Darla Kubb again. Wanted one more chance to talk to her, get her phone number. But there was only one reason why she'd be on the Southwest Chief, and he didn't like thinking about that possibility. The cold was good, would keep him awake. He looked out the window, thought about the old man's rant, about the state of American trains. It certainly was a familiar topic.

America's trains were once the pride of the world—the largest, the most powerful, the most extensive, the most comfortable. They symbolized growing U.S. power. But then came the era of the automobile. The car companies wouldn't brook competition. With the emerging airline industry as an ally, the Big Three worked together to break the back of the railroads. Tracks were bought out and ripped up. Federal subsidies were diverted into highways and new airports. The trains never had a chance. So what if they best conserved energy or transported people and goods most efficiently. Since when did the best triumph?

McBryde had had the great misfortune to miss the golden age of rail. When he was a child playing with his first toy engine, the train companies were already scrambling to get out of the passenger business. Freight remained profitable but people had become an impossible burden. So the companies decided to bankrupt that side of operations and reap the tax benefits. They began to discourage passengers, often with the most ludicrous schemes: discontinuing food service, eliminating security at the stations, setting up schedules that required twelve-hour layovers from 4 A.M. to 4 P.M. You had to be crazy to ride the trains in those days. You had to be a foamer.

When Amtrak began operations in the early 1970s, it suffered tremendously from this legacy. Its cars were dilapidated. The tracks it used were in pitiable shape; still owned by the freight companies, they were best suited for coal and auto parts, not the sensitive rear ends of complaining customers. An inefficient reservation system kept telephone lines perpetually jammed. Put on hold and forced to listen to Muzak, most people gave up and opted for air travel or, God forbid, the bus. McBryde, though he generally dismissed conspiracy theories, suspected a covert plan by the freight companies to strangle Amtrak in its cradle. With more cars on the road and planes in the air, the tracks could then be used exclusively for freight. He believed that the managers of the freight companies who served on Amtrak's board had struck a deal with the government to ensure an undercapitalized system from the very beginning.

But Amtrak didn't die. Somehow, through managerial acumen and more aid from the states, America's passenger train system reconstituted itself. It was still a far cry from Europe or Japan, but the improvements were tangible. Modern engines were bought. The Superliners were added. Some of the tracks were improved, particularly on the money lines in the Northeast. Better food was served, on real plates. The on-time performance grew more reliable. Amtrak began again to attract customers and gradually cut down on its subsidy from the government.

Still, it remained on the dole—a sensitive issue for any foamer. After all, if Amtrak received so much government money, why did it still provide such inconsistent service? As a public official, McBryde had fielded variants of this question dozens of times, usually from those who mistakenly wanted the government to sell off everything, to privatize, to stop interfering in the economy. But these same people usually did not know the extent to which the federal government subsidized the airlines—fifty cents for each dollar of expenditure—with tax write-offs, special contracts, and various other sweetheart deals. The highways, meanwhile, received thirty-nine cents on the dollar. Down at the bottom came little Amtrak, a mere two percent of the Department of Transportation's budget. And with only twenty-eight subsidized cents on the dollar, it was more cost-effective than any other major train system in the world.

In part, Amtrak controlled costs by cutting corners. Despite the addition of new cars and engines, the rolling stock was again deteriorating. The tracks in most locations needed a major overhaul. Without a significant injection of capital, Amtrak would return to its dismal start—discouraging passengers because operating at full capacity was too expensive. No, trains needed more federal help, not less. If the government didn't start investing in trains rather than missiles and in transportation rather than destruction, America would soon find itself outclassed. That was McBryde's philosophy and he hoped his book on Maglev would serve as the manifesto for a new movement.

The Chief was passing through flat Kansas ranch land, the blackness of the landscape only occasionally broken by the small red lights atop silos and water towers. A few snowflakes swirled outside the window. It was lonely country. There were few houses. People lived far apart. They also lived near to the earth, as though they feared being swept off their plots by a sudden gust of wind.

He gazed at this seemingly barren scene with pride. Trains had made this whole region bloom. The tracks, laid out in the Midwest in the late nineteenth century, were like irrigation ditches cut into the desert. On either side of the railbed, civilization took root. Without trains, America would have remained a small agricultural nation concentrated on its eastern seaboard. The train was a magician's rod, Emerson said. With one wave, it transformed the country into a great industrial nation.

A freight train thundered by, going east, buffeting the Southwest Chief. He remembered, with a shudder, the Metro North commuter that had passed so close to him in the tunnels beneath Park Avenue. Trains had roared into people's lives, disrupting them, despoiling them. The men who built the railroad empires—the Vanderbilts and Goulds and Harrimans—were crooks on a grand scale, their immorality so immense that it surpassed evil to become history. The federal government sold these robber barons the rights-of-way for a pittance and threw in great swaths of land on either side of the tracks. The railroad companies made money not only on freight, but on land rent, on loans, on every swindle and scam and power play of the Gilded Age.

If the government poured money into the railroads one more time, how could it avoid the terrible corruption of this earlier era? McBryde had postponed consideration of this dilemma for the final chapters of his book. So far he had no answers. As I near the conclusion, he told himself, I will be inspired.

Conclusion? Hah, he was barely out of the introduction.

Rearranging his feet to prevent a cramp, he kicked his bag. The old knapsack, pressed into service after long years spent at the bottom of a milk crate in a dim closet corner, tipped over on its side. It was very light. He no longer had a gun or a blackjack or a cellular phone. The knapsack contained only two changes of clothes, his Walkman, and a handful of tapes. Of these, all but one contained music. The last was Georgia Huxley's recording of the Lake Shore.

It had not been easy to persuade her. He needed the originals. Because of the embedded signals, they couldn't be taped. Between them, the two tapes McBryde had borrowed came to fifteen thousand dollars. And lately he did not have a very good record of holding on to luggage. But with many assurances from McBryde and no small amount of pressure from the rest of the group, Huxley finally relented.

After the emergency meeting, McBryde had offered Marty Stein a lift home and made his proposition. "I've listened to the first tape a dozen times and I still can't put my finger on it."

Stein glowered in the passenger seat. "I want no part of this."

"Look, Marty, some little noise on this tape is triggering a memory somewhere in my hopelessly muddled brain. I need help getting that memory to the surface."

"You're way over your head, Larry. Why don't you just let the big boys handle this one?"

"Consider it a technical challenge."

"Who needs a challenge? My kid's got the chicken pox, I've gotta spin records at my wife's nephew's wedding, my new program manager's got gefilte fish for brains, and you think I want a challenge? I want a vacation, Larry. Don't give me your stupid cassette. I want a plane ticket to the Bahamas."

"Use some of that fancy new equipment at the station."

"A challenge he wants me to have. Such a good friend." Stein leaned his head against the shoulder strap of the safety belt. "And what do I do if I find your little something?"

"Call me this week. Otherwise, I'll contact you from New Mexico."

So he gave Stein the first tape and kept the latest recording for himself. So far, the deejay had found nothing. This weekend he promised to use a different machine, with some computer-imaging capacities. In the meantime, McBryde would listen to the Pittsburgh segment and see if he could pin down this almost-memory more precisely.

To his left, the old man muttered into his scarf. Around them in this refrigerator car was a symphony of snores and sighs and farts. He knew that he should take advantage of the darkness to roam the train searching for his quarry. But he wasn't sure exactly what to do if he found the pillhead. Turn him over to the conductor? On what evidence? He tried to think the matter through. And discovered that his mind was turning very slowly, like a windmill on a still day. He'd slept through the entire two-and-a-half-hour flight from Philadelphia. In the Kansas City airport, he'd located the one snack bar still open and bought an extra-large coffee. The caffeine had made him so jittery that his right leg shook for the entire taxi ride to the train station.

Now the caffeine had worn off. He felt like burrowing into his parka to escape the tremendous gloom descending upon him. It was time for the Walkman. He dug into the knapsack, pulled a tape out, and fit it into the little machine. Just his luck: the train-accident tape. He was too tired to find a replacement. He tried to concentrate on the familiar sounds but couldn't keep his mind from wandering. He stopped the tape. He bit into his lip. He stared into Kansas. He felt like a clay pigeon, thrown out into the open. He would hear the report of the rifle and frantically try to fly off. But with his wings glued to his side, he couldn't dip or dive. He could only glide in space and await the impact. A clay pigeon. Doomed to crumble in the air or break apart on the ground.

When McBryde next opened his eyes, dawn was breaking. A soft orange glow lit up the clouds in the east. Small derricks bobbed up and down in the Kansas fields. The old man had shifted position, pointing his knees away from the aisle and resting his scarfed head on McBryde's shoulder. McBryde carefully disengaged himself. He shook his head to clear it, pushed the earphones down around his neck. He felt cold and his legs were heavy. His nap had not been restful. The temptation to close his eyelids again was enormous.

But anger over his own failure was stronger. What a fool he'd been! Stay awake, Clarence Brown had advised, and he couldn't even do a simple thing like that. He roused himself, got to his feet.

He picked his way down the aisle, slaloming around sprawled legs and dangling arms. The passengers had gone to acrobatic lengths to find comfortable sleeping positions. A teenager knelt on the floor with her head resting on the seat. A young man had crossed his legs on his lowered tray table, placing his head where the small of his back should have been. A petite woman stretched across two seats, her feet splayed in the aisle and her baby asleep upon her stomach. Whatever their position, the passengers all looked lumpy, like refugees wearing their entire wardrobes.

After three cars of careful footfalls, he came upon the journalist.

He saw her chin from six rows away. Her head was tilted to one side, her eyes closed. The pill pusher was nowhere in sight. Damn it, Jordan had cleared her! Her presence, however, could only mean one thing. She was involved. He approached slowly. All his fear and disgust could not extinguish the spark that stirred in him when he saw her face. Lust, he tried to tell himself. He didn't love this woman, he just wanted to sleep with her. But he knew that he felt more than lust. Whatever name he gave the feeling, it was dangerous.

Frightened by the intensity of his emotions, McBryde quickly walked past her. He still couldn't decide what to do. Was it better to confront her or surprise her in some criminal act? Distracted, he didn't pay attention to where he was going and suddenly found himself in the observation car. With everything still closed, the car was empty. Here too the heat was not functioning. He kept his parka zipped up. He took a seat and watched the sun spread across the Kansas fields. He felt panicked, needed time and space to think. A great private detective he'd turned out to be. In the movies, the hero always got the girl and put the criminal behind bars. But in his movie, the girl and the criminal were the same.

The derricks bobbed mournfully. The ground was covered here and there with thin patches of snow. McBryde briefly considered walking out of his movie and getting off at the next stop. He wanted to be in a different movie, a simpler movie, something perhaps set in a small Kansas town where the men were all heroes, the women were all honest, and the trains all ran on time.

TWENTY-FOUR

Szczymanski **searched for** bugs during the Southwest Chief's journey through Illinois. Without a detector, however, she might as well have been trying to locate a distant star through a magnifying glass. Chaos had offered to outfit her with something that bounced microwaves off every surface. But she didn't want to carry around this "nonlinear junction detector," which was the size and heft of a vacuum cleaner. Travel light and be ready to fight. She ran a forefinger along moldings, reached a hand beneath the metal plates in the vestibule, groped around ankle-high fixtures. The search gave her something to do. But there was nothing in these crevices beyond the residues of ancient chewing gum and the black stickum of oil and dirt.

After washing as much of the grime off her hands as possible, she settled down in her seat to consume the fat corned-beef sandwich her mother had packed for her dinner. On her trip through the train, she had discovered that each car had its own weather system.

Fortunately her seat was comfortably in the temperate zone. She stretched out her legs and watched the cityscapes turn into cornfields. The Illinois earth was hard and winter-dark, dusted with snow like brownies topped with confectioner's sugar. What a pleasure to be working alone again, without some clown making a mess of her every plan.

McBryde wasn't on the train. That was smart of him. There was no point in exposing himself more than was necessary. He certainly could arrange an accident from a distance, his accomplice planting the bugs while McBryde holed up in a safe house and waited for word of the police investigation.

Still, she was disappointed. For some strange reason, McBryde continued to fascinate her. She had had a single conversation with him. Men did not usually insert themselves into her emotions so easily. How could such an awkwardly charming man be a murderer—a mass murderer if you counted all the train accidents? Perhaps the evidence was all wrong. No, that was ridiculous. She had to listen to the facts, not her emotions.

Without McBryde on the train, she didn't know quite what to do. She had no idea what this second plotter looked like. White and male. That certainly narrowed the field. Perhaps she'd flush the quarry in time. She'd keep her eye out for suspicious characters and track their moves. In the worst-case scenario, she would endure the trip, read the generic murder mystery bought from a Union Station bookstore, and pull the emergency brake somewhere in New Mexico. It was an absurd mission: Scramble after a demented saboteur, stop trains immediately before the accident site, and vainly look for clues.

In the morning, after a fitful sleep in which every bump of the train became a derailment and every deceleration presaged a collision, Szczymanski felt even more hopeless than the night before. She lingered over breakfast in the dining car and then conducted another thorough search of the train. They were now speeding through Colorado and she was beginning to grow anxious. It was only on her second trip to the unheated observation car that she took a closer look at a slumped body wearing headphones. Jesus Maria, it was McBryde! Was he feigning sleep? Tiptoeing up to his side, she considered finding the pressure point behind his ear. But before she could make a move, McBryde's head suddenly snapped back and he was awake. He turned toward her, his body convulsing involuntarily. He ran a hand across his face and blinked several times.

"Ah, the journalist," he said, wiping his mouth. "Another conference?"

"Yes, as a matter of fact," she said, sitting down next to him. He certainly was brazen, sleeping out in the open. The most dangerous criminals were the cocksure ones. They made few mistakes and killed dispassionately. She kept her hands free and loose in front of her, ready to move quickly if necessary. "The ozone. In Albuquerque. And what brings you to this particular train?"

"Pleasure."

If the stakes weren't so high, Szczymanski would've laughed at the absurdity of his impersonation. As it was, however, she simply stared at him, uncertain how to proceed. She had the blackjack, the bug, the fingerprint, the proof of his presence on the targeted train. But she wanted his accomplice as well.

Just as she was about to pull out her gun, a family of four entered the observation car. Mother, father, and two small children occupied a bank of seats across the aisle from her and McBryde. The mother complained of the cold, the children bounced on the seats demanding pancakes, and the father tried to explain about the rich mineral deposits hidden beneath the Colorado landscape.

"That was quite a trip on the Lake Shore," Szczymanski said in a conversational tone. She'd wait for the family to leave and then interrogate him at gunpoint. "I didn't see you at the Albany station when we were taken off."

"I decided to continue by a different route."

"Seems like you left in quite a hurry."

He raised an eyebrow. "Should I have stayed behind and gotten framed?"

"Framed? Why framed?"

"Stop playing with me," he said quietly. His face contorted with disgust.

She tried a more direct approach. "Why don't you tell me what the bugs are for?"

"You know as well as I do."

"Oh, I do?"

"I was hoping I wouldn't see you on this train," he muttered. "Where's your psychopath sidekick?"

"What about *your* psychopath sidekick?"

"Who snuffed the kid? You or the junkie?"

She stared at him. "Got a problem with your memory, pal?"

At that moment, the little girl separated from her brother and approached McBryde. She pulled at the earphones looped around his neck.

"What's that?" she asked solemnly.

McBryde smiled, handed her the headphones.

"Karin!" her mother said sharply. "You come here this minute!"

The little girl triumphantly skipped across the aisle with the headphones in her hand. McBryde steadied the Walkman as the headphone jack was ripped from it. His finger accidentally touched the "eject" button and a cassette clattered to the floor.

They both looked down at the tape. The label facing up at them read "Lake Shore."

"You son of a—" she began. The bugs *were* for recording, and the bastard was listening to the accidents. A sicko foamer!

"Give that back to the nice man!" the mother insisted from across the aisle. The little girl approached McBryde again.

But Szczymanski stepped between them. She reached for her gun. The hell with the family. It was time to wrap up this case. Just then, however, the little girl crawled between her legs. Giggling, she stood up to present the headphones to McBryde.

"Stand back!" Szczymanski warned, grabbing the little girl about the waist with one arm and reaching for her shoulder holster.

"Leave her alone!" the mother screamed, grabbing Szczymanski from behind and attempting to pin her free arm.

McBryde ran out of the car.

Szczymanski had to flash her FBI badge to prevent the mother from screaming for help. By the time she could start out in pursuit of McBryde, he had put a full car between them. Finally, in the last coach, she caught a glimpse of the top of his head just as it disappeared down the stairwell. When she too reached the bottom of the steps, McBryde was gone. There were only two possibilities. Either he had slipped into the bathrooms on the left, or he had gone into the compartment to the right marked "Amtrak Personnel Only."

She held the blackjack in one hand—it would be more useful in close quarters than a gun. Warily she slid open the door to her right. The area was filled with suitcases and duffels, most of them piled in a gentle slope against the far wall. Long string-bean bags containing skis lay like felled saplings along the wall to her left. Leaning against the wall to her right was McBryde, his hands in the pockets of his parka.

"Why are you following me?" he asked.

"I could ask the same thing about you."

He moved closer. She kept her eyes on his hands.

"Usually the person in front is being followed and the person behind is the follower." He was unsmiling and seemed nervous.

Szczymanski held her ground, anticipating his move. When it came, she was ready.

McBryde feinted to one side and then came at her low, like a defensive end going for the quarterback. Closed in on all sides by luggage, Szczymanski received the tackle around her midsection but quickly swiveled her hips. "Work with your opponent, not against him," the martial arts instructor had always reminded her. Using McBryde's momentum, she swung him off the ground. They flew together through the air. She was in complete control, had executed this maneuver dozens of times with more determined and experienced attackers. As they fell into the luggage, she made sure that her hipbone connected with his face, that her knees then pinned his chest against a duffel. She twisted his arm at the wrist to release his grasp and, reaching down, caught his neck in the crook of her elbow. They rolled off the bags and onto the cold metal floor.

She was breathing easily but the action had taken the wind out of McBryde. He was limp in her arms. It took several seconds for him to regain his voice.

"Are you . . . going to . . . kill me here?" he asked. "Or will you . . . shoot me in the . . . bathroom with a . . . silencer?"

"Kill you?" Szczymanski was nearly amused. "Quite the opposite, Larry McBryde. I'm making sure that you don't kill me. Or anybody else." McBryde struggled to test her grip but she held him firmly. She knelt on the floor; he lay outstretched with his head in her lap. "You're quite an impressive killer. Jigsaw pumped you full of those drugs and still you managed to plug the kid and jump the train."

"So you're . . . going to frame me . . . not kill me?"

"I have no idea what you're talking about."

He snorted. "I thought journalists knew everything."

"FBI, not journalist."

"One lie's as good as another."

She decided to get whatever information she could. "Why are you making tapes of the accidents?"

"I didn't make the tape."

"Then why were you listening to it? What sick pleasure do you get out of it, McBryde?"

"I told you, I didn't make the damn thing."

"Okay. What about the next accident? Will it take place in New Mexico?"

"Why ask me?"

"Who do you work for?"

"SEPTA."

"Your accomplices," she clarified.

"You need all this information before you frame me?" The fight had clearly sapped his strength. His voice quavered and she could feel the fear in his body.

"Tell me what you know and we'll go easy on you."

"Who's 'we'?"

"I told you, the FBI."

He giggled. It was the laugh of a man about to go out of control. Szczymanski realized that McBryde was not going to give out any useful information. She felt around for the blackjack and found it behind her on the floor. She regretted doing it. Now that he was no longer a threat, she again found him strangely compelling. Jesus Maria, what was wrong with her? She steeled herself, swung the blackjack crisply through the air, and struck McBryde just beneath his ear. He slumped in her arms.

At that moment the door to the baggage room opened.

"This is for Amtrak authorized personnel only," she heard from behind her.

Szczymanski slipped the blackjack down the front of McBryde's parka and twisted around to look up at the conductor. She didn't want to break cover until absolutely necessary. There was still the accomplice to capture. "It's my husband," she explained in a soothing voice. "He's a narcoleptic. Falls asleep at the strangest times! I couldn't carry him back upstairs so I thought I'd just bring him in here to lie down."

The conductor, a tall black woman, looked down on them. Her icy, official manner disappeared. "A narcoleptic? Should I try to find a doctor?"

"Oh no," Szczymanski said, smiling broadly. "He'll be fine in no time at all."

"Well, then, you just stay where you are. We'll make an exception to the rule for you. I'll tell the other conductors. Would you like some pillows?"

"Oh no, no. The floor is really much better for him."

After the conductor left, Szczymanski reclaimed the blackjack. If left undisturbed, McBryde would stay unconscious for at least several hours. She hadn't wanted to knock him out until after receiving the names and whereabouts of his accomplices, but such were the rewards for noncooperation. When the time came to approach the engineer of the train, reveal to him that she worked for the FBI, and explain the situation, McBryde would be handcuffed in the baggage car, safely out of the way. She removed his parka, began to remove his outer shirt. Suddenly she felt odd undressing him, felt a glimmer of sexual interest. Control yourself, woman! This one's a mass murderer. She'd handcuff him and wrap the shirt around the hands as a disguise.

Again the baggage room door slid open.

"Sorry to disturb you, ma'am." Another conductor appeared in the doorway. A large man, he filled the entrance to the car. "You're Darla Kubb, aren't you?"

She nodded warily.

"Fellow on the phone gave me a description and I've been looking all over the train for you. Margaret, she's the conductor that was helping you before, Margaret told me maybe I'd find you here. Attendant in the lounge car has a phone call for you."

"A phone call? On a train?"

"Cellular. It's all part of our new program here at Amtrak to make your trip more convenient." He grinned.

"Who's it from?"

"Afraid he didn't say, ma'am."

He? Was it Chaos? Had he dug up another clue? "I suppose it's important."

"I understand your husband's a narcoleptic. I'd be happy to wait here with him while you take the call."

Szczymanski looked down at McBryde sleeping peacefully. She'd handcuff him when she returned. Chaos wouldn't call unless it was truly an emergency.

The conductor stepped away from the entrance to let her pass. It was only after she reached the lounge car and had conducted a fruitless conversation with the attendant that a peculiar detail floated back to her. Despite his official cap and authoritative tone, the big black man who'd told her about the phone call had not been wearing an Amtrak name tag like all the other conductors.

TWENTY-FIVE

McBryde awoke in a pool of water.

He reared back and snorted the liquid out of his nose, began to splutter and cough. His knees buckled. If his arms hadn't been restrained, he would have pitched forward again onto his face. When the coughing fit passed and he could finally see, he realized that he stood in a small bathroom. Several inches of water rippled below him in a sink. A cut oozed red on his cheek.

The face behind his in the mirror was familiar.

"Good morning," Ron Jordan said in his deep bass. "Have a pleasant nap?"

A pain began to spread up and down McBryde's neck. "Nap?"

"Come on, buddy, wake up. We've got work to do." Jordan tentatively removed his hands from McBryde's biceps.

Now standing on his own in the crowded space, McBryde shivered with pain. It felt as though a blunt nail was being pounded very slowly into his skull. The pain made him nauseous and he had to fight back the rising bile. "Where'd you come from?"

"Heaven. I'm your guardian angel. Here, swallow these." Jordan held out his hand. On the palm rested two round white pills.

McBryde grimaced, still a little confused, the train trips getting mixed together in his mind. "Oh no, no more pills, no more—"

"They're aspirin, Larry."

"Oh." Dutifully he swallowed the pills with a handful of water. The fog began slowly to lift from his mind. They were in the handicapped bathroom, the only one that could accommodate two large people. Jordan, he noticed, wore his Amtrak cap, a gift he'd received several years ago from a friend working in the Philly division. Usually the memento occupied a place of honor on top of the enlarger in his basement darkroom. "What's the getup for?"

"To save your backside, pal. I brought it along just in case. Emergency foamer gear."

"Last thing I remember," McBryde said, trying to impose some order on his memories, "I was lying in the arms of a beautiful woman."

"Not quite. She zapped you one good on the back of the head. From the shape of the bruise, I'd say it was your blackjack."

McBryde now remembered the brief struggle in the baggage room. Too bad. For a moment, he'd truly believed that he'd been relaxing in the journalist's arms as she looked down at him affectionately. He blinked and the image was gone. Now he remembered the half-nelson and the strangulating pressure on his Adam's apple. He said to Jordan, "Seriously, man, what are you doing here? I don't remember you getting on in Kansas City."

"I caught the first flight to Denver, rented a car, and then drove like hell to Trinidad. Took me three hours."

McBryde managed a lopsided grin. He dabbed a Kleenex at his cut. Tentatively he touched the throbbing welt behind his ear. "But why? If you wanted so much to be with me, we could've taken the KC flight together."

"It didn't occur to me until after your flight left. I messed up on the date."

"What date?"

"Today's date. February twenty-eighth. The Raton derailment I was thinking of happened on the last day of February thirty-five years ago. But I forgot that was a leap year. So I hit the books again. Then I found it. The Ural Mountain disaster."

"Refresh my memory."

"Two passenger trains pass in the Ural Mountains, out in the middle of Russia. They set off a shower of sparks. A nearby LPG pipeline has a leak. Major inferno. Four hundred sixty out of twelve hundred passengers meet their maker. You should see the photos, man. Powerful stuff."

"A fluke."

"Today's the five-year anniversary."

Jordan's words finally penetrated. "This is desert out here, Ron. I doubt there's any liquid petroleum gas pipelines."

"Even if there were," Jordan agreed, "it would be too difficult to plan. I figure a different scenario. A westbound passenger train and an eastbound freight train. The freight has an LPG tanker fitted with an explosive bolt on its valve. They attach some electronic gizmo to the side of the Amtrak engine that blows the bolt. The trains pass, the bolt goes, and the explosion destroys everything, including the evidence."

McBryde shook his head, sending a spike of pain up his neck and into his brain. He steadied himself against the sanitary-napkin dispenser. "All because it's a five-year anniversary."

"Whoever's arranging these things is more of an accident nut than me or Georgia. We just passed Raton. Figure on twenty minutes."

As long as McBryde didn't move his head quickly, the pain remained localized just below his ear, the throbbing now receding to a bearable level. He no longer felt nauseous. His sense of cause and effect had returned. The details of the confrontation in the baggage room were clearer. He remembered what he'd been thinking just before trying to wrestle Darla Kubb to the ground.

He'd again flashed to the scene nearly a decade ago when he held the three boys at gunpoint in the Portland rail yards. The youngest was already lying unconscious on the ground, knocked out with the blackjack. He wasn't so lucky with the others. Pulling out his gun, he told them to put down their weapons. Two of the teens held knives—ugly, long switchblades—which they clung to tightly. The oldest boy, tall and blond, pretended to throw his gun to the ground, then aimed and fired. The bullets went wide. McBryde needed only one shot. He had worried all along that the three of them would jump him. They didn't need the gun. That had been their mistake—to rely on distance and to rely on technology.

He would have been able to take out only two of them. The last one could have easily pincushioned him.

There, in the baggage room, he decided not to repeat their mistake. He'd attack her first before she could draw and shoot. He wasn't sure how it happened but what he thought was a good offensive position turned rapidly into a stranglehold. She was certainly no slacker.

"Where's the journalist?"

"Probably looking for you at the moment." Jordan snorted. "Narcoleptic husband!"

"She's married?"

"No, man." Jordan laughed. "I've been tailing her since I got on the train. She brought me to you. I watched you two go at it in the observation car. Then I followed you down to the baggage car."

"You could have helped," McBryde complained.

"Sorry, man. By the time I got down here, she'd already knocked you out. I heard the conversation with the conductor, put on my own gear, and saved your sorry butt."

"Why didn't she put a slug in the back of my head?"

"Maybe that first conductor saved you. Maybe she just wanted you out of the way until the explosion. In any case, I'm sure she won't stay on this train for long."

Shifting position, McBryde noticed the wire running along Jordan's neck. It ran down to the scanner on his belt. "What do you hear?"

"Nothing yet. There's a Santa Fe freight heading east that we're supposed to pass near Las Vegas."

McBryde reached for the door handle. "Let's stop the train."

"Won't make any difference." Jordan laid a hand on his arm. "Freight will still pass us."

"Get the engineer to radio ahead and stop the Santa Fe."

"I have a feeling they won't."

"Why not?"

"They'll call ahead and the dispatcher will tell them that the freighter isn't carrying any LPG."

"Then we have nothing to worry about."

"But there is LPG. My guess is they relabeled the container."

"That's a lot of guesses."

"I checked with the dispatcher at Albuquerque, the point of origin. It has two tankers of domestic water. At least that's how they're labeled."

"Jeez, I don't know, Ron."

"I predicted the Lake Shore, right?"

McBryde nodded. "So what do we do?"

Jordan hunched his shoulders. "That's the big question. We can't just stop the train. And we can't just jump off."

"What about a siding? Or a runaway track?"

Jordan shook his head. "If we were in the cab, sure, we could do that. But we're in the bathroom. We can flush. We can run some water. But we can't move the train this way and that."

McBryde gripped the edge of the sink. "There are four hundred people on this train. We're all going to be incinerated?"

"That's my guess."

"We have to find her before she jumps. She's the only one who can call this off."

"Baggage room?"

"Best place to start."

McBryde poked his head tentatively out the bathroom door and directly into the chest of a fuming matron. She stood, arms crossed, at the threshold, shifting her considerable weight from foot to foot.

"It's about time!" she exclaimed. "These aren't sleepers, you know."

Her expression changed from irritation to mortification when Jordan followed McBryde into the hallway. Turning on her heel and apparently forgetting her need for the facilities, the woman walked stiffly toward the staircase. At the bottom step, as she turned her head for one last withering look at the pair, she walked right into a descending passenger.

"Look where you're going!" she squeaked indignantly. "The rudeness!"

Although she was still unseen behind the turn in the stairwell, the journalist's voice could be heard apologizing. McBryde and Jordan slipped into the recessed space in front of the outer door. When they heard the door of the baggage area slide open, they crept around the corner. McBryde, in front, lunged as soon as he was within leaping distance of the journalist's back—without thinking, without considering the pain in his head or his poor chances of success. He figured the surprise attack would give him the advantage.

It didn't work.

Half-turning, the journalist caught sight of McBryde in mid-air. She ducked and caught him across the span of her shoulders. Then, with a quick arch of her back, she deflected him against a wall of luggage. McBryde tried to grab on to her but couldn't adhere. He knew he should aim his fingers at her eyes, her mouth, her hair. But he couldn't bring himself to fight dirty. Instead, he flew like a soccer ball that's been redirected in midflight into the goal. His right shoulder connected with a hard plastic case and a spasm of pain instantly circulated through his head. He managed somehow to keep from blacking out.

Rolling over onto his knees, McBryde watched through the haze of his agony as Jordan came up behind the journalist, grabbed her wrist in his large hand, and twisted it. He seemed to expend no more effort than if he were plucking an orange from a fruit bowl. She tried to break away but these attempts only brought a sharper twist to her wrist. She sank dejectedly into a squat, her left arm pulled behind her and her hand bent back upon itself. Her other arm dangled free, the hand slowly moving up her chest. McBryde knew what she was attempting to do but could manage only a squeak of warning.

"Don't even think about it," Jordan cautioned. "You reach for your gun and I'll break this hand clear off. Then I'll just fall on you and I can't predict what else of yours will break." The woman dropped her hand in resignation. "Larry, come on over and get her gun."

McBryde hated to see her in this position of submission, even after what she had already done to him. Her blond hair fell across her face, obscuring her expression. But he could gauge from the slump of her shoulders how upset she was. Wincing from the dual pains of head and shoulder, he followed Jordan's order and reached his hand into her flannel shirt. Blushing, he plucked the semiautomatic from the shoulder holster.

"Now," Jordan said, his voice as flat and emotionless as when he had identified the train accidents on the tape. "We want you to radio your accomplices and tell them to disable the explosive."

There was a burst of laughter from the woman. "What are you talking about? What explosive?"

Jordan and McBryde exchanged glances. "If you don't do what we ask," Jordan continued, "we'll tie you up right here and leave you to the explosion."

"What explosion?"

"Will there be a different kind of accident?" McBryde asked quietly.

"Why don't you stop this charade and just kill me right now," she replied.

"Kill you?" McBryde blurted. "We don't want to do that. We just want you to stop the accident."

"Who are you? Who do you work for?" she asked.

McBryde glanced at his friend. "This is what she was asking before. What do you think?"

Jordan wasn't paying attention. Head cocked, he was listening to something from his scanner. His eyes refocused on McBryde. "Listen to this." With his free hand he removed the earphone jack. Static from the scanner filled the baggage room.

"Ninety-two eleven, your train looks good on the north side."

A pause, then the reply came: "Highball forty-three twelve."

"That's the Santa Fe's frequency," Jordan said. "I've been listening in for the freight. They're just past Las Vegas. That puts them less than ten minutes away."

"Damn," McBryde fretted. "She must be bluffing."

"Bluffing or not, she'll blow up just like the rest of us," Jordan said. "I say we hold her until she really starts to sweat. She'll give them the signal."

"You're just going to hold me here?" the woman said incredulously. "And let this accident happen? With both of you still on board?"

"That's up to you," Jordan said.

McBryde tried to see her face behind her hair. But it was hidden from him.

"If you don't want the accident to happen, just stop the train yourselves," she said with growing exasperation.

"As you already know," Jordan said, "that won't solve anything."

Whether Jordan intended to explain his comment or not, McBryde never found out. For at that moment, another message burst from the scanner. Jordan adjusted the volume with his free hand. He must have momentarily relaxed his grip. The woman suddenly reached up her right hand to grasp Jordan's restraining arm. It happened so rapidly that McBryde could just stand and watch, dumbfounded that she would even risk having her wrist broken. He was further amazed when she pivoted and threw Jordan over her shoulder. McBryde had never seen the big man leave the ground, whether of his own accord or through some mischance. But now he watched Jordan topple over her and come down hard on the metal floor of the baggage car, all 250 pounds of him. The impact of his body made the entire carriage shake and several suitcases topple from their perches.

Jordan struggled to say something but the breath was knocked completely out of him. He lay on his back, heaving.

McBryde stepped back and trained the gun on the journalist.

Slowly massaging her wrist, she pointed her chin at him with determination. "I'm going to walk out of this car and I'm going to pull the emergency cord and I'm going to stop this train. If you're going to shoot me, shoot me now."

McBryde's hand wobbled. "It won't make any difference," he said. But he was suddenly so heavy with despair that he didn't try to explain. He didn't think she was going to stop the train. She was simply going to walk out of the car and jump the train, unload as quickly as possible. He'd never see her again. In fact, he'd never see anyone ever again.

"Shoot me now," she commanded, slowly stepping backward to the door.

"Stop," he whispered.

But she was gone. McBryde flicked on the safety catch and placed the gun in the waistband of his pants. He moved quickly to his friend's side. Eyes closed, Jordan was gasping for air. McBryde pulled out a handkerchief and wiped away the sweat trickling down his forehead.

"Did she . . . make . . . the call?" Jordan finally managed.

"No."

"Then what—"

The answer soon came. The force of the deceleration pitched McBryde to the floor beside Jordan. The fluorescent light in the baggage car flickered off, leaving them in darkness. They held on to each other for the minute it took the train to come to a stop. After a moment, Jordan looked at the illuminated dial on his watch. "It'll be here. Soon," he whispered.

McBryde began to shiver. His heart began to race. Now he knew what his nightmare meant. It was a presentiment of his death. Would it feel exactly the same when it came? Would his limbs shrivel and his head ignite like a piece of primed charcoal? He gripped Jordan's arm, but could find nothing to say in the awful silence.

"Buddy, I—" Jordan began.

Then the explosion came.

part three

TWENTY-SIX

Two wooden Indians with faded headdresses stood on either side of the bar's entrance. Inside, the walls dizzied the eye. No more than an inch of wallpaper could be glimpsed between the sepia-toned photographs (Billy the Kid, Doc Holliday), laminated advertisements for curatives and tinctures set in bold capital letters, and rose-hued paintings of reservation and desert scenes. Behind the bar a collection of whiskey decanters shaped like cowboys, Indians, and bucking broncos lined a shelf above the tiered rows of liquor bottles. Two glass-fronted bookcases near the antique cash register contained plastic kachina dolls, garish turquoise jewelry, railroad spikes imperfectly painted gold, and rusty horseshoes from the mail carriers of the Santa Fe Trail. Beneath the coatrack a family of stuffed prairie dogs was outfitted in miniature top hats and doll-size gingham dresses. Bleached animal skulls were affixed to the bathroom doors, a steer for "Men" and a cow for "Women." In a prominent position beneath the bar's television, a framed front page from the *Las Vegas Daily Optic* announced a triple hanging from the windmill in the Old Town Plaza.

T. J. Byron's Saloon was stuffed to its pressed tin ceiling with the artifacts, paraphernalia, and kitsch of the Wild West. It was what the tourists demanded, Szczymanski decided as she rotated on her barstool to take in the decor for perhaps the fifth time that afternoon. The tourists wanted T. J. Byron's bartender to sport a handlebar mustache and pomaded hair parted in the middle, wanted their fellow saloon customers to wear cowboy hats laden with rhinestones. Even when authentic—as Las Vegas, New Mexico, certainly was—the West couldn't help but seem a poor copy of itself.

"This place was wilder'n Deadwood," the man to her right said, after introducing himself as a Taos merchant on holiday. He was what pulp Westerns call an "old duffer"—full beard, twinkling eyes, twangy dialect. His ten-gallon hat, without a crease or a speck of dirt, also seemed to come directly from Central Casting. "Las Vegas was even wilder'n Tombstone."

"I've seen Calamity Jane's grave," she said to prove that Las Vegas was not her first taste of the West.

"Doc Holliday ran a saloon a couple doors down," the merchant told her. He appealed to the bartender. "Ain't that right?"

Without looking up from his newspaper, the bartender removed his thumb from his suspender strap and jerked it at Holliday's photograph above his shoulder.

"Been up to Montezuma?" the merchant asked her. "Jesse James went there once, to take a dip in the hot springs. But they couldn't catch him. Not Jesse."

"Whatcha hear about the accident, Sam?" the man to her left asked the bartender. He, too, wore the regulation cowboy hat and square-toed boots. But he was huge, overflowed his barstool like a cake rising up and over its pan.

"Dead all over the place," Sam the bartender replied, his eyes still zigzagging across his newspaper.

"Collision?"

"Naw," Sam said. "I'd say a bomb. Only a bomb could do that."

"Ragheads?" The man on her left shifted his weight and the barstool squealed in protest.

"Naw. What would they be doing out here, huh?" The bartender gazed at his three customers. "Maybe a robbery gone bad. I don't know. Tell you, though, they shouldn't have gone and sent everybody over to the Casteñeda. That's some good business all going over there. People that ride those trains, they got money. They coulda stayed here at the Plaza."

T. J. Byron's Saloon was part of the Plaza Hotel, Las Vegas's most prominent landmark building. It occupied a prime corner of the Old Town Plaza and had been beautifully restored to its Victorian elegance. T. J. Byron's seemed to be its only concession to the less historically rigorous tourist. It was also, according to Ron Jordan, an ideal place to rendezvous.

"How many dead?" asked the Taos merchant.

The bartender shrugged. "Body parts everywhere. That's what I heard. I'm waiting for Salazar to drop by after his shift. He'll give us the skinny."

Szczymanski resisted the urge to clarify their confusion. First of all, body parts were not strewn all over the place. Second, a bomb had not caused the damage. Third, she was the party responsible for keeping the body count at only two.

Not that she entirely understood what she'd done. Twice Jordan had explained the chain of events and she still found the scenario improbable. If she hadn't stood in the dirt along the tracks and smelled the acrid fumes and heard the distant sizzle of the flames, she would have dismissed Jordan's story as a Rube Goldberg fantasy.

To convince her, Jordan had to give a condensed presentation on braking. She learned that a train has both an engine brake that stops the locomotive and air brakes that stop the rest of the train. When braking, engineers usually press down on the engine brake handle, thus disengaging it so that the locomotives continue to press forward. This way, they eliminate slack between the cars and prevent excessive jostling when the train starts up again. Releasing the handle, however, automatically produces a loud blast of air. To avoid this annoyance, engineers will sometimes "plug the brake" of the engine with a quarter or a small wooden slug, and simply rely on the brakes throughout the rest of the train. Although a clear federal safety violation, plugging the engine brake was never really dangerous.

Except this time—for the unfortunate Southwest Chief engineers. When she pulled the emergency cord, all the brakes throughout the train applied except in the engines. The twin locomotives snapped the air hoses and broke free of the rest of the train. The engineers never heard the uncoupling over the noise of the diesel turbines, never realized during their last mile that they'd left their passengers behind. After traveling one mile, the coupled engines passed the Santa Fe freight. A bolt on the valve of a mislabeled water car was triggered to explode, igniting the liquid petroleum gas and immediately engulfing the Southwest Chief's engines. The explosion destroyed most of the Santa Fe's containers and probably cremated the Chief's engineer and fireman instantly, leaving behind nothing that could be called a body part.

Szczymanski didn't want to know anything about the victims, didn't want to feel the guilt. She tried to focus on the four hundred saved and not the two lost. It wasn't easy. Jesus cared more for the single lost lamb than the comfortable flock. If she couldn't feel guilty, she wasn't even a good Catholic.

The overweight man to her left threw two dollars onto the bar and walked out. The bartender, concentrating on a crossword puzzle, didn't look up. She and the old duffer were now the only customers. He was talking to her, but she wasn't listening, only occasionally nodding and saying "Is that so?" It was four o'clock. T. J. Byron's was clearly not a hip place on a Saturday afternoon. She'd been there two hours and the bartender couldn't have collected more than five dollars in tips. Two hours. McBryde and Jordan should have returned by now. Could there be more than one Plaza Hotel? Could she have misjudged the two foamers after all?

No, she couldn't have made a mistake. Two hours wasn't a lot of time to dig up information. And their stories had more than the usual ring of authenticity. McBryde just didn't make sense as the unsub. First, he was no killer. This she knew in the baggage car when he pointed the gun at her. He could have shot her, but didn't. And she'd known that he wouldn't.

Yet he was also a hero. Both McBryde and Jordan were. They'd known about the accident and still remained on the train. Because they thought they could force her to call it off. Two regular guys from Philly put their lives on the line to save four hundred souls.

She might have physically rescued the passengers, but those two took the real risk. How could she doubt them after that?

She remembered the unmistakable relief and gratitude on their faces as she approached them outside the stalled Southwest Chief. McBryde stood with his hand behind his head, a pained smile on his face. Jordan no longer wore his Amtrak disguise. Two regular guys. Surrounding them on all sides was a flat desert of twisted scrub and hard, cracked earth. The sky seemed immense, a brilliant-blue cloth stretching over them. They stayed a distance away from the other passengers to talk quietly. Their first sentences were taken up with apologies and tentative confessions.

"So you really *are* FBI," McBryde had murmured.

"But if you didn't kill the boy on the Lake Shore, then who did?" she asked.

"Whoever did that," said Jordan, pointing to the fire still raging a mile away down the tracks. The acrid odor of burning oil reached them.

From a distance both the Santa Fe freight and the Chief's engines resembled a ruined Lionel set. Thick black smoke coiled up from the wreck, set off starkly against the white mountains in the background. Firemen scrambled around the perimeter of the flames. While the three of them exchanged their seemingly impossible stories, these little figures managed to extinguish the blaze. A mist of smoke clung like a diffuse halo to the wreckage.

"So I guess this means we're a team," McBryde said softly.

"For now at least," Szczymanski replied. "You've done a pretty good job in staying on the trail."

"Ron's the brains behind this."

"Did you run the data through a computer?"

"Computer?" The large black man sighed.

"In your head?" Szczymanski was astounded.

Jordan cast his eyes down. "I'm an accident man. I just happen to know this stuff. Now, what I want to know is where you learned how to toss guys around like that. I'm no beanpole either."

"I hope I didn't hurt you."

"Mostly my pride."

The buses just then pulled up to take the stranded passengers to Las Vegas.

"We'll be taking you to a hotel, the Casteñeda," an Amtrak attendant shouted through a bullhorn. "New engines will be arriving later this evening and we'll be on our way again tonight. We apologize for the inconvenience. Oh, and would the person who pulled the emergency cord please contact Amtrak personnel on the bus or at the hotel?"

"No one saw me," she whispered.

"Good." Jordan turned to her. "Larry and I will make some visits and get the dope on the Chief. Why don't you check in with the FBI and we'll get together later at the Plaza Hotel bar. It's easy to find." He gave her the directions.

So, after keeping Peña and Metaxas and Chaos and Granite all at arm's length, she'd backed into a partnership with the Laurel and Hardy of foamers. They were far from FBI agents. But if Jordan really had produced a pattern from his memory and McBryde really had escaped the Lake Shore with a head full of Seconal, then she could certainly do a lot worse.

The Taos merchant touched her arm and she was brought back into the present. "Been to the Casteñeda yet?"

"Is that so?" she nodded. Then, embarrassed, she realized that it had been a question. "The Casteñeda?"

"It's a Harvey Hotel, one of the last still standing. Fred Harvey set up hotels and restaurants from Chicago westward. Back in the nineteenth century. Ain't that right, Sam?"

The bartender didn't look up.

"Brought in all these pretty girls from the East. Harvey Girls. Sure you must've heard of 'em. Hell, it wasn't guns that won the West. It was them Harvey Girls!"

"Is that right?" She ran a finger around the neck of her Corona.

"That was back when Las Vegas was the biggest city in New Mexico. Railroads came and everything took off. The railroad built this place."

Great, another foamer. They were suddenly everywhere. It was like the body snatchers; soon she too would be collecting pictures of steam trains, talking about Maglev. And, like those dumb human hosts, she wouldn't even register the transformation.

"You live around here?" The old duffer munched on pretzel nuggets. The crumbs powdered his beard.

"East Coast."

"Mighty big town, that East Coast."

"Washington."

"Been there for an inauguration."

"Congratulations."

"You a tourist?"

She was not in the mood to answer questions. "What do you sell, anyway?"

"Boots." The man turned in his chair to display his red leather cowboy boots. He pulled up his jeans so she could look at the stitchwork. "How 'bout you'n I take a trip out'n' see the train crash. Bet it's pretty spectacular."

"I'm comfortable right here."

"Aw, it's too quiet. Ain't that right, Sam?"

"Viscous secretion," the bartender said, his head still bowed. "Five letters. Middle letter's a 'c.' "

"Mucus," came a deep voice from behind her. She swiveled in her stool.

Jordan and McBryde approached the bar, both smiling. The tension in her stomach immediately eased. She celebrated by turning her back on the Taos merchant and thereafter ignoring him.

"A pitcher of the mystery draft," McBryde said to the bartender.

"Any chicken wings?" Jordan asked.

"Grill's next door. Take a right at Sitting Bull. How do you spell 'mucus' anyway?"

Szczymanski, McBryde, and the pitcher of beer all moved to a corner table in the shadows, leaving Jordan to place a large order for chicken wings and help out on several more crossword clues. McBryde grinned at her and rubbed his hands together. His red hair was unruly. A scattering of freckles highlighted his cheeks just beneath his green eyes. He poured the beer into three glasses and drank off half his glass in a single gulp before turning to Szczymanski.

"God, I needed that." His voice dropped. "Okay, here's what we found out from the dispatcher. Santa Fe's having a fit. They're trying to find out how a tanker of water suddenly became a tanker of LPG. They're more worried about insurance than sabotage. Amtrak, meanwhile, won't find any evidence that the engineer plugged the engine, but everyone knows what happened. What they don't know, and what really sticks in their craw, is why someone pulled the emergency just two miles before the pass with the Santa Fe."

"What do they think?"

"Malfunction."

"They don't see a link to the Lake Shore?"

"They've got hundreds of trains out there every day. Accidents happen."

"What about an investigation?"

"Naturally. But they won't come up with anything."

"It's too freakish. They must suspect something."

"Amtrak'll blame the engineers. They're dead, after all. Won't complain. They'll issue the usual advisory: Don't plug the engine. Santa Fe will come down hard on the yardmaster in Albuquerque for allowing the tank to be mislabeled and not checking the valves."

"What about on board? Did you recognize anybody from the Lake Shore?"

"Only you." Again the grin. McBryde was certainly cute. There was a pixieish quality about him.

"And I recognized you. So we're back to square one. No suspects for the poor kid's murder."

"What about the pillhead?"

"Jigsaw? He works for the FBI. He's a bagman. Don't worry. He's been dropped from the loop. We won't be bothered by him anymore."

"You trust him?" he asked.

"Jigsaw? Of course not. But he's Bureau."

"He drugged me!"

"We still thought you were our fish. We were going to search you."

"What about the paper towel, the screwdriver?"

"Back at the office. Don't worry."

"But they'll connect me with . . ." McBryde began.

"No, no. Only Chaos knows about it. And he won't say anything."

"Chaos?"

"He deciphered the pattern for me. Works for the technical division. He doesn't know much about all this. And he won't talk." She addressed Jordan, who had just returned to the table. "What can you guess about the next accident?"

Jordan paused to take a swallow of his beer. "The number pattern tells us it will be the California Zephyr. We're down to a five-day separation, so it will be on Thursday. The 'w' pattern puts the accident near Elko, Nevada. You'll want to board in Denver on Wednesday morning."

"What's the 'w' pattern?" Szczymanski asked.

Jordan pulled his map from a shirt pocket, unfolded it, and explained the lines.

Szczymanski shook her head. The pattern screamed out entrapment. But what choice did they have? "What will happen near Elko, Nevada?"

"Cornfield meet maybe. Sorry, that's a head-on collision. But I'm not sure. I'll have to hit the archives to get a better sense of it."

"What about a replay of a previous Zephyr accident?" McBryde asked.

"Maybe, although that's not a pattern we've seen so far. The Lake Shore had never before gone off the Colonie Bridge and the Chief certainly never had an LPG explosion. In any case, the Zephyr's been a pretty safe train. It had that head-on in forty-six near Naperville, Illinois, when it was still called the Advance Flyer. And there was that derailment on Christmas night in eighty-eight."

Jordan took a larger swallow of beer. He recalled these accidents as though they were events in his own life. "The most interesting accident was the blizzard. Remember, Larry, those pictures I have of the City of San Francisco up near the Donner Summit? It took them three days to rescue the passengers and another three days to dig the train out of the snow."

"It would be a little difficult for our friends to plan a blizzard," Szczymanski pointed out.

"Precisely," Jordan agreed. "But right now I can't think of anything specific. Maybe you can dig up some leads before Wednesday."

"The tapes," McBryde suggested.

Back at the crash site, she'd been completely absorbed by the story of the tapes, finally understanding the purpose of the bugs. "Do you think your friend will get an offer to buy a recording of this accident?" she asked.

"Perhaps," McBryde said. "Ron, can you get the name and address of Georgia's friend in Colorado? And I'll call Marty to see if he's got anything new from the first tape."

"Chaos gave a radius of three miles for the mikes."

"So there's a receiver set up somewhere near the accident site," McBryde said.

"Or there was," Szczymanski said.

"I'd guess a receiver in a van," Jordan said. "Travels parallel to the train. Hard to detect. Easy to leave town quickly."

"Like a chaser," McBryde added.

"What's that?"

"A foamer who's into photos," Jordan explained. "Chases alongside or ahead of trains to get the best shots."

Szczymanski said, "I want to see a list of people who got off at the last stop. Raton, right?"

Jordan produced a slip of paper from his shirt pocket. "Just so happens . . ."

"Ron can be an awful smooth talker."

She glanced quickly at the list of names. "I'll phone these to Chaos. He can do a check." At least she hoped he would. "And let's do a cross-check with the passenger lists from the other accidents."

"Won't fly," Jordan said. "Unless the tickets were bought with a credit card."

"Still, it's worth a shot. I want some tangible lead before the Zephyr. This'll be the biggie," McBryde said.

"Why do you say that?"

"The pattern. Zephyr's number twelve, and twelve minus thirteen is a negatively numbered train," Jordan pointed out. "Unless they plan to start over again at the top."

At that moment a waitress swept into the bar with a large platter of chicken wings, bright orange from the glistening hot sauce and so spicy that they made Szczymanski cough before she could even bring her lips to their sticky surface. With beer to cut the heat, she managed to eat a few. But she couldn't compete with the foamers.

Eating and drinking with gusto, Jordan and McBryde discussed possible scenarios for the California Zephyr. They traded back and forth a dizzying variety of unfamiliar terms—frogs and humpbacks and rabbits and daisy chains. They raised a number of complicated possibilities involving sabotaged switches, confused signals, and hijacked engines, and then rejected each in turn as unlikely. After initially asking for explanations, Szczymanski gave up and let them speculate without interruption. She'd now drunk four or five beers. Her concentration was dispersing into thousands of tiny droplets.

She glanced every so often at McBryde, watched him strip the sticky little drumsticks with rabbitlike nibbles. It was odd how the features of a face altered so completely when you changed your mind about a person's motives. Before, McBryde had appeared disingenuous, his green eyes open just a little too wide, his mouth too quick to smile, his hair artfully disarranged. Now he looked just like a little boy, a Huck Finn of the railway. Those wide eyes had become irresistible, the smiling mouth fetching, and the tousled hair positively electrifying. He wasn't married. He had mentioned something about an ex-wife and child. But he was probably involved with someone back in Philadelphia.

This was crazy. The alcohol was throwing her completely off balance. She'd practically just met this man, and now she wanted to run her hand through his hair? No, she'd have to keep their relationship strictly business. Emotions only complicated matters. While TB^2 had worked quite well up to that point, it was definitely time for a new strategy. She needed cool logic, not bluster and bravado. Once again, she turned to her deck of personas. Even with the alcohol handicapping her logic, it didn't take long to find the perfect fit.

The Calm Prosecutor.

This strategy from her law-school days had always worked marvelously in court. One separated one's emotions from the case—not so that one became emotionless, but so that one could use emotions strategically to sway juries, to influence testimony, to make impressions upon the judge.

Bracket those emotions, she commanded herself.

"The only witness is dead, right," Jordan switched topics. He was wrapping his pile of chicken bones neatly in a shroud of napkins. "But the kid mentioned seeing two men. Any characteristics?"

"Unfortunately not," Szczymanski replied. "That was my fault. I should have sat him down right then and there instead of going for a long shot. I should have waited for his memory to improve. I feel terrible about his death."

"Me, too," McBryde agreed.

They both turned to their mugs of beer.

"I don't want to sound heartless," Jordan said after a moment's silence, "but there've been a lot of victims. You just happened to meet one of them. Don't let it paralyze you."

"That's a pretty sober view for a churchman," McBryde said.

"Remember, I've seen a lot of premature deaths. I don't know a family in my community that isn't touched by tragedy. Just got to keep moving forward." Jordan checked his watch. "Which reminds me—time to move forward my own self. Hazel's going to be hopping mad if I'm not back tonight. Look, Larry, now that there are two of you, play it cool, okay? You don't have to grab this foamer. Just collect the evidence. The FBI will do the rest."

She hadn't told them about the status of the case. McBryde didn't need to know that she was on a rogue assignment, that the Bureau considered these train accidents a low-priority case, that she'd been led to this impasse all because of an embarrassing sexual-harassment charge. Eventually she'd fill him in on the details, once her situation had clarified. But not until then.

She was sorry Jordan was leaving them. They could use his help. And her libido, it seemed, could use a chaperone.

After Jordan's bus departed for Albuquerque, she and McBryde walked the streets of Las Vegas, going over their mutual misunderstandings on the Lake Shore and the Southwest Chief. It was ludicrous, really, how they hadn't listened to one another at first. But now, as they passed out of Las Vegas's Old Town and into its New Town, they couldn't stop listening to each other's stories. The beer made her loquacious. But not foolhardy. The Calm Prosecutor made sure of that. McBryde pointed out landmarks as they walked. He'd been to Las Vegas before and seemed to know much of its history, at least the railroad-connected parts.

After the well-preserved Western facades of the Old Town, Las Vegas's New Town was a disappointment. It looked like any other small, depressed city. The signs in the stores were discolored, yellow at the edges, cracked. One store was devoted exclusively to T-shirts. "I came to Las Vegas and didn't even gamble. Visit the other Vegas." A red brick building with a turret at its corner was boarded up and abandoned. On the painted advertisement for baking soda on its side wall, a cowgirl sang out "HOWDY," the "H" supplied by a window frame. Except the frame was long gone. "OOWDY," she declared instead.

"As falls the railroad, so falls America," McBryde commented. "So we'll stay here tonight?"

"Tomorrow too," she said. "Then on Monday, let's rent a car and drive up to Denver. That'll give us a couple days to hunt around up there."

"Do you think they're still around Las Vegas?"

"Probably not. They got their sound and then skipped town."

"They'll recognize me. Maybe you too. We're out in the open. This could be the chance they're looking for."

"I have a feeling," Szczymanski said, "that they want us to show up on the next train. And we don't have much of a choice but to follow their bread crumbs. About tonight: this guy in the bar mentioned a Harvey Hotel."

"Fact is, the Casteñeda's where we're heading." McBryde's voice fluttered with excitement. "It was only recently renovated and reopened."

The Casteñeda looked out onto the railroad tracks. It was a two-story, U-shaped building with a covered-arch walkway and a courtyard enclosed on the fourth side by the tracks. Two curvilinear parapets blocked off the roof. Facing the street was an elegant stone cupola. It was a stunning building surrounded by dust and decay. The only other functioning buildings on its street were auto-repair and welding shops, their rusting metal grates pulled down for the night. McBryde pointed out to her a plain, crumbling structure—the Rawlins—the only boardinghouse for the Harvey Girls still standing. The glass in its storefront windows was spiderwebbed with cracks. The windows on the second story were black gaps. She did not have high expectations for its companion Harvey Hotel.

On the inside, however, the Casteñeda sparkled. A chandelier, hanging high above a sumptuous red carpet, illuminated the lobby. The staff wore red velvet dinner jackets and black bow ties. Cabinets lined the lobby area, containing objects found during the renovation—medicine bottles of thick colorful glass, scraps of newspaper, scratched old coins. At one end of the lobby was a huge mahogany reception desk. Behind the desk stood a wooden honeycomb.

"A humidor," McBryde said. "The original. I've read about it."

At the front desk, two women occupied the attention of the main clerk. From behind, they looked vaguely familiar to Szczymanski. Had she seen them on the train, in the lounge car, sitting near her in the coach? As she and McBryde stepped up to the counter, the two women turned around.

Szczymanski stepped back with a gasp.

"Hey, babe, I thought you might come out here," Peña said loudly.

"I—" But Szczymanski couldn't get out another word.

Peña's eyes shifted to McBryde. "We were expecting you as well. Thanks for making our job easier." Her gun was out and trained on McBryde.

TWENTY-SEVEN

They're jacking me up, McBryde thought crazily. The three of them—vivacious Peña, taciturn Metaxas, and even Jennifer Szczymanski herself—were just criminals pretending to be law-enforcement officials. True, they had flashed their FBI badges. But to his untrained eye these could be fakes. They talked about the Bureau this-and-that and discussed contacting various regional offices. But that, too, could be a game. Peña spoke of dragging him back to Washington, D.C. But they probably planned to snuff him out right here in Las Vegas. They'd take him up to a room, drop all the FBI bullshit they'd used to fool the hotel manager, and drill a few new holes in his head.

But then what to make of Szczymanski's behavior? First there'd been that finger-to-the-lips gesture over the heads of Peña and Metaxas as they all stood at the Casteñeda's front desk. Now, as they sat in the manager's office waiting for the suite in the second-floor rear to be readied, Szczymanski was suddenly all innocence.

Metaxas had handcuffed him. Peña leveled a gun at him. And Szczymanski was lying with every breath.

"Oh, he was on the Lake Shore?" she said. "We met in a bar in town and just got to talking about trains and—"

Peña was livid. "Damn it, hermana, why didn't you call in? We put out an APB on this sunvabitch late last night."

"For what?"

"For murder, Fresh Cheese, for murder. The kid on the Lake Shore."

McBryde looked around the office for potential weapons. Could he subdue three agile women with a walking stick and a paperweight? Why wasn't Szczymanski helping him out of this jam?

"I don't understand," she was saying instead. "The police had a suspect—"

"It didn't take long for Max to clear the drifter. Turns out he's got an alibi up until the train stopped. Anyway, Max looked over the scene of the crime, figured out the boy'd been shot before the emergency cord was pulled. Something about blood . . ."

"Distribution and flow of blood," Metaxas clarified. "Showed evidence of the rapid deceleration of the train."

"Whatever," Peña continued. "Checks out with the gearheads in HQ. So then we call up some of the passengers, conduct some interviews. Turns out there was this fellow acting awful strange just before the train stopped. Went to said bathroom just after Albany, then disappeared after the emergency cord was pulled. Dusted for prints—those Albany Doggers didn't even do that properly. Ran some checks. Turned up our boy. Put his pretty face out on the wire."

"And now he shows up in Las Vegas," Metaxas said, staring at McBryde with the heavy-lidded gaze of a lizard contemplating its prey.

His limbs jerked convulsively. He couldn't stop them, could only sit there listening and twitching and trying to figure out what was going on. Could Szczymanski possibly believe these other two? After all they'd already been through together?

"What about the overseas suspect?" Szczymanski asked.

"Max'll tell you about that one later. It was all a computer error. Marinetti's cleared him."

The hotel manager, a soft, boneless man in a dinner jacket, appeared at the threshold of his office to report that their room was ready. He nervously guided them up the service stairs and to the door of their suite. As he retreated back down the hall, he called out, "Please, there's, um, no smoking in our rooms."

They were now alone in the suite. "Are you going to kill me right here?" McBryde asked tremulously.

"Don't tempt me." Peña laughed.

"The FBI doesn't kill its suspects," Szczymanski informed him. Was that a glimmer of warmth in her eye?

Metaxas and Szczymanski sat down in matching armchairs. He was directed to sit on a small wooden chair between them, his cuffed hands in his lap. Metaxas pointed a gun at his head.

"If you move, we shoot," Peña said, stretching out on a bed, propping her back up with pillows and keeping her gun trained on him. "But if you're nice and cooperative, you'll make it to the federal pen intact."

So maybe they were FBI after all. At least he wouldn't be executed gangland-style. They wanted information, not blood. His limbs stopped shaking.

McBryde took stock of his surroundings. Under different circumstances, he would have been thrilled by a suite in the Casteñeda. The rail magnates probably stayed in this great double room, with full view of their property out the bay windows. The suite had been beautifully restored—antique chairs, a bird's-eye-maple dresser, porcelain doorknobs, hand-colored photographs on the wall. Two king-sized beds—an accommodation to modern tastes—were covered by enormous patchwork quilts.

Peña peeled off her shoes with her toes. "Jesus, Fresh Cheese, you're lucky we showed up. There's no telling what he planned to do with you."

Szczymanski blushed prettily. "Oh, I hardly think—"

"Fact is, you got here rather quickly," Metaxas interrupted. "You were supposed to be in Dallas today."

"Fortunately I was still at the Dallas airport when I heard about the accident. Caught a flight to Albuquerque almost immediately."

"Convenient," Metaxas commented.

Good recovery, McBryde thought. Considering her adept

impersonation of a journalist, he shouldn't have been surprised at her powers of deception. But if Szczymanski wanted him to trust her, she was pursuing an unusual strategy. He struggled with the possibilities. If she were behind the accidents, she'd have killed him by now. If she really worked for the FBI and thought him guilty, she wouldn't be lying to her putative colleagues. So she was engaged in some double game. Why trust her? But she had stopped the train. And all Peña and Metaxas had done was browbeat him. Time for a leap of faith.

"I haven't been in Las Vegas for long, but I did manage to get this." Szczymanski produced the piece of paper Jordan had given her. "Names of passengers. That got off at Raton."

"His name on it?" Peña nodded at McBryde as she glanced over the list.

"Maybe a pseudonym," Metaxas suggested.

Peña read the names to someone over the phone. "They'll run a check and get back to us in an hour," she related after putting down the receiver.

Then, after fishing around in her briefcase that lay next to her on the bed, Peña pulled out a glossy magazine. With one hand she flipped through a few pages, murmuring approvingly at several advertisements. With her other hand she kept her gun pointed in McBryde's direction.

"Find out anything else?" she asked Szczymanski.

"LPG explosion. Mislabeled container car. Engineer on the Southwest Chief plugged the engine brake. That's why only the engines blew."

"Yes, we have that information," Metaxas said.

Peña whistled at the page in front of her, an ad for men's cologne. "Nice butt!"

"What's the plan?" Szczymanski asked.

"Plan?" Peña addressed Metaxas. "We got a plan?"

Metaxas turned to McBryde. "Why did you kill Jackson Long?"

"Jackson Long?"

"Lake Shore. Bullet through the head," Peña said. "What do you need, a diagram?"

"I didn't kill him." Keep the answers brief. Tell the truth whenever possible.

"Who did?"

"I don't know."

Peña turned a page. "Get this, Max. At a gala benefit a group of famous young stars show up in the raw!" She peered closer at the photograph in the magazine, then held it up for them to see. "Look, they fuzzed it out. Prudes."

"Where's the next train accident going to be?" Metaxas asked.

"I don't know."

"Come on!" Peña lifted her head from the pictures. "You were on the Lake Shore, you're here in Las Vegas, and you expect us to believe that this is all coincidence?"

"I ride a lot of trains," McBryde answered. "I travel around as part of my job."

"We can connect you to the murder, regardless of what you say," Peña said. "We've got your prints, we've got your motive, we've got your history of murder—"

"Excuse me?"

"Look, McBryde, we've got your whole bio. We know about the kid you iced in Portland."

"Self-defense," he managed.

"In a fucking pig's eye. Cold-blooded fucking assassination. So why don't you go easy on yourself and just tell us the whole story."

"I told you all I know."

Peña leaped from the bed, the magazine flying from her lap like a startled pigeon. She approached, holding her gun by its barrel as though it were a hammer. She swung the handle menacingly. "Bullshit! That's a load of bullshit! And if you don't give us some fucking information, I'm going to make you wish you were sitting with the engineer on that fucking Southwest Chief!"

Metaxas added in an even tone, "It's more than likely that you resisted arrest. And that we had to use some force to bring you in." From her expression Metaxas looked as though she would very much enjoy using that force.

"Ever had a chunk of ice rammed up your asshole?" Peña growled. "Or shit forced down your gullet? Prison tricks. That don't leave any marks."

"Peña." It was Szczymanski.

"What?" Peña turned to her furiously.

Szczymanski shook her head back and forth, once.

"Look, Miss Virgin of Fucking Guadalupe, if you don't want to be part of it, just go down to the bar and get yourself a soft drink. Why do you think we're here tonight and not at the regional office? Huh? Because we wanta gang-bang McBryde? I want this unsub, damn it. This guy's going to talk. I want a confession."

McBryde wasn't sure how much more violence he could handle. His shoulders hurt from where Szczymanski had twice tossed him into the luggage, and the back of his head throbbed dully from the blow of the blackjack. He'd never been very good about pain. A few swipes with the butt of Peña's gun and McBryde would admit to rape, genocide, the assassination of both Kennedys, anything.

"We conduct this investigation by the book," Szczymanski said. "You touch him and I go straight to Granite."

"Well, will you listen to that!" Peña addressed Metaxas in high-pitched sarcasm. "I think she's sweet on him. They had a few drinks and were going to get a room for the night. That's what I think."

"You think wrong, then," Szczymanski said.

"Maybe we should just let you handle the interrogation, Agent Szczymanski. But don't forget the Trojans!"

"Can I please continue with my questions?" Metaxas asked.

But Peña was still after Szczymanski. "I don't like your attitude. For a so-called hotshot you been making a whole lot of mistakes."

"Who are you interrogating, me or him?" Szczymanski asked.

The phone's ringing interrupted the argument. Peña sat back down on the bed to listen to the information, the gun now on her lap. After nodding her head several times, ear pressed to the phone, she pumped her arm in the air. Her face was radiant. "Looks like we've got our man!"

"Who was that?" Szczymanski asked.

"We've got a match on the Lake Shore and the list you gave me from the Southwest Chief. Charles Ulysses Thayer. Crazy-assed name. Ulysses?"

"That your alias?" Metaxas asked him.

"Never heard of it." McBryde pretended indifference. But actually the name sounded vaguely familiar. A Philly Foamer? Someone who called the office?

"Then how come we just turned up that name in credit-card searches?" Peña said defiantly. "All the addresses are listed as 540 Miller Lane. Sound familiar?"

"How can that be?" he said. Then it clicked. Charles Thayer. The name that had appeared on wrongly addressed mail at his apartment over the last several weeks.

"You got off at Raton but came down to Las Vegas to see what happened," Metaxas said.

"Not looking good for you, pobrecito," Peña said. "So 'fess up. Or I'll get the ice-cube trays."

Jesus, he really was being framed. The paper towel, the tape, and now this Thayer thing. He tried to look at Szczymanski without seeming to look at her. Did she believe him? Would she blurt out the real story? Out of the corner of his eye, he could see that she was scanning the room, assessing the positions of the two interrogators, possibly planning something. She'd given him a few signs, had opposed his torture. He could only hope that she was still on his side. They didn't have much time. Tomorrow would be too late. And he didn't think he'd be in any shape to execute an escape with a chunk of ice up his ass.

Peña was again spread out on the bed leafing through her magazine. "Lies, lies, lies. This is the end of the line, Charlie. Why are you setting all these accidents? Life not exciting enough for you on Miller Lane?"

"If you're going to torture me, I'd prefer you did it sooner rather than later."

"Oh, listen to Mr. Bigdick!" Peña held up her magazine again. The photo spread showed the wreckage of an airplane. "What about this, Charlie? Says here that everyone on board was 'pulverized on impact.' That turn you on?"

McBryde didn't answer. Their weapons were a problem. Although he'd given Szczymanski her gun back, she wouldn't draw on her colleagues. So it was up to him. But what could he do without weapons, without free hands, without even a rudimentary plan?

"It's as good as a stroke mag for you, right? Or do you like your victims to suffer more?"

McBryde sighed.

"Wanta know what prison's like? And what the cons do with soft little sickos like you? You wouldn't last a day. They'd spread you on their fucking breakfast toast."

"If you cooperate, we will make sure that things go easier for you," Metaxas added. "If you do not cooperate, we will break you."

"Talk to my lawyer," McBryde said, trying to work out a plan, any plan.

"I was waiting for that," Peña said. "Mr. Thayer has finally remembered his lawyer. Well, kiss my Puerto Rican ass!"

"Peña," Szczymanski said.

"Ah, fuck it. We've got plenty of time for chitchat." She returned the magazine to her briefcase. "I'm hungry. Max?"

Metaxas nodded.

"Chinese?" Peña asked.

"Nothing good out here," Metaxas said.

"Okay, okay. Burgers? Tamales?"

"Pizza," Metaxas said. "It can be delivered."

"Good point. Pepperoni?"

"And garlic."

"Garlic? Jesus, what's Marinetti doing to you? Fucking garlic. We'll stink up the whole room."

The pizza was just the break he needed. Now he had a plan. A lousy, unlikely plan. But he had nothing to lose. Again his limbs began to twitch. He tried to push this anxious energy into his hands. Ta-dum, his fingers thrummed on his thigh. It was agony to wait. If he ever lived through this nightmare he'd have lifelong ulcers.

"Getting a little nervous?" Peña asked.

"Me?" He stilled his fingers.

"We'll give you a slice of pizza if you tell us the truth. Pepperoni and garlic."

"I am telling you the truth."

"Then it's not good enough. And you won't get any pizza. And don't think you're going to get anything to drink either. We'll see how you feel tomorrow on an empty stomach. After being kept up all night. Max and me'll take turns."

His adrenaline level was starting to rise. His heart thumped wildly in his chest. If the pizza didn't arrive soon, his internal organs would leap from their casings.

Finally, after parrying aside the same battery of questions—no, he didn't know where the next train accident would be; didn't know who killed the boy; didn't know who was behind all the wrecks—there came a knock at the door. Metaxas holstered her gun, paid the delivery boy, and carefully conveyed the square cardboard box into the room. He tried to control his breathing and tensed the muscles in his calves.

"Fucking garlic," Peña said, sniffing the air. She kept her gun trained on McBryde as Metaxas approached the coffee table.

Before Metaxas could set the box down, however, he made his move.

Waiting until Metaxas came between him and Peña, McBryde leaped from his chair. Grunting, he barreled into Metaxas with his shoulder and propelled both her and the pizza at Peña. One went high, the other low. Metaxas glanced off her partner's knees and fell hard against a night table, upsetting the desk lamp and sending it crashing to the floor amid the sound of splintering glass. The pizza flipped out of the now open box and landed directly on Peña, covering her gun completely in tomato sauce and mozzarella.

"Maricón!" Peña screeched as she tried to fling the steaming cheese from her wrists and neck. The triangular slices of pizza slid down her shirtfront. They looked like entrails in her lap.

McBryde didn't pause to admire the precision of his aim or thank Vito's for sloppily securing their pizza boxes. Immediately after sending Metaxas sprawling, he spun around toward Szczymanski. She already had her gun out. For one terrible moment he thought she would shoot him. Then he saw her eyes. She looked at him gratefully. "Hurry," she mouthed. He grabbed the gun from her and stepped around to the back of her chair. Circling her throat with his elbow, he still managed to point the gun at her ear. She offered no resistance. He felt a surge of blood to his head as he smelled her hair, her sweat. He pressed the barrel of the gun to her cheek. He hoped that the elbow locked around her throat looked convincing, even though a small space separated the crook of his elbow from her voice box.

"Prick!" Peña said, still peeling the pepperoni slices like circles of raw, scabrous skin off her clothes. Her gun lay on the bed beneath a red-and-yellow ooze.

Metaxas rolled over, blinked several times, and found her gun. A gash at her forehead leaked blood. "Let her go," she said in an utterly confident voice. "I can put a bullet in your head before you even find the trigger."

"Put your own gun down," he instructed her. "Remember, this wouldn't be the first time I've shot someone." Perhaps he shouldn't have said that. Too late. "Not only will I kill the hostage, but I'll make damn sure one of you goes with her." It was a good thing he'd seen the right movies or he'd never have known what to say.

Metaxas's eyes shifted to Szczymanski's. Then she dropped the gun.

"Throw over the guns and your radios." They arrived at his feet. "Now, I want the handcuff keys."

"Fuck you," Peña replied. "Only keys are in D.C."

He poked the gun into the hollow of Szczymanski's cheek. "What are you, stupid?"

"Don't do it," Szczymanski said to Peña in a trembling voice. "He's bluffing."

Jesus, thought McBryde. But then he saw that it was the right thing for her to say after all. Peña looked angrily at Szczymanski and tossed over the keys. Interesting dynamic going on there, but he didn't have time to explore it. He kept the gun pressed into his hostage's face as she unlocked his cuffs. He commanded Szczymanski to cuff her hands together behind her back. Noticing that Metaxas had two more pairs of handcuffs dangling from her belt, he instructed her to attach Peña's wrist to the headboard of the bed and then her own hand to Peña's ankle. That would slow them down a bit.

"I want your car," he said.

Peña watched Metaxas at work with the cuffs. "You fucking burn me."

"Car keys."

"I'm gonna roast your ass. Personally."

"Keys. To the cars and the cuffs."

They clattered at his feet.

"What kind of car?" he asked.

"Red Saturn," Peña spat.

"Yank the phone out of the wall," he instructed Metaxas. She pulled out the cord with such force that he thought most of the wall would follow with it.

It was not easy to collect all the weapons, stow them in the bag, and keep Szczymanski's throat in a death grip. He knew that under any other circumstances she could easily wrestle the gun from his grasp and throw him broken-limbed into a corner—even with her hands cuffed behind her back. But now she moved smoothly alongside him, as if they were do-si-doing at a country dance. A tremendous confidence lifted him. With his free hand, he turned over the key chain and, under the abbreviated list of characteristics, noted that the car was a blue Escort.

"You lied to me," he said menacingly to Peña. Then he mock-tightened his grip around Szczymanski's throat. On cue, she produced a credible strangling noise.

"Red, blue," Peña said sullenly. "Just get the hell out of here already."

"If I see anyone following me, I'll shoot her. Do you understand? When I'm safely away, I'll let your two-faced colleague go."

As soon as they were in the blue Ford Escort and racing out of the parking lot, he slipped the gun beneath his seat. At a stoplight, stalled behind a van, he quickly undid Szczymanski's handcuffs. "Now what the hell was going on back—"

But she cut him off. "Just get out of here now, okay?"

"Denver?" He kept his eyes on the rearview mirror to see if they were being followed.

"Denver. You know where you're going?"

His eyes still focused on the road behind them, he failed to notice that their street had turned into a dead end. Narrowly avoiding a fire hydrant, he swung the car around sharply, his fender glancing off the side of a parked car. Its alarm began to wail. The noise unnerved him so much that he almost swerved directly into a telephone pole. But after shaking his head and concentrating on the unwinding road, he managed to get to Route 518 heading north. The police would look for them on the interstates, not on this little mountain road.

It was late, near midnight, and Route 518 was almost empty. He glanced at her. In profile, her chin jutted out even more coquettishly. He shifted his position in the driver's seat.

"I'm not Charles Thayer."

"I know that."

"I mean, I have no idea how they traced those credit cards to me."

"Don't worry. I know you're being framed."

"How can you be so sure?"

"It's a joke."

"Hardly funny."

"Charles Ulysses Thayer. C. U. Thayer. See you there. On the next train. Someone has a taste for puns."

"So if you were so goddamn confident I was innocent, why'd you lie to them?"

She turned to face him. "I've really screwed up on this one." He could sense the tension knotted up inside her.

He touched the back of her hand and lightly brushed the tiny hairs near her wrist. Then he grabbed the steering wheel again with both hands. The gesture had been very nearly unconscious and it gave him a twinge of embarrassment. He quickly spoke up to fill the silence.

"It's a long drive to Denver. Plenty of time for you to tell me the whole truth and nothing but the truth."

"Hey, you were pretty good back there."

"I nearly crapped in my pants."

She smiled. "The way that pizza flipped out of its box . . ."

"The look on Peña's face."

"Maricón!" Szczymanski screamed and they both laughed long and hard as the blue Ford Escort motored north into the Sangre de Cristo Mountains.

TWENTY-EIGHT

During their night journey northward—ditching the Ford on a Taos side street, hot-wiring a Honda and taking it to Pueblo—she managed to tell McBryde her whole story, starting with Pierre and Rudy Blaine. Putting all of her shame into words was enormously therapeutic. McBryde took the incident very seriously.

"We get at least one case a month, usually female conductors and ticket sellers. Almost every one has led to disciplinary action against the harasser."

"Most men laugh at sexual harassment. Make jokes about it."

"Most men are just boys, I guess. They laugh when they don't know how they should react."

She was impressed. McBryde was a real man for the nineties, almost too good to be true. He was divorced, seemed to be unattached. She was even willing to look the other way when it came to his bureaucratic job and his train obsession. But the Calm Prosecutor forced her to talk about the case, not his private life.

McBryde carefully followed her account. He asked question after question about the FBI, about her interrogation, about Chaos and Jigsaw and Granite.

"You haven't said much about this mole."

"I don't know much about the mole," she admitted.

"Almost every agent you mentioned sounds suspicious."

"It could just be Bureau paranoia. Left over from the Cold War."

"Think there's a connection with our trains?" he asked.

"It was just an accident that I found the equipment at Lucky's."

"Isn't it unusual that microphones are involved in both cases? This Chaos fellow seems the most suspicious."

"But it was an accident that we ever—"

"Accidents can be planned too, you know," McBryde pointed out.

Chaos a mole? It hardly seemed likely. All the information he'd given her had proved accurate and useful. But, then, perhaps he'd sent her on those trips for a different purpose. Perhaps the bullet on the Lake Shore and the premature cremation on the Southwest Chief had both been meant for her. She wanted so badly to trust Chaos. He was the only agent in the D.C. office who'd been nice to her. A nice agent? Rudy Blaine had been nice too. These days, it was best to beware of nice people. Which reminded her.

"I hate to bring this up, but I understand that your hands aren't exactly clean."

"What do you mean?"

"The boy you killed in Portland."

He stiffened. "It was self-defense."

"Do you want to tell me about it?"

McBryde was silent for a few minutes. Then he told her the story of the confrontation in the Portland train yards. "You don't know how terrible I feel about it. Those kids only wanted to steal. But I was so scared. I didn't want to kill him."

"Sometimes you don't have a choice." She felt sorry for him. McBryde just wasn't cut out for this business.

"It doesn't seem right. I should have just given them what they wanted. Lives are more important than things."

"Remember—they probably considered things more important than your life."

"Still, I wish I could just rewind, go back and change things."

She softened. "I feel the same way about Jackson Long. It was my fault he was involved in the first place."

For a time they sat in silence, united by this shared sense of guilt. When they began again to talk, they discussed their chances of escape. They were lucky—no sign of police pursuit. The possibility that Peña and Metaxas were still attached hand to foot tickled her. It might be hard to find a hacksaw on a Saturday night.

Early Sunday morning, outside Pueblo, Colorado, they abandoned the Honda at the bottom of a deserted arroyo. Hiking back up to the main road, they managed to hitch a ride with a phlegmatic Mississippi trucker on his way to Alaska through Denver. Kept awake by amphetamines that did nothing to speed up his monologues, he complained in long whining drawls about the cold weather, the corrupt politicians in the North, and the lousy coffee served up at truck stops. But at least he drove quickly. For a time McBryde talked with him about the relative virtues of espresso and cappuccino. They all ate from a bag of barbecue-flavored potato chips. The overheated cab of the truck smelled of Coca-Cola and unrefrigerated cheese. Szczymanski tried to sleep. But the mole scrabbled at the margins of her awareness, making her edgy, uncomfortable.

The trucker left them on the interstate a few miles from the Denver city center. They attempted to book two rooms at a nearby Sagebrush Inn.

"Only one left," the clerk informed them. "Star Trek convention at the Marriott this weekend."

"This is the Sagebrush," Szczymanski pointed out.

"Spillover. You want it or not?"

"Monday any better?"

"Can't make promises."

They took the room, signed in as Mr. and Mrs. Theodore Judah. Fortunately the room came with two double beds. They were going to spend three nights there and the Calm Prosecutor insisted on the physical distance. She even considered putting up a blanket to separate the beds, as Clark Gable had done in *It Happened One Night*. But the way she was beginning to feel about McBryde, a blanket might not do the trick. Even the Berlin Wall might not keep this prosecutor calm.

They slept through most of Sunday, with their clothes on and the blinds drawn. At dinnertime, they rolled out of their separate beds. McBryde took a shower while Szczymanski went off to buy several changes of clothes for both of them.

Later, when she emerged from her own shower, clean and dressed in a new sweatshirt and jeans, she announced, "I'm going to call Chaos."

McBryde sat at the foot of his bed, watching the television news and playing with the cuffs of his new cotton shirt. "I'm not sure we can trust him."

"But the pattern—"

"We'll have to rely on Ron."

"Anything on the news?"

"Not yet." He used the remote to turn down the volume.

"We're in good shape. It'll take them some time to find the car in Taos. And the Honda outside Pueblo. After that, we've disappeared. Good thing the trucker's on his way to Alaska. We're safe for a couple days. Definitely until the Zephyr leaves Wednesday morning."

"I guess it's best to stay holed up in here, then," he said.

"For you."

"They'll recognize you as well."

She produced a pair of scissors from her purse. "I hate to see it all go. But I think it's time to go punk."

He laughed. "Some red dye would look good."

"Sunglasses. And huge earrings. Very hip."

"It'll be a shame to mess you up like that."

She clipped her scissors in his direction. "At least I'll look better than you."

When she had finished, a prisoner haircut mercilessly exposed his ears. His neck stretched long and vulnerable out of the collar of his new shirt. With the black plastic glasses she later bought him, he could be taken for an earnest but harried college student from the 1950s. For all the disfigurement, however, he was still cute.

And his haircut certainly turned out more flattering than hers.

Working in front of the bathroom mirror, she succeeded in making herself look ridiculous, not hip. Gone were the lovely bangs and the gently curving strands that once framed her face. She'd never valued them until they lay lifeless in the drain of the bathroom sink. Now short and tufted like fur, her hair better revealed the round shape of her head. She had never more resembled a head of cabbage. Adding further to this uglification was the dye job. With its cherry-red flush, her hair looked toxic. But with sunglasses and large plastic bananas swinging from her earlobes, she'd certainly never be taken for an FBI agent.

First thing Monday morning she found an isolated phone booth behind the Sagebrush and called Barnegut at the Birmingham office.

"Girl, where you been?" her friend's voice exploded over the phone.

"Shush. I need a favor."

"A favor? You okay? Where—"

"Shut up a second, will you? I'm fine. What's on the line about me?"

"That you're missing along with some crazy motherfucker. The whole goddamn FBI is mobilized to track you down. I've been so worried, so goddamn—"

"I'm fine. And the crazy motherfucker is innocent. But you've got to keep quiet, okay? I know this sounds strange but we've got to lie low for a while. Trust me on this one."

A pause. "Sure, okay. But Jesus, Jen, where's your head?"

"Still on my neck. Barely. So where does the Bureau think we are?"

"Rio Grande. Looking for a way into Mexico. We've got all the border points covered."

"Listen, could you call this number?" She gave Barnegut Chaos's home number. "Tell him that I'm fine and he better keep his mouth shut. I'll be in touch with him soon."

Later that morning, McBryde called Jordan and discovered several interesting facts from his friend. According to the Southwest Chief's conductor, C. U. Thayer had been McBryde's seatmate from Kansas City until Raton. She listened to the description—an older fellow, wrinkled and bald, who knew a good deal about trains—but she didn't remember such a person.

"Probably because he was all bundled up in clothes," McBryde said.

"But you don't remember him from the Lake Shore?"

McBryde shook his head. "He was very memorable. Unique, even."

"At least we know what to look for on the Zephyr."

"Ron checked on the reservations. Thayer's listed."

"Where's he get on? What's the seat number?"

"Don't get mad. He couldn't find out. He doesn't want to push it. They might get suspicious."

"Jesus Maria!"

"Also, it turns out that Georgia's friend, the one who buys these tapes, is on vacation. Wouldn't you know!"

"And the accident?"

"He thinks a bomb."

"When has there ever been a bomb on a train?" she asked.

"Something obscure. A nineteenth-century train robbery happened on that date. They used dynamite to derail the train and then blew up the safe as well. Destroyed all the banknotes, the fools."

"Likely?"

"Won't be easy to find. You can plant a bomb anywhere on a train. Conceal it in luggage. Train stations don't check stuff like at airports."

They ate pizza in their hotel room that evening. In honor of Peña, they ordered pepperoni, no garlic. With her new disguise Szczymanski felt giddy, unexpectedly excited. They talked and plotted. They teased at the fabric of the case, pulling at the loose ends to unravel the mystery. Time and again, their conversation returned to trains and McBryde poured out his knowledge. It was encyclopedic, a great deal of it learned firsthand.

At one point she blurted, half in admiration, half in frustration at his single-minded obsession, "What, do you live, breathe, and eat trains?"

McBryde grew defensive. "I'm just as serious about trains as you are about your work."

"My work's a job." She chewed on a pizza crust. "Not a hobby."

"Trains aren't just a hobby. Trains make me feel like just after the first coffee of the morning. Or like I used to feel with the first cigarette. A pleasant glow. Anyway, you said yourself that everything you've ever done was preparation for the FBI. Sounds like an obsession to me. Sounds like you're just as much of a foamer as I am."

"It's different," she insisted.

"How many books did you read last year?"

"Huh?"

"How many movies did you see? How many dinners did you cook? How many parks did you walk in? How many friends did you make outside of work?"

She chewed harder. "I was in transition. It was my first assignment and—"

"Look, you don't have to get mad. I was just asking. Ros used to ask me the same questions."

"Ros?"

"Ex-wife. We split up last year. She told me to get married to a locomotive."

"Your wife wasn't a train fan, I guess."

"It wasn't just that. My thing could have been cars or porcelain or purebred terriers. She just didn't want to share it with me. She wanted someone normal. Someone who got excited about everything and nothing at the same time."

She had the urge to reach over and stroke the stubble on his cheek. A scene came to mind—from that old tearjerker *Brief Encounter*. The lonely wife falls in love with the handsome doctor just at the moment he describes his passion for medicine. His passion excites her passion. Now that she thought about it, that movie too was filled with trains! Did everything always return to trains?

That night they slept in separate beds. Neither of them had suggested securing an additional room. She slept little, and so, it seemed, did he. Listening to him twist around in his bedsheets, she pleaded her case in her mind. But the Calm Prosecutor imposed a restraining order, threatened worse if she even so much as breathed in the direction of his bed.

On Tuesday morning, the last day before the fated Zephyr left town, she foraged for clues in Denver while McBryde stayed behind to watch television and grow a beard. She visited a high-tech electronics store, the only one in the area that sold concealable microphones. It was a long shot, but she had no other leads. And the unsub might want to put Charlie Thayer's credit card to good incriminating use.

"Uh yeah," she said to the salesman in her best approximation of punk talk, "like my boyfriend came here the other day and bought some stuff. But, like, he didn't buy enough. Told me to pick up another bug."

The salesman, a thickly bristled fireplug who would have looked better in a wrestling jersey than a tight collar and paisley tie, looked at her with impatience. "Do you know what it is he bought?"

She shrugged. "Something small. He said you'd remember him. Charlie. Charlie Thayer. He's an older guy. I'd, like, recognize the bug if you showed it to me."

The salesman raised his eyes in recollection. "Older guy?" He looked around under the counter. "Bought something like this, maybe?"

The salesman presented a tiny microphone on his fleshy palm.

Her head swimming, Szczymanski nodded.

"Charlie, you said? Nice guy, Charlie. But I thought he said he was from out of state." The salesman looked at her suspiciously.

"Nah, we've been living out in Boulder for a couple years now." She leaned over the counter. "But Charlie likes to make up stories. He's funny that way. What did he tell you this time? That he was from Philadelphia?"

The salesman scratched his bristly beard, wrinkled his forehead in concentration. "No. Taos, I think."

She closed her eyes and swallowed hard. "Taos?" She managed a squeaky laugh. "What a clown. Was he dressed up in that crazy rhinestone cowboy hat of his?"

The salesman nodded. She couldn't wait to tell McBryde.

But he didn't remember the Taos merchant.

"He was at the bar, at the Plaza in Las Vegas," she said, forking out greasy pork lo mein from a take-out container. "We were so close! Didn't you see him? He was the only other customer."

"I wasn't paying attention."

"He had a beard. And there was definitely hair underneath that cowboy hat."

"Two men. That's what the kid said."

"But I don't remember anybody like that from the Lake Shore."

"I guess we're just not observant enough," he said.

"At least we know who we're looking for—one bald, one furry. And a bomb in an unmarked container."

"Should be a snap."

"A breeze."

It was their last night in the room. They sat cross-legged on the carpeted floor eating out of the containers and swigging local brew out of cans. Szczymanski knew that she should feel terrible. They would board the Zephyr the next day at 10 A.M. as marked people. She was taking enormous risks that carried with them extraordinary penalties.

Yet she felt warm and comfortable. The Calm Prosecutor was melting away under the gently corrosive influence of alcohol and soy sauce. The restraining order appeared on the verge of being revoked. Her bed was looking colder, lonelier, and less hospitable by the minute.

TWENTY-NINE

McBryde had hoped and dreamed and prayed that they would sleep together. He'd felt this powerful urge almost immediately, on the Lake Shore, at the first sight of her blond pageboy and beautiful composite face. Even when she was lying to him, throwing him over her shoulder, or surrendering him to her colleagues, his desire simmered on a low flame, refusing to be extinguished. In fact, he seemed to want her most when he trusted her least. Go figure.

The problem was—the feeling didn't seem to be mutual. She treated him like an asexual partner. She'd tried to arrange two rooms at the hotel and seemed terribly disappointed that they weren't available. She adhered strictly to the two-bed arrangement. When she came out of the bathroom after a shower she was already fully dressed, even down to her socks. She wore full-length pajamas to bed.

After she told him about the sexual harassment in South

Dakota, he vowed that he wouldn't make the first move. That brush with her hand on Route 518 was their last physical contact. If she wanted to make love, she'd have to make the pass. Hell, if any woman would, it'd be a ballsy FBI woman.

But no, she seemed to consider their partnership strictly business. Too bad she'd left his copy of *Accentuate the Positive* in Washington. The chapter on confidence in dating, for instance, might have offered some helpful advice. He hadn't felt so adolescently awkward with a woman since junior high school. Most of the time he didn't know where to put his hands, and his laugh was sounding unnaturally loud.

Now they were down to their last evening together. He hadn't slept at all the previous night. While she collected clues in Denver he'd dozed through the daytime soaps. Now, over dinner, he was wide-awake, despite a beery mellowness. It was close to midnight. They were sportively arguing over the rights to the last sparerib when she reached over with a napkin to wipe away a spot of barbecue sauce from his cheek.

"You'll have a proper shadow by tomorrow," she said.

He nodded, close to tears. His limbs twitched with energy.

"Well, we should go to bed early. Lots of work tomorrow."

"Um, right." He giggled, stopped.

"Something wrong?"

"Oh, no," he said quickly, hand to his eyes. "Fleck of dust."

"Hold still." She moved closer to him. He felt her breath on his forehead. "Look up. Hmmmnn. I don't see anything."

"I, well . . ."

There was an awkward pause. She ran her hand through his hair. As if he were a boy, a child. "It's a lousy cut," she said. "But it'll grow back."

"I look like a POW."

"Oh no," she laughed, touching the stubble at the bottom of his neck. "More like a choirboy."

He attempted a falsetto note. "Guess I'm too old."

"And what do I look like?" She framed her face with thumbs and forefingers. She was wearing only one banana earring and the sunglasses were on the bed. "Like a member of the Madonna fan club?"

McBryde tapped the banana, made it swing like a pendulum. "You look cute."

"My face is too round."

He shook his head vigorously. "Just right."

"They called me cabbagehead back in grade school."

"Jerks."

They were sitting within arm's reach of one another. He wanted to tap her earring again. Instead he played with the wooden chopsticks that came with their take-out order. He executed a paradiddle on the metal handle of the fried-rice container.

"What did they call you in grade school?" she asked.

"Nothing."

"No nickname?"

"Carrottop. Red. They didn't stick."

Again she touched his hair. "I could fix it up a little. Make it less ragged." She moved closer to inspect the cut.

Kiss me, he prayed.

"I appeal to the judge," she whispered near his ear.

He licked his lips. "I'm sorry?"

"The prosecution would like to call a recess." She pulled back from him. Even with her weird red punk cut, she was so compelling that the tears again came to his eyes. But he had no idea what she was talking about.

"The prosecution? I don't understand. Did I say something wrong?"

"Talk about trains."

"Trains? Now?"

"It's hard to explain," she said. "You have to distract me. We shouldn't be doing this. Talk about trains."

"Why? I don't really get what you're—"

"The prosecution realizes that given the nature of this case, the jury's sympathies—"

He'd never been one for verbal foreplay. But here she was and she was so beautiful. "Should I talk about Maglev?"

"Anything."

"Maglev stands for magnetic levitation. Is this okay?"

"Yes, yes." She moved a little closer.

"The principle is quite simple. Opposing magnetic forces create a frictionless surface."

She touched his face, spoke calmly. "The prosecution may have to recuse itself from this case."

"Maglev trains can reach speeds of, well, oh, three hundred miles an hour. The trains move very fast but there are no accidents. No. Accidents. At. All." The touch of her fingers against the short hairs of his beard excited him. He touched her chin with his thumb and forefinger. If train talk turned her on, he'd dictate his entire first chapter. Anything to make her stop talking like a lawyer. "Maglev is the future of American trains. It will replace both air travel and our automobile culture. Maglev will make America strong and competitive."

"Yes," she said, unbuttoning his shirt.

"You're so beautiful," he said.

"Trains," she reminded him, pausing mid-shirt.

"Trains are so beautiful," he said. "Trains make my heart beat out of control. Trains turn me on. Trains, oh, oh . . ." She was kissing his chest, running her lips over his nipples.

"Tell me more about trains."

His head felt as if it were going to explode. "I adore trains. I love trains."

"The prosecution rests," she murmured, as they tumbled sideways onto his bed.

McBryde slipped into her embrace. "All aboard," he whispered.

THIRTY

As a teenager, Szczymanski once accompanied a friend's family on a week-long camping trip to Michigan's Upper Peninsula. The friend promised the vacation of a lifetime. Pure, glittering streams with fat bass that leaped onto your fishhook. Wild blackberries so plentiful you could pull pint after pint off the bushes and never see the end. Grilled fish and potatoes baked beneath glowing embers and toasted marshmallows for dessert. Beautiful wild animals—elk and bobcat and bear—roaming at a picturesque and safe distance from the campsite. Wolves howling romantically at night. Story after funny story told around the campfire.

The trip was a bust. While fishing, Szczymanski hooked herself in the calf, had it bandaged, and two seconds later slipped on a moss-covered rock and fell into the frigid brook. She saw no wild animals—except three drunken hunters urinating upstream from their campsite. The blackberry season had already passed, leaving only shriveled kernels of fruit on the thorny bushes. The bass were overcooked, the potatoes hard and raw, and somebody left the marshmallows back home in a kitchen cabinet. In addition to being boring, her friend's family actually seemed to enjoy using the woods as their bathroom. For a long time after this miserable trip, Szczymanski saw the forested beauty of the Great Outdoors only as a vast latrine for campers. At heart, she was a city girl. Six months in South Dakota hadn't changed that.

She was therefore rather pleased that the California Zephyr provided all the thrills of the Rocky Mountains without any of nature's usual hazards. Immediately outside Denver, the train began its long ascent through the foothills, providing passengers in the observation car with spectacular panoramas of sharply etched ravines, scrub-dotted plateaus, and glistening ice-cream slopes. It was a cold but cloudless day. The sun flooded the mountains with light. McBryde had staked out seats in the observation car that allowed them an ideal vantage point. Now this was the way to appreciate nature! If only she could sit back and truly enjoy it.

"Should we be making ourselves so visible?" she whispered.

"Hold hands. No one expects young lovers. Keep looking for your Charlie Thayer and I'll keep looking for mine."

But C. U. Thayer was not Thayer at all. At least in their first circuit through the train she didn't see the Taos merchant in the rhinestone cowboy hat, nor did McBryde recognize his Southwest Chief seatmate. Every bundle in the luggage area, on the other hand, looked like a bomb in disguise. They'd never be able to check each bag and box. Best to concentrate on finding Charlie. They planned to make a loop after every stop to review the new passengers. And soon they'd check the sleepers. But Elko, Nevada, was a long way away and for the moment they sat holding hands and gazing at the scenery.

"Window music. That's what rail fans call it," McBryde said. "I've been on this trip four times, twice each direction, and it never fails to make me . . . I don't know . . . proud, I guess."

"Of?"

"It's a great country. And trains allow us to see it," he said. They'd agreed to discuss only neutral topics in public. "Trains are not just transportation, a way of getting from A to B. They allow us to feel space, to understand space. You can't see any of this from an airplane. You see clouds. And airports. But this?" He swept his arms across the view.

As if to underscore his point, a hawk suddenly took wing from its hidden perch on a branch of a pine tree. It glided for a moment alongside the train before doubling back.

The flight of the hawk caused a dozen cameras to blink. The tourists in the observation car, with their profusion of high-tech electronics, resembled a flock of paparazzi at a celebrity shoot. All around them, passengers snapped pictures and maneuvered video-cams to capture the most scenery with the fewest intervening heads. When a rock face obscured the view on one side and the sightseers rushed to the other, Szczymanski feared that the train would tip over into the gorge below and break open like a piggy bank. But she watched McBryde's face and he wasn't concerned.

The observation car, though crowded, at least allowed her to stretch out her legs. She did not relish a full, anxiety-ridden day in coach. She'd tried to reserve sleepers, but the Amtrak agent merely laughed at her over the phone. Sleepers were booked solid for months. The Zephyr was scheduled to pass through Elko at nearly 4 A.M.—nineteen hours of cramped coach sitting. But at least in coach they wouldn't deal with the question of who slept where.

She wasn't sure how she felt about the previous night. It might have been some strange alchemy of beer and lust and MSG that propelled her into bed with McBryde. She'd never before done anything so weird—using train talk to overcome her better judgment. Today was an altogether different matter. The Calm Prosecutor clocked in after a night off, prepared for a good deal of serious work. Holding hands was okay because it was part of the job. Otherwise, she needed to mothball her emotions.

As the train cut between two towering rock walls, she asked, "When were these tracks laid?"

"About fifty years ago."

"Is this the transcontinental route?"

"That's a couple hundred miles south. It was finished in 1869."

"Over a hundred and twenty-five years ago? It seems impossible. Maybe space aliens came down to help. The same ones that built the pyramids."

McBryde chuckled, then turned grim. "They were like slaves.

Chinese pushing east and blacks pushing west. And the men who owned the companies, Union Pacific and Southern Pacific, they were pigs."

"Slaves and pigs."

"It's easy to forget the evil when all that's left is a clean passage through beautiful wilderness."

"What about your pride?"

"It's funny, the railroads were once the most hated and feared institution in America. Now they're mostly ignored. And I'm never sure whether to be angry at Amtrak for mismanagement or angry at the people who criticize it for not really knowing what they're talking about. Then, when I'm on the Zephyr, I lose all the anger. Any company that keeps up this route, especially when it doesn't make much money, deserves my gratitude."

She gasped as the train rounded a corner and the ground cut away beneath them. At the bottom of this steep decline lay an alpine lake, kidney-shaped and ice-filled, its shores defined by birch and evergreen. The wispy tendrils of a cloud streamed by their window. A videocam panned into her cheek.

"Oh!" the videotaper exclaimed, backing off. "I am hungry!"

"You are sorry," his wife corrected him. They spoke with German accents.

"We're coming up on Tunnel District," McBryde announced, standing up.

The clumsy, apologetic Germans quickly filled their spots.

"Tunnel District?" Szczymanski asked, following him from the observation car.

"Twenty-eight tunnels in a row. It's like a slow strobe light—the daylight flashes on and off as we bore through the mountains. Then we hit the Moffat."

They were briefly separated by a press of people in the aisle. Coming together in the next coach, they reclasped hands.

"The Moffat?" she asked.

"Six miles of tunnel right beneath the Rollins Pass. It's the third-longest tunnel in North America. It used to take five hours to go over the Rollins Pass. Now it's just a ten-minute zip right underneath. We'll be crossing the Continental Divide as well, almost two miles above sea level."

He squeezed her hand. "Put in the earphone. You'll hear them on the scanner." She wore his scanner hooked to her belt, the dial already tuned to the right frequency. She connected up and listened in on the train's engineer. She gave McBryde the codes to translate.

"Tunnel clear," he said. "The length in feet. No snow hazards."

The train entered the first tunnel, throwing them into darkness. Since it was daytime, the train's inside lights were off. She removed her sunglasses. McBryde whispered into her ear as they stood close together in the dark coach. "This is a good time to check out the sleepers. It's dark, we got lost. Very understandable."

As suddenly as they'd been plunged into darkness they were returned to the sunlight as the train shot from the tunnel. The Zephyr hugged a rock face, gliding along a ridge with an embankment falling off sharply to the right. Ten seconds later, as they made their way down the aisle toward the sleepers, the train ducked beneath a series of snow sheds and into another tunnel. The coach wasn't entirely dark. Overhead reading lamps created isolated cones of light. She followed McBryde, their hands still cupped lightly together.

The train reentered the light just as they reached the sleepers. No one stopped them from entering the area. She concentrated on catching a glimpse of a cowboy hat or a full beard from the open compartments they passed. Most passengers sat by their windows, with coffee or bottled water on the table beside them. In this, the economy section, the rooms appeared impossibly small, more like zoo pens than sleeping quarters. And to think that they cost several hundred dollars over and above the ticket price! For that kind of money, you could fly round-trip, throw in three nights at a hotel, and buy a book of color photos of the Rockies.

When they were downstairs among the first-floor sleepers she heard something familiar. Someone was singing inside a closed compartment. It was faint. But it was recognizable.

"In the end, you'll be happy," the voice sang.

"That son of a bitch!" Szczymanski exploded. "Chaos must have told him. I thought I'd never have to see him again."

"It's the handicapped sleeper." McBryde pointed to the wheelchair symbol on the door.

Furious, she hammered the door with her fist. "Jigsaw? You in there?"

The singing stopped, replaced by the sound of shuffling. Then the door opened a crack and the familiar face of the pill pusher appeared. But Jigsaw seemed different, more composed. He smiled broadly on seeing her and swung the door widely to let them in.

"Please, please, I was just about to venture from my shell to find you." He spoke with the smooth flat vowels of a Southerner. "Many apologies for the cramped space. It's for the disabled, but Lord help the cripple! It's more of a parking space than a sleeper." He no longer wore mismatched golf gear but jeans, a polo shirt, and shiny new sneakers. She looked in vain for the plastic bag of pills. She sniffed the air. No rotting cantaloupe. Musk instead.

The handicapped sleeper was larger than the others. Two cushioned seats turned into a lower berth that could accommodate two sleepers. The upper berth, at eye level, was much narrower. On a shelf jutting beneath the window lay a Chicago newspaper. Next to the shelf, a washbasin gleamed white beneath a mirror. In the closet hung a coat with a valise beneath it. A pair of crutches leaned against the valise. There was enough space between the bed and the closet for a wheelchair to maneuver comfortably.

The son of a bitch! She was incensed. Jigsaw would find some way to screw up their plans. Even if his foot was broken. She looked him over; nothing appeared broken.

"I love the haircuts," he said. "You look like a charming young couple!"

Szczymanski stepped close to the agent. "I thought I was clear, damn it. You're off the case."

Jigsaw put out a placating hand. "I'm sorry. I get a little over-eager sometimes." He insisted that they sit on the lower berth and make themselves comfortable. "I have excellent leads for you."

McBryde sat down, but she stayed in Jigsaw's face. "I told Chaos not to give you any more information."

"Don't blame Chaos. I've undertaken this entirely on my own initiative." He looked at his watch and then, around Szczymanski, at McBryde. "How do you do, Mr. McBryde. I'm glad we get to meet again under more auspicious circumstances."

"We were wrong," she said. "He's not the unsub."

"Yes, of course not." Jigsaw again looked at his watch. Then he smiled broadly.

As the train entered the next tunnel and the little room became completely black, she suddenly remembered the Amtrak ticket agent's laughter. Sleeping compartments on all Western trains were booked up for months. For months. Which meant that . . .

"Larry," she began, unsure whether to strike out at Jigsaw or turn back to protect McBryde. The moment's hesitation was fatal. She felt a hand reach into her shirt. Before she could react, her gun was gone. She was shoved hard in the chest and fell backward, striking her hip against the edge of the bed. Above her, the bed exploded into motion and she felt the jab of an elbow in her side. She heard McBryde curse. During the interminable darkness, which could not have lasted more than a few seconds, Szczymanski thought about defending her partner. But she couldn't see who was fighting whom.

When daylight again illuminated the compartment, she saw Jigsaw leaning against the washbasin on the far wall, holding her gun in his hand. His valise now lay between his feet. She turned to find McBryde rubbing his jaw and scrambled up to sit beside him on the seat.

"Are you okay?" she asked.

McBryde nodded. His glasses lay snapped in half at his feet.

"Sorry to be so rough," Jigsaw said. He flicked a switch to turn on the overhead light. "Can't be too careful in this business."

"And what business is that?" Szczymanski turned toward him. But it had all become clear to her—who killed the boy, who planted the bugs. If only they gave medals for stupidity, she'd be the most decorated agent in FBI history.

"Why, train accidents, of course." Jigsaw grinned. "Nothing wilder'n train accidents," he said in the folksy intonation of the Taos merchant. He addressed McBryde. "And I'm so sorry we never had that breakfast together on the Southwest Chief. I always get the Domeliners and the Vistadomes mixed up. I could have learned a thing or two."

"Who are you?" McBryde asked in a pained whisper.

Jigsaw shook his head. "I'm certainly glad I didn't have to bring you back to the compartment with those crutches. Sometimes these disguises are a terrible bother. But I did so much want the larger room. Imagine how cramped we'd be in an economy?"

"You talk like you've been expecting us," she said, feeling sick to her stomach.

"Why, of course! All along. Every step of the way. Naturally we knew that a foamer would crack the pattern. It's not all that difficult, just something complicated enough to fool Amtrak and the police. We did not, however, expect our young agent to get quite so far."

The train entered another tunnel but the overhead light kept the little compartment dimly illuminated.

"Why did you set these accidents?" she asked. "Why kill so many?"

"I do regret the little boy," Jigsaw answered obliquely. "But he threatened to spoil everything."

"You never got off the Lake Shore Limited," McBryde said.

"I knew one of you would pull the emergency. Just a question of which one."

Szczymanski was overwhelmed. Gone was uncouth, rambling, intoxicated Jigsaw. Now he was almost debonair, with delicate gestures and the vaguely Southern lilt to his voice. He stood up straighter and had lost his potbelly.

"I really thought we had you with the Southwest Chief. You were quite lucky about the engine brake. Not very elegant. But very dramatic! Unfortunately I had to get off in Raton, though I listened in to the finale, of course. Quite a showstopper. I must commend you, really." Keeping the gun trained on them, Jigsaw clapped lightly with his fingers against his forearm.

"Fuck you," said McBryde.

"Some people are just not very good at accepting praise." Jigsaw sniffed. "Anyway, you've been so successful at staying alive that we've decided on an encore."

"Who's 'we'? You keep saying 'we,'" Szczymanski blurted angrily.

"Just assume for the moment that I'm using the royal 'we,'" Jigsaw said.

"What did you mean—you knew a foamer'd uncover the pattern?" McBryde asked.

"To pin the blame on you, of course," Jigsaw said with glee. "Poor C. U. Thayer. Not my idea. I detest puns. But the police will appreciate wrapping up the case with no loose ends. And the FBI will be happy to find its mole. Too bad they won't be able to interrogate you."

"Then you're the mole!" she exclaimed. "Why? Who do you work for?"

"So many questions, so little time." Again he calmly checked his watch.

"If you're going to kill us"—Szczymanski's throat clogged momentarily—"you might as well tell us why."

"I never understood why the bad guys always give out all the answers at the end of movies. Too neat. The mark of a lazy writer." He made a theatrical gesture with his free hand.

"We have a long time before Elko," she pointed out.

"Elko? Oh dear, that's right. You're still sticking to the old pattern. Well, patterns change. And Elko is so faaaar away. Wouldn't it be much more fun if the accident were just around the corner?"

"Moffat," McBryde said.

"Bingo, my friend."

"What's going to happen?" she asked.

"Five minutes," Jigsaw said mischievously. "Why don't you relax and turn on your scanner."

"Salerno, 1944," McBryde said.

"Bravo, Mr. McBryde! I can almost forgive you your earlier foul language."

"What?" Szczymanski turned to McBryde.

"It was—"

"Really, you're just as good as your friend Jordan," Jigsaw interrupted. He reached over for a crutch and jabbed it into Szczymanski's stomach. "Turn on the scanner."

She complied, dazed by all the revelations. The radio's static crackled.

"SP detector milepost seventy-eight, detector working." After a few seconds, the flat voice continued, "SP detector milepost seventy-eight, no defects, no defects." McBryde had explained to her the meaning of this repetitive message. Hotboxes distributed at intervals along the rail reported in computerized voices that the journals located near the train's axles had not overheated.

Climbing into the mountains, the train had dropped considerably in speed. Now it moved even slower as it glided through the tunnels. They waited. Jigsaw tapped his foot, dropped the crutch, and shifted the gun playfully from one hand to the other. Szczymanski tried not to watch him too carefully.

She was at a disadvantage sitting down where Jigsaw could shoot her before she even got to her feet. And he'd have no compunction about pulling the trigger. He'd leave the gun behind with McBryde's prints. But what kind of accident had he arranged? What could kill them, yet leave him unscathed? Certainly not a bomb. She desperately wanted to ask McBryde about what happened in Salerno in 1944.

"How will you get out?" McBryde asked gruffly.

"You'll see."

The scanner spit out another series of hotbox checks.

"Is the FBI in on this?" she asked. "Does Chaos know about this side of his friend Jigsaw?"

"I didn't quite expect such a coincidence, that discussion between Chaos and his friend Jigsaw. Fortunately we tapped the line and knew all about their little agreement. Poor Jigsaw is presently stuffed into several garbage cans around New York City. But call me Jigsaw anyway. I love the name."

"You're not Jigsaw," she said, stunned. The train entered another tunnel and the compartment turned gray.

"The Moffat," McBryde said.

"Shut up," Jigsaw barked. "It's coming."

The static increased on the frequency.

"Turn up the volume," Jigsaw demanded.

She did so. A male voice gave out a list of numbers.

"Dispatcher at Fraser," McBryde whispered.

The voice continued, "Hard yellow."

The train slowed.

"Red! Red!" barked the dispatcher.

The train pulled to a stop. Jigsaw braced himself against the wall and the basin. Szczymanski fell against McBryde, then righted herself.

"About halfway," McBryde guessed.

"Six-three-oh-two," the voice continued. "Six-three-oh-two. Read me, Amtrak?"

Another voice responded, "Time estimate?"

"Working on it," came the response. "Working on it."

"Turn that off now," Jigsaw commanded. "And throw it over here." He slipped their scanner into a pocket of his pants.

"You bastard," McBryde breathed. "How'd you do it?"

"Do what?" Szczymanski pleaded.

"We had her waiting on a siding a mile ahead. Plugged the tunnel. Just like a suppository."

"They'll put us in reverse," McBryde said.

"Clarification: two suppositories." Still training the gun on them, Jigsaw pulled out three gas masks from the valise at his feet. One he kept. The other two landed at their feet. "They're defective. The one detail that prevented you from pulling this off. Mine, on the other hand . . ." He dangled the mask as if to taunt them. Then he put it down and began to remove the black rubber molding that encased the window. "By the way, don't even bother trying to walk through the train to the front. The door between this sleeper and the next just doesn't seem to be working. And as Mr. McBryde well knows, there are no—"

Only two steps separated Szczymanski from Jigsaw. She took her chances and leaped off the bed, making sure she kept her head down to avoid the upper berth.

With the mask balanced in one hand, Jigsaw squeezed off a shot at her. She felt a pinprick in her right leg but didn't falter. With his back against the wall of the compartment, Jigsaw planted a foot on her chest and pushed her back down on the floor. She fell against McBryde, his arms surrounding her to cushion the impact.

"The next one will empty your pretty little head. Do you understand, Agent Szczymanski?" All the humor had drained from Jigsaw's tone.

She nodded dumbly from her position on the floor. Despair engulfed her. She felt close to tears, wanted to turn and press her face against McBryde's protective shoulder. Instead, she concentrated on the wound. The bullet had taken a little bite out of the side of her calf. She was lucky that it only grazed her. Blood oozed around the torn fabric of her pants. The wound began to throb.

When she looked up again, Jigsaw had already backed out the window and into the tunnel. A wave of carbon monoxide and diesel exhaust flooded into the compartment. Wearing the gas mask, he waved at them and was gone.

Immediately McBryde jumped to his feet and replaced the window. The thick, oily smell lingered.

He turned to her. "Jesus, are you—"

"The hell with the bullet. What's Salerno?"

McBryde rubbed his face. "Italy, 1944. Train trapped in a tunnel. All four hundred twenty-six passengers asphyxiated."

THIRTY-ONE

Three miles in either direction," McBryde told her. He felt hollow, lifeless. "No one would make it. Not without a gas mask. An intact gas mask, that is."

"How much time do we have?" she asked, examining her wound.

Her blood was staining the carpet. The sight of it, spilling from her leg, made him tremble. His groin tightened as it did when he looked down from a great height. "Is there anything I can do?"

"Forget about it. How much time?"

"Depends." He turned away to locate the towels in the cabinet beneath the washbasin and pressed them into her hands. "With the head-end equipment still operating, we have all the air we need. But I doubt the engine will be on for long."

"Why don't they just switch to auxiliary? That would cut down on the diesel fumes."

"There isn't any auxiliary power," he explained. "Everything runs off the engines."

"Is he going to turn them off?"

"That's my guess."

"Then how much air would we have?"

"Ten minutes maybe."

McBryde crouched on the floor alongside Szczymanski. The diesel fumes did not improve his concentration. He envied Szczymanski's ability to act efficiently, her determination to push forward. The mere sight of her blood reduced him to helplessness.

She rolled the cuff of her pant leg up around her knee, then wrapped a hand towel with Amtrak's logo around her calf. The thin white terry cloth showed a red Rorschach where it covered the wound. He felt like holding her. He wanted to praise her valor. He wanted to lie with her until death came and enclosed them both like a blanket that smothers a fire.

From the passageway they could hear a conductor passing from sleeper to sleeper, reassuring the troubled. They ignored his knock on their door and he continued on. An announcement on the intercom advised passengers to remain in their seats and not to travel between cars. Tightly closing the doors between cars minimized the diesel exhaust. But the fumes still permeated the tunnel. Their compartment smelled like a narrow street at rush hour. But here nothing moved. The announcement explained the delay with its ritual disclaimer—technical difficulties. And why not, he thought. Amtrak was just one big, mobile technical difficulty.

Again he couldn't shake the feeling that his nightmares had anticipated these accidents. Stay away from trains, his subconscious had been urging him. You lost your wife, it told him, don't lose your life as well. He'd been granted two lucky misses. The Zephyr was strike three. It would have been better to die instantaneously in the Chief's inferno. Here, the lights would go out and the oxygen would be relentlessly consumed. The space would darken, become airless. It would not be an explosion this time, but an implosion, his rib cage squeezing his exhausted lungs like a fist. Death would not come quickly. It would be an exertion.

He tried to hold back the despair by thinking about Jigsaw's clues. Why the frame-up? Why the accidents? Why the mole? He'd only tantalized them, given them appetizers but no main course. Hell, even the condemned got full meals before going to the chair.

The worst of it was that they'd been duped. Brilliant deductions? Ingenious sleuthing? Hah! They'd been snapping up the bait like blind fish. Better to have remained bunglers.

"Why don't they just back the train up?" Szczymanski secured the makeshift bandage with a safety pin from her purse. She winced.

McBryde turned his head away, pained by her pain. "The other end is blocked as well."

"What's in front of us?" She rolled her pants down over the wound and elevated her leg by resting it on the seat.

"It was reported as a freight train. There's only one line in and out of here. They jammed the signals somehow and rolled in a box-car or two. Anything longer would have been too conspicuous. Then they—whoever 'they' are—waited for the Zephyr to get halfway before tripping the wire."

"When can the nearest station help us out?"

"It may take them up to an hour to get a crew down here. And even then, who knows how long it would take to get us out."

She sighed with frustration. "At least check with the conductor. See if you've guessed correctly."

"He won't tell me anything."

"For God's sake, don't be such a man!" she exclaimed. "Just ask, damn it!"

"Okay, okay, just relax; don't waste your breath."

The conductor, with droopy mustache and sloped shoulders, stood at the threshold of the adjoining compartment, trying vainly to quiet an increasingly strident couple. When McBryde tapped him on the shoulder, he was momentarily relieved to have an excuse to move on.

"Is it true the tunnel's blocked?" McBryde asked.

The relief was instantly replaced by ill-disguised irritation. "If you'll just stand by and wait, sir, we'll have everything up and running in no time."

Determined to go through with the exercise for Szczymanski's benefit, McBryde checked his watch and asked, "When will they get a rescue crew here?"

Now the conductor grew explicitly angry. "Please, sir, if you would just return to your compartment, we'll be able to do our jobs and get the train moving again. There's really no reason to worry."

This last comment stirred McBryde to laugh. He wondered if

the conductor would still mouth these platitudes as the passengers succumbed, one by one, to carbon monoxide poisoning. His final breath would be wasted on a canned phrase.

The conductor was looking more closely at him. "Which compartment are you in, sir?"

McBryde glanced several doors down. "Seven."

"The Gibsons are seven. And you're not the Gibsons. As soon as we leave this tunnel, I'm afraid I'm going to have to ask you to return to the coach cars."

McBryde balled his fists. "Are you upset that I'm going to die in the wrong section?" And turned his back on the conductor.

He returned to their compartment to find Szczymanski gingerly putting her weight on her injured leg. She looked like a bather testing the water and finding it too hot. Wincing, she muttered something and looked up. "Were you right?"

"Of course. He didn't tell me anything."

"What are they going to do?" She dropped back down on the floor and again elevated her leg.

"It's beyond their control."

"Lackeys," she snorted.

Suddenly the hum of the engines stopped and the lights went out. The sleepers were filled with cries of alarm. He groped his way to her side, touched her arm. "Our last little surprise," he said bitterly. It was a pure blackness, with no grays, no outlines, nothing. Get used to it, he thought to himself and fought the fear.

"You think he shot the engineers?" she whispered near him.

"Probably just opened the cab door and let the train's exhaust do its business. Then he cut the engines."

"Ten minutes?"

"At most."

"If there are only two boxcars, we could push through them, right?"

"If we can get to the cab."

"What about it?"

He felt sluggish. It was getting colder. He tried to calculate. "There are seven cars on the tracks between us, counting all three engines. It takes about fifteen seconds to walk the length of a car. Add another twenty seconds getting into the cab. That's two airless minutes."

"You won't be able to do it," she said flatly. "Even if you could get the train up and running immediately, there's three miles of tracks to go over. That'll take at least another five minutes."

He thought of Melissa. She would grow up with only vague memories of her real father, of Snakes 'n Ladders and choo-choo trains and cold, wintery days at the zoo. He stifled a sob. He mourned his child as though she were about to die, instead of him.

"So we just sit here and asphyxiate? Like those Italians?"

He stroked her arm. "I'm sorry." Sorry because they'd just met and had to uncouple so soon.

"No!" she bellowed. He felt her pounding the floor of the compartment with her fists. Then she stopped. "Do you know where the garbage cans are located?"

"Sure, I guess, but—"

"Find one, empty the bag out, and bring it back here. Make sure you get one without holes."

McBryde knew not to question her. He moved into the corridor, felt his way along the walls, collided with someone in the dark.

"Please return to your seat." The conductor's voice was now hoarse with anxiety. "We'll have everything under control shortly."

McBryde ignored him, pushed on. He heard people crying, calling out, praying. At the end of the corridor, just before the door leading into the vestibule, he found the garbage receptacle inset into the wall beneath the water fountain. He lifted out the plastic bag, dumped its contents onto the floor, inflated it with a swing of his arms, felt its taut surface. Then he made his way back to the compartment, counting the doors to find the right one.

"Jennifer?" he asked at the open door.

"Empty, no holes?"

"Yes." He moved down beside her, handed her the bag. He heard the plastic rustle, felt a wisp of air as she checked for defects.

"Good," she said. "This'll be our makeshift oxygen tank. Will you do it?"

"Go to the cab? With a plastic bag? In the dark?"

Her face suddenly lit up in the dark. She'd turned on a pocket flashlight. "It was in my purse. Didn't want to waste the battery." She turned it off again.

"It's crazy," he said, heart pounding.

"Then I'll do it. You should never have gotten involved in this. It's not your line of business."

"No, no. Your leg. I'll do it." That didn't sound very heroic. "I want to do it. I must do it."

"Good. We don't have much time. The smell's getting worse in here and I feel a headache coming on. Take this and shine the light on me while I fill up the bag. This has to fit out the window."

He helped her stand up, then watched as she gathered air by swinging the bag in a graceful arc. Did he just volunteer for this suicide mission? He swallowed hard, felt faint.

"Start taking in deep breaths," she told him. "Expand the lung capacity."

He drew in the thickening air, pretended that he was about to dive deep under water. The plastic bag of air would never be enough. But someone had to do something. He wished that they could go on this mission together.

"So, I guess I'll see you on the other side." He smiled weakly, inhaled and exhaled. "Of the tunnel, that is."

She stepped forward and kissed him on the lips. The air burst out of him in a gasp. "The first kiss is the last kiss," someone once said. That was wrong. This kiss was as fine as the first, he decided. Perhaps because it promised to be their last.

He let the beam of the flashlight play across her features. So composed, so calm. "I'd love to tell you more about trains."

"I'd love to listen."

"If I die . . ." he began.

"Then we both die," she said flatly. "Don't think about it."

"But if I—"

"Don't think about it!"

He opened his mouth again, but no more noise came out. He began again to gulp air.

While he guided her with the flashlight, Szczymanski removed the glass from the window. He lowered himself to the tracks. It was a short drop from the Superliner to the ground. She handed him the inflated bag, carefully transferring the grip at the top. He caught a last glimpse of her replacing the glass. She looked ghostly in the flashlight glow. The very effort of leaving the train had set his heart to pounding. He resisted the urge to knock on the window for one more breath of air.

He started off through the icy darkness. Four feet separated the side of the train from the tunnel wall, an irregular surface of rough-hewn rock. The flashlight picked out the regularly placed ties and the rock ballast between them. If he hadn't known where he was going, as he had in the New York subway tunnel, McBryde would have been immobilized with fear. But this time, holding the flash-light in one hand and the plastic bag in the other, he chose his steps confidently and carefully. The beam of light played on the ties, and he put his feet into these little spotlights. He heard water drip some-where above him. Holding his breath, he could smell nothing. His throat contracted slowly.

He desperately wanted to fill his lungs from the bag. The blood pulsed in his throat. It felt as though a clamp had been placed on either side of his temple. Each step he took twisted the clamp one notch tighter. Save the bag. He'd need it later.

He wanted to run, to get to the front of the train as quickly as possible. He controlled himself. Lack of oxygen could make you irrational. He concentrated on following the dancing circles of light. What did *Accentuate the Positive* suggest for times of high stress? Stand still and take several deep breaths of air. Fucking book.

By the time he reached the engines, however, his lungs were hot with agony. There was no choice. Pressing his lips to the neck of the inflated plastic, he drank in some of the air, filling his lungs anew. The air was cold, smelled of plastic and banana skins. He tore himself away and clenched the bag tight. He wasn't satisfied, wanted to continue breathing in and out. His headache intensified. His stomach was knotted, his lungs were protesting, his brain felt as if it would trickle out his ears. But he was there, at the head of the train. He touched the warm body of the F40 engine and hoped for reassurance.

With the half-filled bag of air in his hand, he walked steadily ahead. The door to the engine cab was indeed flung open, as he'd predicted. He climbed the ladder up to the compartment and pulled himself in. The flashlight picked out both the engineer and the assistant engineer sprawled on the cab floor, their faces distended and purple. A line stuck out in his mind from his quotation journal:

"The train can reassure you in awful places." But what if the train itself was the awful place?

He sucked the remaining oxygen from the bag, temporarily alleviating the airless agony. With the pocket flashlight gripped in his teeth, he sat down in the engineer's chair and restarted the engine. Even though he'd never driven an F40 before, McBryde knew exactly what to do. He knew the positions of all the controls by heart, had memorized them from pictures, diagrams, from the training video Clarence Brown owned. Of course he'd been on plenty of trains pulled by F40 engines. But for insurance purposes you had to be accompanied by an official watcher in the cab of a moving train. Well, there was no need to stand on ceremony now.

A burning sensation was filling his body. He depressed the throttle and the train jerked forward. Dimly he heard the voices of conductors trying to reach him on the cab's scanner. But he didn't have the energy to respond. Again he wanted simply to exhale and suck in the air. But no air circulated in the cab; it had all leaked out into the tunnel. His eyelids were growing heavier.

Originally he'd planned to bring the engine up close to the boxcars and then gently nudge them out of the tunnel. But he didn't think he could make it. He was very near to losing consciousness. And if he fainted before he got to the cars, the Alertor would stop the train.

The Alertor was an automatic system similar to the dead man's brake. It kicked in if an engineer neglected to touch a control every twenty seconds. If he fainted and fell from the seat, the Alertor would stop the train before they ever reached the boxcars. There was no way he could inform the Alertor of their precarious situation. It performed its job regardless of extenuating circumstances. In the end, a damned safety feature might kill all the passengers and crew.

With his last remaining strength, McBryde pushed the throttle to full and quickly brought the train up to its top speed. If he succumbed, which he felt so close to doing, the engine would propel the train through the boxcars and out the tunnel before the Alertor could apply the brakes. He was too bleary to consider the risks. What if the freight at the tunnel's mouth was a full train and not simply boxcars? What if the boxcars were filled with an explosive substance? These questions hovered half-asked in the haze of his thoughts.

He began to breathe in and out without realizing it. But no relief came from the air he pulled into his lungs. They were still in the tunnel. Everything smelled of exhaust and he grew sleepier. He swayed in the seat, had difficulty distinguishing vertical from horizontal.

The last image he retained was of an explosion and a burst of light. But unlike in his nightmare, this image didn't seem to bother him. He accepted it calmly. He fell, and in falling felt soothed, happy, relieved to be able to sleep at last.

THIRTY-TWO

She had to pull rank to keep McBryde out of the hands of the police. They had him on his hands and knees in the snow beside the cab of the Zephyr, waiting for him to finish vomiting before stuffing him into the backseat of the squad car. Four policemen, young guys, stood in cocky, self-assured stances with their revolvers out and their faces expressionless beneath their mirrored sunglasses. They were joined by several men from the rail crew, who wanted to question McBryde before he was whisked away.

She'd pushed past a protesting conductor to get this far and now, limping, Szczymanski shouldered her way through the circle of men. When one of the bronzed officers tried to stop her, she flashed her badge.

"He's mine," she said, bending over McBryde. It pained her, but she had to continue with the impersonation. "I've been trailing this son of a bitch all the way from the East Coast." She pointed down to her leg. "And he shot me back there. I'm not going back to D.C. without him." She playfully kicked McBryde. "Dead or alive."

"What are you, the first FBI punk star?" someone asked.

"Undercover," she replied, reaching up to remove her banana earrings. She'd forgotten about the disguise. All the more reason to talk tough.

"You the kidnapped agent?" someone else asked.

"Tables turned now." She gazed down and felt a surge of pity and affection.

McBryde looked terrible, all ashen, with blackened mucus leaking from his nose and the corners of his mouth, drops of it trembling at his chin. Finer-spun strands of gray saliva connected his nose to his mouth and his mouth to the snow. His body convulsed like a cat trying to expel a hair ball. Szczymanski waited for the last convulsion. Then she pulled him up by the back of his collar until he was kneeling, his hands reaching out blindly. She crisscrossed his wrists at his back and handcuffed him.

The passengers and crew stood alongside the train, taking in deep gulps of the thin mountain air. The mouth of the Moffat Tunnel lay half a mile back, surrounded by the wreckage of three boxcars and a wooden snow shed. The cab had come through the experience with some dents and nicks. Its front window, however, was completely shattered.

"I need a lift back to Denver," she asserted, continuing on the offensive. TB² revisited. The Calm Prosecutor would have to wait her turn.

"We'd be happy to oblige, ma'am," the oldest policeman said. "But beggin' your pardon, this one's ours."

"These deaths took place in our jurisdiction," his younger colleague pointed out, indicating the bodies of the engineer and his assistant lying some distance off in the gravel by the side of the train. Empty mailbags covered their faces.

"Ten states want this son of a bitch. It's a federal matter. Now either I walk him back to Denver or you help out with a car."

"You've got no right to—" a third officer attempted.

"You're taking me to the regional office," Szczymanski countered. "I'll let you sort out your jurisdictional matters with them." She'd prefer it if they took her and McBryde straight to a hotel, but there wasn't much hope of that.

The youngest officer, who could not have been much older than twenty, pointed at her calf. The blood was now staining her pant leg. "I think we better take you to the hospital."

"You think this is bad?" She glared at him, added more gravel to her voice. "If they find out that you fine young men have obstructed justice in this matter, you'll be hurting from a great deal more than a flesh wound."

They chose the youngest officer to be her chauffeur. The other three remained behind to file a report and help the ground crew. For much of the beautiful downhill slalom back to Denver, McBryde did little more than groan in the backseat. Then he slept, his breathing like a defective auto transmission. She worried about oxygen poisoning. Strange things could happen to a brain choked up on carbon monoxide. In the back with him, she monitored his vital signs, occasionally checking his pulse beneath the cuffs.

When they stopped in front of the regional office in Denver, she promised the young police officer to bring up the question of jurisdiction with the local SAC. "We'll contact you in the morning with the full report."

"Yeah, whatever."

She could tell that he was eager to get back to the action. In fact, he only waited for them to pass the threshold of the FBI building before racing away from the curb. Thank God for the impetuousness of youth.

The desk clerk looked up at them. "Can I help you?"

Szczymanski made sure that McBryde stood behind her with handcuffs concealed. "Is this the Division of Motor Vehicles?"

The desk clerk laughed.

They took a cab to a hotel near the airport. She removed the cuffs on the way over. The cabbie watched her in the rearview mirror but said nothing. When they pulled up in front of the hotel, she leaned over the back of the front seat and slipped the driver two extra twenties. "If anyone asks, you took us to the train station."

Once inside the hotel room, she immediately fell into an armchair, let her arms dangle over the sides. "Sorry about the manhandling," she said to McBryde.

"I took you hostage before. Now we're even." He shook his arms out. Aside from a few small cuts on his face, a residual dizziness, and some stomach cramps, he'd emerged from the whole affair intact.

"Do you remember when the train hit?"

"I must've dropped off."

"Turns out you were right. There were only a couple of boxcars and we smashed right through them. Left only a few slats at the mouth of the tunnel. Did you see the front end of the engine?"

He shook his head, rubbed his wrists.

"A couple of dents. That's all. But a metal rod from one of the cars went right through the window of the cab. It could have gone straight through your head."

"That really would've been a nightmare." He smiled weakly. "And the other passengers?"

"A couple of older people had trouble with their breathing, but nothing fresh air couldn't fix."

"The engineers."

"Poor schmucks."

"How'd you get me away from the cops? All I remember is throwing up."

"Threw my weight around. They knew about us from the wire. But I looked like I was in control of the situation. And they had a whole trainful of unhappy passengers to contend with. Look, you did a real good job back there."

"I was lucky."

"It couldn't have been easy."

"How's your leg?"

"Just a bee sting."

"I couldn't have done it without you."

"Don't be melodramatic."

"No, seriously. You were so brave."

"Practical is all," she said.

He stepped toward her, faltered, then sat on the edge of the bed. He was still pale but managed a weak smile. "Shall we go out on the town? Catch some dinner, a flick?" he joked.

"Why don't you sleep a little. We can order up some room service later." McBryde needed no further encouragement. He crawled into the center of the bed and fell asleep in seconds.

A bellboy brought up the items she had requested from the

hotel's first-aid supplies. In the bathroom, she soaked her injured calf in warm water, disinfected it with hydrogen peroxide, and rewrapped it in a surgical bandage. It was no major disability. But it hurt a lot more than a bee sting. While she cleaned and dressed her wound, she thought about McBryde. For a seat-warming bureaucrat, he seemed to have inner sources of determination.

She'd waited in that dark compartment for five minutes, waited as the voices around her grew more anxious, as the air grew thinner, as even the conductors began to get nervous. After five minutes she admitted defeat. His bag of air ran out, his lungs gave out, Jigsaw had been waiting for him at the front of the train. She prayed to the Virgin Mary. Then she began to cry. The door to the compartment was closed. McBryde was gone. No one would know. Still, she didn't like the idea of meeting her death with tears trailing down to her chin. Her last act on earth was a show of weakness. If not for the leg wound, she'd have taken the plastic bag and the flashlight and the blackjack and braved the tunnel. Better an agent without specialized knowledge than an experienced bureaucrat. But she let him take over. And he'd followed in the footsteps of her last deputy, that poor Jersey boy.

Just as she felt the walls containing her emotions crumble away entirely, the engine began to hum, the lights flickered on, and warm air started to come out of the transoms. The train gathered speed, and her emotions swerved and soared. Goddamn! She began to laugh. The son of a bitch did it! She clapped her hands and laughed with pure delight. She couldn't remember a time when she'd been so happy.

Now she watched him sleeping. The color had returned to his cheeks and his breathing was normal. He lay on his back, arms hugging a pillow to his chest. He looked so vulnerable.

Room service agreed to bring up a late lunch—pot roast, new potatoes, and parsleyed carrots for her; scrambled eggs, chicken broth, and crackers for him. The smell of her meal was indescribably rich. She was hungry and grateful. The noise of the dinner cart woke McBryde. The waiter pushed the cart up to his bed, removed the round metal covers from the meals, and left with his tip.

"Wreck on the main line," McBryde said, crawling over to his tray and eyeing the eggs.

"Are you okay?" Perhaps the fumes had affected him after all.

"That's just what rails call scrambled eggs. Straight up is 'with headlights.' "

Relieved, she pulled a chair to her side of the cart and quickly polished off her meal. McBryde spooned up some of the soup, had stomach for only half the eggs and one packet of Ry-Krisps.

"So my first feelings about the pillhead were right," he said, putting his fork aside.

"He fooled me. Those disguises. That pill act."

"Who's he work with?"

She shrugged. "These days it's hard to tell with moles."

"And we still don't know the why of it."

"We don't know much more than when we boarded the Zephyr."

"Even where to go next."

"No, that we know. Want this?" She plucked the packet of bread sticks from his tray. She particularly liked the ones covered in sesame seeds. "I have an excellent suggestion for our next stop. And the sooner we leave, the better the chances of getting there."

"Philadelphia."

"No, silly: Washington."

McBryde put a hand to his brow. "Tomorrow's Thursday. I nearly forgot. I promised my wife. My ex-wife."

"You can't go to Philadelphia. *We* can't go to Philadelphia."

"I've got to be with Melissa."

"Your ex-wife hardly needs—"

"That's my daughter."

"Jesus Maria, we don't have time for baby-sitting."

McBryde shuddered. "You don't understand. I promised. And Marty might have something new on the tape."

She swore softly. "I think we can track down Jigsaw. Or whoever he is. But we need to go to D.C."

"Philadelphia."

"Why are you suddenly so unreasonable?"

"I feel, well, guilty."

"About what? None of this is your fault—"

"No, I mean about my daughter. During this whole thing I'd almost forgotten about her."

"Then let me remind you—we've just been through two major

train accidents. I've been shot. You've been gassed. Under these circumstances, things can slip a man's mind."

"I'm not being a good father."

"Can we talk about this another time?"

"On the flight to Philadelphia."

"No! Washington!"

He shook his head slowly.

Szczymanski suddenly felt like blackjacking him behind the ear and smuggling her "narcoleptic husband" back to D.C.

McBryde looked out the window at the empty fields surrounding the hotel. "I want a cigarette."

"You said you don't smoke."

"I need a cigarette."

"Going through that tunnel was a good carton's worth."

"Philadelphia."

"Compromise. We fly to D.C. tonight and drive to Philadelphia tomorrow. Deal?"

"I think . . ." He paused. "I think I really like you."

"Look, how about—"

"Last night? Can we talk about that?"

"Later." She looked at her watch. "Flight leaves soon. Do we have a deal, Larry McBryde?"

"We have a deal, Jennifer Szczymanski."

And he even pronounced her last name correctly.

She called the D.C. office and explained to Granite that she'd apprehended McBryde and they were proceeding to the Denver office. That would cut off the heat. Granite asked for details. She put him off, pleading extenuating circumstances and promising the whole story the next day.

When she called the Denver office she was patched through to the Assistant Special Agent in Charge.

"C-c-can I help you?"

She knew that voice. "Doggett?"

"At your s-s-service."

A stroke of luck! "It's Szczymanski. Looks like you got out of Pierre."

"Promotion came through j-j-just last week. But where are you? The police said you brought in the unsub this m-m-morning."

"Changed my mind. We'll be coming in, well, later."

"Later? Where are you?" She could just see Doggett pushing his glasses up the bridge of his nose.

"Don't ask. We'll see you soon, okay? Promise you won't try to find me."

There was a silence on the other end of the line.

"Doggett? The Bureau's screwing me. I was transferred to D.C. but I wasn't promoted. Blaine harassed me. I blew the whistle. Now they don't trust me. But the suspect I've got is innocent."

"I s-s-see."

"You know what you used to say back in Pierre? Suck it up—"

"And d-d-drive on."

"Maybe that worked for you. But it didn't for me."

"Don't do anything f-f-foolish, Szczymanski. I'll see you when I see you."

"You might get a call from national."

"You've got twenty-four hours. Then you b-b-better reappear on the radar screen."

"Thanks." She was about to hang up when she remembered. "Hey, Doggett, what happened to Blaine?"

"He quit. N-n-not long after you left."

Got what he deserved. But if her hunch didn't play out, she'd suffer a much worse fate.

At an airport drugstore, she bought a few items for their trip— aspirin, another pair of glasses to replace what McBryde had left in pieces on the Zephyr, and a baseball cap to conceal her embarrassing hairstyle. The cap, the first one she'd grabbed off a rack in her haste, read "I'm with stupid" and had two arrows pointing to the left and right. McBryde was not amused.

On the flight to Washington, she deliberately avoided talking to him about their "relationship." It was important not to cloud her mind with emotional vagaries. Instead, they talked about the case, going over each aspect with the skillful patience of archaeologists handling fragile shards. There were still too many pieces missing to see the full picture.

They took a rented car immediately to Arlington. Relying on her memory, Szczymanski guided them through the smaller streets to the dark grocery store and the parking lot in the back. At the door to the bar, she gave Peña's knock. Xavier the bouncer appeared, recognized her, and beckoned them inside.

But Szczymanski held up a hand. "I want to see Lucky out here. Not inside." She didn't want to run into any familiar FBI faces.

"Lucky don't do that." Xavier flexed his muscles.

"Tell him I'll fry his balls in olive oil if he doesn't."

Lucky came out, scowling and rubbing a hand over his bald scalp. "I heard you'd been kidnapped and the whole damn Bureau was looking for your pretty head."

"It was just a cover." She guided him to an empty section of the parking lot. "I don't have a lot of time and I need your cooperation, understand?" She described Jigsaw, or rather the several Jigsaws—slob golfer, Taos merchant, suave murderer. "Know the guy?"

"How many guys you talking about?"

"He sings this little jingle." She tried to imitate Jigsaw's Southern inflection. " 'In the end, you'll be happy . . .' "

Lucky hawked and spit. "Okay, yeah, I know who it is."

"Background?"

"Who wants to know?"

"We're about to close you down, Lucky," she bluffed. "Your bar is a security hazard. I can make sure you stay open. But only if I think you're worth it."

The dragon tattoo pulsed on his neck as he tried to control his shock and anger. "You're a real pain in the ass, you know that? Security hazard? That's bullshit." He stopped, seemed to get control of himself. "Okay, listen, he's FBI."

"Office?"

"Floater. Contract work. He's the tap man."

"Meaning?"

"Puts in the bugs. Set up the system."

"In there?" She indicated the bar.

"Among other places."

"How come I don't know him?"

"Keeps low profile."

"Been here recently?"

"Maybe two weeks ago."

"I need the recording."

"No can do." Lucky's face hardened with obstinacy.

"I don't think you understand. This is an emergency."

"Can't give it to you," he repeated. "There isn't one."

"But everything's recorded."

"Everything is. But not for the tap man. He jams it."

"For crying out loud—" She stopped herself. "Was he here by himself?"

"Came with a woman."

"Describe her."

"I don't know, just a dame. I didn't get a good look at her."

"Distinguishing characteristics?"

"I'm telling you. I didn't take a look."

"Ever think the tap man's your mole?"

"The tap man?" Lucky's raisin eyes grew as dark as coal. "Not the tap man. If he's the mole, then we're all moles."

"Why are you so sure?"

"He's been Bureau forever. There's no way, sister."

"Does he have a name, this tap man?"

"Probably."

"Well?"

"Around here we just call him the tap man."

Chaos was even less helpful when they talked by phone. While McBryde sipped chamomile tea in the living room of her apartment, Szczymanski sat cross-legged on her futon in the bedroom, trying to squeeze water from a rock.

"I can't do it," Chaos insisted.

"Just one more favor."

"You're out of control, Szczymanski. Don't think I haven't been following your escapades. You're in too deep. You've fallen for that McBryde guy, right?"

"He's innocent."

"You think you're the first to be suckered by that line? The guy's a psychopath. He's manipulating you."

"Listen to me, Chaos, I know a lot more about this than you do."

"Sure, sure."

"Chaos, please! There's a mole in the Bureau."

"I don't know you."

"I'm this close to catching him!"

"This is a phone, Szczymanski. I can't see how close your fingers are."

"Close!"

"Tell it to OPR. Because they'll be the next FBI office you talk to. Before they put you behind bars."

"I need to know the top guy on wiretaps at the Bureau. I need his profile."

"I'm hanging up."

"They call him the tap man."

"I'm hanging up."

"He killed your friend Jigsaw."

She heard Chaos breathing. "How do you know?"

"He told me. He was the guy I met on the Lake Shore. He just pretended to be Jigsaw."

"Why should I believe you?"

Jesus Maria! If men clung to something more fiercely than their pride, it was their stupidity. "When did you last hear from your friend?"

"Not for some time."

"Just a name and a profile. That's all I need. The tap man."

"No," Chaos said firmly. "Here's where I draw the line."

And he hung up.

She took her mug of tea and joined McBryde in the living room. "Washington's a bust."

"No leads?" He was sitting with his legs crossed, his arms crossed, and his hands nestled in his armpits. Her apartment, she realized, was not very well heated.

"None." She felt desperate. It was becoming increasingly difficult to maintain the composure of the Calm Prosecutor. Behind bars? Chaos wasn't joking. She'd broken so many regulations they could use her in the How Not To class at Quantico.

"Philadelphia might be better."

"Philadelphia?" she snorted. "I doubt that."

"Listen, I was thinking, about last night—"

"I'll make up the couch for you here."

"Oh." He blushed crimson. Her remark seemed to cut his age in half. With his half-beard, he looked like a high school student on a camping trip. "I thought—"

"Let's talk later. I don't have the heart for it now." She instantly regretted this last sentence. It sounded as if she were preparing to shoot a wounded horse. But in fact she didn't know what to feel.

McBryde made a call, talked to his radio friend in Philadelphia. It turned out that Stein had uncovered some lost noise on one of the tapes. They arranged to meet at this fellow's house the next day in the afternoon. While McBryde talked to Stein, she retrieved her backup revolver from the closet. And found the tape recorder she'd used for the Marinetti interview. She should have taken it on the trains to collect evidence. Two could play the tape game. She put it aside to bring to Philadelphia.

Then she pulled out fresh sheets, a clean towel, even a fresh change of asexual clothes for McBryde. "He's manipulating you," Chaos had said. But she was the one who'd initiated their "relationship." Unless, like Jigsaw, McBryde was making her *think* that she was in the lead.

As she was brushing her teeth, the phone rang. It was Chaos.

"Damn it, Fresh Cheese, this is the last time. You understand?"

She swallowed the minty paste. "Understood."

"I have to draw the line somewhere."

"Understood."

"His name's Watson."

"Anything interesting in his profile?"

"Been with the Bureau since fifty-six. He works as a consultant now."

"On what?"

"Something called ARES."

Now *there* was a lead. After their little Philadelphia visit, she'd nail this Watson and nail him good.

"Anything else?"

"Be careful."

"In his profile."

"I can't tell whether I'm helping you or hurting you."

"Anything on ARES come up recently?"

"It's all confidential."

"Doesn't matter. I've looked at most of the files. Any recent requests for the ARES material?"

"Two."

"One was from Peña. Where'd the other come from?"

"Congressional subcommittee."

"I really owe you, Chaos."

"Better cut your credit cards, Fresh Cheese. This bank's not lending any more."

She immediately brought up the topic with McBryde, who was lying on his back on the couch with the covers pulled up to his neck. "What do you know about ARES?"

McBryde snorted. "High-tech garbage."

"Tell me more."

"Instead of investing in real on-the-ground improvements, the government wants to put a satellite up there to monitor traffic."

"What's wrong with that?"

"In principle, nothing. But I bet you the money isn't really for trains. We don't have that many trains to monitor and they all go pretty slow. But what else do satellites monitor?"

"Other countries."

"Spy stuff. Star Wars junk."

"But what does ARES have to do with the train accidents?"

"Let me sleep on it." McBryde buried his head in his pillow. He was acting like a child put to bed without dessert.

She paused at the entrance to her bedroom. "His name's Watson. Our Jigsaw impersonator."

"Don't know him," McBryde grumbled.

"Watson. With a 'w.' He's left behind his mark."

"I don't like his sense of humor." McBryde turned his back on her.

She returned to her bedroom, spent an hour in the dark thinking about ARES and listening for McBryde on the other side of the wall. The couch springs protested his every turn. She pulled her legs up to her chest, shivering. Maybe the radiators weren't fully on.

After an hour she gave up trying to sleep and slid under the covers next to McBryde on the couch.

THIRTY-THREE

Marty Stein's den was a shrine to sound. Dominating an exposed brick wall, an enormous walnut cabinet with glass doors contained the principal pieces of his audio equipment—antique vacuum-tube tuner, phonograph, two tape decks, compact disc player, amp and pre-amp, mixer, and several unidentifiable oblong boxes with yellow, pink, and sapphire lights. A thick cord connected the entire system to a computer on an adjoining table. A second table supported a reel-to-reel with professional cutting board. An electronic keyboard provided a third side to this corner workstation. Leaves of sheet music and composition paper covered the top of the keyboard. Four speakers the size and heft of Easter Island idols occupied the corners of the room. Lining the entire wall opposite the components was Stein's vintage record collection, each album in its own plastic sleeve. A grove of gracefully curved standing racks held his CDs. And a special low wall unit that wrapped around a corner contained his cassettes, the titles neatly typed out on their spines.

Dwarfed by all the audio, the coffee table, single couch, and two stuffed wing chairs appeared merely ornamental, like the framed posters in a dentist's office.

"And here," said McBryde to Szczymanski while Stein was in the kitchen making coffee, "is his collection of toilets flushing."

She laughed. He still felt awkward around her.

"I'm serious. Look." He picked out several tapes and brought them over to the couch to show her. " 'Shinkansen, October 12, 1989, near Osaka station.' Or here: 'Amtrak, April 12, 1993, Empire Builder, outside Chicago.' "

"And I thought *you* were weird," she whispered back.

Stein walked in with a tray. "Espresso machine's on the fritz. But this stuff ain't bad either." He handed over the mugs. "Kenya AA."

"Ten cups a day, Marty?"

"Eight," the disk jockey said proudly to Szczymanski as he sat down in a wing chair to face them. "Two in the morning before work, and then six cups, one an hour, during my show. Keeps the blood running, you know. But hey, now I'm on vacation. So I'm cutting back. Better for the digestion." Stein stretched his legs out beneath the coffee table. "You know where I'm going on Friday for my vacation? That back-and-forth trip I've been talking about. Philly/San Fran/Philly: northern route on the way out, southern on the way back. Other than the couple days in Frisco with my cousins I'll be on the train the whole time."

"Have fun," Szczymanski said.

"I'm sure it'll be great." McBryde tried to offset her sarcasm. "The tape?"

"Right." Stein moved over to the wall of components and flipped a switch, adding a band of green to the rainbow of colored lights. "These new machines at the station are not really designed to do this kind of work. Took me the whole weekend but I managed to uncover a few new sounds. Nothing I recognized, but maybe you'll have better luck."

The tape began and the train came at them from the four corners of the room.

If he hadn't liked train accidents to begin with, McBryde now loathed them with every particle of his being. They offended his every sense—tasted like bile, smelled like the Moffat Tunnel, felt like the slither of spilled brains. Nevertheless he swallowed his urge to gag and made himself concentrate on the half-memory that had tickled and teased him ever since he listened to Georgia Huxley's first tape. He couldn't remember any *thing,* just a sensation: the slightest wisp of familiarity. He listened to the unfolding of the accident as though it were the melody of a hated song.

Then he heard it, felt pierced by it.

"Rewind," he ordered Stein.

He heard it again. "Is that one of the new sections?"

Stein consulted a log of the tape. "About two seconds' worth. Computer indicated dubbing, so I enhanced some of the mid-frequencies, restored a good bit of the lost sound."

"Don't you recognize it?"

"What?" Stein played it again.

"That sound, damn it." McBryde moved to the edge of the sofa.

"Wind, maybe. Somebody opening a packet of potato chips."

"I can't believe it," McBryde said. "That's what I half-caught before. But I just can't believe it."

"What?" Szczymanski turned to him.

McBryde looked at his watch and turned gray. "Christ! Look, Marty, where's your phone?"

"Are you trying to give me a coronary? What's the sound, for crying out loud?" Stein demanded.

"I need to call Ros. Now!" A fear burned at the base of his brain. One call could douse it. Or send it raging out of control.

In Stein's kitchen, he fumbled at the number pad of the telephone, anxiety slurring his motions. Finally he picked out the right digits.

"Ros? Ros? This is Larry."

"And where have you been? I've been calling you at home all day!" His ex-wife's voice went up half an octave when she was exasperated.

"Where's Melissa?"

"She's not here, of course. I thought you had—"

"Where is she?" he shouted into the phone.

"Larry, please control yourself. If you would just let me complete a sentence. Georgia came by just half an hour ago to pick her up. That *is* what you arranged, isn't it?"

"Oh God."

"Georgia said you were out of town and couldn't make it. That she'd baby-sit for the first—"

He hung up the phone. There was no use in explaining. He'd been so stupid! Mooning and spooning and drooling and forgetting completely about his little girl. If only he'd called from Denver, from Pueblo, from Taos, even from fucking Washington, D.C. But no, he'd waited until Cherry Hill goddamn New Jersey before fulfilling his duties. That tiny pea of his pituitary had overwhelmed all the gray matter surrounding it. And now he was paying the price. He smashed his fist against the refrigerator door. The magnets popped off and the notes they held fluttered to the tile floor.

Szczymanski appeared by his side, folded his hand into hers. "What is it?" Stein stood behind her.

He turned to face them. "It's not potato chips, Marty. That's Georgia on the tape. That sound she makes, that asthmatic little snuffle."

"Georgia?" Stein looked confused. "Georgia *Huxley?*"

"She's got Melissa," he told Szczymanski. "My baby."

"But how could it be Georgia?" Stein was asking. "Why would she pay all that money for something she already—" He stopped.

"Where are they?" she asked.

"One more call and maybe we'll find out."

He called his own number, waited for the answering machine to pick up, punched in the retrieval code, and activated the speaker in Stein's phone.

"Larry," the voice of his mother filled the kitchen, "this is your mother. It's not an emergency. I saw the temperatures this morning in *USA Today* and I just hope you bundle up when you go outside. You're at an age now when even minor colds can be dangerous."

He wished he could remember the code for skipping ahead.

"Larry, sorry, man. I just tried you at the hotel but you must've left for the station. But if you call in for messages, well, I don't know how I missed it the first time. Salerno 1944. And you're heading right for the Big Daddy. It's just a guess, buddy, but I sure hope you get this message."

Thanks for nothing.

"It's Monday morning, Larry, and arbitration just broke down. I don't know how he did it but Calhoun's now got support. He's pushing for a council resolution to rescind the fare increase. South Philly's a mess. Call me!"

Come on, Georgia!

"Larry, this is Rosalind, just checking about tonight."

Okay, already.

"Larry, please call. The strike's spread and the phone's ringing off the hook in the office. I need your help!"

And?

"Larry? Screening calls? Rosalind again. You are coming tonight, aren't you?"

And?

"Larry, I'm at home. I left the office. I . . . I couldn't take it anymore. I'm thinking maybe of going to Florida. I'll leave a number."

Jesus, if the next one wasn't—

"This is Georgia Huxley." Szczymanski squeezed his hand. "It's a true pleasure baby-sitting your fine daughter. We thought we'd go to Reading Terminal Market tonight, just the two of us, say around eight P.M. Would you like to meet us there? The side door facing the Convention Center will be unlocked. We'll be in the back, near Seligman's Bakery. Oh, and do bring your friend, your partner in crime, so to speak." She sniffed loudly. "But nobody else—I just hate crowds!"

McBryde looked down at his feet, trying to control himself. How could Georgia have done all this? Not that they'd ever really been friends. In fact, she'd always been remote, always been the most reluctant member of the board. But this, *this?*

"What choices do we have?" he asked finally.

The FBI agent leaned against a kitchen counter. "If this were a standard FBI op, we'd call in the Hostage Rescue Team, position snipers, and blow her away."

"Blow away Georgia Huxley?" Stein blurted out.

"This isn't a standard situation."

"And we don't know who's with her," she said. "I don't buy that 'just two of us' line."

"She was the woman with Jigsaw at that bar," McBryde realized.

"And there's at least one more, the other man with Jigsaw on the Lake Shore."

"Georgia Huxley?" Stein repeated. "Old Miss Priss?"

"We have to consider the safety of your daughter."

"It's the only thing I'm considering," McBryde said. He wanted his gun back, wanted to shoot and kill. Before they'd wanted only things—money, machinery. Now they wanted his own flesh and blood.

"We're going to have to do this by ourselves," Szczymanski said. "Larry?"

McBryde refocused on her. "What if we brought in the other Foamers. They might be able to talk Georgia out of it."

"I'd rather have a SWAT team."

"What could *we* possibly do?" Stein said.

"You got another plan?" McBryde said.

"I can't do it, Larry." Stein looked plaintive. "This sounds dangerous. The tape's one thing. But kidnapping?"

"Marty, it isn't as if—"

"Look, I was against this whole operation from the word go. I warned you, Larry."

He wanted to hit Stein in the jaw. Szczymanski felt him tense his arm and held his hand more tightly. He lashed out verbally instead. "This is Melissa, damn it! She's in danger and all you can do is sit back smugly?"

"Larry, I . . . I'm sorry. But I'm not a brave man." Stein looked as though he were about to cry.

"Okay, okay. At least call the rest of the board, tell them to meet us down at the Market East subway station, near the Greyhound bus depot. Twelfth Street. At ten minutes before eight."

"Maybe the police ought to—"

"Marty, do you know what we're up against? The police won't help. The FBI won't help. If they find out, they'll only arrest me. It's up to us."

Stein swallowed air. "But what do I say's the reason for meeting?"

"That Georgia's flipped and kidnapped my daughter. That's all, understand?"

They left Marty Stein's house a little after 6 P.M. Philadelphia lay right over the bridge from Cherry Hill. They'd have no problem meeting the other Foamers on time. They'd even have time to case the Terminal. God, listen to him. "Case" the Terminal?

The traffic jam began on the long approach to the Ben Franklin

Bridge. One moment McBryde was cruising at seventy-five miles per hour and keeping an eye out for cops, the next moment they were bumper-to-bumper.

"Damn!" He clenched the steering wheel tightly. "Why am I so goddamn stupid?"

"I'm sure it will get better as—"

"The boycott," he cut her off. "It's the damn boycott. Luke's messages. Remember?"

He flipped on the radio and found the all-news channel. It was worse than he imagined. The boycott, no longer confined to South Philly, had spread throughout the city. On the news, they heard the chants of protesters, the comments of drivers forced to leave their buses stranded in the middle of the street, the official statements of SEPTA officials. Earlier that day, the police had hauled off the first wave of demonstrators. But they were quickly replaced by dozens more—young, old, black, white. The trolleys were out of commission. Only the subway still ran, though demonstrators crowded around the entrances to discourage access. The fare increase had struck a nerve, transforming public frustrations over city services into a single hot blast of defiance. The city hadn't been so united since the Phillies won the pennant.

"We can't just wait here," Szczymanski said. "We're inching along."

It was cold and windy on the highway approach road and although the line was only creeping forward, no one got out of their cars to stretch. They'd already passed the last exit before the bridge, there were no shoulders to bypass the jam, and a waist-high concrete divider prevented a U-turn into the eastbound lanes.

They waited. It was 7 P.M.

"What do you think she'll do if we don't show up on time?" he asked.

"Probably nothing."

"Cut off an ear?"

"What are you talking about?"

"Isn't that what kidnappers do to get their money? Cut off parts of the hostage?" He stared straight ahead, white knuckles on the steering wheel.

"Stop it, Larry. Let's get out and walk."

"It's another mile or two to the bridge."

"We could run."

"I'm in lousy shape. And your leg is fucked up."

"What choice do we have?"

"There's a PATCO subway station not too far from here, but still it's—" He caught sight of something in his rearview mirror. "Wait here."

He swung open the door and ran to the other side of the car. Two cyclists were riding through the space between the two lanes of stalled traffic.

"Hey, buddy, get out—"

Their brakes protested, their rear wheels fishtailed, and they nearly collided with him. The three men and two mountain bikes became a tangle of flesh and metal. McBryde was the first to extricate himself. He pointed at his car.

"Let's trade. Three years old, twenty thousand miles, perfect engine." He waited impatiently for the two men to get up from the ground. They were dressed in matching skintight black Lycra. "I want your bicycles. And your helmets too, I guess."

"Fuck you, man." The lead cyclist remounted his bicycle.

"Look, buddy, just get out of the way," his partner said.

McBryde pressed his car keys into the first man's face. "We're in a hurry. Please."

By this time Szczymanski had joined him. Motorists had begun to honk in frustration at the car in their way. "Do what he says. It's a fair deal." She gave McBryde the registration papers to sign over.

The cyclists exchanged glances. "For crying out—"

Szczymanski pulled out her gun and her FBI badge. "A very fair deal."

They left the cyclists standing on the path, holding the keys to McBryde's car and watching their departure with open mouths. "Be careful with the derailleur," one of them shouted before they were out of earshot.

McBryde hadn't ridden in years and these new mountain bikes, with the gearshifts in the handlebars like a motorcycle, baffled him. So he stayed in one gear the whole way. Meanwhile, the strap of the helmet chafed his chin. The seat was so low that his knees crested higher than they should and soon began to ache. His winter jacket was too bulky—it had been a mistake not to trade for their special outfits as well. At least he wore sneakers. Otherwise it would have been even more difficult to use the toe clips. As it was, it took McBryde several revolutions of metal scraping pavement before he managed to insert his feet into the clips and pedal smoothly.

At first he worried that Szczymanski's wounded leg would prevent her from keeping pace. But she was already yards ahead and getting smaller by the second. The wind blew furiously in his face and he tried to keep his head down. How could she ride so goddamn fast? He felt as if he were pushing into a hurricane. He had to stop several times to negotiate the steps and ramps leading up to the walkway across the bridge. But at least he was moving faster than the cars. Considerably faster.

She was waiting for him at the other side of the bridge, rosy-cheeked and breath curling out of her mouth in feathery clouds. "These are good bikes. We're lucky."

"We've really hit the jackpot." Now that he'd stopped, the sweat was cascading down his forehead. His chest heaved, his lungs burned. It was almost as bad as the Moffat Tunnel. People enjoyed this torment? "I feel like such a winner."

"You better go first since you know the way," she said.

He checked his watch. Seven-thirty.

They angled over to Market Street. It was closed off with the sawhorses and yellow ribbons of a police barricade. He could see a dozen buses abandoned along the street. They were huge and dark, like the carapaces of alien creatures. He lifted the yellow ribbon to allow Szczymanski to pass underneath. They moved down the deserted street, cycling around the buses, heading for the Market East subway station.

The subway entrance was surrounded by a dwindling knot of demonstrators. A tall woman with a flowing red scarf chanted energetically into a bullhorn, punctuating her slogans with a clenched fist raised in the air.

"Hey hey, ho ho, transit increases gotta go!"

The demonstrators shouted out this verse with steady enthusiasm, stamping their feet in time to the rhythm. It was seven forty-five. The other Foamers hadn't yet arrived.

Szczymanski grabbed his arm and tilted her head. He looked over her shoulder. Peña and Metaxas were leaning against the wall by the entrance.

"But how?" he whispered.

"They must've been monitoring one of the Foamers' phones. They were just waiting for something like this."

"Let's get the hell out—"

She steadied him. "They can't recognize us. Not with these helmets on."

"But how are we going to get the group together? With them standing there?"

As they stood strategizing beside their bicycles, a demonstrator approached with a leaflet. He was a small man with short hair and a carefully trimmed beard.

"Here, please take a leaflet," the man began his spiel. "The city has gone too far with its latest—" The man's face suddenly jerked up at McBryde. "Hey, I know you. You're Larry McBryde."

McBryde stared at him. He'd never seen the man before.

"Yeah, I know your face from the *Inquirer*. Except now you've got an ugly beard."

He recognized the voice. It was the Timer, the king of complaint. "I'm sorry, buddy. I'm in a hurry right now. Give me a call next week." He got back on his bike and tried to put his feet into the toe clips.

But the little man now held his elbow firmly and with surprising strength. "Guess you had to get your bike out of the garage? How's it feel for everything to be running late, huh?" A devilish grin lit up the man's face. "And what did I tell you about the boycott? Now we've really got you in a corner!"

"Look, pal, I—"

With his other hand, the wild-eyed Timer brandished a slip of paper. "Just today," he read from the list, "the following suburban trains ran late: the Marcus Hook Line—thirty-five minutes; the Chestnut Hill East—fourteen minutes, forty-five seconds; the—"

McBryde tried to shake free. "Why don't you just go back to chanting with your friends."

But the little man could hardly contain himself. He half-turned to shout back at the demonstrators. "Hey, everybody, don't leave yet. I've got the devil by his horns. It's Larry McBryde! He's SEPTA!"

Out of the corner of his eye McBryde saw Peña and Metaxas push off from the wall, guns drawn.

THIRTY-FOUR

Let go, motherfucker!" Szczymanski delivered a blow to the side of the demonstrator's head, knocking McBryde free. "Pump!" she urged into his ear. And shoved him forward.

McBryde wobbled on his seat, still trying to fit his feet into the toe clips.

"Let them scrape, damn it," she insisted. He might be brave but he didn't have an agent's instincts, an agent's reactions. She'd have to be extra sharp to make up for him.

Finally McBryde built up some momentum, with her just inches behind. Pedestrians blurred out of their way. Peña shouted something in the background. Then came the sound of gunfire. Bullets kicked into the pavement on either side of Szczymanski's back tire. Her bandaged calf burned with pain. In fact, the entire ride across the bridge and through the city had been agony. But now she could think only of escape. They'd try to hit the tire, her leg. But they also might miss. Her calf was one thing. A bullet in the base of her spine was quite another.

"Turn!" she shouted ahead at McBryde. Everything sounded so crisp in the cold night air.

He swerved around the corner, nearly losing his balance trying to thread between the curb and a woman pushing a baby carriage. She took the same path, felt the heat of the mother's protest near her ear, heard Peña telling everyone to take cover.

When Szczymanski turned the corner, she found McBryde sprawled on the ground alongside another man, a hand truck, and a huge dented cardboard box. Without coming to a stop, she leaped off her own cycle to gather up a shaky McBryde and propel him forward. Throwing off their helmets, they sidestepped the fallen pedestrian and the dented box.

"Aim for that alley," she pointed ahead. Favoring her bad leg, she trailed a half-step behind.

After turning the next corner, however, they found themselves in a dead-end alley made narrower by rusting fire escapes. The footsteps of their pursuers echoed closer. Without thinking, they raced toward the metal garage doors at the alley's end. And found, behind an overflowing dumpster, a door propped open with a milk crate. The sound of hip-hop music floated out the open door. Szczymanski pushed McBryde inside and then pulled the crate in after her.

They stood in an institutional kitchen, the air thick with the smell of deep-fried chicken and french fries.

A thin young man in a dirty white apron was mopping around the grease-splattered fryers and wall-length freezer units. Taped to the freezer doors were pictures of sun-tanned models in bikinis. The head of the young man was shaved smooth and gleamed bluish-white under the bright kitchen lights. His face was angular and hard, and he looked up unsmiling as they tracked dirt onto the clean wet linoleum floor. "Yo, you can't be coming in here and—"

Szczymanski put a finger to her lips and drew out her gun.

"Shit, if this a robbery, you can have everything, I ain't no hero." He threw down the mop and made as if to usher them out of the kitchen and toward the cash registers in the front of the restaurant.

She shook her head, heard McBryde's labored breathing behind her. "Peña'll go around front," she whispered to him, "and Max'll stay back here." She indicated the door that led from the kitchen into the service area. A corridor connected the two sections, preventing them from seeing what was going on in the restaurant beyond. "Let's first take care of Peña."

Quickly she donned the kitchen mitts that had been hanging nearby on the wall. She grabbed the young man's pail and spilled the soapy suds in a corner. Then she dipped the pail into the trough of one of the deep-fat fryers and flung the tepid oil onto the floor near the entrance. It was impossible to tell where the wet linoleum ended and the oily linoleum began. She was able to repeat the motion once more and return the mop to its bucket before Peña appeared.

"Lookin' cute, Fresh Cheese, in your new 'do." Peña was not even breathing hard.

"Don't come any closer," Szczymanski warned.

Peña laughed. "Oh, Fresh Cheese, you really are a kick! Drop your gun."

With a sigh, Szczymanski complied. She pushed the gun with her foot toward Peña. But not into the oil slick.

Peña hesitated. "What you got planned? Another pizza?"

"We don't need to plan anything to burn your ass," Szczymanski taunted.

"Huh?"

"You're incompetent. Can't even bring an unarmed suspect back to the office."

"Kiss mine, polaca; I got you both now."

"Oh yeah? I'm sure you'll fuck up again."

Peña's eyes blazed. "I'm gonna make you suffer, hotshot. Big time." As she stepped forward to pick up the gun, she kept her eyes on Szczymanski, jabbing a finger in her direction. "Big time!"

Suddenly Peña's eyes widened and her mouth flung open as her feet spun out from under her on the oil. She slid down her back like a first-time skier, the impact of the fall jarring her own gun from her grip. She coasted onto the wet floor where Szczymanski needed only to take a single step to close the distance, reach down, and wrap her putative partner in a half nelson. "Shouldn't let your emotions get the better of you, home girl. Now, what's going on with ARES? Why did Congress ask for the files? What's it got to do with the accidents?"

"Get lost," Peña gasped.

She decided to risk it. "Who's the mole?"

"You're the mole."

"Cut the crap," Szczymanski cautioned. She tightened the hold. "It can't stop at Watson. It has to go higher."

"You're crazy."

McBryde cleared his throat. "We don't have time."

She nodded, removed his blackjack from her back pocket, and knocked Peña out with it. She laid the limp agent carefully down on an oil-free part of the floor and extracted Peña's wallet.

"What about the other one?" McBryde asked.

"This shit real?" the young man with the shaved head blurted out. "I mean, whassup? This TV?"

She showed him Peña's badge. "FBI agents on our ass. Wanta help?"

"Yeah, maybe." He looked uncertain.

"Well, if you don't have the balls to—"

The kid pounded an imaginary boxing bag. "What do I do?"

"Give us a couple seconds, then open that door. Another woman will come charging in. When she heads over to her partner, brain her with this." She gave him the blackjack. "Start shouting for the police. You saw the guns, you thought they were robbers. Can you do that?"

"I got hands. I gotta mouth."

"Don't hit her too hard, okay? Just enough to knock her out." An image of the dead Jersey boy flashed in her mind. "And just be careful, don't do anything stupid. I don't want you getting hurt."

"What are you, my mother?" The kid grinned, held his head at a cocky angle, fingered the blackjack.

She felt for the pouch hanging around her neck. Good, the microrecorder was still there. She removed the baseball cap from her back pocket and placed it on her head. Time for the switcheroo.

They met the manager on the way out. A large man with a spotted face, he stood by a cash register looking anxiously back at the kitchen. "What's going on back there? Where's that other woman?

She told me to wait here, she'd explain later." He moved to block their exit.

"FBI." Szczymanski waved her badge. "Call the police. We're going for backups."

As if on cue, the young man bellowed, "Police! Yo, police!"

The manager stepped out of their way to reach for the phone. They ran out of the restaurant toward their rendezvous with the Foamers. It was just past 8 P.M.

THIRTY-FIVE

McBryde **still loved the**
Reading Terminal Market, even though its connection to trains had
been severed long ago. He loved its history, the very fact of its continued existence. All of Philadelphia's other nineteenth-century stations had been torn down. Only the famous coal carriers' train shed
survived.

The Terminal had been the final stop for the Reading line. Coal
dust once hung thick in the air of the train shed. In the vast room
beneath, Lancaster County farmers sold their produce at makeshift
booths. Formalized around 1905, the Market was the perfect marriage between rural and urban, the garden and the machine. In the
early 1990s, developers threatened to tear down the train shed in
order to make more room for the Convention Center being built
across the street. The Philly Foamers led the protests that turned
them back.

Georgia Huxley knew how much he loved the Terminal. She'd

chosen the site with deliberate perversity. Indeed, she and Jigsaw seemed to have designed the whole escapade in order to sour his taste for trains, to dry up his enthusiasm. Negative reinforcement.

It was working.

Standing in the darkness beneath the scaffolding of the Terminal's Arch Street entrance, McBryde felt horrible. He desperately wanted Melissa back. But he didn't want to go inside the Terminal. The energy that had propelled him past the traffic jam, away from Peña and Metaxas, and out of the Dixie Chicken was now all used up. Only Szczymanski's presence, close by his shoulder, gave him any hope.

"We're meeting her at the back, near Seligman's," he told the Philly Foamers. Ron Jordan, Leticia Gompers, and Clarence Brown stood together, tense and silent. "I want you three to wait inside the door. We've got to be real careful. Melissa's in there and I don't want her hurt."

"Shouldn't we just call the rest of the FBI?" Brown whispered.

"Not on this one," McBryde said. He'd told them the minimum, only that Szczymanski had been assigned to the case. "Georgia's in a pretty unsettled state."

"Who'd have thought she'd flip?" Gompers mused. "She was always Little Miss Uptight."

"Those are the ones that always go first," Brown commented.

They entered the Terminal through the unlocked side door. It was dark, filled with large ghostly objects like an enormous warehouse. Such a contrast with the Market by day—a bright, crowded space with gaily festooned booths, where glistening brown roast ducks hung by their necks at the Chinese food counter, piñatas and Mexican hats decorated La Cantina, tricolor flags surrounded the Italian deli, Amish farmers sold poultry and fresh produce, Korean greengrocers misted the vegetables displayed on their tilted tray tables, and booksellers and spice dealers welcomed customers into their overstuffed areas. At night the Terminal shut down completely. The aisles emptied of customers. White shrouds and heavy tarpaulins appeared over the booths. Chairs were turned upside down atop counters.

A faint light glowed at the back of the hall. He and Szczymanski walked slowly in that direction, she favoring her bad leg. They treaded lightly on the concrete floor, past the sweetshop, the sausage maker, the Salad Express. They tried to approach like hunters.

Then McBryde heard Georgia Huxley.

"It's only a game," she was saying. "And when it's over, and if you've been a good girl, we'll go to Paris as I promised." She snuffled in the silence of the vast space.

Passing the seafood counter on the corner, they came into the eating area that opened up in front of Seligman's bakery. It was the center-back of the Terminal. A row of steel girders ran from the bakery counter to the Market's front entrance, dividing the Terminal in half. The space was filled with cheap metal picnic furniture, the chairs tilted into the tables as though on their knees praying.

In front of a circular bakery display case, Melissa sat in one of these white chairs, her long yellow scarf tied twice around her head, once across her eyes and once across her mouth. The tasseled ends drooped like dog ears over her shoulders. Her feet dangled several inches from the ground. Georgia Huxley stood by her side, dressed in her customary conservative gray flannel dress suit, black nylons, and shiny black pumps. Not one lock of her graying hair, cut close on the sides, was out of place. A single low-hanging lamp lit the scene as though it were in a play.

The sight of the yellow scarf made McBryde's throat tighten. Szczymanski stood a pace behind him. Several tables separated them from Melissa and her captor.

"You're late," Huxley said. "Not like you, Larry."

"Technical difficulties."

Melissa cocked her head on hearing her father's voice. Muffled noises came from behind her gag and she made as if to jump out of the chair. Keeping one hand hidden behind her back, Huxley held Melissa's shoulder tight.

"We didn't expect the boycott," Huxley said. "Even the best-laid plans . . ."

"Tell us about your plans," Szczymanski suggested.

Huxley glared at her. "Thank you very much for coming along. Now please keep quiet. I hate law-enforcement officials. They should be seen, not heard." She gestured down at Melissa. "Like children."

"How could you do this, Georgia?" McBryde asked.

"Let me get to the point," Huxley said. "You're taking the fall for all of this, Larry—the accidents, the murders, everything. Otherwise we kill your daughter. Is that clear?"

She brought her concealed hand from behind her back. It held Szczymanski's Smith & Wesson 1076 semiautomatic, the one Jigsaw had spirited away with him from the Zephyr. With her other hand she produced two pairs of handcuffs from the pocket of her suit jacket.

"You're going to handcuff yourselves together. Then Larry'll get cuffed to this pipe right here." She pointed to a steel pipe running up the side of the nearest pillar. "Your friend—what do you call him? Jigsaw?—he'll be here after midnight to take credit for your capture. Meanwhile Melissa and I will go for a nice weekend outside the city. If you make any mistakes or say anything amiss, she dies. Here are the cuffs." She threw them at their feet. "Now, throw over your gun, FBI girl."

"I don't have one."

"Do you think I'm stupid? Shoulder holster. Take it out, empty the magazine, and throw both the gun and the ammunition over. Do anything stupid and the child dies."

Szczymanski followed the order. Huxley pocketed both the gun and the ammunition.

McBryde cleared his throat. It took a great effort to hold himself back. "Why'd you get involved in this?"

"We don't have time for that."

"I have to know," he pressed. "You love trains and yet you—"

"I hate trains," she interrupted, her voice acidic and her face wolfish. "I've always hated trains. Why do you think I keep all those albums devoted to accidents? I love to see trains crash."

"You hate trains?" McBryde repeated, bewildered. "But all those years with the group, all those meetings—"

"—that I've suffered through. Exactly. They nearly made me sick." She snuffled. "But it got me contacts in the foamer network. To sell those lovely tapes. I don't care what the others are doing it for. I just don't care!"

"Was it just for money, then?" Szczymanski asked from behind him.

"I thought I told you to be quiet?"

"Did something happen to you as a child, Georgia?" He remembered the mystery of her past, the parents who died when she was young. "An accident maybe? Was it your parents?"

"Keep it simple, Larry. Just cuff yourselves and shut up."

Maybe Georgia Huxley was indeed psychotic. All her past mannerisms and idiosyncrasies, dismissed by the Philly Foamers as mere personality quirks, became sinister in retrospect. He'd do anything to save Melissa. But how could he trust a psychotic to keep an agreement?

"If I'm taking the fall for all this," McBryde said, "you better tell me who you're working for."

"Not a chance."

"How do the tapes fit in? How will these accidents wipe out all the trains?"

"This isn't show-and-tell, Larry. But look, a foamer set all these accidents. A foamer taped them. A foamer sold them. A foamer bought them. There's a lot of foamers out there. The public thinks they're all crazy. Who's going to ride trains after this? This will do more damage to trains than the crash of the *Hindenburg* did for zeppelins."

"But you have no proof that I—"

"I'm afraid we do, Charles Ulysses Thayer. Not only the credit-card purchases. There's enough evidence planted in your apartment to keep you in jail forever."

It dawned on him that he'd be lucky to end up in jail. Perhaps Georgia didn't even know that another fate was reserved for them. Locked to the pipe, they'd both be executed by Jigsaw. Mysterious parties would be implicated, no one ever charged. Melissa too. She wouldn't survive the night. Only then would the threat of crazy foamers at large keep people away from trains. Only then could McBryde be trusted to keep his mouth shut. A helpless rage seized him.

"And ARES?" Szczymanski asked.

Huxley pointed the 1076 at her. "What are you, deaf? I told you to keep quiet and I meant it!"

McBryde quickly interrupted. "Where will you go?"

Suddenly Georgia Huxley looked weary. "An island, I suppose. Someplace with boats and no trains."

Melissa scissored her feet beneath her chair and moved her head blindly like a newborn chick.

"You can just give up, you know," Szczymanski tried. "Plea-bargain. You'd get off with maybe a couple years."

Huxley was again prepared to vent her wrath when a voice distracted her.

"What about it, Georgia?" Clarence Brown poked his head above a sandwich-shop counter. "You don't really want to leave Philly, do you?" His voice quavered with fear.

Huxley turned sharply in his direction. "What are you doing here?" She addressed McBryde. "I told you, only the FBI agent."

Leticia Gompers stepped from behind a sushi bar. "Come on, Georgia. You're not seriously going through with this, are you?"

Jordan emerged from the beer garden. "We'll defend you in court. Be good character witnesses for you," he said.

Huxley's head turned this way and that to take in all the new actors in the drama. Her face passed from fury to fear before settling on dismay.

"I . . . I . . ." She raised the gun in her hand.

"If you shoot the child," Szczymanski said, "you'll have nothing. So why don't you let her go."

"I could shoot all of you," Huxley said softly, glancing at the people surrounding her. "I could, you know."

"You really want to do that?" Szczymanski was talking calmly. "My guess is that you'd have difficulty shooting people up close like this. Those train accidents were far away. But could you kill your friends at point-blank range? Why don't you just give us the gun?"

Huxley looked at her in panic. "I'll shoot you first."

"And then Larry commits 'suicide'?"

"No!" A tic pulsed at the edge of Huxley's mouth.

"And then you kill the child too?"

"No!"

"There are a lot of people here to kill, Georgia." Szczymanski stepped forward.

Huxley swung the gun in an arc to keep them back. Brown's head popped behind the counter of the sandwich shop; Gompers slipped below the sushi bar; Jordan crouched behind the low wall of the beer garden.

"Georgia," McBryde began.

Melissa clapped her hands together to get her captor's attention. But Huxley ignored her. Shoulders slumped, she looked ready to collapse. The hand holding the gun fell to her side. "Oh, damn," she moaned, and McBryde could hear the tears in her voice.

The Philly Foamers stepped back into the open, calling out to her in friendly tones.

"I don't know what I'm doing," Huxley said to the concrete floor. She stepped in front of Melissa, looked for a moment as if she were going to pitch forward. "For the first time in my life, I—"

But she never finished the sentence. Her forehead suddenly exploded, spraying blood onto the white picnic furniture in front of her.

THIRTY-SIX

As Georgia Huxley's body crumpled, overturning a table and two chairs as it fell, Szczymanski was already in motion. Keeping low to the ground, she gathered up the trembling Melissa from her chair and dived for shelter behind the sushi bar. Gompers was waiting for her. A second later McBryde slid onto the floor beside them. Clarence Brown and Ron Jordan had disappeared into their former hiding places.

"It's okay," Szczymanski whispered into Melissa's ear. "Just a little game of hide-and-seek." She slipped the scarf off her eyes, smiled at the terrified child, and pressed her into McBryde's arms.

"There's no place to go," a voice rang out. She immediately recognized the muted twang. "The doors are all locked, including the one you came through. If you come into the open, I won't hurt you. But if you don't behave yourselves, I'll just have to punish you."

Szczymanski eyed her 1076, which lay in a pool of Georgia Huxley's blood. Jigsaw/Watson had shot Huxley in the back of the head. Which meant that he was at the far wall of the Terminal, behind the bakery. It was too dark back there to see anyone. The single light illuminated only a small circle of ground at the center of which lay Huxley's body. The force of the bullet had lifted her out of her pumps. She lay face-down, limbs twisted awkwardly.

Szczymanski pointed at McBryde, indicated with hand gestures that he should circle around and make a noise to distract Watson while she retrieved her gun.

McBryde shook his head vigorously. He looked scared, shell-shocked. He clung to his child as though she were a mast on a storm-tossed boat.

Szczymanski glared at him. "Do it," she mouthed. "Now!"

After a moment he nodded reluctantly. After passing Melissa over to Gompers, he began to crawl silently around the other side of the sushi bar to approach the bakery from another angle. Szczymanski felt in the pouch that circled her neck and hung down between her breasts. The microrecorder was still on. But it would be useful only if she survived.

"It's a shame about Georgia," the voice continued. "She really helped our enterprise beyond anything I might have imagined." Slowly the voice was approaching. He must have been directly behind the rotating display case when he shot Georgia Huxley. Szczymanski strained her eyes to see and hoped that McBryde would soon make his move.

Like a ghost materializing, Watson walked out of the darkness. He was nattily dressed in a vest and well-creased pants. Each hand held a gun. It would not take him long to find them. He stepped completely into the spotlight.

A noise came from behind Watson. He stepped backward, turned, and fired with both guns into the darkness behind him. Then came the sound of splintering glass, perhaps McBryde throwing a bottle against the wall. Be careful, she prayed. Watson moved farther into the shadows, circling around the bakery.

There would be no better chance.

Szczymanski jumped into the open, raced to the 1076, and scooped it up. The blood was sticky on its handle. Watson appeared on the other side of the bakery. She picked up a plastic table and heaved it in his direction. Turning her back, she zigzagged around a pillar, took several painful long jumps, and vaulted over a waist-high glass counter. It belonged to the seafood shop that faced the sushi bar across the empty dining area. She heard Watson kick the table aside before opening fire. One bullet struck a garbage can just inches from her body. Another shattered the empty glass case as she flew over it.

A third struck her other calf. Jesus Maria! She knew instantly that this was a more serious wound, that the bullet had ripped into muscle. She lay beneath the counter's shelf, obscured from view. The pillar stood between Watson and the empty display case. On the cold concrete floor next to her were empty plastic buckets and a few clamshells. Shards of glass pressed into her pants. She shook the glass from her baseball cap. She had the 1076. Miraculously the tape recorder was still whirring softly in the pouch. Now she had a fighting chance.

Watson pushed tables and chairs out of the way as he followed her. She twisted her body, looking around for a way out. The only opening lay immediately in his sights. She could feel the blood flowing from her leg and tried to push back the first wave of pain. He'd begun firing again. Slivers of glass and chunks of wood flew above her.

She could roll into the open and perhaps get off one shot at him. But she was at a bad angle and he was firing bullets constantly on either side of the pillar, pinning her down. She might get lucky and hit him in the chest. But she'd probably die in the effort. He was almost at the pillar.

"Hey, mister, over here." It was a man's voice, coming from the sandwich shop. She cautiously peered above the jagged edge of what had been the display-counter window and saw Watson turn around slowly.

"Get down, Clarence!" Leticia Gompers hissed from the sushi bar.

"I'm out in the open," Clarence Brown said, slowly lifting his hands. "I'm giving myself up."

"Well, well," Watson said. His arms wide apart, he aimed one gun toward Brown and one in her general direction. He looked like a policeman directing traffic. "It seems like you're the smartest foamer of them all. Now why don't you all just join your friend out here in the open. I promise not to hurt you."

She checked the 1076's clip. Three shots left. One each for man, woman, and child. The girder was still between her and Watson. His position made a clean shot very difficult.

"I'm waiting," Watson said. "We don't have much time here. And I know your FBI friend is out there with a gun. Come out into the open, Agent Szczymanski, and let's have a nice heart-to-heart."

That was when Clarence Brown took his leap. She saw immediately that he had no chance. Ten feet separated the two men. Watson didn't need to move at all to fire a dozen bullets into his attacker. Brown fell at his feet, a large hole torn open in his chest.

Rolling into the open aisle, Szczymanski squeezed two shots off at Watson. They went wide. But Watson was forced to duck out of the way and that gave her the opportunity to hobble quickly and painfully down the aisle. She knew she was leaving a trail of blood, but couldn't do anything about it. She kept her head down and her gun tightly grasped. Bullets sprayed around her. She clenched her teeth as she ran, prepared for the involuntary twitch of impact. Nothing hit. Finally protected by a row of solid-metal meat lockers, she rose up onto her legs and immediately felt the pain now convulse both calves. She steadied herself and pushed on. The farther she got from the eating area, the darker the Terminal became.

"I wouldn't have done it," Watson explained loudly, pausing in his gunfire. "Except it was self-defense. Now how about it? Am I going to just have to stalk you all? Yes?" He fired a round in all directions, shattering glass, splintering wood, perforating protective cloth covers. "Or no?"

She heard Leticia Gompers crying. She heard the click of switches being thrown. More lights came on. She felt suddenly exposed. The pain in her calves intensified. Keep pushing, she said to herself. If you think it's painful now, just consider the alternatives.

Watson was again moving after her, slowly, methodically. "I left Georgia with only three bullets. Unless my powers of arithmetic have failed me, you have only one left. I'd suggest you use it on yourself. I won't be as considerate an executioner."

She ran as fast as her injured legs would permit, knocking over bookshelves, upsetting small metal tables, pulling loose tarpaulins. Blood trickled down her leg, left a dotted line behind. She was confused by the layout of the Market, couldn't tell whether she was circling back upon herself. The pain made her sluggish. Damn you, she breathed. *Fuck you!* It felt as though she were slogging through sand, as though two relentless dogs had locked their jaws around her calves and she was pulling them both along with her. She had to think of something fast. With only one bullet she couldn't afford any mistakes.

Szczymanski reached a side wall of the Terminal, made for the relative darkness of a greengrocer's. It was a large retail space filled with shadows and long wooden tables. Underneath the canvas on the tables, she could see the outlines of vegetables—rutabagas, carrots, turnips. As she passed by them, she thought how odd it was that the grocers left their stock out on the tables.

But these were the durable vegetables, the ones that were hardiest. The ones that could survive the long haul.

THIRTY-SEVEN

Watson followed her into the dark corner of the Terminal. He moved cautiously, knowing full well that even a single bullet in the gun of a marksman—a markswoman!—could do a great deal of damage. Once he disposed of her, however, the rest would be easy. A turkey shoot. Easier even than those two engineers on the Zephyr. Easier than the countless other victims. And it would be a distinct pleasure to murder a "colleague." It sent a shiver of perverse delight through him.

He hadn't wanted to kill Georgia. She'd been thoroughly reliable up until now, helping to devise the pattern, using the tapes to lure and entrap a foamer. But, at the last moment, she'd proved invertebrate. As he liked to say to his employers, you can't cross a chasm with two leaps. Hesitation killed more people in his business than bravado.

Still, with Georgia gone, the case would tie together much more neatly. Dead McBryde would be blamed for the accidents, dead

Szczymanski made a lovely mole, dead Melissa would tell no stories, and the dead foamers would garnish the main course like so much parsley.

Best of all, he and his assistants wouldn't have to set any more of these tiresome accidents. Public confidence in the railroad had been effectively undermined. His contacts on the Hill informed him that Congress would push for rapid deployment of ARES, if not in this session, then certainly in the next. Funding would be restored, even increased; anything to make the rail system safer. An ARES prototype would be up and running in three years. And within the satellite system's first full year of operation, his organization would be able to freeze all rail movement in the United States.

And, thanks to the work he'd put in on the programming, they would be able to jam every major computer system in the country, from the Internet all the way up to the Pentagon's mainframes. Quite a few countries would pay quite a lot of hard currency for such control.

Long before that, however, he'd retire to the Alps. Practice his downhill. Take off a couple pounds. Get back into shape. Leave the rest of the operations to the other exceedingly well-placed mole, their "second man."

Contemplating this well-deserved retirement, Watson came into the area in front of the greengrocer's cash registers. He immediately sighted Szczymanski's head, her sunglasses glinting in the overhead light, her coat pulled up around her ears, her baseball cap fixed at a jaunty angle. Silently thanking her for being so obliging, he quickly put several bullets between her eyes.

It was only as the bullet pierced his neck that he realized how ridiculous it was for the agent to be wearing sunglasses in the gloomy Terminal. But by that time it was too late to swing around and aim at something other than an artfully decorated head of cabbage.

after

As the train pulled out of West Palm Beach, Primo Rivera tried to get as much chatting time as he could with the new car attendant from Car 4512. She was definitely cute—not too thin, hair held up in the back with a pink butterfly clip—and if he could make an early impression on her, then that wolf Edsall from Car 4507 would never have a chance. It was forty minutes to Okeechobee and the manifest for his sleeper listed a new passenger boarding there. Rivera needed to check the compartment one more time, make sure everything was in order. But still he lingered with the new car attendant, Mindy Ratner. Their conversation drifted onto the topic of the accident warning Amtrak had issued three weeks before.

Mindy Ratner dusted off her jacket, straightened her name tag. "My mother didn't want me to take this job after seeing those accidents on television. But I wasn't worried. Actually, a little accident would be kinda exciting."

"No way," Rivera disagreed. "I was on this train when it went off the bridge north of Mobile. Man, I'm telling you, it was a nightmare. Three cars went into the bayou and an engine exploded in the water. Forty-seven people died. It wasn't exciting. It was terrifying."

Perfecto. He'd managed to fit in the Mobile story without sounding boastful. Now all she had to do was follow up with a question about his heroism and he could modestly tell her how he pulled three children out of the black Alabama waters. Edsall had nothing to match it.

But Mindy Ratner didn't bite. "I wasn't thinking about an accident like that, I guess. Something harmless. Something that doesn't kill anyone."

"If you want thrills like that, go to Disney World," he advised, and was immediately sorry he'd taken that tone of voice with her. "I mean, yeah, I understand how accidents can sound interesting. But the reality is no fun."

"Doesn't matter," she said, blowing at the steam that rose from her coffee. "It doesn't look like we'll have any more accidents like those for a while."

Okay, one more card in the hole. "Did you know I was on the Lake Shore? The one where the boy was shot?"

"Oh?" She seemed more interested.

"I think I even talked with that FBI agent who solved the case."

"I heard about her," Mindy Ratner said dreamily.

"I think she got a medal."

"I wish I could meet her."

The palmetto-strewn landscape passed by the vestibule windows. Sunlight glinted off the metal brackets of the luggage racks. It was another gloriously warm winter day in Florida. Rivera felt good. There was nothing like a Mindy Ratner to improve his job satisfaction.

Before the pause grew too lengthy, he said, "They rigged nearly thirty accidents, did you know that?"

"And recorded them?" She shook her head. "I mean, who would pay so much money for tapes of train accidents? Foamers scare me."

"There was the explosion down in New Mexico and the bottleneck in the Moffat Tunnel and—"

"But I just don't understand how this FBI agent solved the case," she interrupted.

Perfecto! Now he could tell her the whole story, fudging here and there where he didn't know the precise details. "Well, you see," he began, about to reconstruct a story imperfectly remembered.

It was at that moment that his beeper went off. He called in to the lead conductor.

"Smoke alarm, room eight," he was told.

Rivera cursed mildly in Spanish. "It's those smokers," he told her. "You keep telling them that it isn't allowed and they keep lighting up anyway."

He climbed up to the second level and walked through the coach into his sleeper section. He knocked on the door to room 8. Hearing an invitation, he pushed it open.

Inside, Rivera was confronted by a real fire. The flames rose into the air, sending sparks to the ceiling. But the fire, he saw, was contained.

It burned inside a metal wastepaper basket.

A man and a woman sat close to one another on the bed, tearing pages from a book and floating them down into the receptacle at their feet.

"Hi!" the woman said brightly.

The man laughed. "I guess we're not allowed to do this, huh?"

Primo Rivera shook his head gravely. "It's a fire hazard, sir."

"Well, we're almost done," the woman said, holding up the remnants of a paperback. When she stood up to hand Rivera some pages from the book, he noticed how tall she was. And such a round, innocent face. "Would you like to burn a couple pages? The sooner we're done, the sooner we'll be rid of this fire hazard."

He looked at the pages she thrust into his hands. "Work on your own happiness," said one line that jumped out at him.

"This isn't allowed—"

The woman pulled out an FBI badge. "Special operations, conductor. We're destroying evidence."

Rivera stepped back. "Hey, I don't know, I—"

But the woman just laughed. "Relax, my friend. Just ribbing you. I'm on vacation. So just throw those last sheets in and we can celebrate."

Rivera mechanically dropped the pages into the basket, mesmerized by the peculiar scene. He looked more closely at the woman.

Could this be the same FBI agent? He'd lied to Mindy Ratner. He'd been on the Lake Shore the night it pulled up short of the Colonie Bridge. But he never met the FBI agent. Could this be that agent? This woman looked so ordinary in jeans and a T-shirt.

The man produced a champagne bottle and three glasses. He wrapped a towel around the bottle neck and silently popped the cork. He poured champagne into three glasses.

"Can't drink on the job, sir," Rivera said.

They ignored him.

"To your commendation," the man said to the woman.

"Commendation? I was suspended, Larry."

"*After* the commendation. They'll take you back. They have to. Even Peña and Metaxas are on your side now."

"I'm not sure I want to go back."

"But there's still that second guy, the one the kid—"

She interrupted him with a finger to her lips. "Maybe I'll become a private investigator."

The man groaned. "At least with the FBI you get vacations and overtime. I'll never see you!"

"What about all your excursions? Your conventions?"

Rivera wasn't listening to their conversation. His mind was racing. "Are you—" Rivera addressed the woman.

Ignoring him, she tapped her glass with her finger. "The toast?"

"To us!" the man said.

"Yes." They clinked glasses. "And to Clarence Brown."

They nodded solemnly, sipped their champagne.

"Ma'am, were you on the Lake Shore Limited a couple months back?" Rivera asked.

"Lake Shore Limited?" She looked at him as if he'd inadvertently belched.

"Hey," the man said to him. "Did you ever hear the one about the blind xylophonist?"

A voice spoke up. "Oh, Daddy, that's a terrible joke."

Rivera looked up and noticed for the first time a child stretched out on the upper berth. She waved a baseball cap at him. Printed above the bill were the words "I'm with stupid" and two arrows.

"We're goin' to Paris," the blond little girl informed him.

"Los Angeles, Melissa honey," the man corrected.

No, he must be mistaken. This was just another pair of kooky passengers. Best not to encourage them. Rivera smiled and backed out of the compartment.

"The first single-train transcontinental service," the woman said in a singsong voice.

"Fifty-one stops," the man replied, as if in a musical duet.

"Three thousand miles long," the woman said.

"Actually it's three thousand sixty-six," the man corrected.

Not only were they kooky, they also sounded like foamers. Rivera closed the door of the compartment in the middle of her sentence. Crazy foamers, he thought. And hurried back to tell the rest of the train-accident story to Mindy Ratner.

acknowledgments

I would like to thank those who improved this book immeasurably. Karin Lee read through several drafts, helped me untangle many knots in the plot, and midwifed this project from beginning to the end. Train and FBI expert Joseph Wiley appeared deus ex machina to correct many errors of fact and fiction. Kip and Amanda Voytek not only read the manuscript, but also set the stage for the book's eventual publication. Maryrica Lottman and Stan Walker improved the style and content line by line. Andrew Feffer, Elizabeth Griffin, George Justice, Sherri Shultz, and Lisa Gurr all offered careful readings and extremely useful suggestions. Linda Love, Martin Lee, Geoff Tager, Emily Seidel, Liz Orlin, Bonnie Kortrey, Dave Derrer, Carole Mullin, Linda Stern, my parents, and the National Writers Union all lent their skills to help bring this project to completion. Henry A. Sauerwein Jr. and the Wurlitzer Foundation furnished me with a wonderful adobe house in Taos, New Mexico, for three months to finish the manuscript. Finally my editor, Susanne Kirk, copy editor, Erika Schmid, and agent, Susan Gleason, provided considerable polish to the text.

I relied on many books and periodicals in my research on trains and on the FBI. The following were particularly useful: Joseph Vranich, *Supertrains*; Tony Poveda, *Lawlessness and Reform: The FBI in Transition*; James Q. Wilson, *The Investigators*; Donald Itzkoff, *Off the Track*; Robert Shaw, *Down Brakes*; George Douglas, *All Aboard*; Robert C. Reed, *Train Wrecks*; Ronald Kessler, *The FBI*; and Henry Kisor, *Zephyr*. I would also like to thank the National Railway Historical Society, Amtrak, the Delaware Valley Association of Rail Passengers, and the many Philly rail fans who opened their homes and hearts to me.

The errors that have somehow managed to remain in the text are not the responsibility of the above readers and writers. I have no idea where they came from.